"ARE YOU FLIRTING WITH ME?"

"Because this is very serious business. I'm *working*. And I'm never going to finish these cookies if we—"

"That's not flirting," he said, shaking his head vehemently.

"Yes it is. All that arm grazing and chocolate tasting and . . . and I don't like the way you're looking . . . at my lips."

"Maybe I'm looking at your lips because you still have a speck of chocolate right there." He pointed with his index finger and she quickly rubbed at it with her hand.

"Did I get it?" she asked.

He stepped closer and examined the spot closely. "I'm not sure. Let me check." Then he bent his head and kissed her—a light, quick kiss—before stepping back. Examining her closely, he said, "No, it's definitely still there." Then he dipped his head again. This time he cupped a hand softly around her neck, threading his fingers through her hair and bringing their lips together slowly and deliberately in a way that felt exactly right. He tugged her against him, tasting her, kissing her thoroughly, stealing her breath away, making her dizzy and trembling. She stood on tiptoe, straining to kiss him, resting a hand on his chest, where his heart beat steadily and strongly under her fingertips.

Slowly, he moved his mouth near her ear and whispered, "Now *that's* flirting."

PRAISE FOR THE
ANGEL FALLS SERIES

All I Want for Christmas Is You

"A scrumptious holiday treat."
—*Publishers Weekly*

Then There Was You

"A sweet, homespun romance that tugs at the heartstrings in all the right ways."
—*Entertainment Weekly*

"A sparkling springtime romance!"
—*Fresh Fiction*

Then There Was You

"Emotional, heartwarming romance you can't put down."
—Lori Wilde, *New York Times* bestselling author

"A delightful and sexy small-town tale of love lost and found!"
—*Fresh Fiction*

"Liasson ably tugs at the heartstrings with this poignant contemporary."
—*Publishers Weekly*

"One of the best books I've read this year!"
—*Harlequin Junkie*, Top Pick

All I Want for Christmas Is You

MIRANDA LIASSON

An Angel Falls Novel

FOREVER
New York Boston

Copyright © 2019 by Miranda Liasson

Cover design and illustration by Elizabeth Turner Stokes
Cover copyright © 2019 by Hachette Book Group, Inc.

Christmas on Mistletoe Lane by Annie Rains copyright © 2018 by Annie Rains

Forever
Hachette Book Group
1290 Avenue of the Americas, New York, NY 10104
read-forever.com
twitter.com/readforeverpub

First Edition: October 2019

Forever is an imprint of Grand Central Publishing. The Forever name and logo are trademarks of Hachette Book Group, Inc.

The publisher is not responsible for websites (or their content) that are not owned by the publisher.

The Hachette Speakers Bureau provides a wide range of authors for speaking events. To find out more, go to www.hachettespeakersbureau.com or call (866) 376-6591.

ISBN: 978-1-4555-4185-0 (mass market), 978-1-4555-4186-7 (ebook)

Printed in the United States of America

OPM

10 9 8 7 6 5 4 3 2 1

For Ed

Acknowledgments

As I'm writing this, I realize as this third book in the Angel Falls series ends, I'm saying goodbye to the Langdons, who feel very much like family to me. Rafe has been especially close to my heart. I hope he will entertain you as much as he has me! Many thanks to my editor at Forever, Amy Pierpont, who helped me bring Rafe and Kaitlyn to life and let his funny nature and her strong, independent one shine through.

Thanks to Jill Marsal, my awesome agent, and to Estelle, Gabi, Sam, and Jodi, the hardworking and dedicated team at Forever Romance, and to Elizabeth Stokes for the gorgeous covers for my whole series. And thanks to the many people behind the scenes who made this book a reality.

Many thanks to Retired Chief Doyle Jones of the Oberlin, Ohio, Fire Department, who helped me to understand the life and job of a firefighter. The men and women who do this job are amazing!

Thanks to Barbara Talevich of the fabulous West

Side Bakery in Akron, Ohio, who talked to me about what it might be like to create a cookie recipe from scratch and the love and pride of owning a business.

Thanks to everyone who helped name our sweet puppy! I have to thank Anna Katharine Koehler for the perceptive comment that Bandit was the *stealer of hearts*. Jennifer Beck, Jenny Merchant, and Ramona Kekstadt also came up independently with Bandit's name. And Beverly Kee, thank you for the very masculine names that Rafe preferred, like Bear, Gunner, Moe, Harley, and Duke.

Thanks to AE Jones and Sandy Owens, my wonderful writer friends. I'm so glad we can travel together down this crazy path!

To my husband, Ed, thanks for sharing your sense of humor with Rafe and me and for all your love and support day in and day out. And to my kids, thank you for being as proud of me as I always am of all of you.

Lastly, thank you, dear readers, for reading the books, chatting with me, sending me your notes and thoughts, and sharing this amazing journey of the imagination with me. Without you, none of this would be possible.

All I Want for Christmas Is You

There's first love, and then there's *best* love.

—Nonna

Chapter 1

♥

It was a very bad day to take a pregnancy test, Kaitlyn Barnes decided as she washed off the counter at her coffee shop, the Bean, on a snowy late November evening. But she'd taken the test, and in light of how crappy she'd been feeling lately, the bright blue plus sign hadn't come as a surprise.

She was way too busy to even *think* about being pregnant, let alone ponder how on earth it could ever have happened.

Okay, she knew how it had happened. And when. And she wasn't going to lie to herself: the sex with Rafe Langdon had been, after years of dancing around their attraction to each other, epic. But with two forms of birth control, how on earth...Nope. She wasn't going there. Not now, not with worries about her family, her business, and her life at the forefront of her mind.

Mary Mulligan, the last customer in the shop, brought her empty mug up to the counter, her kind but mischievous blue eyes twinkling. "You're good friends with Rafe Langdon, aren't you, dear?"

"Oh, yes, I've known Rafe forever." Kaitlyn squeezed her eyes shut to avoid thinking of his strong, muscular body, his square jaw, his dark, well-defined brows. And other parts of him that she *really* was not going to think about.

"I haven't seen him in here lately. How's he been doing?" Mary asked.

Kaitlyn wouldn't know. She hadn't spoken much to Rafe since what she was coming to call *the incident*, which consisted of one wedding, a few drinks, a rainstorm, and a much too inviting cabin. "I-I haven't seen him," Kaitlyn said with a shrug. "Maybe he gave up coffee."

Yet not even a minute had gone by that she hadn't thought about him, and his nice full mouth that always seemed to be turned up in the tiniest smile.

Oh, that smile. *That's* what had gotten her in trouble—Rafe's ability to take any kind of worry or concern and somehow lighten it up with that easygoing, assured grin. It was irresistible—*he* was irresistible, especially to her, whose life was typically chock-full of worries and concerns.

She blinked to find Mrs. Mulligan staring at her. "I'm sorry, Mary," Kaitlyn said. "What did you say?" She had to stop her mind from wandering.

"I said I hope you're going home soon, dear. You look peaked."

Kaitlyn flicked her hand in a dismissive gesture. "Just a little tired." And nauseated. And losing her lunch on a regular basis. And breakfast. "Want another cup of tea?" Kaitlyn asked. "It's no trouble."

"Oh, no thank you. I know you're closing. I just can't get over how Rafe posed for next year's first responder charity calendar. Mr. December—Chief Walker made a poster of him to help sell the calendars and gave it to a lot of the shop owners on Main Street. Someone even hung one at the base of the angel statue. All the girls in the beauty shop were talking about it. Don't you think he's a hottie?" Mary punctuated her statement with a knowing look.

First off, the police chief, Colton Walker, was Rafe's best friend, and he'd goaded Rafe, a firefighter, into posing for that calendar, knowing full well that including Rafe's image would sell dozens. Second, Colton had not delivered her a copy of Mr. December (not that she wanted one), but she wondered why, since her coffee shop was right in the middle of the main drag. And yes, Rafe was a *complete* hottie, but she knew too well he didn't do serious. So it didn't really matter what she thought.

She skimmed her hand lightly over her abdomen, which was a little fuller than usual but still flat enough that no one would suspect a thing. Another wave of nausea hit her, but she clutched the counter and took a deep breath to quell it. Like it or not, she'd be thinking of Rafe Langdon for a long time to come.

"He's sure going to sell a lot of calendars for Children's Hospital," Mary said, clapping her hands together. "What an inspiration for the Christmas season."

Yes, Christmas. Even now, outside the big plate glass

windows that faced the street, snowflakes eddied around the orange glow from the streetlight. Swirls of chaos that reflected how Kaitlyn felt inside. Someone from the Angel Falls maintenance crew had hung a big lit-up candy cane on each light post, making the Main Street cheery and festive, and she herself had strung multicolored lights around all the coffee shop's windows. She loved Christmas. It was her favorite time of year. But not this year. Not now. She felt anything but festive.

"How's your niece doing, dear?" Mary asked. "I heard she'd gotten into some kind of trouble."

Ah, Hazel. Kaitlyn's older sister, Nikki, had sent her seventeen-year-old daughter to be with family and away from the bad influences at her huge high school in LA. Needless to say, Hazel was beyond thrilled to be dumped off in Angel Falls to complete her senior year far away from home. Kaitlyn knew that Hazel was simply biding her time until she turned eighteen and could kiss Angel Falls and their whole family goodbye.

"She's…settling in. Thanks for asking, Mary," Kaitlyn said. Hazel was having some serious problems fitting in at Angel Falls, but Kaitlyn had learned a long time ago not to feed the gossip mill of their close-knit town, no matter how concerned and kind her customers were.

Suddenly the shop bell tinkled, bringing in a few eddies of snow as well as the police chief himself, who was holding on to Hazel's bony elbow. With her thin frame, big brown eyes, and delicate bow-shaped mouth, Hazel still reminded Kaitlyn of a pixie, a sweet, fragile creature. Except it was difficult to get two words out of her now, and personality-wise, she nowhere near resembled the little girl who used to love spending summers here. Catching Colton's worried eye, Kaitlyn braced herself and set Mary's tea mug on the counter with a *thunk*.

"Colton. Hazel. Is everything all right?" She wiped her hands on her apron and bolted around the counter.

"Thanks for the tea, sweetie," Mary said, blowing Kaitlyn a quick kiss. With a wave to Colton and a wink at Hazel, Mary astutely let herself out the door.

Kaitlyn approached her niece and held her by the upper arms, a move that forced Hazel to face her. Hazel's eyes met hers with their usual stoic look of well-practiced indifference. But just for a flash, they might've held fear, until she made her expression go flat again.

Colton gave Kaitlyn a sympathetic look. He practically made a second career out of helping the misguided youth of their town, so she knew whatever Hazel had done, it must've been serious for him to drag her in at closing time like this.

"Tell your aunt what happened, okay?" Colton said. It came out as more of a command than a question.

Hazel crossed her arms and tossed Colton a glare. "Why don't *you* just tell her? You're the one who insisted on bringing me here."

Kaitlyn braced against another wave of nausea, willing it away. *Oh, please, oh, please*, she prayed. *Not drugs. Anything but drugs.*

"Okay, fine," Colton said, blowing out a patient sigh. "Hazel here decided she wanted to get a magazine over at the pharmacy—without paying for it."

Kaitlyn frowned. "A magazine?" She turned to Hazel, who was nervously shifting her weight from one foot to the other, a move that showcased her Chuck Taylor high-tops. Under her coat, she wore a burnt-orange sweater with a crazily patterned scarf that looked straight out of the seventies. A thief with fashion flair. "I could've given you the five dollars."

Hazel's face flushed, which Kaitlyn took as a sign that maybe there was the teensiest bit of the old Hazel left in there somewhere.

"Mr. Barter said this isn't the first time," the chief said. "He's looking to press charges."

Kaitlyn gasped. Oh, this was not good. "Colton, no."

"Hazel, do you have anything to say?" Colton asked.

"I didn't do it."

Struggling not to roll her eyes, Kaitlyn looked at Colton. "Can I talk to you—privately?"

She pulled him off to the side, next to a vintage life-sized sign of Santa holding a cup of coffee up to his mouth and winking. "Look, I've been...preoccupied the past few weeks. I should've been looking out for her more." Guilt pummeled her. "I'll hire her here...as punishment. And to keep an eye on her." Not exactly the best plan to recapture the relationship they once had, but what else could Kaitlyn do?

Colton narrowed his observant cop-eyes at her. "You okay? You look almost as bad as Rafe."

"What are you talking about?" she asked, narrowing her eyes right back.

"It's no secret you two have some kind of tiff going on."

"It's not a tiff." She really didn't know *what* to call

sleeping with someone you never should've slept with in the first place, someone you couldn't avoid because his sisters were your best friends and his family was just like your own. Complicated and awkward—yes. But a tiff—no.

"Well, whatever it is, he looks like crap too." Colton dropped his voice. "Look, you told me Hazel's done this in LA. That makes her a repeat offender. Letting her slide again isn't going to do her any favors in the long run."

"I'll be more diligent. I won't let her out of my sight. Please, Colton. If you tell Mr. Barter that, he'll listen."

Colton grimaced. "You can't be responsible for everyone, just to let you know."

Colton was well aware of Hazel's situation, and Kaitlyn appreciated his understanding, but still, she felt like she'd been too wrapped up with her own...issues. She'd left the tending of Hazel to her mother, and that had been a mistake. "Thank you, but...I can handle it."

He let out a heavy sigh. "It's against my better judgment, but okay, I'll see what I can do. But next time..." He made a cutting motion across his neck with his hands...accompanied by the faintest lift of his lips.

"Thank you," she said, giving him a hug.

"And you'd better go get some sleep. Or make up with Rafe or something."

She ignored that, then walked back over to the table where Hazel sat drawing patterns in the sugar she'd dumped from packets onto the table.

"So, are you throwing me in the clinker?" Hazel

asked, her mouth pulled up in a smirk. Kaitlyn tried not to be upset.

"You're going to work here," Kaitlyn said. "Every day after school."

"What?" She sat up and shot Kaitlyn an outraged look.

Kaitlyn forged on. "That's the deal. And when your shift is done, you'll do your homework in the back. And if your fingers get sticky again, I won't be able to stop anyone from pressing charges. That will look bad on your college apps."

Hazel snorted, and Kaitlyn knew why. Because there were no college apps. And possibly because of the fact that she'd said "sticky fingers," as if she'd been watching too many old mafia movies.

The point was, Nikki had worked long hours and sometimes multiple jobs to give Hazel everything a kid needs. But she'd struggled, and funds for college were simply...not there. And with Hazel getting into trouble recently, both with her grades and with the shoplifting, her shot at a scholarship or a free ride to college had slipped away.

At parent-teacher conferences a few weeks ago, Hazel's teachers had said she was bright but undisciplined. Unfocused. She didn't seem to care. Maybe that was because she didn't think anyone else did.

"I'd like to go back to Gram's now," Hazel said, not looking her in the eye.

"I'll drop you off on my way to the station," Colton said.

Kaitlyn thanked Colton. "I'll see you here after

school tomorrow," Kaitlyn said to Hazel, as Colton ushered her out the door. She didn't get an answer back.

Kaitlyn locked the door after them and dimmed the lights. Then she sat down at a table and put her head down on the cool wooden surface.

She had to do something to help Hazel before it was too late. But she couldn't help wondering if maybe she was already too late, that Hazel's decisions so far had set her on a certain course and changing that would be almost impossible.

Kaitlyn had no experience in her own life to compare—she'd always been responsible, a good daughter and a faithful sister. Nikki had always been the more emotional, more impulsive one. She'd gotten pregnant at eighteen and had ended up marrying her high school sweetheart, but things hadn't worked out.

Kaitlyn had always been determined not to allow her emotions to rule her decisions like her older sister had. But hadn't the same thing happened to her? She'd acted rashly with Rafe. She'd gotten swept away. How could she not, when every time he looked at her, her pulse skittered and desire rushed through her like a tidal wave?

In the darkened coffee shop, the strings of Christmas lights were as cheery as always, and the blinking lights from the ice cream shop across the street continued to remind her that life was going on as usual for most everyone else.

That crazy night with Rafe had led to something that would change—was already changing—her whole life. She was going to be a *mother*, something that, at nearly thirty-two, she was beginning to think might not happen. A baby—hers and Rafe's—was growing inside of her right now. That was overwhelming, frightening, miraculous, and...awesome.

She imagined how Christmas next year would include a whole brand-new little person in their lives...a sweet bundle to hold and love and carry around, tiny arms outstretched toward all the shiny ornaments on the Christmas tree.

She wanted to be a mom more than anything, even if the circumstances weren't perfect. She was going to do all she could to make smart choices so her baby would have the best life she could give it. That meant growing up, setting aside her misplaced feelings for Rafe, and focusing on securing her business.

She reached into her apron to examine the clipping she'd ripped from a baking magazine earlier in the day. *Win $15,000 Plus Three Months of Pastry Classes for the Best Christmas Cookie Recipe!* the headline read. Kaitlyn tapped the clipping on the table. She had to start thinking of sustaining her business. Becoming a real businessperson. Growing. Winning this contest would give her a chance to put her café on the map. And it would give Hazel a shot at college.

As for pastry classes...well, Kaitlyn had always dreamed of taking those. She'd always wanted to expand her baked goods section, which was popular. Plus, she knew exactly the recipe she'd submit—one for the most amazing Christmas cookie in the entire world. Her grandfather's chocolate snowcap cookies, which were slightly crunchy on the outside, gooey on the inside with melted chocolate, and coated with powdered sugar that cracked in the oven so they looked like snow-covered mountains. She'd grown up eating them after school in the Bean, her grandfather placing a warm plate full of them before her and Nikki and asking them about their days.

She had to start securing her future. Because she hadn't needed a pregnancy test to tell her that she was going to have Rafe Langdon's baby.

Chapter 2

♥

There's our pretty boy," Jonathan McDougal said, as Rafe walked into the Tap, a flurry of snow swirling in as he shut the door behind him. Jon was the owner of the popular neighborhood hangout, and apparently, he had seen the calendar.

"Pretty boy, Jon?" Rafe said, raising a brow.

"Oh, he's just jealous," Jon's wife, Maggie, said, brushing her gray hair aside as she slid some menus into the holder on the wall behind the bar. "We all know Rafe's more than just a pretty boy—he's *Mr. December*."

"Ha ha, right. Thanks, Maggie," Rafe said. Maggie was also a paramedic, and he was used to her ribbing. Off to his right, he heard a giggle. Two young, pretty women sitting at the other end of the bar were looking at him and whispering to each other. One of them wiggled her fingers in a little wave.

He smiled back, but it wasn't genuine. Not his usual lady-killer smile. But the woman flashed him a big smile back, and he knew that if he wanted to, he could land her number in a heartbeat.

Not that Rafe was cocky or arrogant. He just...knew women.

Well, some women. But definitely not one woman in particular whom he couldn't figure out for the life of him.

It was really unlike him to get his suspenders in such a twist. He should be excited that Mr. December was bringing him new dating opportunities, but he just...wasn't. He was losing his touch. Had been for the past few months. What was *wrong* with him?

Across the bar, the women stood up and began to head to the door. The one who waved at him earlier was trying to make eye contact, but he made sure not to look.

"Mr. December?" Eli Nelson, a carpenter buddy who was sitting at the bar, chuckled as he took a swig of beer.

Evan Marshall, the full-time police deputy who sat next to Eli, teased him. "December's going to be a great month for you—every day will be like Christmas with all the women you're going to meet."

"He had on Santa pants and a cute Santa hat," Maggie said, gesturing excitedly as she handed Rafe a beer, "and the only thing hiding those amazing abs was a tiny little kitten. Next December's going to be my permanent calendar page." Her voice faded as Jon stared at her.

"Oh, honey," she said, kissing her husband on the cheek and lovingly patting his beard, "you'll always be my favorite Santa." Everyone knew that Jon played

Santa for the women's shelter Christmas party every year.

"Aw, look at that," Rafe said, watching Jon's ruddy complexion turn even ruddier with a blush.

Jon smiled at his wife, mollified. Turning to Rafe, he said, "Maybe you should do something with all that Santa talent."

"Yeah, like what?" Rafe asked, taking a sip of his beer.

"How about taking over being Santa this year for the women's shelter?"

"How come you're not doing it?" Rafe asked. Jon had the great beard, the deep laugh, and the stockier build. The perfect Santa.

"One of our kiddos has a Christmas program that night," Maggie said. "As much as we love helping out the shelter kids, we've got to pass this year."

"So how about it?" Jon said. "I've seen you with your niece and nephew. You're a natural."

Being a fun uncle was one thing. But playing Santa for an entire roomful of shelter kids was another thing entirely.

"The only people who get to sit on my lap are single women." Rafe grinned to punctuate the joke and left it at that.

Evan and Eli howled, and Jon threw up his hands.

Maggie, however, shook her head. "I'm glad you're having fun being a pinup now, Rafe, but sooner or later you'll be happier to have a wife at your side and a baby on your lap."

He flashed his brightest smile and used his most joking voice, but deep down, he meant every word. "Don't hold your breath, Maggie. Sorry." Because it would never happen.

Rafe had been there, done that, and vowed to never go there again. Eight years ago, his fiancée had died in a car accident, on the way to a doctor's appointment. She'd been eight weeks pregnant, a fact that only a few people knew.

Rafe understood himself pretty well, and he knew he was not capable of surviving that kind of loss again. And if joking about never settling down made him seem calloused, or insensitive, or whatever, he was okay with that. He knew his limits.

"Hey, a couple of us are going into Richardson tomorrow night to have some fun," Evan said with a grin. "Want to come?"

"Thanks, Evan, but I'm busy this weekend," Rafe said. He wasn't that busy—he just wasn't in the mood to pick up women. Which was odd because usually he was all in for that.

But lately, all he could seem to think about was Kaitlyn.

Kaitlyn, whom he'd known forever. Who was best friends with two of his sisters and practically part of his family. Whom he'd impulsively slept with after they'd had too much fun together at a wedding because he'd been unable to resist her. And he'd regretted it ever since.

If he were completely honest with himself, over the past couple of years, on top of their friendship, there'd been something else brewing. Attraction. A certain...

fondness. *Feelings.* Somewhere along the line, Kaitlyn had gone from that nice-enough girl who always hung out with his sisters to a funny, vivacious woman who made him laugh and who sometimes knew him better than he knew himself. It was no wonder they struck up an even closer friendship after she broke up with her last boyfriend. But he knew from the start that he had to draw a thick line in the sand, one that could never be crossed.

He'd tried to keep her at arm's length, but he'd let his guard down that night—and the unthinkable had happened. But it would never happen again. Sleeping with her had messed everything up—their easy conversation, the jokes and banter he looked forward to every day. And now he had no idea how to get them back to the fun and easy friendship they had.

Because not having Kaitlyn in his life ironically made him think about her more. And that was ruining his mojo. He *hated* having his mojo ruined.

"C'mon, Rafe," Eli said. "You're scaring us. Snap out of it, because wingmen need love too."

Rafe turned to Evan and Eli and sighed. "Buy me another beer and that might twist my arm."

For the next half hour, Rafe managed to laugh and make small talk and buy another round. So maybe he wasn't really in the mood to do any of these things, but what was it that his mom used to say? *Even if you don't feel like doing something, do it anyway—and you'll be surprised how your mood will change.*

Have to take your word on that, Mom, he thought, lifting his beer a little in salute. She'd been gone a long time, but one thing he remembered: his mom had used humor to make people feel better. The only trouble with that was that people expected you to be funny all the time, regardless of what you were feeling underneath.

A half hour later, the beer gone, Rafe said his good-byes and walked out into the cold. It was snowing pretty heavily now, the flakes big and fat, the kind that stuck to your eyelashes and your coat. The cold air felt good—it woke him up and pulled him out of his thoughts, made him focus on something other than Kaitlyn.

His truck was parked in the lot, but he didn't get in, just kept going. He told himself he needed a brisk walk to clear his head, that he didn't care where his feet led him. But he did care. And he knew exactly where he was headed.

* * *

The Bean was closed for the night, but Rafe found himself on his way there anyway. Kaitlyn was probably inside tidying up before tomorrow's morning rush. He missed seeing the way she tucked her pretty blond hair behind her ear and smiled. And talking to her about everything and nothing. He missed *her*, period.

And, God help him, he missed the thing that had ruined their friendship. Sinking onto her softness, murmuring her name as he brushed his lips against her soft full ones, hearing her little moans as she kissed him back and came apart in his arms.

He shook his head to clear the images. But he

couldn't, and they'd already affected him, if the tightening in his pants was any indicator.

He told himself he was going to the Bean to set things right. Because she meant too much to him to let things continue as they were. After all, they'd been best friends until *that* had happened.

"Rafe?" a familiar voice said. "What are you doing out there?"

Kaitlyn. Startled, he realized he'd been standing in front of the Bean's big plate glass windows, staring in. He wasn't sure for how long.

She was fussing over him, tugging him by the arm. "It's freezing, and you haven't even got your jacket zipped. And where are your hat and gloves? Geez, you're covered with snow." Her busy hands dusted off the coating of snow that had accumulated on his hair, his coat.

"I was at the Tap for a while," he said. He'd never admit it, but he enjoyed her fussing. Her *touch*.

He wondered if this was how it was going to be, that they were both going to pretend everything was normal between them, like they hadn't been avoiding each other for months.

As she pulled him inside of the warm, deserted café and steered him over to a table, he noticed she smelled good, like dark rich coffee. And apples and cinnamon.

She placed a hand on a hip and assessed him. "Did you eat dinner?" she asked. "Don't even answer. I'm making you a sandwich. And I've got some chicken soup left."

"Why are you still here?" he asked. "It's Friday night.

Don't you have a date or something?" Oh no. Why did he say that?

"I was...going over some numbers," she said.

"You look pretty," he said. *Oh, even worse.* Why had he come here when it was clear his foot was going to spend the entire time in his mouth?

She halted halfway to the kitchen and turned. "Rafe Langdon, are you drunk?" She frowned and tiny lines appeared between her eyes. He wanted to smooth them with his fingers. No, he wanted to kiss them away.

What on earth was he thinking? He had to stop being an idiot.

"Just a little," he said. He wasn't at all. But if saying so would help excuse his foot-mouth situation, so be it.

"Are you okay?" he asked. Getting the attention off himself was a relief, but he was genuinely worried, noticing the dark circles rimming her eyes. He could swear she blushed at his question.

"Of course I am." She sounded fine—maybe a little too fine, in his opinion. Like she was trying hard to convince him. "Why would you ask that?"

He shrugged. He knew everything about her too well. The way she blushed when something was bothering her, the way worry filled her blue eyes and made her press her lips together in a tight line. "Just that you look tired." On the table was a clipping from a magazine. He lifted it up. "What's this for?"

She took it out of his hands. "Nothing. It's...nothing."

He snagged it back and read it. "A recipe contest?"

She shrugged nonchalantly, but her fingers tapped

restlessly on the table. "It's just something I'm thinking of entering."

He searched her eyes as he slid the clipping back in her direction. "I've been worried about you."

"Rafe...don't."

"My sisters told me your niece is having some problems. Everything all right?"

"Yes. Everything's fine." She lowered her eyes. "Actually, just between the two of us, she got caught tonight trying to lift a magazine from the pharmacy."

Her pretty blue gaze flicked up at him. *Between the two of us.* What would it be like for there to actually *be* a *two of them*? But he knew better than anyone that there was no chance of that ever happening. After he'd lost Claire and their unborn baby, he'd made a pact with himself...never again. *Never. Again.*

No matter how much he cared about Kaitlyn or how sometimes he had moments where he thought they'd be amazing together...she deserved someone normal. Unscarred. And capable of love. Which he was not.

"Just a magazine?" Rafe asked.

Kaitlyn frowned. "There's no such thing as 'just a magazine.' Plus, you know she was caught shoplifting in California too."

"What I mean is, if you're going to be bad, why not go for the cash register? Or the narcs."

"Rafe!" Her voice sounded horrified but it was clear she was suppressing a laugh.

He grinned. It was so easy to loosen her up, to make her smile. He felt a sudden surge of pride that he hadn't lost his touch with her at least. "Wasn't she supposed to get a job to teach her some responsibility? And you know, so she wouldn't have time to shoplift?" he asked. "I thought that was the deal your mom made with her."

"My mom never insisted on it. So *I* just hired her." Kaitlyn sent him a look that he knew meant *What have I done?* But she'd never say that.

He blew out a breath. "Kaitlyn, that's kind of you, but—you sure that's a good idea? It sounds like the kid needs more than a job."

"I'll be able to keep a better eye on her this way. And maybe I could...I don't know. Try to figure out what's going on with her." She dropped her voice. "I couldn't just do...nothing."

He nodded sympathetically. Kaitlyn was known for taking on lost causes—stray cats, lonely customers... him. Before he could say anything, she'd jumped up and run into the kitchen. She came back a minute later with soup and a sandwich, which tasted like the best he'd ever had, and he thanked her.

"So why the recipe contest?" he asked as they sat together while he finished eating. "Don't you have enough to do?"

She heaved a sigh. "My grandfather had this recipe for chocolate snowcap cookies that was *amazing*. I *know* it would win the contest. But it's...lost. No one knows where it is and my mom doesn't remember how to make them."

"And this is important why?" Her voice held an edge of passion, and something else—desperation, maybe?— but for a recipe contest?

Kaitlyn blushed. "Nikki makes too much money for

Hazel to qualify for full financial aid for school. So she'd have to take out massive amounts of loans. If I win this contest...voilà...college money."

"Is Hazel going to take pastry classes too?" He tried not to sound skeptical, but he hoped this scheme wasn't all for Hazel. He knew how much Kaitlyn loved the Bean and how she always wanted to experiment with new recipes.

"Those are for me. For the Bean's future. I know it's crazy and a long shot but...it's a shot I want to take."

"Well then, you've got to take it." He sat back and smiled—because he couldn't help it.

"What? What's so funny?"

"Just that it reminds me of that time you invented that coffee milkshake to sell in the Bean."

She put a hand to her forehead. "Don't remind me. That tasted terrible!"

"It wasn't that bad. You looked pretty hot serving it up to everyone who walked by wearing that stuffed coffee bean costume."

"What?" she said, rolling her eyes. "That stuffed bean costume was *not* sexy."

"I mean, I'm just joking," he backpedaled. "You always look nice." Okay, he was blathering, and he needed to stop. Right now. Even though the coffee bean costume *had* been kind of hot—with her long legs in yellow tights under the stuffed bean part. But why he was even thinking about that he had no idea.

Frankly, right now, she looked more than nice. And that way she had of nervously worrying her lower lip was making him crazy. He wanted to stop talking about baking contests, reach over the table, pull her into his arms, and kiss her sweet full lips. He had a few other ideas too, about how to get her to relax. All of which were completely out of line.

Instead, he gave a nonchalant shrug. "The point is, you went for it. And I think you should follow your instincts on this too. Why not?"

She smiled. "Well—thanks for your support. It means a lot that you don't think I'm crazy."

"You are crazy but...Nothing ventured, nothing baked." He quirked his mouth in a wry grin.

She gave a snorty, sudden laugh. "Okay, you're crazy too."

"Probably," Rafe said, setting down the clipping. "You look tired. Are you sleeping okay?" He'd said that already—probably because he was too afraid to say what was really on his mind.

Kaitlyn swallowed and dropped her gaze from his. "I'm fine. How have you been?"

He ignored the question and placed his hand over hers on the table, and she immediately stiffened. But he cut to the chase anyway. "Kaitlyn, I—miss you. I miss how we used to talk. I miss my...friend."

"We became more than friends that night at the wedding, Rafe."

He smoothed his thumb over the back of her palm. "That part was...That was really good too." What was he doing? He had no business touching her. *Wanting* her. Or allowing her to believe he could give her what she wanted. "Not that I remember much, that is. I mean, we'd both had too much to drink, and..."

"Yeah," she said, sitting up straighter. "I mean, I don't either. Remember, that is."

"Oh." She didn't? The truth of the matter was he remembered *too* much. The way she felt, soft and warm in his arms. The way she kissed him, breathless and passionate, their kisses breaking down a mountain of forbidden feelings between them.

At least that's how it had been for him.

But he couldn't tell her that because he had no intention of acting on any feelings he might have for her. He didn't *have* feelings.

He pushed down his irrational disappointment and continued. "It was obviously a mistake. One we won't be stupid enough to make again."

"No, of course not," she said hurriedly. Disappointment riffled through him, settling in his stomach. She didn't care about him like that. So why wasn't he relieved?

"I value our friendship a lot," she said, sounding like she was letting him down gently.

"Me too. I would never want anything to mess that up. Especially not a dumb...mistake." It *was* a dumb mistake, right? He almost expected her to cut in, interrupt him. *Deny* it. "I mean, I'd never want to ruin our friendship by trying to have a...relationship."

"Rafe, I'm not one of those women you have to try and get out of things with." She squeezed her eyes shut tightly. Great. He knew what that look meant— that she was 100 percent serious about something. "I don't...expect anything from you."

He sat there, tapping the tips of his fingers together

anxiously. Of course she wouldn't be demanding or pressure him for more. She was different than other women. Still, her low expectations of him niggled in a way he couldn't quite explain.

"So how about we go back to being...just friends?" That he could handle.

"We'll always be friends, Rafe." She looked right at him, her pretty blue eyes deep with feeling. But he couldn't shake the sense that she was rejecting him. Writing him off. "But after what happened, I can't...It can't go back to the way it used to be. Things are...different now."

"They don't have to be." He sounded a little desperate, but he *needed* things to go back to the way they were before. Their relaxed, easy friendship. Sharing laughs, hanging out. Talking to her about the latest crazy news around town or really anything that was on his mind. Surely they could put this inconvenient...attraction aside for both their sakes. They *had* to.

Kaitlyn sighed. "Well, they *are* different. Look, I have something to say, and I'm just going to come out and be honest. I'm—"

She was interrupted by Rafe's phone ringing. On the phone a photo came up beside the caller's name. It was of him and a woman he'd met at a bar with his friends, his arm around her, both of them smiling for a selfie. He pressed *ignore*, hoping Kaitlyn didn't see it.

Too late. Kaitlyn glanced from his phone to him but didn't say anything.

"What were you saying?" he asked.

"The night of the wed—"

His phone rang again. Same woman calling. Again he pressed *ignore*.

"Maybe you should get that," she said. "It looks important." She nodded toward the picture on the phone.

"I doubt it. She's just someone I met out the other night." Someone who was clearly interested.

"You two look pretty cozy."

His first impulse was to tell her the truth. That it had been the woman's idea to take a selfie together and put her number into his phone. And that he'd rather sit all night with Kaitlyn than answer a call from someone else.

But what good would that do? He knew the answer to that, and he also knew what he had to do. He picked up his phone and pressed a few buttons and looked Kaitlyn dead in the eye. "I always do that when someone wants my number."

"Do what?" she asked innocently.

"Take a selfie so I don't forget who she is." He pocketed the phone and stood to go, trying not to wince at what he'd just said. "I'm glad you don't hate me, Katie. Your friendship means too much to me."

Friendship, he reminded himself. Just that and nothing more.

"Rafe, you're such an idiot. But I could never hate you." She stepped forward and hugged him. Her voice sounded a little funny, a little cracked.

Only she would hug him after he'd been such a jerk. He inhaled the sweet smell of her hair, felt the softness of her cheek as it brushed past his. Deep down, his stomach ached from the lie. After a few seconds, he pulled back and held her at arm's length: "You know I love you, Katie." Then his phone rang again, vibrating from his pocket. "What was it you were going to tell me?"

Kaitlyn was staring at him, her eyes a little watery. "Oh, just . . . just that . . . that your friendship means a lot to me too. And . . . and we'll figure out where to go from here."

Where to go from here? That didn't sound good. But he had faith they'd figure it out, now that he knew she didn't hate him. "We will." Then he tossed her a wave and headed back out to the street.

His phone buzzed yet again. He was a second away from blocking the number when he hesitated. Took a deep breath of frosty air. This time when he picked it up, he decided to follow his mom's advice again. "Hey, Jade. Yeah, I've been thinking about you too."

Maybe if he willed that to be true, he could drive all thoughts of Kaitlyn out of his head for good.

Chapter 3

♥

Kaitlyn was one of those people who always suffered a gut-clenching case of anxiety before doctor's appointments—complete with sweats and cold, clammy hands. Not to mention she also felt like she was about to throw up, but honestly, she was actually getting used to that feeling.

It wasn't just that she hated to see the doctor in general. Her doctor was her best friend. She loved her doctor! But her doctor also happened to be Rafe's sister Sara. She'd desperately wanted to tell Rafe before this visit, but she'd gotten distracted by Selfie Woman. Which had drilled into her head what she already knew—that he was nowhere near ready for commitment, and certainly not with her.

But it had been so good to talk with him again too, especially after they'd done a great job avoiding each other the entire fall. He'd appeared concerned about her and encouraging about the recipe contest. And he truly seemed to miss their friendship, just as she had.

But big changes were in order, and she had to get herself and her business together. With a resolute pang, she understood the hard truth that they could never go back to the easy-breezy friendship they'd had.

The waiting room was decorated with a tabletop fiber-optic tree that was softly twinkling its array of ever-changing colors. But it was side by side with a tabletop snowman that kept flashing Merry Christmas on its belly, a disconcerting sign that made her clutch her own belly and reminded her of why she was here. The practice's longtime nurse, Glinda, startled her further by calling her name and motioning her back to the exam room.

Glinda was probably the only nurse left on the planet who still wore a white cap, but she wore it proud and she wore it well. But today the white cap was replaced by a festive Santa hat. They passed the countertop of the reception area, laden with several large trays of Christmas cookies, reminding Kaitlyn she had to get on that cookie contest. As they passed the reception area, she patted a poster taped to the edge of the counter. There was Rafe's gleaming smile beaming at her from under a tilted Santa cap jauntily set on his head, his cool gaze following her every move as she turned the corner to the exam rooms.

Wasn't it enough that Mr. Hottie Firefighter filled every waking thought? But seeing his image here was just…disconcerting. Geez.

Glinda led her into an iceberg-cold exam room. Why were exam rooms always so freezing?

"Hello, dear," Glinda said, pulling the blood pressure

cuff from its wire basket on the wall and preparing to wrap it around Kaitlyn's arm. Kaitlyn automatically lifted her sleeve. She knew the drill. "So you're here for your annual?" Glinda asked as she put her stethoscope in her ears and inflated the cuff.

"Yes." She could not bring herself to tell Glinda the truth. She was saving that for Sara. She'd lived in this town long enough to know that today's casual conversation could easily turn into tomorrow's gossip, regardless of HIPAA rules.

"Still taking your birth control pills?" Glinda asked, holding an electronic tablet and ticking down a list.

"Um, I stopped. I was going to talk to Sara about that."

"Okay," Glinda said, typing that information into her tablet. "When was your last period?"

"Um, a few weeks ago?" Try two *months* ago. Oh my gosh, she was lying. In a doctor's office. On her medical record. Could you be arrested for that?

"Any new sexual partners since last time?"

"Nope. No. *Definitely* not."

"Any burning, itching, discomfort, discharge?"

Just pregnant. "No, no, nothing like that." *Please, let this be over.*

Glinda closed the tablet. "How's everything at the Bean?"

"Business is great." Passable, anyway. But she would need it to do even better to secure her—and her baby's—future. And help steer Hazel in the right direction.

"Back in your grandfather's day, everyone sat down

and had coffee. Now people grab it and go. But Gabe would've loved that you made it a welcoming place to sit and chat and kept that same sixties feel."

That "sixties feel" was only because she couldn't afford to replace the old furniture…yet. And her one full-time employee, Gwen Hardy, had been there nearly as long. She was a little quirky but she totally got the Bean's friendly, small-town vibe. "I wish he could be here to see it too," she said. That was the great thing about living in a place this size…people remembered. They still spoke fondly of her grandfather, and that touched her and reminded her that she was determined to carry on his legacy. Make him proud of what she was doing to keep the Bean successful. She hoped she'd inherited the same innovative head for business that he'd had.

Glinda gathered her tablet and opened the door. "Put on the gown, sweetie. The top goes on with the opening in the front. Doctor will be with you in just a minute."

"Thanks, Glinda."

Kaitlyn busied herself by checking her phone and then, to distract herself, considered the office décor. The office had been remodeled recently and the walls of the exam room were painted a nice, soothing gray with tasteful art prints that were supposed to be calming. One was an abstract painting of a colorful spiral. But staring at it for more than ten seconds made her feel like she was falling down Alice's rabbit hole.

She sort of had, now that she thought about it. Funny how everything seemed so normal, but just by uttering a few little words—*I'm pregnant*—her life was

going to be changed forever. That included her friend-
ships with Rafe's sisters and the rest of his family, whom
she really regarded as her own. Not to mention what
her mother would say and how her teenage niece would
see her...

Kaitlyn made herself sit up straighter on the exam
table. Which was really hard in bare feet, dressed in a
too-small paper top she had to hold closed and another
rectangle of paper she had wrapped around her bottom
half like a towel. All her pride and dignity had been
stripped away with her clothes. And the fact that she
would have to tell Sara the buck-naked truth.

Well, so be it. At least Sara wouldn't judge her...or
would she? Rafe was her brother, after all. Gabby,
Sara's younger sister and Kaitlyn's other best friend,
had suspected something had happened with Rafe that
night at the wedding because Kaitlyn and she had
roomed in a cabin together. But Sara...Kaitlyn wasn't
sure what she knew.

The worst thing was that Rafe didn't even remember
what had happened between them that night. He'd said
so himself. Yes, they'd had a few drinks. But *she* remembered, all right—every touch, every kiss, *everything*.

And now she needed to erase those memories from
her mind. So that she could finally, *finally* move past
the ridiculous fantasy she'd been harboring that maybe
someday they'd be more than friends. There'd been
times when he'd looked at her and she'd seen something
wonderful there—something that made her believe over
and over again that there was a chance for them. But
now she knew...she'd been wrong.

A knock on the door pulled her out of her thoughts as Sara, four months pregnant herself, walked in, smiling. Marriage to the Angel Falls chief of police had been good for her. She was radiating contentment and happiness. Kaitlyn wished she could borrow just a little.

"Hi," Sara said. "I almost called you to ask you to bring me some of that good decaf you made me last week, but then I thought maybe that was being a little diva-ish. How are y—"

It all suddenly felt like too much. Kaitlyn bit her lip to keep from crying, but it wasn't working, and she suddenly burst into tears.

"Kaitlyn. What is it?" Sara grasped Kaitlyn's hand and squeezed. "What's wrong?"

Kaitlyn swallowed and cleared her throat. If she was going to be a mother, she would have to learn to be brave.

"I'm pregnant," she blurted.

Sara's expression went from concern to disbelief to wide-eyed surprise in seconds. "You're—pregnant?" she echoed.

"That's what the stick told me. But I came in to make sure I was doing all the right things. I've already started a prenatal vitamin and—"

"Have you told Steve?" Sara asked.

Kaitlyn bit her lip again. "It's not Steve's," she said levelly. It would be so easy if it were. She'd dated Steve, a teacher and coach at the high school, for a year and a half, the longest she'd ever dated anyone. He'd been campaigning for them to get back together ever since she broke up with him last year, as Sara knew all about.

"Maybe you should sit down," Kaitlyn said.

Sara sat on the wheeled doctor's stool. "You're scaring me a little. Look, if you had a one-night stand with someone, I swear I won't judge you."

Did a one-night stand after years of trying not to act on her attraction count? Technically, it *was* a one-night stand. But to tell Sara that when she knew how Kaitlyn had always felt about Rafe... *gah*.

"Rafe is the father." There. She'd said it. But she felt anything but relief. Her heart was pumping crazily, making blood whoosh loudly in her ears. She had one more really hard thing to say. "Whatever happens, please don't—please don't stop being my friend. I couldn't bear it if that happened."

"Oh, Katie," Sara said, getting up and wrapping her in a big hug. No one ever called her Katie, except her grandfather. And Rafe, who actually called her that quite often. But when Sara said it just now, it brought more tears to Kaitlyn's eyes. Or maybe that was just the fact that suddenly it felt really good to share the burden of her secret with someone. Or terrible. She couldn't quite decide.

"You're like my sister," Sara said. "I would never stop being your friend." Judiciously, Sara paused. "Does Rafe know?"

"I tried to tell him last night, but some woman kept trying to text him."

"Oh dear." Sara looked... horrified.

"It's all right. I know Rafe is the world's greatest commitmentphobe. I knew better, but I slept with him anyway." That night, it hadn't seemed to matter, but now the stakes were much higher and it did matter. A lot. "I plan to tell him as soon as possible." As soon as she got up the nerve again.

"Rafe really cares for you," Sara said gently. "I can see it in the way he looks at you. But he's never been the same since Claire died."

"I've tried to get him to talk about that, but every time I bring it up, he shuts me down and I've never pushed him."

"I know," Sara said. "We've all tried to get him to talk about it, but he just won't. We can all see he's avoided getting involved with anyone since the accident." She sighed. "I'd hoped things would be different with you."

Inside, Kaitlyn's heart broke for Rafe, who had lost so much at a very young age, but she forced herself to keep her tone matter-of-fact. "I stupidly thought he was past that *because* he never talks about it. But who could ever get over something like that?"

Sara gave a shrug. "Rafe's going to have to if he wants to really live his life."

"Well, I'm not holding my breath," Kaitlyn said resolutely, sitting up straighter on the exam table. "I'm prepared to raise this baby on my own."

"Oh, honey. You won't be alone." Sara squeezed her hand. "And I wish I could say Rafe will step up, but I . . . I just don't know."

"Don't worry about me. I—I'm happy about the baby—about being a mom." Just saying those words melted her fear a little. A *baby*—something she'd feared she'd never have. "I'm trying to focus on that part, you know?"

"How far along do you think you are?" Sara took a little cardboard wheel out of her pocket, a pregnancy calculator of some sort, and began lining up numbers and dates.

"It happened at the wedding...in September." Kaitlyn had accompanied Rafe to his cousin Stephanie's wedding, and it had been a blast. Clearly, too much of a blast.

"But...but Gabby and I *talked* to Rafe about behaving himself that weekend. We..."

"It's not his fault any more than it was mine. We were having so much fun, and we'd had a couple of drinks, then the blackout happened..." That sounded insane. Irresponsible. But if Kaitlyn was anything, she was *not* irresponsible. "I've never missed a pill and we used a condom. What are the odds of this happening?"

"Are you sure you're pregnant? Of course we'll repeat the test today, and..."

"I thought I had a period in October but it was weird, you know? And nothing since. Plus I've been throwing up at least twice a day and I can't stand the smell of perfume, onions, garlic, spaghetti sauce, make that just about all food..."

Sara gazed at her with compassionate eyes. "Okay. Let's do an exam, and blood work, and I can bring the ultrasound in here and we can get an idea of dates and check the heartbeat."

Kaitlyn felt the blood drain from her face. An ultrasound? Seeing that little speck—teeny tiny, barely visible—would make this real and...well, and once she saw that, there would be no mental turning back. She was going to have a baby.

Sara, who must have seen her hyperventilating, squeezed her hand again. "One step at a time, okay? And you have my word that I won't say a thing to anyone."

Kaitlyn nodded, unable to speak. She squeezed Sara's hand back to let her know how grateful she was.

Because she was going to need all the friends she could get.

Chapter 4

♥

"Looks like Mary Mulligan's dachshund had another seizure," Rafe said that evening, riding shotgun to Randall Ames, his good friend and partner for the night, as they took the EMS vehicle to a call.

"And you know what *that* means," Randy said.

"Man, I am not crawling under her porch to get that dog again," Rafe said. "It's *your* turn."

"I'm just getting over bronchitis," Randy said, giving a pathetic cough. "See?" The windshield wipers seemed to squeak in agreement as they swished rapidly back and forth. It was a cold, damp night, the rain on the verge of freezing into sleet.

"No," Rafe said. "Just no. We flip for it. Come on, man, I got all muddy dragging that dog out of there the last time."

"Yeah, but you live a lot closer to the station than I do. You can change your clothes easier. Plus, you don't want me to catch pneumonia, do you?"

"Well, I may not care all that much but I'm sure Janis

does," Rafe said. Randy had been seeing someone for a couple of weeks now, and all he did was talk about her.

"Jan-*et*," Randy said. "Janet. Get it right, dude."

"Sorry." For a long time, Randy was hung up on Rafe's sister Gabby, who'd just married Cade Marshall, an author and English professor at the local college. But Rafe suspected that Randy really liked Jan-*et*, based on the number of times he'd corrected Rafe on the pronunciation of her name.

Rafe was happy for him, but it also made him feel that the last of his good friends were off the market. First Colton, the most confirmed bachelor he knew, fell for Rafe's older sister Sara, and now Randy...Who would be next?

Not him. *Definitely* not him.

An image of Kaitlyn entered his mind, poring over that newspaper clipping. She'd looked so...earnest. He felt like he'd let her down in a million ways. He hated the way he'd left things with her. What had she said?

I don't expect anything from you. Why should she? He'd made her think he didn't remember what had happened between them. If only he could tell her he remembered *everything*.

That night in the cabin—no, not a night, just *moments*, really—were forbidden, stolen, frantic—and mind-blowingly amazing. Before Rafe could relive the memory for the thousandth time, he shut it down.

Randy hit him playfully on the arm. "You're awfully quiet. Who're you thinking about?"

That brought Rafe back to reality. "Just a muddy wet

dog that you're going to rescue while I drink tea with Mary."

At the top of the stairs, Randy dug into his pocket and produced a quarter. "Let's do this fair and square. Heads or tails?"

"Heads," Rafe said, watching Randy toss the coin and slap it on his forearm.

Randy looked from the coin to Rafe, a slow grin spreading across his face. "Sorry, buddy," he said, not looking sorry at all.

Rafe didn't have a chance to say anything back because just then the door opened, and a sweet gray-haired woman in her late seventies answered, wringing her hands in distress. "Come in, boys. Georgie had a seizure and barfed all over the kitchen floor. I sat with him for a while until he started to come to again. Then I went to get him a drink of water. And that was when he disappeared."

"Disappeared," Rafe asked, looking around as she led them into the kitchen. Was it okay to hope that this time Georgie had "disappeared" somewhere in the nice warm house instead of outside in the weather from hell?

"I was coming back from taking out the garbage when it happened and I must've left the back door open a crack. Anyway, I can't find him! I've been calling and calling." She stepped out onto the tiny porch outside the back door. Rain blew in through the kitchen door. It was *nasty* out there. "George!" she called. "Georgie!"

No answer. Rafe pulled up his hood and walked onto the back porch, the wind blowing ice-cold rain into his face. He shined his flashlight into the backyard, but no dog in sight. "Why don't you go back inside, Mrs. M.?" Rafe said.

"He's probably in his special hiding place," Mary said.

Right. His special hiding place in the muck under the porch, no doubt. Rafe hoped he had a clean uniform at home, because he was going to need it—and a hot shower—by the time this was over.

"We could stay warm in here and have tea," Randy said to Mary. "And I could tell you about my new girlfriend."

Rafe rolled his eyes and continued checking out the backyard. "Thanks, Randy, dear," Mrs. Mulligan said, "but I'm too nervous to stay inside." She gave him a knowing smile. "And do you mean Janet? She's a lovely girl. You should stop by the statue one day and let me take your picture."

Mrs. Mulligan was the official Angel Falls photographer, and after years of taking pictures of couples at the falls, he supposed he couldn't fault her for believing in their local legend. It still amazed him how many people believed getting their picture taken in front of the big bronze angel statue on the bridge and dropping a coin into the falls would guarantee them true love forever.

As if. Rafe snorted. The legend was a clever way to fill the town's coffers, in his opinion.

Rafe walked down a set of wooden stairs and shined his flashlight under the porch. There was a large hole underneath one of the latticework panels where some animal had clearly been trying to dig his way under.

"I'm not strong enough to get those wood panels off," Mary said from the top of the steps. "That's why I called. I know it's an awful night to come out."

Awful is right, Rafe thought as rain dripped from the porch roof down his neck. "Hey, we're used to it. Don't you worry, Mrs. M." Rafe turned to Randy, who was behind him, and dropped his voice. "Why don't you get her to go into the house? I'll look under there."

"I heard that," Mrs. Mulligan said. "I'm not budging until we find him."

"You're not going to be of any help to George if you get sick, right?" Rafe said. "I'll let you know as soon as I see anything."

Rain pelted his face, but he managed to pull the wood panel off and squatted down, shining his flashlight under the porch.

A sweep of the space revealed puddles of water, lots of dead leaves, and...one frightened-looking dachshund. Shivering in the far back corner.

"Found him," Rafe called.

"Oh, thank God," Mary said. "How's he look?"

"A little scared, but okay."

"Oh, I'm so glad. Can you get him to come?"

"George, buddy," Rafe said in his calmest voice. "It is one miserable night to be wanting some alone time." Suddenly Rafe choked and drew his hoodie up over his nose. "Wow, something really smells under here," he said.

The dog whined and went belly and ears down, causing Rafe to chuckle. "Sorry to insult you, George. I know you're having a bad day."

"Rafe?" Mary said. "How's it going down there?"

Not good. George wouldn't budge. "Um, he's not really wanting to come. Any suggestions?"

"He's always so confused after he has a seizure."

Rafe edged a little closer, talking more nonsense to the dog. "Your mama's waiting with all the dog treats you can handle. Want a biscuit? Cookie?" Rafe patted his pockets. Sometimes he actually carried dog treats, but right now they were empty. "C'mon, buddy. It's really gross under here. Come with Uncle Rafe."

George was still not having it.

"You and I are going to have a talk," Rafe said as he squatted at the entrance of the crawl space. "Now, don't you want to go back inside and climb into your nice warm bed? Come on, now." Then suddenly he shuddered and tried to flip his jacket collar up as rain rolled straight down his neck.

That was the final straw, making Rafe do what he did not want to do—crawl toward the dog on his hands and knees. He sloshed through puddles of icy water and mud until he finally managed to grab hold of the dog by the collar. All Rafe's irritation faded when he discovered the dog was shaking so hard his teeth were rattling. "It's okay, Georgie, I got you," he crooned, petting the dog's back.

"Rafe?" Mary called from somewhere over him, her voice cracking. "Have you got him?"

"Yes, ma'am," Rafe said, trying not to breathe through his nose. Or let go of the muddy, slippery dog.

"Oh, I'm so relieved," Mary said. "How is he, Rafe? Are you coming up now?"

"Got him. Be up in just a minute."

Rafe felt Mary holding her breath. After a long pause, she finally spoke again. "By the way, I saw Kaitlyn the other day."

Rafe nearly stopped in his commando-crawl tracks. "Kaitlyn Barnes?"

"Why, yes, your Kaitlyn, of course. We were talking about how nice you looked on that poster."

Rafe was about to protest, but she kept on talking. "And poor thing, she was so nauseated. I could tell she was doing her best to pretend she was fine, but she brought me a bowl of soup with my tea, and I could tell the smell was really getting to her."

Had Kaitlyn been ill? He thought back to their discussion the other night. She *had* looked thin, and she'd had circles under her eyes.

"Funny, but the only time I remember odors bothering me like that was when I was expecting."

The little wiener dog slipped right through Rafe's hands and landed back in the mud with a splash. "Sorry, George," he said, getting a better grip on the dog and his own emotions.

Expecting? Kaitlyn? Uninvited images flashed through his mind of the night of the wedding. He'd started to walk her back to her cabin, but it had been pouring and they'd ended up back at his instead. They'd been talking and laughing and then suddenly the lights had gone out. He'd reached for her out of instinct—but once he touched her, he couldn't seem to stop.

It was as if all the denying, all the times he'd told himself *no, not her, never her*, had been cut loose, and for that brief time neither of them were able to deny what they'd been fighting all along.

Still, they'd used protection. She was on the pill and he'd used a condom. So if she was pregnant...

His heart suddenly took a plunge and an icy feeling spread through him that had nothing to do with the frigid conditions under the porch. *Steve.* The high school football coach she'd dated up until last year, who made no secret he wanted her back. Who always seemed to be a little jealous and irritated at Rafe because he and Kaitlyn had hung out so much together after she and Steve broke up.

"Of course, that nice Steve Connolly has been stopping by the Bean a lot lately. Why, when I was in there the other day he'd brought her a bouquet of red roses for her birthday. And it isn't even until next week."

Rafe scowled, and not just because he knew she preferred daisies. Could she have gotten back together with Steve? Who would blame her, after Rafe had pulled away and had done his best to avoid her?

The dog barked, and Rafe looked up to see that he was nearly across the width of the crawl space. He told himself to calm the hell down and to stop letting his imagination run wild. If he listened to the speculation of every neighbor in this town who thought they knew everyone's business, where would he be? Maybe Kaitlyn was fighting the flu. It was going around town. No need to jump to crazy conclusions.

From the far corner of the crawl space came a noise so faint Rafe thought he'd imagined it. Sort of a cross between a squeak and a cry. Great, now that he was worked up over Kaitlyn, he was hearing things.

He kept slogging along with the dog, who was now squirming like a greased pig in his arms. He heard another noise. This time it was a whimper.

He called to Randy through the deck slats above his head. "Hey, Rambo, come down here, okay?"

He thought Randy was going to give him grief for making him come outside, but no questions asked, he soon came clattering down the stairs. That's what made them such good partners.

Rafe handed him the dog. "Ask Mary where her washtub is. I'll be right up."

Randy scanned his face. "You need help?"

Rafe shook his head and pointed behind him with his thumb. "There's something else in there. Whatever it is, it's whimpering."

Randy took the muddy dog and Rafe reentered the dark space. Another noise from the back corner made the hairs at the back of his neck stand up. He flashed his light systematically over the entire rectangular area. Leaves. Spiderwebs. Dirt—correction, make that *mud*.

Suddenly his light caught the red flash of two retinas. Tiny, close-together retinas. Whatever it was, it was *small*.

He startled, and almost lost his balance, but managed to flash the beam back into the corner. "Holy…what the…Are you a…" He'd had encounters with bats before, and he knew rabies was a concern with them and any wild animal. And a raccoon could be just as dangerous. Suddenly out of the piled-up leaves came a…

"Dog?"

He ventured a few steps closer to examine the bundle of mud with eyes. It was whining pathetically and shivering with cold.

This was no dog. It was a fricking *puppy*.

"Oh man. You've got to be kidding. Who would—"

His brain stuttered, filled with rage and wonder at the same time. He'd seen a lot of crazy things as a firefighter, but...who would abandon a puppy? Leave him to perish in this weather? Or was it possible the animal escaped from somewhere...someone's house?

Rafe lifted the little bundle and held it against his chest. It was...tiny. Quivering. Freezing cold. The animal gave him a look that seemed to say, *I'm not real sure I trust you, but you're the best I've got*, then went still in Rafe's arms.

"Hey, now. Don't give up the fight. Because you're in luck. I'm a firefighter. I've got resources. Come on, pup."

The puppy felt limp in his arms, and Rafe felt a desperation cut through him. "No giving up. Okay, boy? Or girl. You're too muddy to tell."

All he knew was it was small and helpless and he had to warm it up and...and get it somewhere. Where it could be checked over and looked at and...saved. Nobody, human or animal, was going to die on his watch.

Finally he was back to where he'd entered the crawl space. He clutched the puppy close and crawled through, then ran back up the stairs.

Mary was waiting for him in the kitchen, beside her cellar door. "Randy took Georgie down for a bath. And—oh my goodness! What on earth—" She ran over, grabbing a towel from a kitchen drawer on the way and examining the dog as she rubbed it down.

The dog didn't fight, but it was awake, and stared at Mary, wide-eyed.

"Look at the paws on you," Mary crooned. "Big paws. And look at the black coat and the white snout and the patches of gold on your legs...Who on earth would abandon a purebred?"

Rafe frowned as he readjusted the puppy, now wrapped in the kitchen towel. It poked its head out and cast him a baleful look. "A purebred *what*?"

"This is a Bernese mountain dog," Mary pronounced, wiping off its head. The dog shook its head, splattering Rafe with more mud. Not that it mattered now. "They can be quite expensive."

Just then Randy came up from the basement, Georgie bounding up the stairs with him, showing off his new clean self. George stopped in front of Rafe to sniff at the puppy. "Hey, George," Rafe said, bending down to pat him on the head. "You did good." To Mary, he said, "George saved this little guy."

"He must've known the puppy was under the porch," she said, looking quite proud.

When they finally left Mary's house a little while later, Georgie was happily curled up in a blanket by the fireplace. Which is exactly what Rafe would have liked to do, but he had a whole night of work ahead of him.

"What are we going to do with our little friend?" Randy asked. "Want to take him back to the station?"

"I think we should drop him off at the vet hospital," Rafe said. He had no idea how long the animal had been out in the cold. "Then get back to work."

As Rafe walked out to their vehicle, the dog burrowed against him, into his warmth, tucking his head into the inside of Rafe's jacket.

"Aw, look at that," Randy said, laughing. "He likes you."

That made Rafe shake his head. Cute as can be, but not for him.

"Hey, he's probably abandoned or something, you think?" Randy asked. "Maybe you can keep him. Kaitlyn likes dogs, doesn't she?" Randy asked.

Frowning, Rafe got in. Oh, Kaitlyn liked animals, all right. Like an entire litter of kittens that decided to be born in back of the Bean behind the trash dumpster. She'd fed them every three hours for a month and had wanted to keep all of them. "Kaitlyn and I are not together," he said. *No Kaitlyn. No dog.*

Thinking about not wanting Kaitlyn instantly brought back thoughts of her in full force. As he started the car and turned on the wipers, he hoped it was a hellishly busy night to get him out of his head and distract him from wondering about Kaitlyn. Pregnant. *Kaitlyn pregnant.*

Nah, she couldn't be. Yet Rafe had to admit that if Mrs. M. was right, he'd gotten exactly what he'd asked for. He deserved Kaitlyn moving on without him.

* * *

The next morning, Rafe decided to stop by the vet's office on his way home to check on the dog, which they'd learned last night, after all the mud was finally cleaned away, was a *he*. "Hey, Dr. J.," he said, walking into the waiting room. Dr. Jasmine Drake looked up from her paperwork and smiled. Rafe had known her since he was a kid and his family used to bring their Labrador retriever mix in for checkups.

"Good morning, Rafe," Jazz said. "On your way home to bed?"

Rafe nodded. "I was just wondering how the puppy's doing." Not that he wanted a dog at all. But he was curious. Where had it come from? How had it ended up in the mud under somebody's porch?

She draped a stethoscope around her neck and left the desk. "Why don't you come back and see him?"

Barks and yips emanated from the back room even before she opened the door. They passed three dogs in crates: a Chihuahua, a bichon, and a big dog with floppy ears that looked like a cross between a husky and a German shepherd. And then there was the puppy, fast asleep on its stomach, oversized paws splayed out in all four directions, as if it had fallen asleep suddenly and went slack all over.

Something in Rafe's chest squeezed at the sight of the small and completely relaxed puppy. He couldn't help chuckling. "It's a good-looking dog," he said, noting its glossy black coat, golden brows, and the white streak down its face and snout. "A whole lot cleaner than yesterday too. And look at those big paws."

"Berners were bred to be working dogs," Jazz said. "They're all muscle. Back in the day, they used to pull carts in the Swiss Alps. They grow huge, but you'll never meet a gentler dog."

The little guy was pretty darn adorable. So adorable he thought he'd better leave before he did something stupid like ask Jazz if he could bring it home.

The puppy suddenly woke up, blinking his eyes until he became aware of them staring at him. Then he scrambled up and stuck his nose between the bars and gave Rafe a baleful look that Rafe imagined meant, *Bust me out of here already, would you?*

"Any word on where it came from?" Rafe asked, letting the puppy sniff his fingers.

"No, but we've gotten a handful of adoption inquiries already, just by word of mouth," she said, gazing at him steadily. "But I have a strict rule about Christmas puppies."

He shot her a quizzical look.

"Oh, you know. At this time of year, everyone wants an adorable puppy, but not everyone *should* have one, if you know what I mean. Although most people are well intentioned, not everyone realizes what a commitment it is to have a pet—a baby one, no less. Truthfully, I'd love this little guy to go to a good home—the home of someone I know and trust. You interested by any chance?"

Just then the puppy stood up at the bars, tail wagging a mile a minute.

Rafe squatted down. "Hey there." He put his fingers between the bars to rub his silky snout, and the puppy licked at them. Rafe moved his fingers, and the puppy swiped at them. This game continued. "Frisky," Rafe said.

Jazz laughed. "All the staff have fallen in love with him."

Well, who wouldn't? Rafe gently scratched the dog behind the neck. The puppy rubbed up against the bars for more.

"How much longer does he have to stay here?" Rafe asked.

"I'm keeping him a few more days to see if anyone claims him and to keep an eye on him. From a health standpoint, everything seems fine."

The puppy swiped at Rafe's hand. When he reached in to pet it again, the puppy flopped on its belly for more.

Wow. Cuteness overload.

Jazz opened the cage. "Here," she said, bending down to carefully gather up the puppy. "Give him some TLC. He needs it."

"Oh no, I really don't think—"

Jazz unceremoniously placed the dog in his arms. "There you go, sweetheart. Meet the big strong fire-fighter who rescued you." She looked up at Rafe. "Can I take a picture to post in the office?"

"If you want, but I—" Before Rafe could protest, the picture was taken.

"So, you sure you wouldn't want him?" Jazz pressed.

"I couldn't." He wasn't the type to form attachments—with women or pets. "I'm gone twenty-four hours and then home forty-eight."

"The home forty-eight part sounds perfect, if you can get somebody to take care of him when you're at the station."

"I really don't think I—" Rafe suddenly burst out in laughter. The puppy was licking his fingers, one by one. "Hey, crazy dog, what are you doing?"

The puppy gave him an innocent look. When Rafe turned his attention to Jazz again, the licking continued.

"He likes you," Jazz said. "He definitely likes you, Rafe. Reminds me of that time you found Jack. How old were you...around nine?"

Rafe kept his attention on the dog. He didn't want to remember.

"That dog was full of mud, matted, full of fleas," Rafe said. "It was barely potty trained and it didn't know any commands."

Jack had followed him home from baseball practice one night about a year after his mom had passed. His father had not wanted to take care of a mangy dog on top of four rambunctious children, but he'd relented, and Jack had become a part of the family.

He'd loved that dog. They all had, but Jack was *his* dog, first and foremost.

"I believe that sometimes animals find us when *we* need them most," Jazz said, "not necessarily vice versa."

"Jack was a great dog," he said. "I like dogs. But I'm just not ready for one." Truth was, he'd avoided any type of emotional commitment since the accident.

There was a knock on the door. Jazz scurried over to open it. It was Kaitlyn with a cardboard carrier full of coffees and a bag filled with something that smelled like cinnamon.

"Hey, Jazz," she said, a little out of breath. "Hi, Rafe." He examined her carefully, trying to figure out the puzzle that had been preoccupying his mind. She didn't look especially tired or drawn—quite the contrary. Her hair was swept up in a no-nonsense ponytail with some wisps coming undone around her face and her cheeks were a little flushed from running down the street. Her apron was her trademark brown one with a giant cartoon coffee bean on it holding a cup of steaming coffee. She looked...pretty. But then, she always looked pretty.

But *pregnant*?

He found himself fighting not to cringe, thinking of Steve. He was an okay guy, but not for her. She deserved someone who did more than just watch football August through the Superbowl. Who understood what she said before she said it. Who could tell what she was thinking from across a room without her having to say a word.

Geez. Listen to him. Steve was a nice guy and he was acting...jealous. Which he had no right being.

"Hey, Kaitlyn," Jazz said, lighting up at the sight of Kaitlyn bearing coffee. "You didn't have to run these over. I could've gotten them myself."

"I figured you were busy, so I thought I'd save you the trouble." Kaitlyn caught sight of Rafe with the dog and nearly spilled the carrier, quickly carting it over to a desk and setting it down. "Besides...everyone's talking about the puppy." Her mouth turned up in a smile as she walked over. "I had an ulterior motive."

Her gaze flickered between him and the puppy, who was settled in the crook of Rafe's arm in a nirvanalike state, nearly fast asleep. Her big blue eyes shone as clear and true as the lake on a cloudless spring day, causing a strange stirring inside him that caught him completely off guard. She bent her head close enough for him to catch a whiff of her shampoo, which smelled clean and fresh, like the winter air when you come in from outside. "What a cutie-pie," she said, curling her fingers in the puppy's silky coat. "You're keeping it?"

"No," he said quickly, telling himself to *snap out of it.* "Just checking in."

"No one's claimed it yet," Jazz said. "But my hunch is no one will. This isn't the first time someone's dropped off a puppy passing through town."

"In the middle of winter?" Rafe asked. "That's just crazy."

"Weird," Kaitlyn said. "It's amazing he did so well." She bent close to the puppy, who stirred briefly and sniffed her face. "You're a Christmas miracle," she said to the puppy. To Rafe, she said, "Looks like you made a friend." She carefully avoided his gaze as she stroked the puppy. "He likes you. And it looks like you like him too. A good match."

He smiled a little. The old Rafe might've said something smart-alecky to get her goat, but that kind of jocularity seemed all wrong lately. Truth was, he was kind of enjoying the fact that the puppy had snuggled right in and fallen fast asleep. Even if it was just temporary, it was very...soothing. Unlike the flares of emotions igniting all over his insides from the woman standing quietly in front of him.

"What a sweet bundle of fur," Kaitlyn crooned. "You're so pretty, yes you are."

Though the dog was nearly asleep, his little tail rotated once around at the sound of Kaitlyn's praise. If Rafe were a dog, his tail would be wagging too. "What are you going to do?" Kaitlyn asked Jazz.

"Wait and see if anyone comes forward," Jazz said,

returning to a spot behind the desk. "We've got notices out everywhere. Would you want him?"

Kaitlyn laughed and held up her hands. "Um, no thanks. I've got my hands pretty full right now."

A vision popped into Rafe's head. Kaitlyn and Steve sitting around a fire, bouncing a drooly, round-cheeked baby, a Christmas tree in the corner, the puppy lying on the rug.

Geez. He was too tired. He needed to go home and go to bed.

"I've been working on Rafe here," Jazz said. "This little guy has certainly taken to him."

"Are you going to take him, Rafe?" Kaitlyn was searching his face in that thorough way she had, like she could read him from the inside out. Sometimes he felt like she could.

He hesitated a moment before saying, "Nah, my hours are too messed up." Quickly, he passed the dog back to Jazz, who took him and deposited him back on the blankets in the crate. "Hey, I've got to go," Rafe said as he headed toward the door. "Thanks for letting me visit him."

He took one last look at the sweet, sleeping puppy, nuzzled into the blankets. It was super cute now, but one day that dog was going to be huge. He could only imagine the food bill. Even as he said it, he saw a picture of himself as a nine-year-old, his father saying the same things. Since when had he turned into his dad?

Chapter 5

♥

Tell him, a voice inside Kaitlyn's head urged as she stood taking orders behind the counter of the Bean. She barely heard Bing Crosby dreaming of a white Christmas in the background or noticed the festive garland she'd twined with multicolored lights that she'd put up behind the counter. Or the string of cute little plastic snowmen lights blinking above the cash register that all the little kids in their mothers' arms loved so much.

The Christmasy details were lost on her, with Rafe sitting just feet away having a late-afternoon meet-up with Colton, Eli, and Evan. Occasional laughter burst from the table as the guys discussed...whatever guy-talk they were discussing.

"Hazel's in the back," Gwen said, pointing with her thumb, "and I'm almost out of here." Gwen had been hired as a teenager by her grandfather years ago and knew the shop and the customers inside and out. Which was a blessing. The curse was that she nearly always spoke exactly what was on her mind.

"Is Hazel...okay?" It had been a rough day so far, and Hazel had seemed jittery and full of nerves. On the plus side, though, she'd taken a lot of notes, so she was clearly trying.

"Let's put it this way," Gwen said, "I'm thinking of having a cigarette and I haven't had one in fifteen years."

"That bad, huh?"

"Mind if I take off a little early?"

"Of course not," Kaitlyn said. "I'll be fine."

In the past, Rafe often stayed after his friends left—sometimes he helped her close down the espresso machine, wash the milk pitchers, and do the other closing tasks, but sometimes they just sat and talked over coffee. But he hadn't hung out like that since "the incident." Still, she knew if she asked him to stay, he would. She could sit him down and tell him about the baby.

And then he would freak out.

She steeled herself for his reaction. She was frightened out of her mind but also thrilled beyond belief at the thought of having a baby. Sara had shown her a few blurry, whitish blips and a heartbeat on her office ultrasound machine and had given her the name of an OB in the next town over who would want to do a better ultrasound. But there was no doubt—the baby was *there*, inside her, growing. It was a mind-boggling miracle.

As if Rafe could sense the intensity of her thoughts, he looked up from his cup of coffee, caught her eye, and smiled.

Something low in her belly flipped. She suddenly realized she'd been wiping off the old Formica counter so vigorously she feared she might've rubbed a hole through it. So she made herself stop and gave herself a firm scolding to shut off whatever hormones caused that twinkly, starstruck rush to spread through her. She could do this, fight these wayward feelings. She must train her mind, then her body would follow. Like yoga.

She had to. Because she did not want to be attracted to someone who was into good times and fun and not around for the hard stuff—the *real* stuff.

Like her father.

She knew firsthand what it was like to want your father to be there when you needed him, and she wanted more for her baby. Even so, she understood why Rafe ran. Why he'd run from any woman—because he was still so torn up about the fiancée he'd lost. She got that. But their baby needed someone who was capable of stepping up.

"Hi, sweetheart," Mr. Iocona, an elderly man who was one of her regulars, said, walking up to the counter. "I'd like a ham sandwich, please."

Despite Kaitlyn trying to tempt him with multiple other offerings, Mr. Iocona insisted on ordering the same thing every single day: ham, cheddar, lettuce, and a pickle on a plain white bun.

A terrible thought occurred to her. Rafe was *her* ham sandwich. The habit she had to break.

"How about a bowl of soup, Mr. Iocona?" Kaitlyn asked—more like shouted so he could hear. "It's broccoli cheese."

"You say you want a *squeeze*?" The old man leaned forward, speaking just as loudly. "Oh, if only I were fifty years younger."

Gwen, who was bringing more cookies in from the back, rolled her eyes at his comment. She caught Kaitlyn's gaze as Kaitlyn eyed the bakery case.

"Do *not* give him another free cookie," Gwen said.

"I love you too," Kaitlyn said, blowing Gwen a kiss as she slipped a cookie from the bakery case onto his plate.

"Fine. Why don't you just give everyone free cookies?" Gwen mumbled.

"Have a nice evening," Kaitlyn said. "Go to your yoga class. No cigarettes."

"Yeah, yeah," Gwen said. She sounded grumpy, but Kaitlyn didn't miss her tiny crack of a smile.

Suddenly Kaitlyn became aware that Rafe had joined the line, dressed in his navy Angel Falls Fire Department uniform, his big biceps visible under his short sleeves. He was frowning.

She *knew* what Rafe was thinking—that she was too nice to all the seniors, and that they mooched too many free cookies from her, but she didn't look at it that way at all. If she could ease a few people's loneliness, she'd give away dozens.

"Hey," he said, giving her a concerned smile.

"Hey," she said, managing to make her voice neutral. "That puppy sure was cute," she said, grasping for a neutral topic.

"Yeah," Rafe said. "I'm sure Jazz will find it a good home." He scanned her face with careful scrutiny, as if he sensed something was off. It made her nervous.

She nodded and fiddled with the cash register. "Of course." She gave him only the briefest glance, or else she'd run the risk of getting lost in the warm dark depths of his eyes. No thinking about how his hair, the color of rich, black coffee, had the slightest wave in it—how she'd seen pictures of him as a toddler in a sleeper with bunny feet, his hair a curly riot. An olive-skinned baby with curly dark hair and big brown eyes. That's what his child—*their* child—would look like.

She accidentally hit the St. Jude donation jar next to the cash register with her hand, causing it to crash from the counter, change rolling and spilling everywhere.

Oh shh... sugar.

"Are you okay?" Rafe asked, leaning his tall frame over the counter as she scooped change off the floor.

She gave up and stood, fighting a sudden wave of nausea by gripping the countertop.

"You sure you're feeling all right?" he repeated.

Okay, this had gone on long enough. "Yeah, but we really need to—"

"Hi, gorgeous," said a deep voice. She looked up to see her ex, Steve, right beside Rafe, who nodded somewhat curtly. The two men were like oil and water. Steve hated that she'd become such good friends with Rafe after their breakup and Rafe...well, he didn't care for Steve either. Which was odd because Rafe liked just about everybody.

"Steve. Hi." She cleared her throat. Steve was a super nice guy—the nicest she'd ever dated. Faithful, steady, and solid. Too nice in some ways because he had no...edge. He didn't make her laugh hysterically or finish her sentences or get her stupid jokes...like Rafe did, of course.

"I've got tickets to that weird little indie band you like so much," Steve said. "They're coming to the House of Blues this weekend for a holiday concert. Want to go?"

"That's sweet, Steve, but I'm out of town this weekend." She knew she should be more direct, tell him more clearly that she wasn't interested since he kept persisting in trying to get back together. But as usual, she was having trouble finding the words.

"Maybe we could grab dinner before you go."

"Hey, speed the line up." Rafe, now in line right behind Steve, was holding up his coffee mug, probably for a refill. For the life of her, she couldn't understand why he insisted on antagonizing Steve, who suddenly turned beet red under his collar.

Steve turned around and glared. "Hey, where's the fire?" he asked in his most irritated voice.

Now Rafe turned red. "Time-out, coach," he said, making the time-out sign with his hands, which seemed to anger Steve even more.

When Steve took a step toward Rafe, Kaitlyn knew she had to act. "Okay, Jacob and Edward, enough."

Rafe burst out into laughter at her silly barb. Steve just looked puzzled.

Kaitlyn hated confrontation—the number of cookies she gave away for free every day proved that. It was probably all the fights her parents had had growing up—terrible, unresolvable ones with lots of yelling and sleepless nights where she and her sister would climb in bed together and cover their ears.

She pulled out two cookies and gave each guy one. "Behave yourselves now," she said, hoping that would diffuse things. "And please move out of line. People are waiting."

Suddenly there was a giant crash and a clang as something hit the ground behind the counter. "I suck at this!" Hazel cried. "I never wanted to work here in the first place. I never even wanted to *be* here. I want to go *home*!" The girl, in tears, ran through the door leading into the kitchen.

Kaitlyn turned and froze for a second, staring at milk spilled on the floor and spattered over the lower cabinets. In that moment of hesitation, she suddenly found someone at her side—Rafe. He squatted down and picked up a steel milk pitcher.

"Please, let me help." He grabbed a towel from her hands. "You shouldn't be doing this."

What? That was a weird thing to say, but she stepped aside and let him help. "Thanks."

Suddenly everything felt a little overwhelming. This idea that putting Hazel to work would cure all her ails was far-fetched. Being pregnant was exhausting. Feeling like the world was on her shoulders was too.

"It's just her first day," Rafe said.

Kaitlyn dropped her voice. "You heard her. She hates working here. She hates being in Ohio. She's constantly on her phone and biting her nails and sending me evil looks like I'm the worst aunt in the world. Maybe I am, because I can't get her to talk to me. I have no idea how to help her."

She batted back tears as she grabbed another towel and wiped up more of the mess. He walked to the utility closet and came back with a bucket and a mop.

"Thanks for helping," she said, trying to take the mop, but he wasn't letting go. "I've got it. Go back and sit down with your friends."

He gently placed his hand back on the mop, their hands grazing. Which sent unwanted zings up her arm. "I have another idea. Let me get the floor and the customers and you go take care of Hazel."

For a moment they both stood there. Then he slid his hand over hers and squeezed. "Go on."

"Thanks," she said, surrendering the mop and walking through the swinging door into the back.

The Bean had been a small restaurant at one point, and it was equipped with a full-service kitchen complete with professional-grade stainless-steel countertops. Hazel was sitting at a small wooden table pushed up against the sidewall, zeroed in on her phone, which sat atop a pile of schoolbooks. Hazel's work apron dangled halfway off the back of her chair, allowing Kaitlyn to admire the cute green floral jumper she wore with tights and combat boots. The outfit struck her because most days, Kaitlyn's biggest fashion decision was which sweater to toss on top of her jeans.

"Hey, sweetie," Kaitlyn said. That was when her mind went blank. Now what should she say? She wasn't a parent; she had no idea. At one point she moved forward to hug Hazel, but her niece quickly shifted away.

"Look," Kaitlyn said finally, "I know things might seem jumbled up and a little hopeless." Now that was something she could relate to. "But things aren't hopeless. Angel Falls is a great place. People care about each other here. Your family cares about you. We *love* you."

Kaitlyn couldn't help but draw the parallels. Her family loved her as well. So did Rafe's. Somehow, everything would be okay.

"I can't do this," Hazel finally said. "I don't know anything. Cappuccinos, lattes, macchiatos, espressos. It's a different language."

"I thought all teens spoke Starbucks fluently," Rafe said from the doorway. How long had he been there?

Kaitlyn shot him a frown, but she also bit her cheek to keep from laughing a little.

"I hate it here," Hazel said. "It's cold and I have no friends and school sucks."

"You're just the new kid right now," Rafe said, pulling up a seat next to Kaitlyn. "Things will get better."

Wait…Rafe offering advice? Shouldn't he be cracking jokes?

"No, you don't understand," Hazel said. "I don't even care about the friend thing because I'll be gone from here as soon as I graduate. But school really sucks. And I'm flunking my stupid math class." Tears welled up again.

"I'll talk with your teacher," Kaitlyn said, placing her hand over Hazel's. Her niece flinched and moved her hand away, revealing some kind of flower inked on her wrist. Kaitlyn's mother would have skewered her if she'd showed up with ink at Hazel's age. Undeterred, Kaitlyn said, "We can come up with a plan."

"The plan is I have to pass or I won't graduate." Tears were flowing freely now.

"Hazel, I'll do anything I can to help you," Kaitlyn

said. "We'll hire a tutor. So you can graduate and plan for college."

"I'm not going to college," Hazel said, not making eye contact.

"Maybe we should just focus on passing the class right now," Rafe said, clearing his throat. "I'm pretty good at math. Why don't you let me have a look at it?" He turned to Kaitlyn. "Is Hazel done for today? Maybe we'll go out front and work. Colton always enjoys a challenge." He gave Kaitlyn a wink.

"Okay," Kaitlyn said reluctantly. Rafe had an easygoing way about him that Hazel seemed to respond to. Plus she didn't remember enough algebra to save her life. "Sure."

By the time Kaitlyn finished cleaning up the mess, Rafe and Colton were battling it out over multiple sheets of paper torn from Hazel's notebook. Rafe finally took to Googling the type of algebra problem on Kaitlyn's iPad and, after filling several more sheets of paper, set down his pencil to rake his hands through his hair.

"Ready to call it a day, fireman?" Colton asked.

Rafe picked up the pencil again and cracked a smile. "Not on your life, copper."

"How many cops and firemen does it take to do a math problem?" Kaitlyn asked, refilling their coffees for the second time.

Rafe looked up and laughed.

She couldn't help laughing too.

"Too many," Colton said, tossing his pencil onto the table. "I give up. Let's call Sara. She's smart."

Hazel stood and gathered all the papers. "Thanks, guys, for trying to help. I'll just go in early tomorrow and ask my teacher. I'm going to head into the back and get the rest of my stuff."

Colton looked at his watch. "I'm going to take one last cruise through town and head home myself."

Then it was just she and Rafe across the table. "I know someone who might be a good math tutor," he said. "Mind if I ask?"

"Sure," Kaitlyn said. "That would be great. I'm going to speak with Hazel's guidance counselor. She might have suggestions too."

"Good idea," Rafe said.

"I just wish I knew how else to help her. I want to show her that I believe in her. How do I do that?"

Rafe shrugged thoughtfully. "Support her dreams."

The sensitivity of his remark caught her off guard. "I don't even *know* her dreams because she won't speak to me. She doesn't trust me. I'm hoping I can get her to loosen up a little when I take her to your parents' place this weekend. If she'll go with me, that is."

"You're going to the lake house?" His brows lifted in surprise.

Kaitlyn felt her cheeks heat a little. "They invited me. For my birthday."

"Oh." He looked surprised. "I have to work. Sorry I'm going to miss it."

"That's okay." She paused and looked him in the eye. "Rafe—I was wondering if you could have dinner with me sometime soon—maybe tomorrow? I thought we could—have a talk."

He scanned her face, and she swore he went pale. "Okay, sure. How about you come to my place? I'll cook."

"You don't have to do that." She'd rather talk to him at her place, where she could at least be in her own territory. And not have to drive home alone when things went south. "We could just order pizza."

"No, I want to cook. I'm off." He paused. "Is there anything you've been craving?"

Craving? Oh God. Did Sara tell him about the baby? No, Sara would never go against her word. Rafe always asked what she wanted to eat when he cooked for her. She needed to get a grip. "No, whatever you want to make is fine."

Just then Hazel walked out of the back, her satchel of books slung over her shoulder. Her gaze flicked from Kaitlyn to Rafe and back. "I—um—I washed all the pitchers. And the syrup bottles. And sanitized the ice machine. I'm heading out now. See ya!"

Kaitlyn stopped her by calling her name, which made Hazel halt but not turn around. "Are you headed back to Gram's?" Kaitlyn asked.

"Actually"—she slowly turned around—"I was going to drive out to the quarry and smoke some weed and get wasted."

"That's not funny," Kaitlyn said.

"Don't you trust me to go home?" Hazel's tone held a mixture of boredom and outrage, but Kaitlyn could see a glimmer of hurt in her eyes.

Kaitlyn held the line. "I just want to make sure we're both clear about curfew."

Hazel crinkled up her nose as if it smelled really rotten in the café. "*Curfew?*"

"That's where you're in by ten thirty on a school night." Kaitlyn glanced at her watch. "And it's ten o'clock now."

"I'm just going to Gram's, okay?" she said with a slash of irritation. "Call her in five minutes if you don't believe me."

"I believe you," Kaitlyn said, but she could tell Hazel didn't buy that. "And you may not think this, but you did a good job today. First days are always challenging."

Hazel shot her a look that was half *I don't believe what you're saying at all* and half *Can I leave now?*, before she gave a quick wave and scooted out the door. The final slam made Kaitlyn jump.

"Well, I screwed that up," Kaitlyn said.

"Hazel will be all right," Rafe said.

One glance at him showed he seemed perfectly confident. "How do you know that?"

One side of his mouth turned up, a move he made when he was about to joke. He tapped his temple with an index finger. "I can see it in her eyes."

"You sound like Nonna."

"She's frustrated and confused, but I think she's really trying." He shrugged. "At least, that's my take."

"I didn't mean to act like I don't trust her, but... I guess I really don't." Kaitlyn sighed heavily. "I'm trying to give her structure and discipline. And love. She definitely needs that. But I'm just not really sure *what* I'm doing."

"You know what Nonna used to tell us when we were kids."

"What was that?"

" 'I'm your grandmother, not your best friend.' I mean, somebody's got to be a little firm with her. Not me, of course. I'm just here for the comic relief."

Kaitlyn squinted at him. "Don't sell yourself short. You were good with her. I'm not exactly getting through to her. She thinks I'm mean."

"You're the kindest person I know." His tone, sincere and steady, melted her.

She scanned his face again—was he joking? Because he nearly always was. Kaitlyn looked away. "I need her to know that life is serious. She has to choose a good path—the *right* path. If she keeps going on the one she's on now, she'll have a terrible life."

"I agree with all of that." He rubbed the back of his neck. "Parenting sucks. All this reminds me of why I never want kids."

The warm fuzzy feelings their conversation had stirred suddenly dried up faster than summer dew, and Kaitlyn's stomach took a leaden plunge.

With that he got up to go, and she didn't stop him.

Chapter 6

♥

When Kaitlyn walked into her mom's kitchen that night after work, she found her busy at the table cutting shapes out of red and green construction paper and singing along to Michael Bublé Christmas songs. A fat yellow cat rolled around in the thin curls of paper on the floor.

Kaitlyn kissed her mom on the cheek and sat down at the old red table with aluminum trim. The cat stopped rolling around and stretched its body out, batting its paw on her thigh.

"Hi, Melvin," she said, brushing the paper strips off his fur.

"How are you, sweetie?" her mom asked. She wore dangly Christmas tree earrings that swung back and forth in time to the music. And a Christmas sweater, circa 1990, also sporting a Christmas tree, with enough colored sequins to delight a four-year-old. Appropriate for Charlotte Barnes, who seemed to possess all the enthusiasm and excitement of a child, which was probably why she spent her spare time helping her neighbor with craft projects for her preschool class.

"Want some tea?" her mom asked. "It's Christmas Calm—decaf, of course."

That sounded kind of...good. Especially the *calm* part. And since Kaitlyn couldn't stomach much, maybe the tea would stay down.

"You want some too?" Kaitlyn got up to fill the kettle. A quick glance around revealed more mail, extra boxes of tea, a box of Girl Scout cookies, and a poinsettia plant...and that was on the countertop alone.

"Kaitlyn, take a look at how cute this is." Her mother held up green and red paper circles. "They're wreaths. We're going to dye rice green, and the kids are going to mold it over the wreath circle to make their own ornament. Then we're going to have them put these little faux velvet berries on them. Aren't they the cutest things? And their picture goes in the center."

"Cute," Kaitlyn said. Her mom had clearly missed her calling to be a preschool teacher. Which was why she not only helped out with the crafts, but also spent her occasional Friday afternoons off from her insurance company auditor job helping out in the classroom.

"I was going to experiment on the rice recipe next. Want to help?"

"No thanks, Mom. I'm kind of tired." Usually she enjoyed watching her mom get carried away with all kinds of artsy stuff—and she enjoyed spending time with her. But right now Kaitlyn just didn't have the energy.

Her mom looked up from cutting. "You *do* look tired. Everything all right?"

"Everything's fine." She would tell her mother soon, but not until she told Rafe. She wasn't sure that was how she wanted to play it, but truthfully, she was too tired to think about it.

She made tea and glanced over at her mom, guilt dealing her a double blow—one for succumbing to Rafe's charms and allowing this to happen and another for how her news was going to cause her mother all kinds of concern and worry.

Concern and worry led her to wonder about her niece. "Did Hazel seem okay when she got home?" Kaitlyn asked. "She had a difficult night at work."

Her mother looked around, a little startled, as if she'd forgotten where she was. "Goodness, I've been so involved with this project that I'm not sure if she's back yet."

"Mom, I know you haven't had a teenager around in a long time, but Hazel needs to be kept track of— diligently." She could fall into doing drugs or hanging out with bad kids or get picked up by seedy guys coming out of the Tap late at night or…

"Oh, you're such a worrywart. She always checks in with me before she goes to bed. I'm sure she's fine."

"Mom, she's a shoplifter. She's troubled! We have to know where she is, like, 24-7!"

"Hazel needs to feel like we trust her. It's not good for us to be breathing down her neck like that."

"I wish she would trust me enough to talk to me," Kaitlyn said. "She seems so…lost." Again it occurred to her—for all that she couldn't seem to understand what was going on with her niece, she and Hazel weren't all that different. Kaitlyn was a little lost too.

"She told me tonight she's flunking her math class, and if she fails, she won't graduate. Do you know what she's planning to do when she graduates?" *If she graduates* crossed Kaitlyn's mind, but she didn't say that out loud.

"Well, I have no idea," her mom said in a slightly exasperated tone.

"Graduation is six months away."

Her mom sighed. "I expect she'll do what everyone does—figure it out."

"She's smart. She can go to college. We need to guide her into making the right choices." Kaitlyn got herself through college—while working full-time at her grandfather's coffee shop. She'd been the first one in her family to attend college. She needed Hazel to know that she could do the same.

For the hundredth time, Kaitlyn wondered if she should've simply had Hazel move in with her instead of with her mom. Her tiny apartment over the coffee shop was just that...tiny. But maybe she should've done it anyway.

Just then the front door opened and Hazel walked in.

"Hi, Gram. Hi, Aunt Kate." Hazel waved to her grandmother but assessed Kaitlyn with a cool, detached gaze.

"Hi, sweetie," Kaitlyn's mom said. "I heard you had a bit of a rough first day."

"It was peachy," Hazel replied, deadpan. Kaitlyn's mom was too absorbed in her crafting to notice her scissor-sharp tone.

"You did great today, sweetie," Kaitlyn said. "There's a lot to learn and I'm sure—"

Hazel yawned loudly. "I'm really tired. I was just going to grab a glass of milk before I hit the sack."

Hazel's fragile-featured face looked as hard as the rock at Stonehenge. Lord only knew the hostile thoughts she was thinking.

"Did you eat?" Kaitlyn's mom asked. "There's some Chinese left in the fridge."

"I had dinner at Aunt Kate's."

"Did *you* eat?" her mother asked Kaitlyn.

She took a sip of the tea, which she actually found soothing and palatable. The urge to retch had not resurfaced. "I'll have something later. This tea is really good."

Ignoring her mother's scrutinizing look, she turned to Hazel. "Hazel, are you doing anything this weekend?"

"Well, let me see," she said, leaning up against the counter and folding her arms. "I'll have to check my busy social calendar."

"I hope that means you're free," Kaitlyn continued, undeterred. "Because my friends have invited me to their lake house for the weekend to celebrate my birthday, and I wondered if you'd like to come."

"To hang around with your friends?" she asked, pulling a hang-around-with-old-people face.

"Well, it's actually a family. My two best friends and their parents. Their older sister and her children will probably be there too."

"Hmmm. Little kids. Sounds fun."

"Great," Kaitlyn said, ignoring the sarcasm. "I'll pick you up Friday at four thirty. Be packed."

Hazel stopped leaning on the countertop. "Thanks, but I'm just dying to get started on *A Tale of Two Cities*. I've got a ton of studying to do this weekend."

"Is Rafe coming?" Kaitlyn's mom interjected.

"No," Kaitlyn said a little too quickly. "He's working." It was a good thing, to not have him there, because he'd only be a distraction. Even if it was her birthday. And his not being there was making her a little...sad. But then, he didn't want kids and she was having *his*, and that made her feel even worse.

"Have you met Rafe yet, Hazel?" Kaitlyn's mom asked. "Oh, he's the most handsome guy. And he's sweet on your aunt."

"I met him," Hazel said. "They look at each other all googly-eyed. And they laugh at dumb *Twilight* jokes together."

"He's not 'sweet on me,'" Kaitlyn interjected. "Rafe and I are *friends*." How on earth was she going to make them believe this friends thing once they found out about the baby?

"You started out as friends," her mom said. "Anyone can see that you two have feelings for each other."

"Yes, Mom. *Friend* feelings." Oh, what was she doing? Digging herself into a hole, that's what.

"How come you haven't brought him by lately? And you've been stumbling around all mopey. I hope you haven't put him off."

Put *him* off? Geez. Why did everyone adore Rafe so much? She knew exactly why. He was handsome and charming and funny. But he did not want kids, and he was about to get one. She wondered what her mom would think of him if she told her that. But she wouldn't, of course.

She knew down to her core that Rafe was a kind person. Surely he would be good to their child. At least she'd thought that *before*.

Kaitlyn suddenly became aware of her mom and Hazel staring at her as she'd zoned out of the conversation. So she said, "Mom. Rafe and I aren't dating."

"Oh, don't you give me that." Her mom waved her hand dismissively. "You used to spend almost every free evening together. You had season tickets to the Broadway musicals series at Playhouse Square. And when you two went to that wedding as a couple last September, it took you two weekends to find the perfect dress. That's dating behavior, if you ask me. And the way that man looks at you when you're not looking! It's swoony."

Hazel's brows arched up into question marks. "You and Rafe hang out a lot, but you don't date?"

"That's what Kaitlyn says, but I don't buy the friend thing for a moment," Kaitlyn's mom said. "I like him so much better than Steve. He's just what you need to lighten you up—always finding something funny to joke around about. So polite and helpful too. He plays rummy with Dorothy and remember when he helped me carry all my craft boxes up to the attic? And he's from a good family. Honestly, Kaitlyn, I do hope you'll give him a chance. Rafe is one of the good ones."

Yes, Rafe had certainly charmed their elderly neighbor Dorothy, as he had 99.9 percent of all women. *Ugh.* But being a genuinely nice guy did not necessarily make for good husband and father material. And the fact was, Rafe didn't *want* to be a husband or father.

"Aren't you having dinner with him tomorrow?" Hazel asked. "I heard you two talking about it. He's cooking."

Someone. Was. About to have their neck wrung.

Her mom clapped her hands together. "See? I knew it. Wonderful!"

"Anyway." Kaitlyn quickly shifted topic and addressed her niece. "This weekend is just a birthday dinner with my friends, and then they do fun stuff like moonlight hikes and sledding and bonfires, and games inside by the fire. And I think they're getting their Christmas tree too. We'll take the last ferry back Saturday afternoon, so you can still get your homework done."

Hazel opened her mouth—probably to say no. But then Kaitlyn's mom said something surprising. "I have my colonoscopy scheduled for Saturday morning." She added green food coloring to a bowl of rice, focusing intently. "So, Hazel, if you stay behind, you can keep me company while I prep."

Kaitlyn set down her tea. Wait...did her mom just *intervene*? More important, was she sick?

"Why do you have a colonoscopy scheduled?" Kaitlyn asked. "Is anything wrong?"

"It's just routine," her mom said, looking up and giving Kaitlyn a wink while Hazel dug around in the fridge. "But I have to drink gallons of this stuff that tastes like gasoline. It's supposed to clean my whole system out. Like a *massive* cleanse. And they say once it gets going...look out!"

Hazel emerged from the fridge door holding the milk carton and looking dubious.

"We can watch movies," Kaitlyn's mom continued, "if you don't mind pausing every so often while I run to the bathroom."

Hazel might've blanched. "Um, Aunt Kate, if I can get some reading done at the lake, maybe I can go—I mean, if it's okay with you, Gram."

"Oh. Well, sure, of course." Her mom even managed to sound a little disappointed. "I guess I probably wouldn't be much fun anyway."

"Great," Kaitlyn said. "So four thirty then." At first she thought it was a great idea to bring Hazel to meet the Langdons. But she was telling Rafe about the baby tomorrow. What if Rafe wanted to tell his family this weekend, while she and Hazel were at the lake house? How would all that be for Hazel to witness?

She'd have to tell him they'd do it after her birthday, at a time when Hazel wasn't there. So at least this weekend would be free of conflict—one last weekend with the Langdons where she could pretend her whole life hadn't completely changed.

With a quick nod, Hazel said good night, gathered up her book bag, snagged an apple from a bowl, and headed upstairs.

"Do you think it's a good idea to make her work in the coffee shop?" her mom asked as soon as Hazel was out of range. "Especially since she's had problems?" She made air quotes around *problems*.

"Yes, Mom, I do. I think she's bored and miserable and she isn't socializing."

"Well, now that you've got her working every day, how is she going to find friends? Or keep her grades up?"

"I'm not sure yet." Oh, geez. Was *this* what parenting was like?

Her mom sighed. "She *has* been pretty wretched here. Counting down the days until she can leave. She's mentioned going to New York to work in the fashion industry. She loves watching *Project Runway*."

"Oh, is that right?" Kaitlyn said, surprised. But the more she thought about it, the more that made sense. "She certainly has a flair for fashion."

Her mom shrugged. "She's talked about taking sewing lessons. I mean, Nikki taught her to sew, but she wants to learn advanced skills. I told her I thought it was an interesting idea."

"I'm going to go in and speak to the guidance counselor. Maybe she'll have some ideas on how we can use Hazel's interests to get her back on track. Hazel's got a lot of decisions to make about her future. I don't want her to miss an opportunity to apply for scholarships or aid."

"That's a good idea." Her mom, sounding distracted, was staring at her. "Are you sure you're all right?"

"Yeah. Why?"

"I don't know. You just look...tired. Thin. Something...something seems different."

Oh no. Kaitlyn's mom had always had a mother's sixth sense about what was wrong with her, mentally and physically.

"I'm fine, Mom. Really. Do you actually have a colonoscopy on Saturday?"

Her mom looked up, a mischievous glint in her eye. "Of course not. But I do have one scheduled. It saves lives." She pushed the box of tea toward Kaitlyn. "Take the tea with you. Your complexion looks a little greeny."

Kaitlyn picked up a cosmetic mirror that was tucked into the fruit bowl at the center of the table and looked at herself. "Greeny?" Was that even a word?

Kaitlyn felt her mom's quietly assessing gaze for a few more beats. Then her mom said, "The tea's got mint in it. That was the only thing that settled my stomach when I was pregnant with you."

Chapter 7

♥

That Thursday evening, Kaitlyn pulled her boots off at Rafe's front door and looked around at the set dining room table and the fire in the fireplace. Jazzy Christmas music played in the background, and she could smell warm bread, which actually seemed to calm her stomach for once. It was a picture-perfect evening. And she was going to shatter it with her news.

"You went through too much..." she said.

"No trouble," Rafe said quickly, before she could finish. "You know how I'm always trying out new recipes for the station." Rafe set pot holders down on his dining room table and walked over to take her coat. He hung it up in the closet, frowning. "Hey, where's your *winter* coat?" he asked.

"I'm plenty bundled, see?" She flapped her hands, which were covered by the arms of her long wool sweater.

"Aren't your feet cold?" he asked as he looked down at her thin socks.

"Don't worry about me, Mom," she said emphatically. "I'm *fine*."

He grinned. "Hey, I can't help myself. It's all those years of being mothered by three sisters. I'm a mother hen in disguise. Come on in."

She stepped into the open space that included his living and dining areas, surveying the minimalist furniture, the open floor plan, and the brand-new couch in front of the fireplace. She'd helped him pick out that couch months ago. He'd agonized over beige versus brown for twenty minutes until she finally told him the darker color was probably more practical. She had no idea if that was really true, but Rafe also fretted over domestic decisions like a mother hen.

"What do you think?" he asked, watching her reaction carefully.

"You've knocked down some walls since the last time I was here," she said. "And you bought the couch! It looks very...nice. Except for one thing."

"What's missing?" he asked, knitting his brows.

"Christmas decorations," she said. "Are you going to get a tree?"

"I haven't thought that far ahead," he said.

"Rafe, it's three weeks before Christmas. How much time do you need to think?"

He shrugged off her comment, and dimly, she wondered if he was avoiding getting a tree. Come to think of it, he hadn't had one last year either.

"Look," he said suddenly, holding her by the shoulders and interrupting her thoughts, "I'm glad we're having dinner together. You know you can tell me anything, right?"

She frowned. "Right. Of course." Did he suspect something? Maybe she just looked worried—he had a way of sensing her moods.

"Great. Have a seat. I'll bring out the food."

Rafe went into the kitchen and came out holding Santa oven mitts. Surely those had been a gift from Rachel, his stepmom, or his Italian grandmother they all called Nonna. She couldn't imagine him being *that* domestic all on his own. He set down a steaming pot full of a very savory and robust-smelling...cheesy, meaty sauce.

Uh-oh. Her stomach twisted in protest. *Not tonight*, she warned it as if it were actually going to take heed.

"I made pappardelle from scratch. And Bolognese sauce. Remember when we had it that night in Little Italy and you kept saying how you wished you could have this at home?"

She *did* remember that night. The waiter had thought they were a couple and kept joking with them (which of course put Rafe right in his element) and bringing them different things to try, including a giant piece of tiramisu on the house that they'd split. They'd had such a fun time—and the Bolognese had been awesome. Now, though, all she could think was, *Oh no. Meat.*

The smell...made her stomach flop over like a beached seal and brought a wave of nausea that had her mouth producing saliva and frantically trying to swallow it down.

Focus on how pretty the table is. The candles flickering. Rafe's solemn face showed that he was clearly looking for her reaction in response to all his efforts. He'd even made the pasta himself. Who did that?

No one had made her such a fabulous meal before. She'd dated Steve for a year and a half and the best he'd ever done was speed-dial takeout and laugh about not being able to boil an egg.

"It's—wow. Amazing, Rafe."

He laughed, and his eyes shone deep and dark in the candlelight. She missed the days when she felt that laughter resonate deep in her chest, when she felt so comfortable with him that she wouldn't think twice about laughing along too.

"Look, Rafe, I—I have to talk to you about the night of the wedding."

It was nearly impossible to tell when Rafe was flustered, but even in the candlelight, Kaitlyn could see a flush start at his neck and overcome his face.

He cleared his throat. "Look, there was definitely too much wine involved. We—we both agreed we got carried away."

Just then he opened the lid to the sauce and a wall of meaty aroma hit her head-on. For a moment the room spun. *Breathe deep, breathe deep*, she chanted to herself, focusing every bit of concentration on keeping her stomach contents where they belonged.

Please God, let this pass. Not *now*.

"Are you okay?" he asked. "You look a little…gray."

"Rafe," she said, inhaling deeply. "Rafe. I have to tell you something. I'm—"

Suddenly she was doubled over, her stomach trying to leap out of her body. And there it came. Right on his shoes. And his beautiful new rug.

* * *

Kaitlyn grabbed a napkin and raced to the bathroom, which was down the hall off the family room. Rafe found her caressing the toilet bowl. The EMT in him raced into action, placing a cool cloth on her neck, offering her water to rinse her mouth, even going so far as to bend down, prepared to scoop her up and take her to lie on his bed.

"Rafe—no," she said, splaying out her hands so he didn't get too near. But he seemed oblivious to the fact that she was a mess, rewetting the cloth, leaning her head back against the wall, making her take sips of water.

He sat across from her against the door, his long legs filling up the bathroom space.

"Come lie down," he said insistently. He was great in a crisis. But what she was about to throw at him...well, she could only think that the barf was just the beginning.

She shook her head to clear it, unrolling some toilet paper to wipe her eyes and blow her nose.

"Let me get you something to drink," he said. "Want some Coke? More water?"

"Rafe," she said, her voice raspy and hoarse. The acid stung her throat, but that was nothing compared to the ache in her heart. She wanted to rewind, to go back to the lovely set table and all the homemade food and pretend... well. She pushed all that out of her mind. Actually, she wanted to go back to that wedding and start all over again. "I'm fine. Listen." She grabbed his hands.

Now he was looking at her with eyes narrowed, concern written all over his face. "You sure you're okay? Maybe you need to go to the ER or something? Maybe I should feel your abdomen."

"I don't have appendicitis. I don't have a GI bug." Oh God. Her heart was a bongo drum, resonating loudly between her ears, threatening to pulse out of her chest. For one last second, she scanned his face, wanting to remember what it was like before she said the words that would change everything between them forever.

"I think I know what you're about to say," he said, holding up his hands to halt her words, "and I just want you to know I'll be there for you whether you're with Steve or not."

Puzzled, she stared at him. "You will be?"

He nodded and took her hand. "I'll always be here for you, no matter what. Have you... told him?"

"Told who... what?"

"Have you told Steve you're... expecting?"

Oh no. He thought... "Rafe," she said grasping his hands and looking dead into his eyes. "I haven't slept with Steve. I broke up with him a year and a half ago."

"But he's always in the coffee shop, bringing you flowers..." Rafe's eyes suddenly widened. His expression shifted subtly—the creases between his brows deepened. Confusion clouded his eyes. "Steve's not... Steve's not the father?" he asked. "Then who..."

Kaitlyn closed her eyes. She wished that, like Dorothy, she could click her heels and spin around a few times and disappear. Going back to Kansas would be great right around now. Staying here for this fallout...not so much.

"Whose baby...is it?" He spoke slowly and deliberately, and he seemed to be staring intensely at the drawer pulls on the bathroom vanity. Which she recognized as the oil-rubbed bronze pulls she'd helped him pick out a few months ago. Why the image of them strolling through Ikea came to mind now she had no idea.

She rested her hand on his arm until he looked at her, all the emotions rampant on his face.

"It's our baby, Rafe," she said softly. "Yours and mine."

* * *

The baby was his? "That's...but you're on the pill. I-I used a condom." Confusion clouded his vision and made his voice sound an octave higher than usual. "How...?"

Kaitlyn looked ghostly white, her eyes big and round. He understood that his reaction was important, that she would remember whatever he did or said in the next few moments for a lifetime. Yet he felt like he was watching himself in a movie.

"That box of condoms Randy put in your suitcase," she said. "Did you check the dates?"

The box of condoms. He lunged forward, opened the cabinet below the sink, and scavenged violently through his bathroom supplies. He tossed aside rolls of toilet paper, double boxes of toothpaste, a spray bottle of Pine-Sol, a giant bottle of shampoo. He was nothing if not prepared—but the condoms were not his doing. From the depths, he pulled out a box of thirty-six condoms, now minus one. The same box Randy had buried as a joke in his suitcase the night of the wedding. Gabby had seen it and thought he was preparing for a wild weekend, but he hadn't been. He'd spent all his time with Kaitlyn, eating and dancing and having fun, and he'd never even cared to look at anyone else.

Women had been texting him too, also the result of his buddies' prank. He hadn't told Kaitlyn that though. He'd used the constant texts as an excuse to get the heck out of that cabin after they'd . . . well.

Rafe examined the box, rotating it in a dozen different directions to read the fine print.

He let out a long breath he didn't realize he was holding as he held it out to her. A sense of knowing dread flooded through him, flowing ice-cold through his veins. "July 2017. These expired a year before the wedding."

Images from that night came flooding back. The rain pouring down in sheets, clattering down on the tin roof of the cabin, the thick velvet darkness of the blackout dark and deep. Kaitlyn's lips, so sweet and warm, the feel of her under his lips and his hands. The way she moved beneath him, so responsive to his every touch.

Kaitlyn clutched her stomach as she sat leaning against the wall, as if she were steeling herself for another attack of nausea. "I never missed a pill," she said, pressing her lips into a thin line. "But after I picked up my prescription, I might've left it in my car for a day or two. Sara told me the heat might've made them less effective."

He looked up suddenly. "Sara knows?"

She nodded. "I saw her in the office. I'm two and a half months along—well, twelve weeks technically because they count from the last period, not from when it happened."

Rafe put his head in his hands. A strange involuntary sound emanated from him, a mixture of a moan and a sigh.

A baby. *His* baby. Not Steve's. His and Kaitlyn's.

She hadn't taken her eyes off him. She was waiting for his reaction, seeming almost to hold her breath for it.

He didn't want to hurt her, but she knew him too well. He couldn't hide what he was feeling, which was shock and fear.

He desperately wanted to meet her honest blue gaze and smile like he nearly always did, every time she needed a laugh, every time she had a worry or concern. She could count on him to make her laugh. That was what he did. What he was good at.

But now…now he was out of jokes.

The other day he'd told her that he didn't want kids. He'd meant it—he'd very carefully planned that that would never be in the cards for him. And yet here they were…A baby was coming, whether he was ready or not.

Kaitlyn must be nervous. Fearing his reaction.

Maybe even a little afraid. He got that, he understood that. He always wanted to help her, to rally for her, but he just... couldn't.

He'd always suspected he could never love again, and this was proof... because something was wrong with him, deep inside. He wasn't reacting the way a normal person should. He wasn't feeling anything, just remembering a long-ago morning—the morning of the accident. Seeing himself on that glorious, sunny summer day, everything perfect in his life. He was about to be married and he had a baby on the way, and that had been the icing on the cake.

And then everything went black.

Kaitlyn cleared her throat, and he realized he'd zoned out.

"I'm fully prepared to do this on my own," she said, lifting her chin. "I know this is a shock, and I know you don't want kids. But I've had time to think about it and I'm... I'm okay with it. I'm going to give this baby the best life possible. We—we're good friends and—we can raise this baby with love. Or I can raise this baby alone with love. It's your choice."

Just like that, the ball was back in his court and again, he had no words. His heart could not love like that again. He just didn't have it in him.

She was blinking fast, like she had something in her eyes, and he knew she wanted to cry. Before he could scramble to his feet to help her, she got up and ran out of the bathroom.

He ran after her as she flew into the kitchen, returning with a roll of paper towels and a bucket to clean up the mess.

He walked over and took the roll from her. "Let me get this," he said.

"Rafe, you are *not* cleaning up my barf," she said.

"And you are going to sit down and rest."

She took the bucket back and got to work. "I'm *fine*." When she was done she took her coat from the closet.

"Don't go," he said, concern etched all over his face.

"I think we both need some time to process this," she said, putting on her coat. "I'm sorry I ruined the nice dinner."

As her gaze swept over his face, he saw it all—the fine frown lines, the holding back of tears, but mostly—the disappointment.

"Bye," she said quickly and headed out the door.

"I—I want to help," he said, but she didn't hear.

Rafe waited until he heard Kaitlyn's tires squeak against the packed snow as her car rolled down his driveway. Her beat-up Toyota Corolla probably needed new tires for the winter, and he made a mental note to check the tread ASAP.

He grabbed the wine bottle from the table and sat down on his couch, taking a big gulp, then another.

The wine didn't take away the realization that had finally sunk in, deep down to his bones.

He was going to be a *father*.

Chapter 8

♥

A few minutes later, Kaitlyn pulled into her parking spot in front of the Bean. It was marked by a sign with a pink cup of steaming coffee on it that read "Owner," which had been a gift from the town council when she'd first reopened the Bean after her grandfather died. The council was grateful that she'd saved it from being made into a chain coffee shop.

Every time she pulled into this space, she reminded herself that what she'd accomplished with the café had been risky and scary. She tried to derive strength from that for this next big challenge on her plate. But the sign wasn't reassuring her now, and the thought of going up to her apartment alone was giving her the shakes. So she drove to her mom's instead.

She dreaded telling her the thing she'd been warned against her entire life... getting pregnant with the wrong guy. Her mom had gotten pregnant in college with Kaitlyn's older sister and had ended up marrying Kaitlyn's father, which had turned out to be nothing short of disaster. He'd left when Kaitlyn was ten. Nothing in Kaitlyn's own experience had proven to her that men stick around when the going gets tough.

Still, Kaitlyn hadn't given up on the idea of finding a good man. She'd dated some questionable guys before Steve, but Steve had been a genuinely nice guy. He'd wanted to *marry* her, for goodness' sake. And yet Kaitlyn couldn't move forward with him, couldn't put thoughts of Rafe aside. And look where that had gotten her!

She'd told Rafe she was capable and prepared to take on the responsibility of a baby with or without him, and she'd meant that. She was strong and she would get through this just fine. But sometimes, a girl just needed her mom.

"What's up?" her mom asked as she let her into the tiny Cape Cod–style house. She was wearing a brown fuzzy robe that had reindeer antlers sticking out of a hood at her back. "Aren't you usually crawling into bed with a book and the remote by now?"

"I—" *Mom, I'm pregnant* didn't seem like the greatest lead-in for a conversation. "I was wondering if you've been able to find Grandpa's snowcap cookie recipe anywhere." Okay, maybe she wasn't quite as brave as she thought.

Plus, she'd been the daughter who hadn't made waves. Who was goal-oriented and capable and practical. And she couldn't shake the feeling her mother was going to be very disappointed in her choices, no matter how much her mom loved Rafe.

"Oh! I did dig up something from the attic." Her mom

walked over to the dining room table and brought a big cardboard box back to the kitchen, where Kaitlyn had just sat down. "Here you go. Have at it. I was going to give this to you for your birthday, but there's no sense in waiting. Also, I bought you and Hazel Christmas robes." She lifted the fleece-lined hood of her robe over her head. Two padded reindeer antlers stuck straight up. Eyes and a bright red nose accompanied the antlers. "Do you want this style or one that has a penguin face on the hood?"

Guilt stabbed her again, as she realized that elevating the conversation from reindeer robes to babies was going to rock her mom's world. "The robe is cute," she said. "I love it. Hazel will too."

Kaitlyn opened the box, which was full of old spiral-bound cookbooks and a stack of gallon-sized plastic freezer bags stuffed full of yellowed clippings and hand-written recipes—in her grandfather's handwriting. That made her tear up.

She carefully thumbed through the old recipes. Hot cross buns, Swedish coffee ring, blueberry muffins. She remembered those blueberry muffins. She'd have one warmed up, dripping with butter, every Sunday when she visited him at the café.

"I've gone through all the clippings and loose papers for that darn cookie recipe," her mom said, setting tea bags into Santa mugs. "But you're welcome to search again. I asked Aunt Bea and all the ladies in my sewing club if they might have it, because we used to trade recipes all the time, but no luck."

Kaitlyn got up and hugged her mom, maybe a little too tightly. "Thank you for doing this. I love looking at old recipes, even if the cookie recipe's not in here." Images of ones she could create—low-fat versions, vegan versions, gluten-free versions, organic versions—danced through her mind...Experimenting with baking was sort of Kaitlyn's crack. Thinking about it centered her a little.

"Your grandfather was planning to put all his favorite recipes into a book for you, but then he passed so suddenly..."

Oh no. That choked her up a little too. "This is the next best thing." She sat back down and forced herself to look her mom in the eye, ignoring her clammy hands and pounding heart. She spoke past the wad of cotton balls in her throat. "Mom, I need to tell you something..." she began.

"Oh dear, what's wrong? I know that look. Just come out with it," she said clutching her hand. "Did someone die?"

"I'm pregnant," she blurted, then held her breath as the words processed. Her mom's eyes grew wide.

"Well, I wondered. You've looked a little green around the gills." She squeezed Kaitlyn's hand with both of her own and looked at Kaitlyn with eyes full of love and concern. "Tell me, sweetheart."

"Rafe and I slept together at that wedding a few months ago," she blurted. "It was...impulsive. A mistake. We used protection but...it didn't work. I want you to know even though this isn't the most ideal way for this to happen, I'm thrilled, and Rafe..."

"Rafe what?" her mom asked, frowning. Her mom tightened the death grip on her coffee mug.

"He and I are going to raise this baby as friends."

"As friends," her mom murmured incredulously. "You're kidding yourself if you think you two are just friends. Anyone can see the chemistry between you."

Kaitlyn shook her head. "I know how he is. He's not the kind to settle down. Like I said, it was a one-time thing. I—"

"One-time things don't come out of nowhere when you two have been such close friends."

"I don't think he will ever get over what happened with Claire."

"But that was years ago. And he was so young."

"It devastated him. He still won't even talk about it. And he doesn't have to. I'm okay with raising this baby on my own. He doesn't want a relationship. And I—I don't either. I've always had a thing for him, but it was a fantasy. It's time I put those feelings aside and grew up anyway. I just—worry that I've let you down."

"Oh, sweetheart," she said, clasping Kaitlyn's hand across the table. "You can never let me down. When I found out I was pregnant, I quit college. You've got your degree and a thriving business. You're far more mature and capable than I was at your age."

"I don't feel very mature and capable right now."

"I'm glad you're not going to jump into marriage with issues to work out. But I'm not sure you should give up on your relationship with Rafe either."

Kaitlyn shook her head. She had to set her mother straight on this. "I know you love him, Mom, but there is no relationship."

"In some ways, you're the opposite of me—so capable

and independent. Just don't be afraid to need somebody else."

Capable and independent was a compliment, right? Was there actually such a thing as being *too* independent?

"I'm thrilled. You'll be a wonderful mother. And I'll be a wonderful grandmother!" She left her chair to hug Kaitlyn, tearing up again.

It felt so good to be wrapped in her mom's embrace that Kaitlyn started crying again too.

"I saw the softest, cutest yarn today in the craft store," her mom said. "I can just imagine it being tiny baby booties and a little sweater and hat. And maybe even a matching baby blanket. I'm going to go back and buy it and start looking for patterns." Then, she said softly, "This is wonderful news."

"I love you, Mom," she said. "And thanks for the recipes."

"I'm excited to see what you do with them. Your grandfather would be so proud."

Because life would go on, despite this little bump in the road.

* * *

"What's your impression of me—as a guy?" Rafe asked. He glanced over at Colton as they both jogged up the hill they jokingly referred to as El Capitan, the biggest incline in town.

"I'm not sure if I understand the question," Colton said, breathing hard.

The sun was bright and warm despite the cold, the light reflecting off a coating of fresh snow like millions of diamonds. Only the brilliant day did not come near to penetrating Rafe's pensive mood. "Like, do I strike you as a mature adult that can be counted on?"

"Yeah, in a bar fight," Colton said, laughing. Then he looked over and saw that Rafe wasn't smiling. "Counted on to save someone's life? Yes. To be a good brother and son—sure. To haul your ass up this hill— maybe. I mean, you *are* a little bit of a wimp about that."

"You're just saying that because I beat you last time." They jogged in silence for a while. "I mean as far as being reliable and dependable."

"I'd trust you to bring milk home after work. Rafe, I have no idea what you're talking about."

"I mean as far as with women. Do I strike you as the kind of guy you can count on?"

"Oh," Colton said, going radio silent.

"Colt?"

"I'm trying to think how to answer that. Because you're ... complicated. And why are you asking me this? Why don't you ask Kaitlyn?"

"What makes you think this has anything to do with her?"

"Because it's no secret you two were spending a lot of time together until recently. You know you could talk to me about that if you wanted to, right?"

"Just answer the question, okay?"

Colton sighed. "Most people would say you're fun and easygoing. That you're young and sowing your wild oats. But I've known you for a long time, and I'd say that's probably only half true."

The pavement below Rafe's feet was punishing, and the cold air felt like fire in his lungs as they fought their way up the steepening incline. Colton knew his history better than anyone, and Rafe knew he wouldn't judge him.

Rafe thought Colton was done talking, but he eye-balled him from the side. Judging by his dead-even gaze, he was about to say something Rafe wouldn't like. "The truth is, you haven't had a real relationship in years. Seems to me that you shy away from anything serious."

"Well, I can't this time."

Colton slowed down and, on seeing the expression on Rafe's face, came to a dead stop. "What do you mean?"

"Kaitlyn's pregnant."

Colton cast Rafe a bewildered look. "Whoa."

Rafe doubled over to catch his breath and hold his side. He looked over the guardrails on the side of the road to see hills dotted with pine trees, a perfect winter postcard. But inside his head, nothing was picture per-fect. "Sara knows. Kaitlyn had a doctor's appointment with her."

"I see." He paused for a long time. "I had no idea you two were...you know."

"We weren't." Rafe forced himself to continue. "I mean, we only did it one time."

"Rafe, are we talking about sex here?" Colton asked. "Just to be clear."

"It happened at Stephanie and Everett's wedding."
Rafe held up his index finger for emphasis. "One time."

Colton blew out a big breath. "That's all it takes."

"Tell me about it."

"It's clear you two like each other a lot," Colton said.

"We were best friends," Rafe said. "I mean, she's
easy to hang around with and talk to and kind and cute
and...sort of the whole package...if I was the type of
guy to want a relationship, that is." Which he was not.
If he ever needed confirmation of that fact, his reaction
to Kaitlyn's news about the baby solidified it. "Plus you
know how close she is with Sara and Gabby. I knew to
stay away, you know? And after it happened...things
got weird. I never meant for it to happen. I should have
kept it to friends."

Colton snorted.

"What?" Geez, he was looking for some support
here.

"Come on, Rafe. You've never looked at her like any
kind of friend, even a bad one. Surely even you get
that."

"It was just the booze at the wedding, the blackout,
the...why are you looking at me like that?"

"Rafe, it's too late for excuses," Colton said gently.
"What are you going to do now?"

Rafe raked his hands through his hair. "Last night
after she told me I was just...speechless. Dumbstruck.
I tried to say the right things but I just...couldn't. I've
already let her down."

"Shock is understandable. But only to a certain
point."

"I'm going to do the right thing," he said, straightening. "I—I'm just not sure I got that across." He'd fumbled badly. He'd done an awful job of showing any support.

Colton's gaze was sympathetic. Maybe a little pitying too, which Rafe hated. "You know, it wouldn't be the worst thing to try a relationship."

Rafe shook his head, the sweat dripping off his face. "Not that. I can't do that."

"Why not? She's a great woman. You get along. And clearly you have chemistry together."

"I'm not cut out for that. For a relationship."

"Rafe, I ought to kick you in the butt. How do you know that?"

Rafe couldn't answer. Finally he looked Colton dead in the eye. "You were there. You know why."

Colton put his hand on Rafe's shoulder. "Let them go, Rafe. Don't let the past prevent you from living a good life now—a *great* life. Two years ago I never imagined I could have the life I'm living now—with the woman of my dreams and a baby on the way. Love changes things. But you've got to make yourself vulnerable enough to let it in."

Rafe stared at his friend. Saw the look in his eyes change as he spoke about Sara and their baby due next May. Kaitlyn's and his baby would come along a month or two after that, he imagined.

A baby. His and Kaitlyn's *baby*.

"I can't tell you what to do," Colton said. "But if you tell her you don't want to try a relationship, she'll move on. She's not the type to sit around and pine after someone." He slapped Rafe on the back. "Even if it's your pretty face."

An image popped into his head, clear and bitter as the cold air, of Kaitlyn carrying a toddler with a tumble of blond curls and big blue eyes...right over to Steve.

Another man with her. Raising their daughter. Or son, whichever it was.

Okay, he was not having that. He might be the unworthiest person to be given the opportunity to be a parent, but over his dead body would he ever surrender that responsibility to somebody else. Especially to Steve, who didn't know what made Kaitlyn laugh or that she secretly loved those bloody horror movies where the teenagers all do stupid stuff to get themselves eaten by zombies or even how she took her coffee. I mean, how could you be with someone who didn't even know how to fix your coffee?

And he might not be able to do a relationship, but he could do everything else.

Suddenly he realized he hadn't told Kaitlyn any of this. That a baby was a blessing. That a baby was a miracle and a privilege. That thinking about that made him scared out of his mind but also...hopeful.

Hopeful of what? That he could maybe one day live the life he was once denied?

No. He couldn't even go there. But the point was, he could do better. A *lot* better.

Suddenly he knew what he had to do. "Last one up the hill buys the beers," he said, and took off running.

Chapter 9

♥

"*Why* are we going to these people's house again?" Hazel asked, her voice resonating with annoyance as they drove to the ferry.

"Because they are dear friends of mine, and they want to celebrate my birthday tonight," Kaitlyn said in her most patient voice.

"But your birthday isn't until Monday," Hazel said.

"Aw, you remembered my birthday?" Kaitlyn said, glancing over at the passenger side. Hazel's response was the tiniest head tilt that might have meant, *Yeah, so what?*

"I get to celebrate again next week with you and Gram." It was true that the Langdons were a second family to her. With their encouragement, she'd taken over her grandfather's café at age twenty-four, something she never would've had the courage—or know-how—to do otherwise. Dr. Langdon and Rachel had given her advice and encouraged her to take a few business classes—but it was their moral support that had made a huge difference. And they'd loved her like a daughter.

She was only too aware that her relationship with this family that she loved was about to change big-time. Once they found out about the baby, there would be no turning back. She feared they would go full-court press to convince Rafe to marry her, and she didn't want that. She would never force a relationship on him. It was enough he had to adjust to being a dad when he'd made it clear that was not what he wanted.

Thank goodness Rafe wouldn't be there this weekend. Soon, they would have to tell their families the news, but she didn't want to think about that just yet.

For the next twenty-four hours, she wanted to focus on Hazel. On giving her the experience of a kind and loving family and trying to loosen her up a little so they could actually communicate.

Speaking of communicating, Kaitlyn hadn't told her sister about the shoplifting. She knew she should have, but Nikki was so anguished about everything—wanting Hazel to be all right, trusting that Angel Falls would be the place to turn her around.

Kaitlyn couldn't fail at helping Hazel. She planned to put all her efforts into helping her. And for just this one weekend, focus on getting their minds off their problems and have a little fun.

As they approached the gravel lot at Crystal Lake, the low, deep bleat of a boat horn sounded. Opening the car door as she scooped up her mittens and purse, she said, "We've got to hurry. Captain Jake is getting ready to pull out and that's the last ferry until tomorrow."

Kaitlyn pulled her thick multicolored knit cap down over her ears and handed Hazel her scarf. "I know it's freezing, but would you want to go out on the deck and see the sunset?" she asked, her boots clanging on the metal stairs as she walked up to the open deck.

"Freezing is an understatement!" Hazel said, accepting the scarf and twining it around her head and neck. The skyline over the lake had turned a fiery salmon color that took Kaitlyn's breath away. Or maybe that was the icy wind that was blowing full force into their faces. "Isn't that beautiful?" Kaitlyn exclaimed, pointing to the horizon. "There's nothing better than a winter sky at sunset."

Kaitlyn drew in a lungful of the cold, crisp air. She closed her eyes against the wind and tried to concentrate on the fresh air filling her up, blowing away all the negative thoughts and worries of the past few weeks. For a moment she let herself get lost in the beauty of the brilliant sky. If Rafe were here, he'd say it was orange, and she'd say no, definitely salmon. Then he'd quote the old sailor's saying, "Red sky at night, sailor's delight" and tell her all the explanations behind why that was more than just an old saying.

Suddenly she found herself smiling at the thought of Rafe explaining that to a child. He had so many qualities that would make him a great dad. She saw that so clearly, even if he couldn't.

"How can you smile in this weather? Can we go inside now?" Hazel asked, her teeth chattering.

They spent the rest of the time inside the enclosed seating area with about ten other people, most of them scrolling through their phones. Kaitlyn bought them each a hot chocolate, a tradition on the ferry. On the way back to Hazel, Kaitlyn did a double take. There, on one of the interior walls of the seating area, was a poster of Mr. December. Rafe in his Santa pants, the contours of his perfectly sculpted chest on full display, a killer smile on his face showing off his perfect white teeth. Kaitlyn squeezed her eyes shut and shook her head, trying to block the too-handsome image out of her mind.

Kaitlyn suddenly realized that she didn't like the Mr. December shot—it was man candy, a sexy, flirtatious Rafe for anyone to enjoy. And it *was* gorgeous, because Rafe was a gorgeous hunk of a man. But it was only one side of the Rafe she knew. Sadly, it was the side he put forward to a lot of people. Especially women. She preferred the side he didn't show very often—the one she saw when he looked at her sometimes when he didn't think she was looking, the one that popped up when they were watching TV or talking about their fun childhood memories or just hanging out.

Kaitlyn handed Hazel her hot chocolate and they sat by the windows sipping it and listening to Christmas carols in the growing dusk.

"So are you and Rafe a couple?" Hazel asked. "He's pretty cool. I totally get why you sneak around with him."

Sneak around? Oh, that sounded...awful. "What do you mean...sneak around?" she asked.

"Gram told me about the baby," Hazel said, glancing up and then out at the water. "I think it's cool you and Rafe are getting together."

"Well, we're . . . we're actually not getting together in that way."

"Oh," Hazel said, a frown creasing her forehead. "I'm confused."

Kaitlyn was definitely not getting the role-model-of-the-year award. "Hazel, I've known Rafe a long time. I grew up with his sisters and he was always . . . around. But when I moved back to town after college and took over Grandpa's café, I started to look at him . . . differently."

"I can see why. He's *hot*." Hazel flapped her hand in front of her face like she was fanning herself.

That he was. Kaitlyn bit back a smile, because what she needed to tell Hazel was serious. "Well, Rafe's never been interested in me that way. After I broke up with Steve, we started to hang around more, but he's always made it clear he's wanted to just be friends. What happened at the wedding was . . . an impulsive mistake. On both our parts."

"Oh."

"We used birth control. Two kinds. As you always should, not that you're ever going to have sex, but . . . but it's really important to do that. But somehow . . ." She bucked up her courage. "Somehow it failed. And here we are. Rafe is still getting used to the idea of being a father. This has been kind of a shock to everyone, and we need some time to get used to the idea before we tell his family. He's not going to be at the lake house, so we don't have to worry about things being awkward." So there you have it . . . She was the worst aunt in the world. Her sister would probably kill her, having sent Hazel to

Angel Falls for guidance and good examples. But what else could she do but tell the truth?

"So...I'm actually excited about this baby," Kaitlyn said. "I've always wanted to be a mom, but I was afraid it would never happen. And I'm working to make the Bean even better, and I plan to prepare in every way I can to give this baby the best life ever."

Hazel flicked another glance in her direction, but this time it stuck. A small smile lifted one corner of her mouth. "I think you and Rafe will be great parents," she said.

Oh, she hoped Rafe would be a good parent. Because she wanted him to want this baby, not just for her sake, but for his own. Rafe had such a big heart—if only he wouldn't be afraid to open it.

"And I think you're handling all this stress pretty well, considering," Hazel continued.

"Oh." Wow, that sounded...beyond her years. "I'm trying," Kaitlyn said with a smile, giving Hazel a side hug. Did Hazel just pay her a...compliment?

"Yeah and...I could help you more at the Bean. If you're sick or tired. Just let me know."

"Thanks. The best way you could help me is to...be happy. Find your direction." Kaitlyn worried about sounding parental or being obvious about sneaking in the preaching after she'd spilled the complications of her own life. But she needed to let Hazel know she mattered. A lot. "We love you and want to help you. That means I'm happy to listen anytime. You know that, right?"

"Right," Hazel said dismissively, suddenly standing up and walking over to the windows and pointing.

Kaitlyn could see the lights of the dock ahead. "Are we almost there?" Hazel asked.

Kaitlyn was aware that the window of opportunity to reach Hazel was now closing, and she had no idea if she'd gotten anywhere. "Almost there," she confirmed, pulling out her phone and texting Gabby with their ETA so someone could come pick them up, to which Gabby texted back, Got you covered.

Then suddenly the boat docked, and they got caught up in the rush of people exiting, arms full of overnight bags and satchels and, in her and Hazel's case, sacks of food as well. Hazel didn't complain when Kaitlyn handed her a bag, but she did crinkle up her nose and ask, "You have to cook your own birthday dinner?"

Kaitlyn laughed. "No. But I thought the least I could do for our hosts is bring the coffee and dessert."

"What kind of dessert?" Hazel asked, poking her head inside the bag.

"Oh, just something chocolatey and warm and delicious," Kaitlyn said with a smile.

"Have a good weekend, folks," Jake said, as they exited the ferry.

"You too, Jake," she said, waving. Because she wasn't looking, she nearly ran into Hazel, who'd stopped dead on the last step. "Whoa. What's the mat—"

"Well, Aunt Kate," she said, talking over her shoulder but looking straight ahead, "it looks like your baby daddy decided to come after all."

Baby daddy? Oh good grief. As Hazel pointed, Kaitlyn's gaze shifted over to a lone lamppost at the end of the dock. The wave of people rushed by, hauling bags, packages, and suitcases, chattering to waiting family and friends who'd met them. Surrounded by light flurries of snow, a man leaned against the pole, bathed in white light. His height made him slightly intimidating, as did the stoic expression on his face and his stance, hands in pockets. He wore a red-and-black hat with earflaps, looking tall, formidable, and handsome enough to be a J. Crew model.

Her heart leaped at the familiar sight, and a flush of heat suddenly infused her core and spread through her limbs despite the freezing temperatures. *Rafe*. He was *here*? Before she could process that, he caught sight of them nearing him and waved. The shock of seeing him caught her off guard, and she actually slipped on an icy patch on the gravel. He immediately stepped forward, his strong arms steadying her, his gaze grazing over her and making another flare of heat rise up inside. It seemed to take forever before she could catch her balance and step away.

"I thought...I thought you had to work this weekend," she said, holding him at arm's length.

He pulled back and casually shrugged, averting his eyes. "Change of plans."

* * *

Kaitlyn looked shocked to see him, which oddly pleased Rafe. He felt the same pull as ever at seeing her, even though she was bundled in an almost comical ski hat with a huge pom-pom on top and her nose was red from the cold.

"Rafe?" he suddenly heard her asking. "You can— let go of me now. I'm fine."

"Oh sorry," he said, dropping his hands.

He'd been thinking about her—well, as far as the baby went—a lot. He was over the initial shock. And he wanted to rewind and start again. Tell her he was okay with it. More than okay. And that he would be there for this baby, do everything possible that he could.

Except . . . could he love it?

He honestly didn't know if he could get there.

But he'd do anything for Kaitlyn, and right now he needed her to know she wasn't alone in this.

"Why are you here?" Kaitlyn was asking. And she looked . . . confused.

"I—misread my work schedule and realized I could come out for your birthday after all." Which was not true—he'd switched his shift. He'd been a part of her birthday celebrations, voluntarily or otherwise, since she'd become friends with his sisters long ago, and he wasn't about to miss one now. Especially not now.

He placed a hand on Kaitlyn's back to steer her toward his truck, which he'd brought over on the ferry. Much to his chagrin, that light touch through a thousand layers of clothing seemed to burn straight through his gloves. "You ever been to Crystal Lake?" he asked Hazel to distract himself.

"Nope," she said, looking around at the dock, the nearly vacant parking lot, the forest of pine trees. "But it sure looks exciting."

"You'll like it," he said with a friendly wink, more for Kaitlyn's benefit. He knew how worried Kaitlyn was about this girl.

He opened the door of the truck for Kaitlyn, and

she climbed in. He always tried to keep it neat as a pin, the firefighter in him, he supposed, since they spent so much time cleaning the station, their gear, the trucks. He'd even hung a little tree air freshener in a Christmas pine scent, something he thought Kaitlyn would appreciate as him getting into the Christmas spirit.

Instead, she choked a little and crinkled up her nose.

"I thought you liked fresh pine," he said.

"I do like fresh pine. It's just very...potent." She waved her hand in front of her face.

"Oh." He reached up and snapped the air freshener off the elastic thread and tossed it out the window.

"That's littering," Hazel said.

"So is vomiting in someone's clean truck," he said in a low voice as he pulled out of the lot.

The deep frown Kaitlyn tossed him made him want to laugh, but thank goodness he didn't. One glance over at her showed she was putting her head between her knees.

"Lose something?" he asked in a tone that was far more casual than he felt.

"Nothing. I'm fine," she said, taking a big breath. She opened her bag to reveal an enormous box of saltines. "Would anyone like a cracker?" she said with false cheer.

"Sure, I'll take one," Hazel said from the back seat. "Everything okay up there, Aunt Kate?" She took a cracker from Kaitlyn.

Kaitlyn seemed to be struggling—hard—not to upchuck. He opened the car window a crack and rubbed her back a little, just to let her know he wished he could do more.

He *needed* her to know he wanted to do more. Right now. "I just want you to know—I've got your back," he said quietly to Kaitlyn.

She glanced sideways at him, her head still between her knees. "You don't need to rub my back," she said.

"No, I mean—" He paused. She definitely wasn't getting what he was trying to say. What he'd come here to let her know. "I want to be with you every step of the way."

"Okaaaay." The look she flashed him was not relieved or grateful—it was—suspicious. Like she didn't believe a word he was saying.

"We're going to work this out," he continued.

"Work *what* out?" she asked, trying to sit up but thinking better of it.

"I'm going to help you with"—he sneaked a quick glance back at Hazel, who was engrossed in her phone—"the baked goods in your oven."

"I have perfect control of my own oven, thank you very much," she said. "I can handle all the baking myself."

"Okay, fine," Rafe said. "But I *want* to help. You shouldn't have to *bake alone*."

"You guys are weird," Hazel said. A glance in the rearview mirror revealed she was still playing on her phone. "Also, I know about the baby so you can stop speaking in code."

"Did you see the sunset on the boat? It was orange," Rafe said, changing the subject.

"Salmon," Kaitlyn said, popping her head up for a second.

"I beg to differ. Definitely orange." He glanced at Kaitlyn and was relieved to see she was smiling. He took it as a sign that maybe she'd forgiven him for the stupid way he'd responded to the baby news.

Now he just had to pretend that he also wasn't worried about the thousand things that could go wrong during a pregnancy—because they could. But he didn't want to ruin her joy over the baby with his tangled-up feelings about the past.

"Aren't they, like, the same color?" Hazel asked. "Orange and salmon?"

"Whatever you want to call it," Rafe said, "it means no snow."

"How the heck do you know that?" Hazel asked.

"It's an old sailor's rhyme, and it's true. If the dusk sky is *salmon*"—he glanced at Kaitlyn to show her he wasn't beyond compromise—"it's probably going to be clear the next day. Good sailing. We tend to watch the weather pretty closely out here because of the ferry. You don't really want to get stuck for days if you have to be at work on the mainland."

As he pulled the truck up to his parents' lake house, he was hoping to catch Kaitlyn alone, but as soon as the car stopped, Kaitlyn was out of there, running to the front door just as it opened and most of his crazy family flooded out of it. The shake-sided house was decorated with wreaths and a single candle lamp in every window. He felt certain, knowing Rachel, his stepmom, that there'd be a giant tree inside too. Rachel greeted Kaitlyn with a huge hug, and his dad joined in too while Rafe hauled all the bags into the house. His sisters and

Rachel were chattering and exclaiming over how Hazel had grown up since they saw her last, but the girl stayed awkward and stiff even under all that hugging.

His nonna gave him a squeeze before he could even put down all the bags he was carrying. "What a surprise, Raphael," she said, patting his cheek. "We weren't expecting you."

"I'm here," he said. "And I'm hungry."

"Now that Kaitlyn's here maybe you won't mope around anymore," his sister Gabby said.

"The only reason I'm going to mope is if there's no chili left." He escaped Nonna's perusal by walking into the big farm-style kitchen. Rachel followed him and started examining the bags Kaitlyn brought. "There's a chocolate cake in there," she exclaimed.

"Yes, and I need to heat it up in the oven. It's served warm and it has a gooey middle."

"I knew there was a reason we decided to invite you to celebrate your birthday this weekend," Rachel teased.

"A gooey middle," Gabby said, elbowing her brother. "Just like you, Rafe."

"What does that even mean, Gabriella?" Rafe asked. Gabby was the sibling he argued with more than the others, but she was also the one who got him the most. Which suddenly bothered him more than usual.

"It means you act all tough on the outside but inside you're a softie."

"Not to you," Rafe said with a wink. "How are you feeling, by the way? You look good." Gabby and Cade had gotten married recently and she'd just learned that she was pregnant.

Gabby rubbed her nonexistent belly and gave Rafe a kiss on the cheek. "Six weeks already," she said. "And I feel great, thanks. I thought you said you weren't coming."

"I cleared my schedule," he said, hugging his sister. "How could I miss Katie's birthday? Plus I heard Rachel made her chili." His gaze slid over to Kaitlyn, who was placing a deep cake pan in the oven. "Of course, your birthday is far more important than Rachel's chili."

Kaitlyn closed the oven door and rolled her eyes.

"Happy birthday, sweetie," Nonna said, coming over to give Kaitlyn a kiss and a pat on the back. "Did you bring some of that good coffee for us? I've been looking forward to it all day." Nonna's mild dementia made her forget some things but never excellent coffee.

"Of course, Nonna. I'll make us some right after dinner."

"Oh goody," she said. "And did someone say chocolate cake?"

"Yep," Gabby said. "And we're going to put birthday candles on it."

"*Lots* of birthday candles," Rafe added, since Kaitlyn was, after all, three years older than he was.

Kaitlyn shook her head and laughed. Thank goodness she wasn't holding against him the fact that he'd reacted like an idiot to the baby news.

"So, you're getting the hang of things at the café?" Rafe asked Hazel, who stood leaning against the kitchen countertop picking the dark blue nail polish off her nails in bored indifference.

She stopped picking long enough to spare him a glance. "Yes, indeedy." Then went back to picking.

Rafe met Kaitlyn's concerned gaze over Hazel's head, so he tried to engage Hazel. "You'll be good when we play charades later," he said, but Hazel wasn't picking up the bait.

"Oh, I love charades," Nonna said, clapping her hands. "When can we play?"

Hazel barely flicked her gaze up, but Rafe persisted. "You know why, don't you?"

The teenager shrugged.

"See?" Rafe said, mimicking her gesture. "You win."

There might've been the tiniest trace of a smile on Hazel's face, but Rafe couldn't be sure.

"Okay, everybody," Rachel said, herding people out into the family room. "Chili's heating up. Let's go sit down while the men start the fire."

He saw Kaitlyn swipe at her eyes as she carried some groceries into the adjoining mudroom.

"Everything all right?" he asked, following her in.

"I'm fine. Just a little...emotional."

"Because it's your birthday?" Please let it not be because of his behavior the other day.

"No," she said in adamant protest. "Of course not."

"Oh. Just wondering, because you *are* really old today." He felt desperate to make her laugh. To make her see he cared and was sorry for his bad reaction.

"Shut up, Rafe," she said, punching him in the arm.

"If I say it's because you're pregnant you'll really hit me, right?" he said, rubbing his arm.

"Don't even go there." The warning look she gave him showed him she meant it.

He pulled her aside, out of everyone's earshot. For

a second, he caught her gaze, and what he saw there tore him up inside. It held that same suspicion and disappointment. He hated that he'd let her down. She didn't deserve his... baggage. He'd hurt her because of it.

He took a deep breath and plunged in. "Look. I've had some time to think and I just want you to know... I'm really sorry about the way I acted. I—I want you to know I'll be here for you. And for—the baby. One hundred percent. We'll do this together." There. He'd said it. He wanted to be upbeat and positive and *there* for her—in the best way he could be.

She scanned his face, seeming to look carefully for clues. Could she tell that underneath the calm expression he manufactured he was freaking out? He hoped not.

He responded to her reluctance by talking more. "I was shocked. Having kids wasn't in my game plan but I'm... readjusting." For her. For this coming baby, he would *have* to somehow readjust. He could manage responsibility, taking care of what was his, because that was who he was. But love, bonding, joy... those were other things entirely.

"I don't want you to look at this baby as a chore or a responsibility," she said in a tone that was clear there was no compromise. "Because I'm perfectly capable of taking care of this baby on my own."

"That's not going to happen." He paused, hoping the matter was closed. "So why were you getting teary in the kitchen?"

"It's just... everything's going to change. Especially with your family."

"No," he said, using his *of course not* tone. "*Nothing's* going to change. They love us."

"You have no idea, do you?" she said, shaking her head. "They're going to take this baby to mean there *is* an *us*. They are going to push for an *us*—hard. It's going to be relentless."

"Well, they've been doing that for the past few years. I don't expect them to stop now," Rafe said. "Trust me, they'll be so thrilled about the baby they'll be fine with whatever else we tell them—which, by the way, I think we should do right after dinner."

"Tonight?" Her voice rose to an unnatural octave, and her pale skin turned paler. "Now?"

"Everyone's here. Why not?" His family would only take this baby news as a source of joy. He knew it down to his bones.

"Because…because I'm not ready. Because…because we're on an island with a ferry and the next one isn't until tomorrow night!" She threw up her hands, clearly getting worked up.

He took her hands so she would stop flailing them. "Relax. Breathe. This is family. I say we do it now and get it over with."

She closed her eyes and shook her head in a way that told him she was stressed. "Okay, we can wait a little," he said. "We'll do it when you feel comfortable, okay?" He'd caused her enough stress. He could do this the way she wanted to do it.

She blew out a big breath. "Great. Thanks. We'll do it very soon, just not tonight."

Just then Dr. Langdon came in from outside, stomping the snow off his boots. He was carrying four narrow brown bags, two in each hand. "Kaitlyn, my dear," he said, "I've got an extra special surprise for your birthday." He side hugged her and steered her toward the family room.

"What is it, Dr. L.?" she asked, looking over her shoulder at Rafe, who gave her an encouraging thumbs-up.

Yes, his family certainly loved Kaitlyn. Looked like his dad had made her a batch of wine.

Wine. Something she could not have. Rafe followed close behind them as they left the kitchen.

"You know about my wine-making hobby, right?" his dad said. "Well, I made a special vintage just for your birthday. It's called 'Kaitlyn 2019.'"

"Nice name," Rafe said. "But *four* bottles, Dad?" Rafe's heart sank, for Kaitlyn's sake. He knew she was nervous about telling his family, and the wine issue would force it for sure.

"I've got more in the shed if we run out," his dad said. Turning to Kaitlyn, he asked, "Are you surprised?"

Kaitlyn's gaze drifted reluctantly over to his. He knew her too well not to see the dread, fear, and panic there. Rafe knew exactly what she was thinking—that the "surprise" was going to be on all of them, and there was no way to stop it now.

Chapter 10

♥

Dr. Langdon led Kaitlyn into the family room, where everyone had gathered around a big stone fireplace that contained a lively, crackling fire. Rafe's oldest sister Evie's two kids, Michael and Julia, colored in front of the fire with Cade's little daughter, Ava. Nonna settled into a big easy chair nearby, propping her feet up on an ottoman, her bull terrier, Rocket, nestled in at her side. On the other side of the room, against the windows facing the lake, stood an enormous Christmas tree waiting to be decorated.

The peaceful scene was shattered by what was going on inside Kaitlyn's head. That Dr. Langdon's special wine was going to blow this happy holiday gathering to dust, and she had no way to stop it. There was no way they would be able to avoid spilling the baby news once the wine was poured.

Watching her friends with their husbands didn't calm her either. Sara sat on a couch with Colton, his arm wrapped around her shoulder. Kaitlyn caught them exchanging a little secretive glance filled with love and contentment. Gabby handed Ava some juice and then sat down next to Cade, their hands intertwining. Both of her friends looked so happy, and she couldn't help the little twitch of envy that shot through her.

Kaitlyn picked a spot near Hazel, who was absorbed in her ever-present phone, despite attempts by Sara and Gabby to engage her in conversation.

Rafe gave Kaitlyn a sympathetic look and joined her. "Hey, Hazie," he said. "Checking the weather?"

Hazel—and Kaitlyn too—gave Rafe an *Are you crazy?* look. After which Hazel resumed scrolling. Rafe gave Kaitlyn an *I tried* shrug.

"Michael, that's my crayon," Julia, who was six, suddenly said to her little brother.

"We're *sharing*, Julia," Michael said.

"I'm going to tell Mom you're using my special pink," she said.

"I want pink too," Ava, who was four, chimed in.

Rafe left the couch to interrupt potential crayon wars. He got down on all fours, pawing and roaring. "I'm a big, hungry lion," he said, "and I need to *eat*. And you three look like the perfect size."

"The perfect size for what, Uncle Rafe?" Michael asked, approaching slowly. Julia, older and less cautious, came even closer. Ava eyed Rafe suspiciously and lingered near the crayons.

Rafe grinned and, still in lion mode, licked his chops and swiped a paw in the air. "The perfect size...*for a snack*!" He let out a playful roar.

Michael and Julia screamed and tackled him by jumping on his back. Ava, who was not used to Rafe's antics, dropped her crayons and hid behind Nonna's chair.

"Okay," the big hungry lion said. "Maybe two will be enough."

Kaitlyn laughed and noticed that Hazel couldn't help but laugh too. The shenanigans were a buzz of distraction from the dread that was coursing through Kaitlyn's bloodstream.

"Ava, it's okay, sweetie," Gabby said, getting up and peering behind the chair. "Uncle Rafe is only playing." She turned to Rafe. "Aren't you, Uncle Rafe?" She pantomimed to Rafe to say something to make things better.

"It's okay. Ava," Rafe said loudly. "Come on out and you can help me eat your cousins."

"Rafe!" Evie, the oldest Langdon sibling, said at the same time as Gabby.

"Uncle Rafe, you're silly," Julia said, giggling.

"I don't think violent play is appropriate," Evie said, but by this time, the kids were in full lion mode themselves, including Ava, who ran out from behind the chair roaring.

"Maybe it's just about having fun," Joe, Evie's husband, said as he scooped up his son and tossed him over his shoulders.

Evie laughed in spite of herself. Rafe was such a goofball—but a kind goofball. Kaitlyn hated the out-of-control feeling that threatened to overtake her as she watched him with the kids, like all her resolve to steel herself against his charm was melting around the edges. Yet she could not tear her gaze away.

From across the room, Sara caught her looking at Rafe and sent Kaitlyn an encouraging smile. Gabby waggled her brows when Rafe took his seat right next to Kaitlyn. Ugh, it was difficult having your two best friends watching every move.

Just then Rafe leaned his head close and whispered, "When the time comes, just pass the wine this way."

"Okay," she said, swallowing hard and trying not to notice despite all her worries how good he smelled, like fresh air and some spicy shaving cream.

"His last batch was pretty good," he said with a grin. "And besides, I like wine."

"That's what you said last September and look where *that* got us," she mumbled. Oh, did she really just say that? He gave a little chuckle and looked at her with amusement glinting in his dark eyes.

"Not funny," she whispered, her mouth curving up a little despite herself.

He shrugged, looking…adorable. "It's a *little* funny."

Okay, it was funny. In a horrifying way that was going to soon play out in front of his entire family.

"Happy birthday!" Rachel called, suddenly carrying in the cake, fresh out of the oven and lit up with a thousand candles. Everyone sang the birthday song, with Rafe bellowing loud and long, hamming it up for the kids, who loved it and followed right along.

"Make a wish," Gabby prompted.

Kaitlyn closed her eyes. She didn't wish for herself. She wished for her baby. That he or she would know they were loved, no matter how the rest of it turned out. That one day he or she would laugh and play with cousins in this same room. And that Kaitlyn would be strong enough to navigate her relationship with Rafe— whatever it was. She opened her eyes, making sure to focus on the cake and not look in Rafe's direction. Until he spoke.

"Hurry up, Katie," Rafe said. "Unless you need some help blowing those out, now that you're thirty-two. Geez."

She tried to look annoyed at him, but he was sitting there, tossing Michael upside down while the other two kids clamored for their turn.

"Don't frown," he teased. "You still *look* young."

She finally did the honors amid clapping, cheering, and well-wishing. Hazel plucked off the candles, licking the icing off the bottoms of a couple and shocking Kaitlyn by saying how amazing it was.

Everyone was laughing and exclaiming over how delicious the cake looked. Their faces were happy, expectant, kind.

"Rachel, would you mind cutting the cake?" Kaitlyn asked, passing over the knife Rachel had brought from the kitchen. "I think I'll start a pot of coffee."

She walked into the kitchen, certain that no one thought anything of her leaving just then. She just needed a minute to get her head straight.

Tonight's celebration wasn't unusual. She'd been part of this family since she was ten years old. But despite Rafe's belief that his family would take their news in stride, she couldn't help but think it would dramatically change things, change her place in the family. And oh, what if they really did push for her and Rafe to get together for the sake of the baby?

She'd just started the coffee and then leaned on the island, taking a big breath, when she heard a familiar voice behind her.

"Hey, need some help?" Rafe asked.

She spun around at the sound of his voice. "Oh. Rafe, hi. Just starting a pot." She thought about how great he was with those kids...yet how he'd said he didn't want to be a father. He was filled with contradictions, and she couldn't help but wonder if that was a line he used to protect himself—to protect his heart.

"Okay, just wondering." His gaze rolled over her in that way he had, not missing a detail.

He walked into the pantry, grabbed a brown paper bag with handles, and pulled out a pretty silver box, wrapped with a red bow. "Happy birthday," he announced. "From me."

Her already sensitive stomach plunged. "You didn't have to get me a gift," she said.

He leaned close, his hand propped on the counter beside her. "Open it," he said, nudging the box toward her. "You only turn forty once."

"Will you stop with the teasing?" She waited for him to parry, to jest. But he didn't. He just stared at her with an odd look that she couldn't quite read.

Finally, he cleared his throat and said, "Okay, no more teasing. Just open the gift, Katie."

She turned the box over in her hands. "What is it?"

He gave a secretive smile and shrugged. "You'll have to see."

"It's pretty," she said, shaking it, noting that it was a little heavy.

"I wrapped it myself."

This was saying a lot, because the bow on top was curled by hand. "Since when do you know how to make bows?"

"Since YouTube taught me. Open it already."

She set the package down on the distressed oak table and ripped open the paper. Inside was a coffee maker. A high-end, expensive one, the kind you'd buy a couple for a wedding gift.

"It's a coffee maker," he said.

"You're kidding," she said with mock surprise.

"Do I ever kid you?" he quipped right back.

"Um, all the time."

"Not *all* the time." He flashed a Rafe grin. Sweet, adorable, and irresistible. She immediately shifted her gaze back to the gift.

"It's a very nice coffee maker," Kaitlyn said. "But Rafe, I own a coffee shop, remember?"

He laughed. "And yet you don't have a coffee maker like this."

She looked at him, perplexed, as he tapped his finger on the text on the side of the box. "'Brews a single cup or a whole pot,'" she read. "'Thermal carafe. Grinds the beans.' Great features."

He shook his head at her sarcastic tone, took the box out of her hands, and pointed to the picture on the side like she was just not getting it. "It's programmable. Charges your phone too."

She looked at him. Was he crazy?

"You can set it, and your coffee will be ready at four thirty a.m. on the dot."

"Oh. I see," she said softly. The gift was thoughtful. It was nice. And she knew exactly where he'd gotten this idea. She'd told him how hard it was to wake up so early, and how she never had time to make herself coffee before she headed out to open the café.

It was an odd gift but also oddly...touching. And she didn't have the heart to tell him she wouldn't be drinking any coffee for a while. Instead she made the mistake of looking at him. His face held a look of careful anticipation. That look—innocent, hopeful, and more than a little boyish—undid her.

Heck, he could have given her spray-painted rocks and she would have gotten emo about that too.

Before she could think, she kissed his cheek. It was rough with stubble, and warm, and he smelled like simple Dial soap and shave cream and...Rafe. She lingered a few seconds too long, unable to pull back. He stiffened, and she thought he was going to pull away.

Suddenly his arms came around her, encircling her waist. She sucked in a breath. Or was that him? Unable to move, she stood frozen in place, searching his eyes.

"Happy birthday, Katie," he whispered, his voice soft as spun silk.

And oh, she felt the current between them, strong as always, brought on by camaraderie and banter, but sustained by pure, unholy chemistry. She found herself tipping her head toward him, drawing closer, *needing* to kiss him. He drew her in despite her will, pulled her right in like a magnet, to a place where she forgot time and space and who she was, replacing all her worrying and fretting with a desire so potent it made her tremble. The urge to cradle his face in her hands nearly overcame her. She had to ball her fingers into fists to stifle it.

His dark gaze bore right through her then flickered to her lips.

His mouth came down on hers, direct and bold. He softly stroked her lower lip with his tongue, and when she opened her mouth on an uncontrollable sigh, he curled his hand around her neck to pull her closer.

She breathed him in, all of him, his wonderful, masculine scent, while it took her less than a second to respond to his kiss, tangle her tongue with his, and press herself against his warm, solid body. He tasted like...Rafe, like an indescribable, unforgettable essence she knew as him and only him, and it took her, straight as an arrow shot, right back to that night in the cabin, to every last, desperate kiss, every urgent touch.

The memory flooded her with a bittersweet panic. Her hands flew to his chest to find balance, to try to make sense of the onslaught of sensation coursing through her, but she was lost, the breathless feeling of being in his arms once again nearly overtaking her. His heartbeat pounded under her hand, strong and rapid, matching her own as it hammered in her ears.

Rafe's hand wandered under her sweater, skimming the bare skin of her back. Weak-kneed, she leaned into him, worried she was no longer capable of standing on her own. He didn't seem to care, his kisses turning more urgent, deeper, *hungrier*.

"Hey, everyone sent me in here for the coff— Oh,

whoa!" Hazel had walked into the kitchen and saw them, then suddenly covered her face with her hands.

Kaitlyn jumped back but Rafe stayed in place, somehow managing to look completely nonplussed. Without missing a beat, he calmly stepped away and began taking down coffee mugs from the cupboard.

"You're not—you're not interrupting," Kaitlyn said, fighting the urge to tidy her hair, her clothes, her *life*. "We were just—getting the coffee, right Rafe?"

He cleared his throat. "Right," he said, before he gathered up all the red stoneware mugs and set them together on the island. "We'll be right in."

Hazel had beelined out of the kitchen. Amid the *chink*ing of the mugs as Rafe organized them, Kaitlyn forced herself to take deep breaths, to slow down her furiously pounding heart. She was busying herself with finding sugar and creamer when she felt his hand on her arm.

"I didn't mean for that to happen," he said. His words made her heart crack a little and caused a sudden burst of anger to well up from somewhere deep inside. Scanning his face, she found it impossible to know what was behind his impenetrable mask that only a moment ago had been so different, so tender, so *expressive*.

Of course he didn't mean it. Because that was typical Rafe. But for a few moments, there had been a different Rafe. One who'd affected her more than any other man she'd ever known. Kaitlyn straightened up, unwilling to let him see her confusion, her *hurt*. "I didn't either," she said indignantly. As usual, she'd gotten too close, allowed him in too far.

She *knew* better than to give in to the currents of attraction that had always seemed to flow so fast and strong between them.

Gabby walked into the kitchen, coming to a sudden halt when she noticed the dead silence and Kaitlyn staring at Rafe, who was turned away, his hands on the island, head bowed.

"Hey," Gabby said, offering Kaitlyn a little smile. "I can take those coffees."

"Oh, sure," Kaitlyn said, her voice full of forced cheer, gathering the cups—and her senses—as she pulled out a tray and Gabby helped her load it.

They'd done it again. Gotten carried away. Rafe was capable of sweeping her away to a place where the consequences of behavior like that didn't seem to matter. But it *did* matter, as the rest of their world was about to learn very soon.

* * *

What had just happened? Rafe leaned over the kitchen counter as he struggled to pace his breaths and slow the ferocious rhythm of his heart. Why couldn't he keep his hands off her? In his parents' house, no less?

Struggling to grasp hold of some sense of control, he walked into the small mudroom. On impulse, he shrugged into his coat and walked outside, sucking in deep breaths of the icy air and hauling several good-sized stacks of wood to the back door, grateful for the physical labor. He contemplated going for a walk to clear his head but decided returning to his family and doing his best to pretend nothing had happened would be the wisest tack. As he hung up his coat, he nearly ran right into Hazel. The overhead fixture was off, but in the borrowed light from the kitchen, he could see her standing right near the door, in front of a shelf under the window that held bags of cans and bottles that needed to be recycled.

And Gabby's purse. Which, he was sorry to see, Hazel had her hand inside of.

She made two mistakes. One was to withdraw her hand quickly, and the other was to let him see the look in her eye, which was a mixture of guilt and fright.

If she was going to become a criminal, she'd have to work on that tell.

"Need something?" he asked, keeping his voice calm and even.

"Just looking for a cigarette," she said.

"Yeah, Gabby smokes those all the time now that she's pregnant."

He crossed his arms, playing tough scary adult, stalling for time as he debated how to handle this. He wondered if this—catching someone red-handed and wondering what the hell to do next—was what Colton felt like on a daily basis. Rafe suddenly felt grateful he was a firefighter and not a cop.

"Gabby doesn't smoke, obviously," he said. "And that happens to be her purse."

"How do you know this isn't *my* purse?" she asked.

"Because it's not." Because he noticed things. Because Gabby's purse was peppered with buttons with weird sayings like "Squeeze the Day" and "Orange You

Glad It's Friday?" Plus it had a bright pink faux rabbit's foot attached to the handle, compliments of Cade's little daughter.

Hazel sighed. "Please don't say anything," she said in a hoarse whisper, not looking him in the eye.

Rafe looked at the girl. She was skinny, and with her pale complexion and charcoal-black hair, she gave the impression of being small and easily breakable and...alone.

Now what? He didn't want to keep secrets from Kaitlyn. Their relationship was confusing enough without him doing anything that she would interpret as a betrayal. But how would she feel to know that this girl she'd done everything to help was still up to her same old ways? Wasn't Kaitlyn dealing with enough right now?

"Okay, fine," he said.

Hazel let out a big breath.

"But," Rafe continued, "there's a price to pay for my silence."

Frowning, Hazel asked, "What do you mean?"

"What I mean is, now that you have an income source, you should be saving some money so you don't have to—um—find it in other places. So every Friday go cash your check and bring me forty bucks."

"You're going to take forty dollars from me every week? That's extortion!"

"Relax, kid, I don't want your money. We're going to put it in a bank account for you so that you have a place to go for money instead of other people's pockets. As for what else you can do...I'm not sure yet. Let me think on it. But this has got to stop. Your aunt's trying to help you, you know?"

Hazel screwed up her face, and he couldn't tell what she was thinking. What was clear was she was done with the conversation. "She might think you're hot, but she doesn't really think of you as boyfriend material," Hazel said over her shoulder as she walked back into the kitchen.

Rafe understood Hazel's words were meant to bite, a last parting volley. And he had to admit that her statement was accurate. He *wasn't* boyfriend material. Then why did her words sting?

Chapter 11

♥

Rafe entered the room and sat down next to Kaitlyn, smelling like fresh piney air. He didn't look at her or speak to her, which made her both relieved and irritated. Looking around, she saw that everyone seemed to be more into eating chocolate cake and coffee than noticing there might be something off with them. It seemed to Kaitlyn that the fact that she'd just kissed Rafe was written all over her face. Or that he'd kissed her. Oh gosh, they'd definitely kissed each other. Rafe focused all his attention on the kids, praising their drawings and threatening to bring back the child-eating lion, which brought squeals of mock horror.

Then Dr. Langdon stood up and looked at Rachel, who gave him a reassuring nod. Someone had plugged in the giant tree, showing off strings of multicolored lights, awaiting decoration.

"Now that everyone's sitting down," Dr. Langdon said, "I want to say how excited I am that you all could be here tonight." He poured a few glasses of wine and passed them out, first to Rachel, then to Nonna. "Rafe," he said, handing him a glass, "glad you made it this weekend. Hazel"—he gave her a glass, looking over at Kaitlyn to get her approval—"you've grown into a lovely young woman, and we're so happy to have you join us."

Hazel looked a little shocked at being given a glass of wine, but it was a tradition in this big Italian family, and Kaitlyn wasn't going to make a big deal of it.

Dr. Langdon poured seltzer for Sara and Gabby, but for Kaitlyn, he poured a generous glass of wine, full up to the rim. Sara got a weird expression on her face, like she was going to turn into the doctor police if Kaitlyn tried to take a sip.

Kaitlyn's heart began to knock hard against her chest. Panic rose, clogging her throat, making it hard to swallow. Next to her, Rafe seemed oblivious of any impending doom, reclining back on the couch, the picture of relaxation. Except for a tiny muscle in his jaw, which kept twitching.

They hadn't really discussed what to do once that wine got poured. That's what happened when you were too busy kissing to discuss important matters. She prayed that one sip would make Dr. L. happy and buy her more time.

Finally, Dr. Langdon raised his own glass and turned to Kaitlyn. Everyone in the room followed suit. "Kaitlyn, we consider you our fourth daughter." Dr. Langdon looked over at Rachel, who nodded in agreement.

"We're so proud of you—as a hardworking entrepreneur, a capable business owner in our town, but mostly because you're you—kindhearted and beautiful inside and out. We're proud of you, we love you, and we wish you an amazing upcoming year."

"So, sweetie," Rachel said, "here's to a *big* year to you and the Bean."

It *was* going to be a big year. Except the bean Kaitlyn was thinking of was a tiny little speck. A little bean. Not a coffee shop.

Little Bean. Big year. Yes, on both counts.

"We couldn't be more proud of you, sweetheart," Rachel said.

"Cheers," Dr. Langdon said.

"Cheers!" everyone echoed.

"*Salute*," Nonna said, lifting her glass.

Kaitlyn took a tiny sip of wine. So tiny, in fact, she wasn't sure if she even tasted it. Her throat had dried up so badly she could barely swallow, and her hand was shaking.

"This is awesome," Colton said. "Sorry you can't have any, honey," he said to Sara, who frowned.

"We'll drink theirs for them," Cade said, clinking glasses with Colton.

"It's really smooth," Rachel said. "Very nice, Walter."

"Delicious," Kaitlyn said. "Thank you so much for the special wine."

There, she'd handled it. That wasn't so bad. Everyone was tasting the wine and exclaiming about it, and now it was over. The fire was blazing, and the tree was huge and brilliantly lit. Everyone was chilled out and relaxed, the picture of holiday calm. Crisis averted. All that worrying for nothing.

Rachel came around, handing out round straw baskets to the adult kids. Kaitlyn looked a little puzzled when Rachel handed her a basket.

"These are all Rafe's ornaments that he made in grade school," she said.

Rafe rubbed his neck, a sure sign of embarrassment. "Oh, how sweet," Kaitlyn replied, carefully picking over the various Popsicle-stick creations and glittery treasures and viewing the elementary school pictures that were glued to many of them.

"Oh my gosh, look at this one!" Kaitlyn exclaimed. "Rafe, you looked so cute with glasses. And check out that sticking-up cowlick!" She picked up another. "Look at this buzz cut. And this one—no tooth!" She pointed to her own teeth to demonstrate to him where the gap was, and he flashed her a look of death.

Just wait until she got to the beanpole, gawky-looking middle school ones. Unable to bear it any longer, he tugged the basket from her hands. "Let's look at the girls' ornaments. They're prettier," he said, then hid it behind the couch.

"Hey, I was enjoying making fun of you," she said. Seeing him squirm made her feel a little better.

"Wow, look at this one," Colton said, dangling an elaborate glass ball covered in sequins and sparkly beads. He grinned at Sara, who was sitting next to him on the couch. "An overachiever, even back then."

"I was very…focused," Sara said. "Gabby's and Evie's look even better," she continued with a smile. "They got the artistic genes in the family."

While everyone was exclaiming over the ornaments,

Dr. Langdon came up beside her. "You've barely had any wine," he said. "Go ahead, sweetie, take a *real* swig and tell us what you think."

The smile slid from her face. She was aware of Rafe shifting his position, sitting up straighter, clearly aware of her discomfort. She blew out a breath and steeled herself, then stood. "I—I have something to say."

Rafe stood too. He flashed her a tight smile, then took up her hand.

"*We* have an announcement." He looked around the room. "A *big* announcement."

Rafe's warmth seeped into her, and she felt the absolute strength of him. But she didn't dare even consider borrowing that. She had her own strength, thank you very much.

"Kaitlyn and I are going to have a baby," Rafe said.

For a second, the room turned deadly quiet. A log on the fire snapped, and sparks flew up in the grate like mini fireworks. Rocket gave a quiet snuffle as he stirred in his sleep.

Gabby let out a shriek, which woke up Rocket, who hopped down from Nonna's chair and began zooming around the room.

"Oh my goodness," Nonna said, clutching her chest. "Walter, more wine."

In the distance, a wineglass dropped. Someone, maybe Evie, gasped. Rachel exclaimed and cheered.

Through it all, Kaitlyn was aware of Rafe's hand encircling hers. She had to admit, it was a comfort. But she didn't need him to watch out for her or protect her—or *take over* their announcement.

She worked her hand free. Startled by the movement, he turned to her.

"You okay?" he asked.

"You hijacked the baby announcement," she whispered.

"I wasn't hijacking it," he whispered back, fully facing her now and looking irritated. "I was *helping* you."

"Helping me? Helping *me*? It's your announcement too." *What the heck?*

Oh no. They were getting into a fight, right in the middle of the baby announcement. And the funny thing was, they almost never fought.

Why was that? Probably because in the past, she'd let him get away with this kind of thing. Because she'd had stars in her eyes. And yes, he was trying to be kind, trying to "save" her...but she didn't need to be saved.

And she needed to let him know that. Because things were different now. She was going to be a mother, which meant that she needed to stand on her own two feet. For herself *and* the baby.

Around them, commotion had erupted. "Praise Baby Jesus," Nonna said, lifting her hands in the air and coming over to give Rafe a big kiss on the cheek. "You two are finally getting married!"

Kaitlyn had just opened her mouth to respond when Rachel clapped her hands, looking completely thrilled. "Oh my gosh, that's wonderful!" she said as she ran over and hugged and kissed them both.

Evie burst into happy tears and threw her arms around Kaitlyn. "When's the wedding?" she asked. Everyone was crowding around and talking animatedly.

Even Rocket was barking up a storm, and there wasn't a second to get a word in edgewise.

Gabby ran over to hug her. "We must be due around the same time," she said.

"I'm due in June," Kaitlyn answered.

"Wait—we're July." Gabby's eyes grew wide. "You're due *before* me! I can't believe it! How did that hap—oh my gosh." She clapped a hand over her mouth. Dropping her voice, she whispered. "The wedding? You got pregnant at Stephanie and Everett's *wedding*?"

Kaitlyn only had time to shrug when Sara walked over. "Our babies will all grow up together," she said. "Except mine will be the oldest," she added pointedly.

Gabby smiled and shook her head. "Sara, is your kid going to be as competitive as you are?"

"Hope the baby looks like Kaitlyn," Colton said, clapping Rafe on the back.

"This is a very fertile family," Gabby's husband, Cade, added, looking a bit taken aback by all the commotion.

Gabby laughed and put her arm through Cade's. "It's about time these two got together," she said. "Finally!"

Evie joined all the huggers and congratulators. "I just realized I'm the only woman of childbearing age in this family not pregnant," she said.

"And that's just fine with me, honey," Joe said hurriedly.

"You two!" Rachel said. "Making everyone believe you were just friends. You had us all fooled."

Kaitlyn met Rafe's gaze. He looked a little panicked as he rushed to say, "Yes, well. About that..."

Rafe's dad stood. "I'd like to propose another toast."

"Walter, no," Rachel said. "Fifty percent of the women in this room can't drink."

Oh no. They had to tell everyone the whole truth right now. "You're the one who wanted to make an announcement," Kaitlyn whispered to Rafe. "Say something. Tell them the rest of it. That *we're not together*."

He gave a mock bow. "No, please. Feel free."

Suddenly Nonna was at Rafe's side. "When is the wedding?" she asked.

Rafe glanced at Kaitlyn then at his grandmother. "We're not getting married, Nonna," he said in a low voice. Thank goodness. They needed to put an end to this before it spun out of control.

Nonna cupped a hand over her ear. "What did you say?"

"I said, we're not getting married."

Nonna looked confused. "What do you mean you're not getting married?" she asked. "Don't you love her?"

"Of course we love each other, Nonna," Kaitlyn said hurriedly. "As friends. We're going to raise this baby as friends."

"*Friends?*" Nonna said in an exasperated tone. "Friends don't make babies together."

"Trust me, Nonna, we're better as friends," Kaitlyn added. "Neither of us wants to get married."

Rafe cleared his throat. "Hey, everyone. Listen. We're still getting adjusted to this big news. Kaitlyn and I need some time to process this. We aren't getting—"

"Oh." Nonna stood up, a blank look on her face. "Ooooh!" she exclaimed. "A baby...is always good news," she said, her voice fading a little toward the end. Suddenly she clutched her chest. "Oh my," she said. "I-I feel a little dizzy." She swayed a little, coming dangerously close to the Christmas tree.

Rafe quickly moved to Nonna's side just as she wobbled again, lost her balance, and face-planted into the tree.

The tree rocked precariously, lights and all, and seemed to cushion her fall. Pine boughs swished as the tree crashed to the floor. Glass balls shattered, ornaments tinkled, and some rolled away, Rocket in pursuit. Rachel let out a little cry.

Rafe's father and the other guys rushed over to help. Together, they pulled Nonna gently out of the tree and laid her down on the carpet as everyone gathered closely around. An ugly purple bruise on her forehead was starting to swell.

"I'm going to get her some ice," Rachel said, moving to the kitchen.

"Those needles hurt like the dickens!" Nonna said. "I told you we should have bought that pretty white fake tree on sale after Christmas last year."

Rafe knelt by his grandmother's side. "Are you still having chest pain, Nonna?"

"Oh my chest!" she said, almost as if with all the commotion, she'd forgotten. "*Dio mio*! Feels like a semitruck ran over it."

Rafe and his father exchanged knowing glances before Rafe pulled out his phone. "We're going to have to get a medevac team out here," Rafe said, dialing 911 as he took Nonna's pulse, in full paramedic mode now.

"The volunteer squad will take her to the ferry parking lot," his dad said. "The helicopter can meet us there."

"Oh no," Rachel said, her voice pinched and panicked.

"It's okay, Rachel," Nonna said, lifting her head. "I've always wanted to take a helicopter ride. I just wish it wasn't nighttime so I could see better. But do I have to go? I think I'm fine now." She looked up beseechingly at Rafe and his dad.

Rafe's dad gave Rachel a reassuring look. "Nonna," he said, placing a hand on her shoulder, "we're going to take you to the hospital to make sure you're okay."

"I could be having a heart attack," she said solemnly. "Or a stroke."

Rafe patted her arm, clearly struggling to stay calm himself. "Well, those are the worst things. But we'll need to get you checked out, okay?"

"Okay," she said. "Hurry, I feel faint."

Sirens sounded outside. "The squad will be here in a minute," Rafe's dad said. "Let's give them room."

Rachel handed Kaitlyn ice wrapped in a towel, and she passed it to Rafe. As he took it, they looked at each other. Now was not the time to tell the family they weren't together, no matter how badly they wanted to set everyone straight.

* * *

Rafe was sitting with the family outside the ER several hours later when his father walked into the waiting room with news of Nonna's condition. Rafe had ridden with Nonna in the medical helicopter while the rest of the family had gotten the ferry captain to make an emergency trip back to town. By the time they all made it to the ER, it was the middle of the night. Everyone was sitting on the uncomfortable vinyl chairs drinking coffee or dozing, including Hazel, who'd seemed very worried about Nonna and was lying down across two chairs she'd put together, covered by Dr. Langdon's and Rachel's jackets. Kaitlyn, who was sitting next to Rafe, had fallen asleep, her cheek on his shoulder. He stayed as still as he could to not wake her. Feeling her weight against his arm and hearing the soft, rhythmic sounds of her breathing were oddly calming.

"Nonna's fine," Dr. Langdon said. "She's doing great. No heart attack. No broken bones."

Everyone let out collective murmurs of relief. Hazel rubbed her eyes and sat up. Rafe let out a huge sigh. Kaitlyn, awake now, suddenly hugged him, whispering, "Thank God."

"Yeah," he said, trying not to register the feel of her in his arms, her silky hair grazing his neck, her sweet scent enveloping him. "Thank God."

"Don't get too happy," Rafe's dad said. "She's asking to see you. Insisting, more like."

Rafe got up immediately, running an agitated hand through his hair.

"You too, Kaitlyn," Rafe's dad said.

Kaitlyn looked startled. *She should be*, Rafe thought. He had a very bad feeling about this.

As Rafe passed his father, he said, "The good news is, she wants ice cream and to watch her 'stories.'"

"That sounds like Nonna," Kaitlyn said, sounding relieved.

"Yes, very encouraging," his dad said, frowning and looking sternly at both of them. "They didn't find anything wrong, but they're still going to do a full cardiac workup to make sure nothing's happening with her heart. So whatever you do, don't excite her any more. Or upset her." He dropped his voice. "She's worried for some reason that you two aren't going to get married. So whatever you tell her, keep her happy. Lie a little if you have to. Okay?"

"We won't upset her," Rafe said. Telling her that he and Kaitlyn were going to raise the baby as friends clearly had. He'd steer clear of any talk about the baby this time.

"Thank God she didn't break anything when she fell," Kaitlyn said as they walked down the hallway to Nonna's room.

"And that she didn't have a heart attack." Rafe felt terrible. What if she had because she was unhappy about them not being together? He never would have forgiven himself.

Nonna was sitting up in bed wearing a hospital gown, a cardiac monitor suspended above her beeping out a regular, reassuring rhythm. An IV bag hung half-full on a pole, making her look small and more than a little frail.

She looked up from scraping the bottom of a paper cup of ice cream and set down her spoon. "You two. I'm glad you're here." She gestured them over as though she were holding court. "Kaitlyn?" she said, extending her skinny arm, which looked all the more pitiful with the IV tubing and a big bruise from an attempted needle stick.

Kaitlyn took Nonna's hand and helped fluff her pillow.

"Rafe, give me your hand too," she said, extending her other arm. "I may not have much time."

"Nonna, you have plenty of time," Rafe said. "You're doing great. You're going to be able to go home really soon." Hearing Nonna talk like that was...scary. He didn't even want to think of that.

Nonna looked from Kaitlyn to Rafe and back. "I'll say this quick. Nothing makes me happier than seeing the two of you together—finally. If I die right now, it's my final wish to see you two marry. Promise me you will." She joined their hands together in front of her. "*Promise* me," she repeated solemnly.

"Nonna, I—" Rafe halted midsentence as Kaitlyn gave him a singular look.

"*Promise* me," Nonna insisted, looking from one to the other and squeezing both their hands with considerable strength.

"Yes, of course, Nonna," Kaitlyn said, ignoring Rafe. "Anything."

"My heart feels better already just knowing you've created a new life to bring into our family. Now I can die a happy woman."

"Nonna!" Kaitlyn said, squeezing her hand back. "Don't talk like that. You're not going to die."

"Kaitlyn's right, Nonna," Rafe said. "You're going to be fine. The doctors said—"

"Hush!" Nonna said. "I always knew it would take someone special to make my Rafe open his heart to love again. And I'm so glad it was you. I've always loved you like a granddaughter."

Rafe's breath caught. It was the *again* that got him. Nonna never mentioned his past, but this was clear evidence that she thought of it. She had strong opinions about what she believed he needed. And he did not want her to go there.

He didn't want to agitate Nonna, but he also could not outright lie. Surely she could accept that they would raise the baby as friends. "Nonna, we all love Kaitlyn, but I have to tell you—*oomph*." Rafe grabbed his side where Kaitlyn had drilled him a hard right jab with her elbow.

"You're like a grandmother to me too," Kaitlyn said.

Nonna set her gaze on Rafe with laser precision. "Get married *now*. Soon. Pronto. Promise me, Raphael." She tapped her fingers impatiently.

Rafe took a few breaths. One look at Kaitlyn told him that she was on board with playing along, crazy as it was. He could not risk upsetting Nonna again. At least his grandmother's short-term memory was terrible, and she'd forget it all soon enough. "Okay, sure."

"Say it. In complete sentences."

Rafe shuffled. "Okay, fine, Nonna. We'll…get… married."

"Say 'I promise I will marry you as soon as possible.'"

"Nonna, I—" He recalled promising *I will not talk in church* and *I will not hit my sister* among his past penances.

"I think my heart pain is coming back." Nonna's voice got weaker as she clutched her chest.

Rafe turned to Kaitlyn.

"Don't forget to take her hand," Nonna said.

As he did as instructed, Kaitlyn whispered, "Just do what she wants."

Looking down, Rafe was struck by how small Kaitlyn's hand was compared to his. And that brought out an elemental urge to protect her and their child. But protecting and marrying were two different things. "I promise. To marry you." He said it quickly enough that the words slurred.

"And now a kiss," Nonna said, waving her hand in the air. "On the lips."

For a second, Rafe scanned Kaitlyn's face. She looked tired, and her hair was a little mussed on one side from sleeping sitting up in the waiting room. But she looked...she looked—beautiful. One hundred percent determined to do anything for Nonna. In that moment, he was full of some kind of feeling—gratitude, maybe—that Nonna was okay, that Kaitlyn was okay, and that somehow despite all this craziness, everything was going to be...all right.

He kissed Kaitlyn full on, intending a quick peck but getting lost in the feel of her lips, soft and pliant beneath his, the taste of peppermint gum, and the fact that she was definitely kissing him back. *Kissing him back*— not clamping her lips together, not backing away.

That simple kiss broke every rule he had about not feeling, not thinking, not *wanting*. Because every time he touched her he felt all those clichéd things that peo-

ple talked about…fireworks, sparkles, explosions behind your eyelids. The warmth spreading everywhere,
the quickening of his pulse, the knowledge that this one
kiss would never be enough.

He must have gotten a little too caught up in that
kiss, because suddenly Kaitlyn was pulling back, clearing her throat, and looking a little flustered. Which
brought him back to reality and made him wonder what
the heck he was doing. It was fine to promise to be there
for the baby but *marriage*? This was going way too far.
Even for Nonna.

Nonna sat back and crossed her arms, blowing out
a deep breath. "Well. Now I can relax. Rafe, will you
scoot that tray table over here? I want to finish my gra-
ham crackers."

Rafe did as he was told. "And can you change the
channel before you go? *Real Housewives* of something-
or-other starts in five minutes." She reached up and
patted his cheek. "Now that I know you've found true
love I can rest."

They left her happily watching her show. In the hallway, Rafe walked a few doors down and leaned up
against the wall. "Whew. That was a little crazy."

"Yeah, crazy," Kaitlyn said, touching her lips as she
stepped back. "I mean, could you imagine us getting
married? We'd be a *disaster*, but I'd say anything for
Nonna's sake. I just hope she doesn't remember anything about this tomorrow."

Disaster? Something deep within him bristled. Not
that he would ever want to get married but…a disaster? Was the thought of being with him that awful?

"I'm sure by tomorrow it'll be completely out of her mind," he said. But Rafe wasn't so sure. Nonna had been very adamant—the most stubborn he'd ever seen. "It wouldn't be *that* bad... would it?"

"What?"

"I'm a pretty good catch. In general, I mean." He had a great job and he did a lot to support their small-town community. And while he might have come to terms with the idea that he wasn't cut out for marriage... Kaitlyn thinking that and calling him out on it? He was not okay with that.

Kaitlyn glanced down the hallway. Sara and Hazel had gone into Nonna's room. "Come on," she said, "let's go tell your family what we've agreed to so they can play along in front of Nonna." With that, she started to walk ahead of him down the hall.

They barely got back to the waiting room when the whole family flooded the doorway.

"There you two are!" Sara said. "Nonna just spilled the beans!"

Rafe caught Kaitlyn's eye in time to see her wince.

"What took you so long to tell us?" Gabby asked, squeezing his hand. "Congratulations!" She grabbed him and Kaitlyn by the elbows and dragged them back to Nonna's room, the whole family in tow.

"A birthday and an engagement, all on the same day," Dr. L. said, hugging Kaitlyn.

"Hey, everybody," Rafe said, "Nonna is just getting a little carried away..."

"She certainly is," Sara said. "She called me on her cell and told us all to get right in here."

"I'm so thrilled," Nonna said, looking very pleased. "This is the best day of my life." *Oh no.* Getting her a cell phone had been *his* idea.

"Now you'll be our legal daughter," Rachel said to Kaitlyn as she hugged her, "not just the daughter of our hearts."

Kaitlyn, surrounded by his family, stole a look back at Rafe, and what suddenly struck him was that he could see the panic in her eyes.

Panic over getting stuck with him. *Ouch.*

Nonna was holding court and everyone was congratulating them and exclaiming and there was no way he could set everyone straight right now.

"Hey, congratulations," Colton said, slapping a hand on his back. He scanned Rafe's face for a beat too long. "You okay?"

Rafe barely managed a nod, because at that moment, Sara hooked an arm in Kaitlyn's and led her away, with Evie, Gabby, and Rachel close in tow. "We want to hit all the wedding dress places this weekend," Sara said. "And Gabs and I still have lists of caterers and halls and bakers and photographers... We'll fix you right up!"

Kaitlyn seemed to turn white under the bright lights of the hospital room. He saw her nodding and pretending to smile, but he knew by the way her jaw was clenched that she was not happy. At all.

She was pale and drawn—clearly over the panic of suddenly being fake-engaged to him. Yet another feeling besides panic suddenly took hold of him—a feeling that wouldn't leave him, and he'd finally figured out just what it was—disappointment.

Not about the fake engagement. That was still registering a 10 on the shock-o-meter.

It was just that he'd expected her to...to *want* him. That was it. *That's* what was bothering him. Maybe even more than the fact that his entire family thought they were engaged. Even though he knew he had no right to be disappointed in her reaction.

She really didn't want him. And that bothered him way more than it should.

Chapter 12

♥

Kaitlyn was doing all she could to stay calm when Rafe drove her home from the hospital just before dawn, but her mind was doing cartwheels. The Langdons had dropped Hazel off, leaving Kaitlyn to catch a ride home with Rafe. "Well, that went well," he said, exhaling a deep breath as his fingers held a death grip on the wheel.

"For Nonna, it *did* go well, and that's all that matters," Kaitlyn replied. "We can deal with the rest." A quick glance showed him looking exhausted after the long night. "Look, Rafe, I want you to know I'll do everything I can to straighten this mess out with your family as soon as possible."

"I tried to pull my dad aside before we left," he said, "but it was impossible with all the commotion."

"I can tell your sisters, and when Nonna's out of the hospital and everything calms down, we'll have to tell her too." She pointed out the window. "Oh, look. The lights are so pretty."

Strings of lights were strung high across the street and around lampposts. Tiny white ones were wound tightly around the branches of trees to create a magical winter wonderland. It was a world away from the tension she was feeling and what she was certain Rafe was feeling too.

"It *is* pretty," he said. They drove in silence for a minute. Her head was spinning, and it was good to take a breath...and a time-out.

Rafe glanced in her direction. "Hey, you know we'll figure this out, right?"

"Right," she said, trying to sound like she believed it. "I didn't expect things to get so...complicated."

"We went from baby news to engagement news faster than it takes me to slide down the pole for a three-alarm fire," he said. "You're right—that's pretty complicated."

"I mean, they think we're...*together*. Going to get married. They were all so...happy."

Kaitlyn rubbed her forehead. Instead of the familiar surroundings of their town, she saw the faces of Rafe's family, smiling and teary-eyed.

"Rafe, don't miss the last turn," she said, pointing out the window and tapping him on the arm.

"Oh, sorry," he said, rubbing his cheek. It made a scratchy sound from the stubble that had grown overnight. He looked exhausted but very masculine, a thought she immediately tried to erase. He dropped his hand just then and it accidentally landed right on hers between the two seats. She intended to jerk away, but his hand felt so...good. Warm and soft, the feel of the callouses on his palm comforting. A sign of strength. If only she could believe he had the kind of strength she needed. That she could count on.

As usual, at his touch, her pulse ran as rampant as a corral full of stampeding bulls, and a thunderbolt of attraction skittered up her arm and invaded her entire body with heat. Sort of like their kiss in front of Nonna. That kiss had been...amazing.

This was why she didn't touch Rafe.

Or why when she did, disaster struck.

His hand lingered over hers for seconds too long. He gave her hand a squeeze, which she didn't return. But she didn't pull away either.

As he pulled into one of the diagonal spaces in front of the Bean, he looked over at her. "We're in this together, okay? *Together.*"

She sucked in a deep breath—that was a surprise. It had come out of nowhere, yet he'd sounded adamant and sincere, his voice cracking a little at the end. She managed to toss him a quick nod before she tugged her hand away, busying herself with gathering up her purse and gloves.

"Thanks for the ride," she said, collecting her things and wrapping up her scarf.

"Wait a minute." He turned off the car and pulled out his key. "I'm walking you up."

She stifled a yawn. "Rafe, you are not walking me upstairs. Go home." She flicked her hands in his direction. "Shoo."

"I'm walking you up," he said more firmly. He tried to cut the edge of his words with a smile, but she could tell he meant what he said. He'd always hated her living alone. Downtown was a friendly place, but no one really lived down here.

"If you insist, but it's very safe. No one even bothers to lock their doors."

He had one thing to say about that. "You'd better lock yours."

* * *

He opened her car door for her and walked her up a narrow staircase accessible from the inside of the building. They reached the top of the stairs and Kaitlyn turned to him. "No one's around. You can stop pretending to be my fiancé."

They were at the landing now. The dim, orangey hall light was buzzing loudly over her door.

Rafe frowned and reached out to touch her arm. "Katie, I know I didn't handle the baby news well. But I'm trying here...trying to show you how much I do care about you and this baby."

She glanced from her arm to his face and she looked...surprised. But also skeptical. Untrusting. He didn't blame her. He'd given her no reason to think otherwise.

"Okay," she said. "Well. Thanks for walking me up, but—"

Rafe gently took the key out of her hand, opened the door, and flipped on a light. Of course everything was fine. But he wanted—no, needed—to show her he was all in for her. He wanted to be the man she could count on, not one who made her go pale with dread.

He walked over to the windows and looked at the little town beneath them, literally glowing with lights—with Christmas joy. He tried to focus on the joy, the thrill—that Kaitlyn and his family felt at welcoming this baby. Babies were awesome! He squeezed his eyes shut and tried—willed himself—to channel that joy.

One day, everything could be fine, and the next day, everything could be . . . gone.

He ran his hand absently down the sides of the windows, feeling the cold air seep in from seemingly everywhere. "These windows are drafty." He began tinkering with the sash, looking under the drapes, running his hand along the caulking. "Really drafty."

At the same time, she said, "It's really late," and yawned. "Or rather early."

He hadn't realized how intensely he was inspecting everything until she made him stop by tugging him by the arm. "Tomorrow is another day for home inspection, Mr. Firefighter. Go home and get some rest."

"What's your plan with the baby's room?" he asked, glancing into her bedroom as she guided him toward the door.

"Oh. I thought I'd give the baby my room and move my bed out here." Her apartment had some nice architectural elements, like an exposed brick wall and really beautiful crown moldings. But it had just one bedroom, right off the main room.

He sighed. "You probably wouldn't consider moving?"

She smiled. "From this beauty? It's close to work and *free*—what more could I ask for?"

"Um, a place where the heating pipes don't wake you up at night, where the plaster's not crumbling, and where you aren't the only human being around?" Rafe moved toward the bedroom. "Mind if I have a look?"

"Now?" She thought he was out of his mind. And after the long night, he must be. But he didn't want to leave things like this. He couldn't fix himself, but he could certainly fix her apartment.

"I'll just take a quick look." He examined the room that would one day become the baby's, flipping on the wall switch, which lit up a small bedside lamp. The tidy double bed and a stack of books on the bedside table didn't surprise him—Kaitlyn always made her bed, and she was always reading. In his mind he saw her reading in bed after a long day. He'd come sit on the edge and gently tug the book out of her hands—and show her what else they could use this space for.

Whoa . . . where did that thought come from?

He cleared his throat, took a step back, forced himself to look at the ceiling. "No overhead lighting in here."

"No but that's okay. I can make do," she said, suppressing another yawn.

"I'd like to come back tomorrow and see if I can run some electrical wires into the attic crawl space. What do you think of some track lighting in here?"

She took his arm and guided him through the living room to the front door. "I don't need track lighting."

"You should have some," he said. "And I'll caulk your windows too."

"Hmm," she said, tapping a finger against her cheek.

"My kitchen faucet is a little drippy. And the dryer's making a funny noise."

"I'll look at those too."

"Thank you, but I'm kidding. Everything's fine. See you later, okay?"

He looked her in the eye. "I meant what I said. About being here. Being involved. I—I want to be involved. We'll get through all of this—together. We'll straighten out this thing with my family. I promise you, it's all going to be all right."

She nodded, but her lips were pressed together in a thin line. He knew her well enough to know that she didn't believe him, that she was humoring him. She opened the door for him.

"Good night, Rafe."

Chapter 13

♥

Is anyone with you today, sweetie?" the ultrasound tech asked in the darkened exam room. "I'm Carly, by the way." She busied herself flipping switches on the ultrasound machine, gathering the probe, and adjusting the TV monitor so Kaitlyn could see it from her semireclining position on the exam table.

"Just me," Kaitlyn said with the biggest smile she could muster. She didn't want anyone feeling sorry for her. She'd *decided* to come today by herself. Which might have been selfish, but she needed some space from Rafe.

Between the fake engagement and his wanting to fix everything in her apartment not tied down and the fact that she just wasn't sure what was motivating him to be so solicitous...she just needed a breather. The family was understandably worried about Nonna, who was still in the hospital getting cardiac tests, and she and Rafe were on hold about telling them the truth. But right now all she wanted was some room to think.

She was perfectly fine with doing this whole baby thing on her own. And secretly, maybe she preferred it. Anything was better than Rafe's strange hovering behavior and nervous energy.

Carly took a seat on a stool, reached for the ultrasound probe, and adjusted settings on the machine. "Okay," she said, grabbing a plastic bottle and explaining that she was going to squirt some gel on Kaitlyn's lower abdomen.

The gel hit her skin just as a text went off on her phone.

I'm at your place doing some work. Okay? Let myself in.

Rafe. Working in her apartment again, as he had all day yesterday too. Okay, she typed back, guilt running through her, cold as the gel.

She should have told him about this test and asked him if he wanted to come. But he was so…zealous about helping her and worrying about everything. He'd gone from being shocked about the baby to trying to prove to her that he was all in. She didn't buy it. Oh, she couldn't deny that he wanted to be a part of this baby's life, but something just wasn't sitting well. It was as if he was driven by his own strong sense of responsibility instead of his heart being in it.

It made her afraid he wouldn't be able to really love this baby.

The screen flicked on, and fuzzy gray-and-white images filled the screen. She forgot all about Rafe and how weird he was acting and all her confused feelings because the room was filled with a loud *whoosh whoosh whoosh* sound.

Kaitlyn swallowed. "Is that..." Her voice trailed off as her throat suddenly tightened.

"You bet," Carly said, adjusting a few nobs and dials. "That is the strong and regular heartbeat of this little person," she said, pointing. Up on the screen was the profile, clear as day, of a *baby*. With arms that were moving and legs that were kicking. And a little nose and mouth and tiny moving fingers.

Something in her broke. A tide of overwhelming emotion washed over her. And just like that, Kaitlyn fell in love. An overpowering, relentless love that made her breath catch and her eyes well up with tears. She swallowed hard. "Is she—is she sucking her thumb?"

"Yes, he or she is."

"Can you tell? If it's a boy or a girl, I mean?" Kaitlyn asked.

"Not until the twenty-week ultrasound. That's much more detailed." She pointed out what features could be seen—organs, tiny fingers and toes.

It was the most amazing thing Kaitlyn had ever seen. Something she and Rafe had made, a part of her and a part of him.

Carly pressed keys on a computer keyboard. "Your little one's heart is beating one hundred sixty times a minute, which is awesome. All the organs appear to be in place. The placenta's right here. All the measurements indicate your due date is spot-on."

Kaitlyn pressed her lips together and focused on the

screen. She wasn't going to miss a single second of meeting this baby.

Her first impulse was to text Rafe, to share this like they'd shared so many other moments. But of course she couldn't. She should have invited him here. To show him what this was really all about. And maybe he would have fallen instantly in love too.

* * *

When Kaitlyn returned to her apartment, Rafe was on a stepladder in her bedroom fiddling with wires that were sticking out of the ceiling. When she saw him, her first re-action was, *Who's the hottie in the flannel shirt fixing stuff?* It wasn't the worst thing, having him around, doing things for the baby. She liked that he'd wanted to fix the baby's room. And maybe—just maybe—it had also been a little nice that he'd walked her to her door the other night, and had caulked her windows, and was even talking about help-ing her pick out a paint color for the baby's room.

She could come to like this behavior—well, *some* of this behavior—a lot. Too much, really. That was why she wasn't going to put much stock in it. Because what-ever was making him feel guilty was going to pass, and they'd go back to Rafe being Rafe and her going it alone. And that would be all right. Better to get used to things being that way between them than hoping for more. The other scenario was way too dangerous.

"I hope you don't mind I came over and got started," he said, flashing a smile as he looked down from his high-up perch.

And oh, that smile. It might've even affected her if guilt hadn't crept through her. Ugh, she was a terrible person.

"No, of course not," she said. There he was, spending all his spare time fixing up her apartment for the baby, and there she was, going by herself to their baby's ultrasound. She was the *worst*. She took the ultrasound images she'd been holding in her hand to show him and slipped them under her mouse pad on her desk. She *wanted* to show him—at the right time, when she could explain.

"I've been Googling a few things you might be interested in," he said as he stepped down from the ladder, pulling out his cell phone. "Do you know how many micrograms of folic acid are in your prenatal vitamin?" He scrolled through his phone intently. "Because there needs to be four hundred to prevent spina bifida."

"I've been on a prenatal vitamin for quite some time," she said. It was suddenly coming back to her why she'd needed some alone time.

"And did you know you shouldn't eat uncooked hot dogs?"

"I don't eat hot dogs, Rafe." Hot dogs? He'd been reading about *hot dogs*?

He dug into his jeans pocket and pulled out a sticky note. "And do you get twelve hundred milligrams of calcium a day? If not, you might need a supplement."

"Ice cream is my favorite food. I'm pretty sure I don't have a calcium deficit." Was this what it was like to have someone really be concerned? She wasn't used to this. Steve, being a football coach, had been concerned about the outcome of all football games, local and otherwise—but she'd never had this level of obsession directed at her.

"Have you been checked for diabetes?" That list Rafe was reading from must be a mile long. She fought a sudden urge to toss his phone out the window.

She crossed her arms and frowned. "Are you implying that I eat *too much* ice cream?"

He glanced up, still dead serious. "Of course not. It just says here that you have to be checked. And how much fish do you eat a week? Because fish have mercury in them, especially big fish. You know, the ones at the top of the food chain. I had no idea you had to watch out for that."

"I don't really like—"

"I forgot the most important one. Have you had your flu shot? Pregnant women who get the flu are at high risk of complications. Basically, your immune system sucks when you're pregnant."

"Rafe, stop. Enough Googling." She tugged his phone out of his hands, forcing him to look up at her. "You're freaking me out."

"Oh." Oh dear. He suddenly looked...hurt. Hurt? This was a strange side of him, one she'd never seen before, and she had no idea where it was coming from.

She softened her tone and touched his arm. "Look, everything's fine. I feel great. There's nothing to worry about. I've got to take a shower and get to work, okay?"

She needed a little breather from his obsessions. Because he was driving her completely batty.

* * *

Rafe heard the shower whoosh on and the old pipes screech and clank as they struggled to supply hot water. Yes, he was acting like a mother hen. Yes, he was worried about…everything. But not because he felt guilty about their relationship—or rather, their lack of one. The truth was, Nonna's health scare had brought him back in time. To Claire. And their baby. And now he was scared to death. About everything. Kaitlyn's health. Her safety. How could he tell her that every fear, every list of everything that could possibly go wrong in a pregnancy, was running at warp speed through his brain 99 percent of the time? That he was terrified that he'd lose her too.

Man, he needed to get a grip. His obsessing over everything that could go wrong wasn't making things any easier, and now he'd gone and freaked out Kaitlyn too. He pulled out his tape measure and climbed the ladder to take a ceiling measurement but ended up coming back down and scrubbing a hand over his face.

He knew repairing everything in sight wasn't a substitute for talking about the elephant in the room. Which was that he couldn't stop thinking about the baby from so long ago. And this time, he wanted to do everything right so that everything would *be* all right.

Logically, he understood life didn't work like that. But he had to do something. The last time he was young and focused on himself and look what had happened. The worst. He was determined for things to be different this time.

Not on my watch was what kept running through his mind.

Deciding to make coffee, he walked into the kitchen. For a few minutes, he lost himself in figuring out the complexities of the new coffee maker that he'd set up for Kaitlyn and even found a bag of beans in the cupboard.

As the pleasant gurgles and the rich aroma of brewing coffee filled the kitchen, he walked into the main room and sat down at Kaitlyn's computer desk. Maybe if he Googled signs of a healthy pregnancy he'd be able to calm down. Kaitlyn was right—she was doing great, and he was letting his imagination carry himself away. He tapped the space bar to wake up the screen and shook the mouse.

That was when he saw them. Edges of thin paper sticking out from underneath the mouse pad. He lifted it up to find a couple of grainy black-and-white images—*ultrasound* images. His hand paused in midair, a mishmash of feelings pitching and yawing inside him.

Rafe swallowed hard. Heard the shower turn off down the hall and the pipes shudder one last time. He reached for the photos but suddenly withdrew his hands as if they would burn him. He took in a few gulps of air. With shaking hands, he finally picked them up.

The fuzzy image of a baby viewed longways from the side was plain as day before his eyes. It was the clear outline of a tiny human being, with miniature hands and feet. He could make out facial features too, and the hands were near the mouth.

A baby. Not a pregnancy, but a *baby*. His and Kaitlyn's.

He heard his name. Kaitlyn was standing there in leggings and a bulky sweater, watching him. For how long he didn't know. Her eyes were wide with surprise, wariness, maybe even shock, but she said nothing.

He swallowed, but words failed him. His hand was shaking, but he hid that by setting the images down.

"I—I had an ultrasound today," she said.

He cleared his throat. "I see," he said, his voice tight. He was disappointed she hadn't told him and relieved at the same time.

"You're upset with me," she said, walking over to him.

Instead of waiting for her, he got up and walked into the tiny kitchen. He opened the fridge and pretended to search for milk but then shut the door and stood there, in front of the closed fridge, trying to think of what to say. The images would not leave his head. *Ultrasound images.* Of a baby, plain as day. Like the ultrasound Claire never got to have.

"Rafe, I didn't ask you to go because...because I feel like you're doing all this because it's expected of you." She waited for him to turn around. "And I appreciate all you're doing, but you're just being super... super hovering about everything. I-I just wanted some space. I'm sorry if I hurt you."

"Hovering, huh?" he said, anger making his voice sound higher than usual. This was getting worse. She didn't want him at the appointment, and she didn't want him here doing things.

"I—appreciate your help," she said firmly. "But I don't need it."

"You mean you don't *want* my help." He turned to

the coffee maker and started punching buttons, determined to get at least one thing right today.

"I don't want you to feel like all of this"—she gestured to all of his projects—"is an obligation. I want you to *want* this baby."

His heart sank. "It's not what you think," he said. It was complicated. It wasn't about wanting or not wanting. It was about being scared out of his mind.

"Then what?" She threw up her hands, frustrated with trying to read him. "What is it? You want your old life back? Then take it back. I'll be fine on my own."

"Stop." He quit fidgeting with the stupid coffee maker and rested his hands on the counter. He couldn't look at her. "I need to tell you something."

* * *

Kaitlyn scanned Rafe's face and saw that it was full of...struggle. Which surprised her, because he was always the one to break the tension in a hard moment, always the one to find a reason to laugh or crack a joke.

He wasn't cracking any jokes now. He looked so at odds that she placed her hand on his arm. He stared at it, seeming to gather his thoughts.

Suddenly he took up her hands and looked at her intently. She couldn't help the feeling that he was about to reveal something raw, something awful, and every muscle braced for impact. *Please, please*, she thought. *Please don't say you don't want this baby.*

"There was a baby," he said, his voice barely audible.

She barely heard him. "Excuse me?" she said.

His grip was desperate, his face full of anguish. "Eight years ago—there was a baby."

She echoed his words, comprehension dawning slowly. Suddenly she got what he was saying. Eight years ago. With Claire. A *baby*?

"Claire was eight weeks along when the accident happened. We hadn't told anyone yet. She was—she was driving herself to her ultrasound appointment."

"Oh no, Rafe. No." Without thinking, Kaitlyn wrapped herself around him and hugged him, hard. Dear God in heaven.

"I'd gotten called to a fire. It was at the washer factory in Richardson, and mutual aid calls went out to four counties. So I called her on the way and told her I wasn't going to make it to the appointment. I didn't even take the time to tell her I loved her." His voice broke. "Truth was, I was more interested in heading to my first big blaze."

Kaitlyn clung to him, her cheek pressed against the scrape of his rough one. Losing a fiancée was catastrophic. But a baby as well... A whole new understanding dawned. "I'm sorry," she murmured into his shoulder. "So sorry."

They stood together in the tiny kitchen. She wanted to be strong for him, to take away his pain. A pain that must surely stab him in the heart every time he thought of *their* baby.

His eyes searched hers. She thought he might say more, but he didn't. Or maybe he couldn't. For a man who wielded his sense of humor with such proficiency, she understood how hard it was for him to be serious.

"I'm sorry about the way I've been acting," he said again. "I don't want this to—I don't want this to drag down a happy time."

She ached for him, for the family he'd lost—no, for the *life* he'd lost. She struggled to say something light-hearted, as he might—but failed. "I can't imagine your pain," she said. "But thank you for telling me." Her head was spinning. Everything she'd thought about him—the fun Rafe, the happy-go-lucky guy, always ready with a quick joke—that wasn't really who he was. The humor was a front, a mask to hide all this heartache.

She held him by the arms and met his troubled gaze. Before she could analyze what she was doing, she found herself desperate to fill the silence. "I saw the baby kicking today—I mean *really* kicking, even though it's too early to feel a thing. They said the baby's growing well and everything's in its place and the heartbeat is strong. I-I'm really sorry I went without you. I hope next time you'll come so you can see everything too." Maybe she was blathering. Maybe he didn't want to hear about it. But it was the one way she could think of to give him the only thing she could...hope.

He nodded, but he still didn't say anything, so she kept talking. "No matter how difficult this whole situation is for either of us, we created something...good." She took his hand and placed it on her abdomen, leaving her hand atop his. "This baby is joyful and good."

She looked at his ashen face. The dark circles under his eyes. She'd never seen him so weary.

He nodded and attempted a smile. For a moment,

he pulled her close and held her there, finally planting a brief kiss on her forehead before releasing her. Then he glanced at his watch and mumbled something about getting back to work.

Now she understood that her entire perception of Rafe as an easy-breezy ladies' man was entirely wrong.

Just as Rafe never crossed the line of intimacy with anyone, she'd never leaned on anyone or let anyone help her. Maybe he *wanted* to help her—maybe he hadn't just been saying that. Maybe it would be healing for him to help her, and to see that this baby was going to be just fine. From now on, she was going to give him the benefit of the doubt.

She understood that Rafe had locked his heart away to prevent it from feeling any more pain. She got that. The trouble was, this Rafe—the *real* Rafe—was making her feel all the feelings again that she'd worked so hard to shut down.

* * *

It hadn't been so awful to open up to Katie. His secret was out in the open now. But it would be naïve to think she could save him, that she and this baby could somehow take away all the pain he could hardly bear for all these years. The way she'd felt in his arms—so sweet and full of love and understanding—it nearly undid him. But how could he allow himself the luxury of accepting her comfort when he could give nothing in return?

Rafe walked into the room that would one day be

their baby's and shut the door, Kaitlyn's words echoing in his mind. *This baby is joyful and good.*

Like its mother, he thought.

Rafe got back to work, wanting only to lose himself in his project. When Kaitlyn knocked to tell him she was headed downstairs, and that she had an appointment to see Hazel's guidance counselor today, he nodded and waved, pretending to be engrossed in whatever was playing in his earbuds. But the truth was, there was nothing there but dead silence, his own brain working overtime.

It dawned on him what Kaitlyn had done just by being herself—she'd made him want to find a way through this pain. For their baby. And who was he kidding? For *her*.

Kaitlyn was like sunshine, offering warmth and sweetness and…hope. The scary part was that she made him wonder, what would it be like to dare to step into that light?

Chapter 14

♥

Later in the Bean, Kaitlyn was trying to force-feed cookies to anyone she could, starting with her mom, Sara, Gabby, and Gwen. She had her notebook nearby, where she was recording all the different ways she'd altered the recipes for three separate batches of cookies she'd just baked. This was the one good result from her talk with Rafe: it was making her bake like crazy. Anything to avoid thinking of all the feelings he'd stirred up with what he'd confessed this morning.

The Christmas lights were on around the windows, and Hazel had helped Kaitlyn loop more light strings all along the ceiling, wedging the wires between the ceiling tiles. They'd also strung ornaments from fishing line, making the ambience in the Bean welcoming and very Christmasy. On the mounted TV in the corner, the movie *Elf* was playing, and a group of seniors were drinking their happy hour two-for-one Christmas drinks and chuckling at the antics of Buddy, the very tall and very misplaced elf. Several tables of teens were doing homework and watching too. One boy kept surreptitiously watching Hazel as she worked behind the counter.

Hazel stopped by to steal a cookie. "Not bad," she said, flying past on her way to take someone's order. Worry gnawed in Kaitlyn's stomach even as she smiled at her niece. She'd intended to show Hazel a quiet weekend with a nice family and instead the teenager had gotten family drama over the baby announcement, Nonna's nosedive into the tree, and a midnight ferry ride to an all-night hospital marathon. But despite all the tumult, Hazel seemed...better. More settled. Happier? And she certainly was getting the hang of making coffee drinks.

"What's this one?" Gwen asked, examining the first of three plates of chocolate cookies.

Kaitlyn lifted the plate and held it out. "Taste one and tell me what you think."

Mr. Iocona, probably lured by the word *cookies*, perked up immediately and walked over from his usual spot at the counter. "I'll try one."

"Here you go, Henry," she said, handing him one. "Now," she addressed the others, "I've made several batches using different fats to make them cakey versus crispy. I was trying for crunchy on the outside and cakey and a little gooey on the inside. Then I used different leaveners—baking soda and baking powder. So try a bite from all three plates and tell me which one you like best." She'd been trying to bake away her thoughts about Rafe as he'd been this morning—vulnerable, wounded, a man with depth and feeling. She'd never seen him that way before. And she had to admit, it made him *way* too attractive.

"Wow," Sara said, tasting one. "Who knew baking

was such a science? It reminds me of organic chemistry lab."

"This is like *The Great British Bake Off*," Gabby said, selecting one from the first plate and taking a bite. "I'll be Mary Berry. *Quite good, I'd say*," she said in a very bad British accent.

Kaitlyn, always amused by Gabby, laughed.

"None of these really *look* like your grandpa's," Gwen said flatly, making Kaitlyn's smile fade. At least Kaitlyn could count on her to be bluntly honest. "Gramps's were big and chocolatey and they had patches of white snow on them." She held a cookie up and rotated it as if she were examining it under a magnifying glass. "Hence the name, *snowcaps*."

"Well," Kaitlyn said, "I rolled them in powdered sugar, but maybe I didn't let them sit in it long enough. So for today just focus on the taste."

"Your grandfather would be proud," her mom said judiciously. "They're all quite good."

"But?" Because she'd definitely heard a silent *but* in there.

"I'm still trying to decide," her mom hedged. Kaitlyn's heart sank—she knew her mom well enough to know that none of these recipes were close. Her mom was just too nice to say it.

"Mom, don't you remember anything about Grandpa making them? Maybe even some buried memory of him mixing some special ingredients together that I might be missing?"

"I'm sorry, honey," she said, taking another bite. "I always avoided anything to do with the kitchen."

"I think this one's chocolatey and velvety, with a buttery feel," Gabby said, biting her lip to keep from smiling.

"This one's simple, light-bodied, dry, and crisp," Sara piped in, propping her chin on her hand and tapping her lips in consideration.

"And this one's sweet, earthy, and intense," Gwen added. "Oh, and don't forget oaky. *Definitely* oaky."

"You people!" Kaitlyn said. "You're supposed to be helping me. The winery's thirty miles west of here."

"Bottom line is, they're all good," Gwen said. "But none of them has that special gooey, melty, chocolatey goodness that I remember. And you do know about the secret ingredient, don't you?"

"No. What secret ingredient?" Kaitlyn picked up her pen. Finally, she was getting somewhere.

"I actually don't know *what* it is, but I do remember Gramps mentioning it," Gwen said. "I remember him talking about adding a special something and saying, 'This is my best cookie. And it's got a little something to give it an extra kick.'"

"Marijuana?" asked Gabby.

"My grandfather didn't smoke weed!" Kaitlyn rolled her eyes. At least, she didn't *think* he did. She was surrounded by jokesters and people with bad memories. Great.

"We're sorry we can't be more helpful," Gabby said, gathering up her purse. "But thanks for the chocolate snack."

Gwen got back to work and Sara, Gabby, and her mom left, leaving Kaitlyn alone with her notebook. She was tasting bits of the cookies and writing down what she thought was wrong with each one, when the bell tinkled and Rafe walked in.

"Hey, beautiful," he said, sitting down.

Kaitlyn felt a full-body flush coming on, and that tingly feeling she always got when Rafe was still yards away. Maybe these pregnancy hormones were just playing tricks on her. It wasn't unusual for him to joke around and call her beautiful or gorgeous or some other name. But a quick glance up at him showed he looked... serious, which confused her more than ever.

That reminded her of their discussion this morning, and all her turmoil came tumbling back. She broke her gaze and looked around the café. "Hey, there's no one around." She dropped her voice. "No need to pretend."

"I'm not pretending." He paused and adjusted himself on the stool. "I've been thinking about...earlier. I'm really sorry for going overboard with the worrying." In his eyes, she saw how difficult the admission was for him. "I'll try harder to rein it in."

"And I'm sorry about going alone to the ultrasound." She patted his hand, which felt like a weak gesture when what she really wanted to do was hold him. Find a way to take away all his pain. But that would probably scare him, and besides, she was at work. Instead, she said, "Really sorry."

"I'm glad everything was okay—with the baby," he said. "I don't think I told you that."

"Me too." Silence lay like a heavy blanket between them, and she hesitated, unsure of what to say next. "Well then, we're good," she said as cheerily as possible, then flashed him a little smile. Which was easy to do because she would've done anything to make him smile in return.

She dug into her apron pocket and pulled out a piece of computer paper. "So...I'll give you some cookies if you look over this list of math tutors I got from the high school guidance counselor *and* help me find a sewing machine for Hazel." She pushed a plate toward him.

"Good deal," he said, taking a bite out of one. "But why the sewing machine?"

"Turns out Hazel's interested in fashion design. Did you know she makes all her clothes?" Kaitlyn felt embarrassed that she didn't have a clue about Hazel's interests. But now that she was armed with that information, she was going to use it wisely.

"That right?" Rafe said, taking another bite.

"The guidance counselor suggested we give her access to a machine. She said there's a contest Hazel could enter."

"What's with your family and contests?" Rafe asked, one corner of his mouth lifted in a smile. A really nice smile.

"Nothing ventured?" she answered with a shrug.

Rafe rubbed his chin. "Nonna has a sewing machine. I'm sure she'd let Hazel use it. She's coming home from the hospital and I'll be spending the night over at her house one night this week. I can ask her." He reached for another cookie. "Hey, these are pretty good."

Rafe happened to be looking at her as he was chewing. Which made her feel awkward and too aware of him, even though she *knew* he was talking about the cookie. "See? Exactly," she said, tapping her index finger on the counter. "*Pretty* good. Not *wow* or *totally orgasmic. That's* what I'm going for."

Suddenly his phone clattered to the floor.

He picked it up and cleared his throat. "You want a cookie to taste...orgasmic?"

"Yeah. Because I can't win a cookie contest without that, Rafe. It has to be the best darn cookie anyone has ever tasted. One that makes you feel like..."

He'd just taken another bite of cookie, and now he raised a brow. "Like..."

"Like you have never had better."

He stopped chewing and stared at her. Then he swallowed and studied the tutor list intently. "This is the guy I told you about. Logan Burroughs," he said, pointing to a name. "Going off next fall to study engineering at Ohio State. In fact, he's sitting right over there with those kids."

The boy Rafe had singled out was the same one who had been staring at Hazel. "Oh, is that Bob and Angie's son? Last time I saw him he was playing Little League." They were both leaning over the counter, their shoulders all but touching. She straightened up and moved back.

"He's a nice kid."

"Great. Thanks." She started tapping her pen against the counter because she needed to get busy doing...*something*. And because Rafe was still way too close.

"By the way," he said, casting her a sideways glance. "You'll find the *wow* recipe. I have faith in you."

She just nodded because…because sometimes he knew exactly what to say.

He took another bite of cookie and considered it. "This one's definitely *almost* a *wow*. But not quite."

"Well, if I don't elicit a *wow*, I'm not doing my job," she said. As soon as the words came out, she froze. A hot flush crept wretchedly up her neck.

He stared at her for a long time. He couldn't be remembering…no, of course he couldn't. Because he didn't remember any of that. *Did he?*

Just then the bell above the door tinkled, and three teenage girls walked in wearing tons of makeup, skintight jeans, and expensive ski jackets.

"Oh, hi, Hazel," said a pretty girl with long dark hair who stood in front of her friends.

"Hi," Hazel said, her tone guarded. "What can I get you?"

"I'll have a grande half-caf seven-pump toasted white mocha with no whip and extra sprinkles," said one.

The second girl chimed in. "And I'll have a venti triple almond milk chestnut praline latte with no whip."

"And I'll have a grande peppermint mocha with extra whip and extra drizzle at a hundred twenty degrees," came the third order.

Hazel scribbled something down, but the orders came fast and furiously.

"Those girls know this is not Starbucks," Kaitlyn whispered, fisting her hands. "And their orders are ridiculous. I'm going in."

"Easy there, Mama Bear," Rafe said, holding her back by gently taking her arm. "Let her handle it."

"But—"

"Shh," he said, nodding his head toward Hazel. "Just look." Hazel was calmly making the drinks, with Gwen looking over her shoulder. Then she delivered them carefully to the counter.

"We're going to a really fun party tonight," the dark-haired girl said as she paid. "Too bad you can't come."

Oh, these girls, Kaitlyn thought.

"Actually, she *is* coming, Emma," someone said. It was the boy who'd been watching from the table—a very cute boy with an athletic build who'd just walked up to the counter. "With me."

"Logan! What are you doing here?" asked the leader. From the tone of her voice, Kaitlyn could tell whatever he would say mattered to her.

"Saying hi to Hazel," Cute Guy said, turning all his focus onto her niece. "By the way, love your shirt. You look pretty today."

Hazel blushed furiously. Kaitlyn glanced at Rafe, who shrugged. The mean girls left with their fancy-schmancy drinks, thank goodness.

"You could've told those girls you're just going to be my math tutor," Hazel said to the boy. "They think—"

"I don't really care what they think," he said, and then he smiled. Which made Hazel blush some more. "Are you almost ready?"

She nodded and looked over in Kaitlyn's direction. "Let me make sure it's okay to leave."

This time Kaitlyn did go up to the counter. "You did an amazing job with those drink orders," she told Hazel.

"Thanks," Hazel said. "But Gwen helped."

Gwen walked out from the back. "You *did* do a great job keeping everything straight."

"Without you," Hazel said, "I would've had no idea what they were asking for."

"Well, I have years of experience. And those orders were wacky."

"Everything about those girls was over the top," Kaitlyn said.

"That's okay, boss, I fixed their wagon," Gwen said, a very self-satisfied expression on her face.

Kaitlyn spun to face her, her stomach churning with dread. "Wh-what do you mean?"

"I might've used super high-altitude blend in those drinks. By accident, of course. So it'll be like they're drinking a few cans of Red Bull . . . each."

"Gwen, no. You didn't—"

"She's kidding, Aunt Kate," Hazel said, smiling.

Gwen raised her brows. "Or is she?" she said before disappearing behind the counter.

Hazel walked around the counter and lowered her voice as she spoke to Kaitlyn. "We're going to grab a burger down the street at Lou's and study there," she said. "Is that okay?"

"Sure. As long as you're back by curfew."

Hazel rolled her eyes, but she was also smiling a little. "Okay, fine."

"See you later," Kaitlyn said, as they left out the door. She didn't realize it, but she was wringing her hands. Rafe steadied them by putting his hand over both of hers.

"She's doing better," he said. His grip was firm and steadying, and his voice low and calm in a way that instantly made her feel calmer too.

"You think so?"

"Yeah," he said, biting back a smile. "And the good news is she's found her own tutor."

It was Kaitlyn's turn to roll her eyes.

"My hunch is that she wants to show you that she's trying." He released her hand but stayed where he was, his dark gaze melting her and discombobulating her thoughts. "Hey, I have to tell you something. Not a big deal, but I don't think you're going to like it."

"Now you have me worried." Her hand flew up to her chest as she braced herself.

"When I went up in your attic to do the electric work for the new lights, I noticed you have a type of very old insulation up there called vermiculite." Rafe's tone was slow and patient, which she took as a little foreboding. She must've looked puzzled, because he added, "Have you ever heard of that?"

"I might've heard the name before, but I don't really know what it is. And this building is from the 1890s. So I have no idea how old the insulation is."

He pressed his lips together, his expression serious. "Yeah, well, vermiculite is not the kind of insulation you want to have."

"Maybe that's why my place is chilly. I'll have someone come and add some more—maybe that kind they blow in through the cracks. That should take care of it, right?"

"Unfortunately, the problem is more complicated

than that. Vermiculite contains asbestos. So the question now is how much. Your apartment needs to be tested. You might need abatement."

Kaitlyn dropped down on the nearest stool. "*Asbestos* abatement?" Oh, she got it now. Dollar signs appeared in front of her eyes. Thousands of dollar signs. "That sounds like a major, horrible ordeal." Oh, she did not have the time for this, or the money.

"It could be complicated. Or it could be nothing. I'd like to send a guy over there to check it out, if that's okay."

"Okay, fine. But it's just insulation, so can it wait... like, until spring or something?"

"Well, I drilled a hole for the can light in the ceiling and unfortunately some dust dropped down." He shot her an apologetic look. "So..."

Dust? Potentially toxic dust? Floating around her apartment? "Rafe, what are you saying?"

"You can't go back there," he said in an *absolutely not* tone. "I may have aerosolized some of it. It's not safe."

Oh, this was getting worse and worse.

"No." She rubbed her forehead, trying to smooth out her stress but failing. "This is... this is terrible."

He touched her forearm. One look into those coffee-brown eyes showed he was cool as a cucumber, while she was freaking the heck out. "My mom has no room with Hazel there. I'd have to sleep on the couch. Or ask Sara or Gabby to put me up for... for how long?"

"A week. Maybe two. If they can get to it right away."

"I suppose I can use the kitchen here to keep working on my cookie recipe. There's only a week left before the contest deadline. This is...awful."

He placed his hand on her arm. "I have a better idea. Come stay with me. I have a freshly painted extra bedroom and a brand-new kitchen. You can bake all the cookies you want. Plus you'll have the place to yourself every third day and night while I'm at work."

She perused his handsome face. He was looking at her kindly. His mouth was quirked up a little, as if for some insane reason he was slightly amused by all this. "I don't think it's a good idea for me to—" For her to what? Move in with Rafe, whom she was suddenly finding more appealing than ever?

"I think it's a great idea. It—would be my privilege to have you stay at my house. All right? So I've got a mask in my truck. Tell me what you need from up there and I'll go in and get it. Sound like a plan?"

She squeezed her eyes shut and shook her head in dismay. She started to tell him that she was definitely not going to let him riffle through her underwear to get her stuff. But then she saved her breath, because she knew he'd fight her to the death about it.

The last thing in the world she wanted was to live with Rafe. But what choice did she have? Stay in her mother's crowded place, or bother the newlyweds? When she opened her eyes, he was still looking at her, solemn and unblinking. "Okay, fine. I accept your offer."

"I was wondering something else too," he said, snagging another cookie.

"What's that?" she asked, frowning. She couldn't take much else.

"Would you want to...hang out? Maybe go check out all the shop windows, grab a bite...before we head back to my place? I thought we could maybe watch a movie tonight."

She fiddled with her apron tie just to look somewhere else besides at him because...how many surprises could she take in one day? She tried to keep her cool. "You want to...hang out?"

"Yeah," he said. "Hang out, talk? Like old times, only—different. Better."

Better? What was he telling her? That he was going to try to get their friendship back on track? *Or more?*

Back then, they'd had discussions over just about anything—the origin of life, global warming, how glass is made, how the rocks got to Stonehenge—but they'd left anything truly intimate untouched. Now, for the first time, she wondered if maybe that could change.

She suddenly realized she *wanted* it to change. And she allowed herself to feel hopeful that it could.

"Okay, sure. Sounds fun."

He broke into a smile, which made the bottom drop out of her stomach.

"Great. Terrific," he said as he stood up from the stool. "I've got to get back to the station. But I'll stop by on my way out."

Doubt still clutched at her. He must have sensed the conflict in her, because he said, "This has nothing to do with you having to stay with me." He was looking at her in a way that gave her goose bumps. "It has everything to do with the fact that I miss you. I have for a long time."

"Oh," she said, more than a little surprised.

That sounded friendly. But it sort of felt like a...*date*. She couldn't contain a strange feeling that had taken hold. *Excitement*.

"What can I bring?" she asked.

"Just yourself," he said, his gaze sweeping her up and down in a thorough way that made her entire face go up in flames. Fortunately, a rush of people came through the door, along with a nice cold gust of air to cool her off.

When she looked back at him, he was gone. And so were all the cookies.

Chapter 15

♥

When Rafe arrived to pick Kaitlyn up at the Bean at six p.m., he stopped dead in his tracks. She was waiting for him near the door, not her usual behind-the-bar position, where she was always finishing up a hundred things before she could get out. She'd even ditched her apron with the cartoon coffee bean. Instead she wore a black sweater dress with tights and big hoopy earrings, which she must've dug out of the suitcase full of clothes and cosmetics he'd thrown together for her earlier. Her hair was down and she had on red lipstick.

"Wow," he said without thinking, then winced. Another foot-mouth moment. "I mean, wow, you look terrific," he said carefully, "but you didn't have to dress up."

"This isn't dressed up," she said, grabbing her coat off a nearby chair. "I just wanted to look nice."

She looked more than nice. She looked amazing. Sexy as hell. *Gorgeous.* He pried his eyes off her. "Oh, I almost forgot," he said, handing her a bundle wrapped in green paper.

She ripped open the paper to find daisies and sent him a tentative glance. "Oh, Rafe. They're beautiful."

"Pretty," he agreed. But it wasn't the daisies that were beautiful to him. "Not very Christmasy, though."

"No, but they're my favorites."

"I asked at the flower shop what daisies mean."

She carried them behind the bar and reached below it for a tall stainless-steel carafe for cream. "What did you learn?"

"Childbirth, motherhood, new beginnings." He wasn't eloquent enough—or courageous enough at the moment—to tell her that the *new beginnings* was what had stuck with him. He wanted to spend time with her and get back to what they'd once had. But as far as taking an entirely different kind of step with her...could he do it?

She filled the carafe with water and set the daisies in it, and took a minute to fluff them out, or whatever a person did with flower arrangements. "Nice," she said, admiring them on the counter as she walked around and let him help her with her coat. Her awful, worn coat.

"Where are we going?" she asked. "I'm a little bit starving."

He raised a brow. "You're starving, huh? That's a nice change."

She nodded and smiled. "Now that I can eat, everything tastes amazing and it seems I'm hungry all the time."

"I thought we'd take a walk through town and decide where to grab dinner. Is that okay?"

"Sounds like a plan." He held the door for her as he'd done a million times before, but this time it felt different. He felt excited and awkward at the same time, like he was back in high school taking a girl out for the first time.

They walked out of the Bean and onto the street, which was crowded with Christmas shoppers, even though it was a little after six on a weeknight. To navigate them around a group of shoppers in the middle of the sidewalk, he took her hand, but after they'd passed, he didn't let go, even though he could have.

As they walked for a block or two, Rafe was vaguely aware of the lights, the decked-out windows, and all the shoppers laughing and talking, their arms laden with shopping bags. Kaitlyn occasionally exclaimed at something—the vintage train set chugging around the tracks in the hardware store windows, the animated snowman and the fake snow in the ice cream shop window, and the digital light displays in the computer repair shop. But most of his awareness was focused on the woman next to him. He loved seeing her excited, pointing out things that caught her eye, relaxed for the first time in a long while.

"We've walked this street a lot of times," Rafe said.

She turned suddenly and gave him a strange look.

"Just never holding hands," he said.

At that, she blushed and immediately tried to retract her hand, but he kept a good hold on it.

"I—like it," he said, lifting a brow. "Do you?"

She looked down at their hands and then at him while he held his breath, thinking himself an idiot for asking. "I—um—yeah," she said. "It's nice."

"Good," he said, letting out the breath and adjusting his grip so their hands fit together more comfortably. "Me too."

He tugged her toward a clothing shop. "Let's go in here."

She pulled him to a stop. "You want to go inside a women's clothing shop?"

"Yeah. For Rachel." Fortunately, she didn't question that.

Rafe walked down aisles of expensive, dramatic clothes. He stopped to view a bright orange scarf wrapped around a mannequin. It was made of some kind of material with soft tentacle-like appendages that stuck out everywhere—like the shaggy chenille fibers on a shower mat. Plus they were sparkly. The mannequin wore a matching hat too.

"You need this," Rafe said.

She laughed. "Actually, I think that's more up Hazel's alley. It's very...creative."

"And orange," Rafe said. "Very orange."

Rafe walked up to the owner, who stood behind the counter sorting sparkly jewelry. She had coal-black hair done up in a smooth bun and wore an elegant print dress with high-heeled boots.

"We'd like to see that," Rafe said, pointing up at the mannequin wearing the ridiculously orange boa-scarf-whatever-it-was.

"No, Rafe," Kaitlyn whispered. "We really *don't* want to see that."

"Yes, we do," he insisted, then turned definitively to the shop employee. "The coat. Do you have her size?" He gave a nod in Kaitlyn's direction.

The woman looked Kaitlyn up and down. "He's kidding," Kaitlyn said, waving her arm dismissively. "He's a big joker."

"I'm not kidding," he said. "What's your size?"

"Young man," the woman said, walking down an aisle and producing the coat in Kaitlyn's size. "This is a designer coat. If you're not serious…"

"Oh, we're serious," Rafe persisted.

Kaitlyn tried again to protest. "Rafe, I really don't want—"

He held it out for her to slip into. After a moment's hesitation, she finally tried it on. It was camel-colored, which looked great with her hair, and double-breasted and long—below her knees. He didn't know much about fashion but it looked elegant and classy and a million times better than that thinly lined thing she'd been wearing for the past five winters.

"It fits you quite well," the saleswoman said.

"What's it lined with?" she asked. "It feels like goddess material," she said with a grin.

Rafe nudged her toward a full-length mirror. "Take a look." She *was* a goddess, and he wanted her to have this coat.

As she examined herself in the mirror, he saw her brows hike up for just a second as a look of surprise crossed her face, but then she carefully schooled her features to neutral and shrugged the coat off. "It's really pretty. Thank you for letting me try it," she said, handing it back to the saleswoman before she turned to Rafe. "Come on, Rafe. Time to go."

She practically dragged him out of the store and back onto the street.

"That coat looked terrific on you," Rafe said.

"It was beautiful. But—"

He stopped her by putting a hand on her arm. "Are you always like this?"

"Like what?" Maybe her coat really was getting thin, because he swore he felt the heat of her right through it.

"You never let anyone do anything for you," he said. "Or take care of you."

"I'm not going to let you buy me a coat, if that's what you mean." Stubbornness and pride made her chin tilt up. "I can buy myself a coat. I just haven't gotten around to it."

"Yeah, yeah. You don't need it. But what if someone just wants to do something nice for you?"

"There are a lot of nice things that don't cost a month of rent."

"It wasn't that much." He squeezed her arm a little, until she looked up at him. "It's okay to let someone do something for you just because they want to."

She shrugged and looked uncomfortable. "I—I guess I'm not used to that."

He sighed. "Someone should make you feel special every single day."

* * *

"Want my milkshake too?" Rafe asked a little later, holding out his chocolate shake as they sat in a booth at Lou's, the local teenagers' hangout.

"Ha ha," Kaitlyn said, holding up a hand to refuse. She'd just eaten a double cheeseburger, fries, and an entire chocolate shake. "That was amazing," she said, putting a hand on her stomach. "The most delicious burger I've ever eaten."

Rafe pulled out his phone and took a picture of her empty plate.

"Are you posting that somewhere?" she asked, sort of horrified as he continued doing something on his phone.

"Not yet," he said, glancing up. "But I think this is the first time you've ever eaten more than me, and I wanted to document it."

"Not funny," she said, fake frowning.

"It's a little funny." He paused and looked up, showing her his phone. "Or at least, fifty of my friends on Snapchat think it is."

"Rafe..." she said, grabbing for his phone.

"Kidding, I'm only kidding," he said.

After Rafe paid the bill, they left the restaurant. Kaitlyn felt full and content. But not just from the food. Everything between them felt different. She wouldn't even describe their friendship as back to the way it used to be—not that she believed it ever could be, after all that had happened. But Rafe was right—it *was* better, but in a way she couldn't quite put her finger on. Everything between them felt charged with a different energy. With what she could only describe as a hopeful anticipation.

Maybe it was the fifties Christmas music they'd played from the old jukebox in Lou's while they were eating—Elvis and "Jingle Bell Rock" and Alvin and the

Chipmunks and "Rockin' Around the Christmas Tree." Or maybe it was that Rafe was back to holding her hand again and his smile was finally reaching his eyes. And when he looked at her, she saw something there that she thought she'd never see—things she didn't even dare to vocalize.

On the way home, they passed a roped-off parking lot filled with fresh-cut trees, a sharp piney scent filling the air. "Let's get a tree," she said on impulse.

"Just like that?" He sounded surprised.

"It would make your house look a little Christmasy." She put her thumb and index finger together and smiled. "A *tiny* bit of Christmas."

His look softened. "Okay. But I don't have any ornaments."

"Maybe I can ask Rachel for that basket of ornaments you made as a little kid."

Rafe laughed, good and loud, a deep sound that hit her low in her stomach. "Anything but that."

She grinned because she knew he wouldn't refuse her. But she also knew he was going to love it. She'd make sure of it.

They walked down an aisle surrounded by tagged trees on both sides. Rafe immediately pointed to a tall, narrow tree. "How about one like that?"

She wrinkled up her nose. "It's so...skinny. That doesn't feel like Christmas to me," she said. "Maybe it's because I'm pregnant, but I like the rounder ones."

"You're not going to want one as wide as Rachel's, are you?" he asked cautiously. "Because that took an hour to set up."

"No, not that big. Just not…lanky." She pointed out a fuller tree. "That's a nice one."

"Yeah. Nice firewood," he said under his breath.

"I can't believe this," she said, rolling her eyes. "You're Mr. Fun. What have you got against live Christmas trees?"

"You have to haul it home," Rafe said as they walked. "Then you have to saw the trunk to get it to fit into a stand. Plus the needles get everywhere."

"Wow," she said. "We aren't tree-compatible. I had no idea." She slowed her steps as they neared a group of wider, rounder, fuller trees. *Now they were talking!*

"The truth is," Rafe said, examining the boughs, "I'm a firefighter. We know too much about the hazards of having live trees."

"I'll make sure to water it."

"And keep candles away from it. And keep it three feet away from the fireplace. And toss it in a few weeks."

"Yes, yes, and yes." His grinchiness left her undeterred. "Now, which one should we get?" Suddenly she felt something cold on her neck. She looked up to find Rafe had shaken the snow off a pine bough onto her head and was laughing at her.

"Hey, why'd you do that?" she said, dusting off her hair and coat.

He looked down at her and smiled and set to work swiping the snow off her hair. Suddenly he froze, fingering a strand.

His lids lowered. She got tangled up in noticing his long lashes, unfair for a man, really, and the look in his eyes, which had turned dark and dangerous. Her legs

suddenly felt like spaghetti, and she grabbed his forearms to steady herself. He homed in on her lips and
lowered his head and oh my, right here in the middle of
the tree lot, he was going to . . .

She felt Rafe grab her arms and jerk her to the side,
out of the middle of the aisle, just as an enormous nine-
foot tree—tall *and* plump—fell right at their feet with a
giant *whoosh*, scattering snow from its boughs around
their feet.

"Oh my gosh, that scared me," she said, still clinging
to him, her hands on his chest. She was wrapped up in
him and enjoying it way more than she should. And she
was a little startled, but definitely not frightened.

"I saw it falling," Rafe said. "You okay?"

Okay? How could she be okay when her pulse was
racing a mile a minute and adrenaline was pumping
through her veins? Being close to Rafe had driven all
other thoughts from her mind. She vaguely registered
the pounding feet of Boy Scouts coming to the rescue.
"I'm perfect," she blurted. "I mean, *it's* perfect. The
tree, that is."

He looked at her and then at the fallen tree, a puzzled
expression on his face. "What do you mean?"

She shrugged and met his gaze. "That's our tree. It's
fate. It fell right at our feet."

He peered down at her from his tall height. "That
sounds like something Nonna would say. And it nearly
fell *on* us, by the way. I'm not sure I'd interpret that as a
friendly sign."

He kept his big arms around her when the Boy Scout
leader began apologizing profusely and offered them a

deep discount. She snaked her own arm around Rafe's lean waist—just for balance, of course.

"We'll take it," Kaitlyn said, looking up at Rafe. "If it's okay with you?"

He half rolled his eyes and half smiled. "What the lady wants," he told the Scout leader. "Wrap it up, guys."

They ended up buying a few boxes of ornaments and strings of lights that the Scouts were also selling. Rafe insisted on paying for everything and didn't even accept the Scout leader's promise to give them a deal for their trouble. Distracted by deciding which colored balls they should buy, she suddenly saw Rafe discreetly hand the leader something when he thought she wasn't looking. A small box?

"What was that?" she asked.

"Nothing," he said, a little too dismissively. "We need a tree topper," he said, picking up two boxes. "Star or angel?"

She shrugged and pointed to the angel, which was shiny silver and smiling. She liked the idea of an angel smiling down on them. "Well, this *is* Angel Falls. And your name *is* Raphael. So—obvious choice."

"Yeah. I think—let's get the angel," he said. As he turned back toward the cashier, he continued in a voice almost too low to hear. "To watch over the baby."

His words made her freeze. Did she hear that right? A glance over at Rafe showed he was already paying for the ornaments, tipping the Boy Scout, telling him that he was an Eagle Scout and that the library garden was his Eagle Scout project.

But wait—did he just pick the angel to watch over

their *baby*? She turned away and pressed on her chest, which suddenly seemed tender. And blinked her eyes, which were getting watery. All sorts of melty, gushy feelings were threatening to spill over from her heart, and somehow she had to keep them contained.

It was an impossible task. She realized that she was tired of containing them. What if she allowed them to spill over everywhere into the entire rest of her life? What if she stopped denying her feelings and admitted the truth—that she wanted *him*?

No, no, no. What was she thinking? This was all a dream. A fantasy. It couldn't be real. Happiness wasn't something she was used to or even expected. But this... this was dangerous. These feelings left her heart completely unprotected. Exposed.

The trouble was, she couldn't seem to stop them.

Kaitlyn quickly swiped at her eyes and got it together before joining Rafe at the register, where he was watching the Scouts carry the tree off to the bundler machine. Then she and Rafe began the walk back to Rafe's house to get his truck. She was really hoping the walk would clear her head.

As they crossed the bridge that ran over the falls that gave their town its name, they noticed couples were getting their photos taken in front of the angel statue by Mary Mulligan. A children's choir was standing off to the side singing carols, and people were gathered around listening. The sweet voices of the kids and the backdrop of the light garlands strung across the bridge made everything look magical. Part of her wanted to linger and listen and enjoy the holiday spirit.

But the other part saw that Mary was headed straight for them. "We've got to walk faster," she said to Rafe.

"What for?" Rafe asked, slowing down instead. "Do you have to get back? Are you cold?" He started to unzip his jacket. "Want my coat too?"

"It's not that. It's—"

Just then Mary grabbed Rafe's arm.

Too late.

"Congratulations, you two, on the big news. When's the date?" Mary winked at Kaitlyn. Oh dear. Mary knew. That meant the whole town probably did too.

"Well, actually—" Kaitlyn began, but Mary interrupted.

"I visited your nonna in the hospital and she told me all about the engagement and the baby. I've never seen her so happy." She chuckled as she fiddled with her camera. "Don't know what you two are waiting for with a bun in the oven, but that's young people nowadays. Anyway, all proceeds from photos this month go to the shelter party for Christmas presents for the kids. So how about puckering up for charity?"

"For charity," Rafe said. "Of course."

"Of course," Kaitlyn said, as Rafe slid his arm around her back. And oh, she felt his warmth, right through her coat. The dangerous warmth that she was afraid to feel.

"This has gotten out of hand," she whispered in Rafe's ear. "We really should say something."

"Yeah," he said, staring at her lips and sounding very unconcerned. "We'll clear everything up . . . later."

She didn't protest. She was too busy staring right back at his nice full lips too. Wait. *What was she doing?* What were *they* doing, buying trees and ornaments, walking around holding hands, and now *this*? And was it wrong to want to keep that magic going just a little while longer?

Mary positioned them so that the statue was directly behind them. Rafe still had his arm around Kaitlyn. If only she could have a little breathing room so she could think, because everything was so muddled in her head.

Suddenly there was the sound of money hitting the ground, pinging and scattering at their feet. A quarter hit one of the iron posts on the bridge and ricocheted into the water.

"Oh-oh," Kaitlyn said. They all knew the legend: drop in some money, kiss your honey, true love forever, yada yada.

Rafe looked down, searching for the source of the change.

Kaitlyn blushed. "Some change just fell out of my coat pocket," she said. She didn't say both pockets had holes, because he'd have a field day with that.

"You don't have to kiss me," she rushed on to say. "After all, that quarter plunged right into the falls, just to let you know." She pretended to laugh, but for some reason she wasn't finding anything funny.

"I don't care about the folklore," Rafe said. "But I do care about kissing you." He tugged her closer and, smiling, he looked around, scanning something behind her head.

"What are you looking at?" she asked.

"Just making sure no other Christmas trees are about to fall on us."

She couldn't help laughing. Rafe was so...ridiculous.

Funny. Unexpected. Wonderful. Yes, sometimes he was just wonderful.

"Did you say a quarter fell in?" Mary asked. "They say you need two for the legend to count."

Kaitlyn could feel her face turning red from embarrassment, but Rafe just chuckled. Probably because Mary always did her best to increase donations for the city treasury.

At Kaitlyn's feet, perched precariously on the edge, another quarter suddenly winked up at her, the water under the bridge rushing and gurgling as it ran over the falls. Impulsively, she scooted her boot closer to the cement edge of the bridge and let the other quarter tip in. It was a crazy thing to do, she knew. And she must be out of her mind for doing it. She blamed her crazy behavior on all the confusion she was feeling.

"Smile now, kids!" Mary said, holding up her camera. "Say 'onesie!'"

* * *

Then suddenly Rafe was leaning in, Kaitlyn's heart skittering as it always did at his nearness. She let her gaze drift upward, thinking how tall and handsome he was, and how somehow the story he'd told about his past had changed everything between them. And despite the fact that she was pretty freaked out about it, she felt something else she hadn't felt in a long time…a sense of wonder. Of awe. Of…happiness.

Was *that* what she was so afraid of?

Rafe smiled a devilish smile, curled a hand around

the back of her neck, and pulled her in. His hands were cold but his lips were warm and soft, and his kiss was slow and lingering without getting indecent in front of Mary. Kaitlyn couldn't help but close her eyes and lean in to him, his hard muscle, his strength, his warmth. Her head spun, her breath becoming ragged as the kiss took away her breath and her sense.

Then Mary's flash went off and Kaitlyn remembered she was standing on a bridge with icy mist from the falls hitting her in the face. The white twinkly lights strung through the trees surrounding the bridge blurred with the stars, and she saw her whole world spin. When Rafe pulled back, his eyes were shining with mischief, but also something else. A tenderness she only recently learned to see. A crack in the walls that surrounded his heart.

She was suddenly filled with the need to tear down those walls whichever way she could to find the man who'd been in there all along.

"Oh my goodness!" Mary exclaimed. "No wonder you two are...um, expecting. That is some positively ferocious chemistry! Lordie, pass me a fan!"

The photo was cute and, sure enough, Kaitlyn's foot was twisted just a little from nudging that final coin into the falls. But she would be the only person to ever notice such a thing.

For the first time in their relationship, she wasn't squashing all her feelings down somewhere where she refused to feel them. She was daring to let them out. And it felt more than a little like they just might be two people falling in love.

Chapter 16

♥

It was around eight when they got back to Rafe's place after collecting the tree and set it up. While Kaitlyn went to change, Rafe finished stringing the lights and lit a fire in the fireplace.

Kaitlyn hadn't asked him to light the fire; he just thought it would be fun. The truth was, his entire body was humming with energy that he needed to work off. His thoughts wandered to sitting on the couch together, watching a movie with the tree lights on, putting his arm around her, *kissing* her.

He wanted her. And that kiss in front of the falls—it had cemented the fact that no other woman had ever made him feel the way she did. There were moments—times like tonight—when he could imagine the fog that he'd lived under for so long lifting and being able to relax and do the things that normal people did, like walking around together holding hands, enjoying Christmas, *making love*.

Still Rafe understood that committing to a relationship with Kaitlyn would be sort of like falling off a cliff. He would have to take risks with no safety net, and the consequences of putting his heart out there again could be fatal. But there was something about being with her that made him feel like himself—the self he'd left behind a long time ago and never thought he'd regain. She made him feel like the man he could have become if tragedy hadn't struck.

He struggled to clear his head, pacing nervously to the kitchen and noticing the transformation his apartment had undergone in the past hour that Kaitlyn had been in it.

Her purse stood open on the counter, and her earrings were tossed into his wooden salad bowl. Her boots sat lined up next to his shoes near the front door, and her ratty old coat was slung over his couch. Her scent was in the air—a warm, delicious vanilla that reminded him of Christmas cookies and...well, of her.

He was used to living without clutter—at work they had protocols about leaving everything in perfect order. But having this little trail of her things around him...it felt good in a way he couldn't even articulate. A feeling of peace and contentment overcame him—of rightness. Like *she* was the missing thing that this place had been waiting for all along. Like she was the one he'd demo'd this old place for and painted and put in a new kitchen and two sinks in the master bathroom. And a second closet with organizers.

"Still up for the movie?" she asked as she entered the kitchen. She was wearing a way-too-big sweatshirt that read "Love is Love" and leggings and furry gray slippers—and she looked adorable and at home.

"What about decorating the tree?" he asked, looking at the plumpish tree strung with lights and nothing else.

"It's so pretty," she said, assessing Rafe's work on the lights. "Maybe we could water it and save the rest for tomorrow? I'm a little tired. And hungry. Want some popcorn?"

"Sure." He bit back a smile.

In the kitchen, he reached to the right for the big wooden bowl, remembering to take out her earrings—while she reached left into a cupboard for a bag of popcorn. She put it in the microwave while he poured them some sparkling water with ice. This dance they did—moving around his kitchen, passing each other, reaching for things yet never once bumping into each other—was a familiar one. One that played out very much the same in her tiny kitchen as here in his bigger one. He'd forgotten how much he missed it.

She took the popcorn out of the microwave, opened the bag, and dumped it into the bowl. They both reached for some at the same time, their hands grazing.

"I had a great time tonight," he said, unable to hide how he felt. "I'm glad you're here."

She scanned his face carefully, as if she was making sure he meant it. "Me too," she finally said, "on both counts." She reached into the bowl for another handful of popcorn and cracked a smile. "Race you to the couch."

It was something that started because the old couch in her apartment had a broken spring that tended to stick up and pinch whoever sat on it. They each tried to be the one to claim the opposite side.

He grabbed more popcorn. "New couch, remember?"

She took the bowl from him. "Well, I'm picking my side anyway."

They sat for a while, watching the fire and enjoying the tree, eating mostly in silence. For the first time in he couldn't remember how long, he realized they were just being themselves.

"Rafe," she said, between handfuls of popcorn, "I really like sitting here, staring at your bare Christmas tree."

"*Our* tree." He waited to see how she would react to that, but her only response was lifting a brow in question. "I mean, it fell right in front of us."

"Maybe we don't even need the ornaments," she said, putting her hands up like a pretend frame. "It's pretty without them."

He reached behind them, moving aside a couch pillow. "Well, we need at least one." He held out the box. "For you."

She stopped chewing and stared, wide-eyed. "What's this?"

He shook it a little. "Open it."

She traded him the popcorn bowl for the box. And as soon as she saw what was in it, she darted a glance over at him, put her hand over her mouth, and teared up.

"Kaitlyn, geez." He put an arm around her, which meant he had to move a little closer, which was fine with him. "Don't cry." He hadn't expected a big reaction. He'd just thought she'd say it was cute and hang it on the tree. This display of emotion threw him—in a good way.

She wiped her eyes on her sweatshirt sleeve and sniffed while he took the small ornament out of the box. It was a tiny painted kangaroo—obviously pregnant, with "Welcome Baby" and the year painted on the side.

She was ugly crying now, her head bent on her arm. Finally, he tugged on her sweatshirt sleeve and pulled her into his arms.

"Don't cry," he said, smoothing her hair, which was so soft and silky.

"I love it," she said, wiping her cheeks. "It's adorable. And very thoughtful. Thank you."

"You're welcome," he managed, but he could barely concentrate on the ornament. Because all he could think of was how much he wanted to kiss her.

But how would that be different from just a few months ago, when he'd acted without thinking? Yet he was drawn to her in a way he'd never been drawn to anyone before, even Claire. Kaitlyn stirred him and challenged him and accepted him—but what could he give her in return, and would it be what she deserved? Once he acted on his feelings, there would be no going back. Things would change between them again—this time for good.

* * *

The cheery popping and snapping of wood on the fire was a bit muffled by the bursts of stellar gunfire and the swish of light sabers, which made the peaceful ambience of Rafe's living room a little startling but still fun. But Kaitlyn was too affected by the man next to her to concentrate much on the movie. They'd had such a fun evening. It seemed almost like old times. Except it didn't.

A few times, her hand brushed Rafe's in the popcorn bowl, sending her pulse skittering and leading her to move her hand away as quickly as possible. Sometimes, their legs brushed too, and Rafe seemed just as anxious about keeping some space between them as she was.

Maybe Kaitlyn was able to maintain that space physically, but mentally she was a wreck. The more galactic firepower, the more sparks seemed to fly between them. These disruptive urges shattered her concentration in the movie, which fortunately she'd seen too many times to count anyway.

Sleep caught her unawares, as it often did during this pregnancy. When she awakened much later, the room was dark except for the softly glowing tree. The fire had died down to embers. She had a blanket over her, tucked up under her chin. She tossed off the upper half of it and stretched out her legs only to bump into Rafe's long ones next to hers on the couch.

She felt under the blanket to find the rest of Rafe right next to her—her hand finding his hard chest, encased in warm flannel, his long, muscular legs in jeans...Yes, it was definitely Rafe, all six two of his delicious body running the length of hers.

She turned to find his face very close to hers. Even worse, he was lying there, propped up on an elbow, looking at her.

A disconcerted feeling flashed through her at the thought of him watching her sleep. Frowning, she asked, "How long have you been staring at me?"

"Not for long," he said, his voice a little low and gravelly, which made him sound even sexier than usual. He rubbed at his eyes. "I fell asleep too."

She should move, because it was impossible not to touch him, and the only alternative was to fall off the couch.

She willed herself to move, say good night, and flee quickly to his tidy spare room down the hall. But one glance into his eyes prevented all movement and wiped out all thought. Their gazes locked and she got lost in their dark beauty.

Her heartbeat accelerated dangerously, causing a loud, steady drumbeat in her ears. Heat was consuming her, even though the fire was out and the room had taken on a chill. And it also seemed to be radiating from Rafe's big body, which was so close and so, so tempting.

What was the reason she'd agreed to stay here with him again? She couldn't remember. Hadn't she known she'd be unable to guard her heart from him? The real Rafe was a dozen times more appealing than the handsome joker always ready with a quip.

She forced herself to make a move, but his arm came around her, freezing her in place. He took up her hand in his big one, his long, graceful fingers twining with hers.

"The movie was good," he said, but his eyes told a different story—one not connected with *Star Wars* at all. Or any movie, for that matter.

"I—missed the end," she said, wanting to look away but unable to.

"I could explain it to you," he said quietly, his voice lulling her with its deep, soothing tones. "Leia loves Han, but he's frozen in the carbon-freezing chamber. Luke is down a hand and shocked that Darth is his daddy, but he'd rather die than join the Dark Side. He's got some brother-sister force thing going with Leia and she sends Lando to fly by to save him."

"I—I've seen it before, like, five times. With—you." For some reason it was hard to talk, her words pushing out of her, sluggish and breathless.

"Kaitlyn," he said, his tone solemn. Somehow hearing the syllables of her name roll off his tongue sent a tiny thrill to her core.

She swallowed. "Yes, Rafe?"

"You—look very peaceful when you sleep."

"That's because this baby makes me sleep like the dead." *Keep this light*, a voice inside her head warned. If only he wasn't holding her hand, aimlessly twining and untwining their fingers. That was causing sparks of sensation to zip and zag up her arm and spread through her entire body. "I've never slept so deeply in my life."

"It's—it's not a good idea, for you to look like that."

"Why not? Was I drooling?" She lifted a hand to swipe over her mouth. "Snoring? Sleeping with my mouth open?"

He cracked a faint smile. "No. Nothing like that. It's just that you're—beautiful."

Before she could back away, he cupped her face in his hands and brought his lips to hers.

Their lips touched, sending a shock wave through her limbs. Rafe readjusted his body on the narrow couch, his knee settling between hers. Their tongues met and slid together, their bodies shifting to deepen the kiss so that they were suddenly flush all down their lengths.

This was the kiss by the angel statue times ten. This was her twining her fingers through the thick layers of his hair and running her hands under his shirt along the solid muscular contours of his back, and him nipping at her lower lip and then sucking on it and grabbing her backside with both hands and letting out a low growl that thrilled her to the core.

It was their breath getting ragged and their hands frantic and kiss following upon kiss, devouring and insatiable.

It was like the *wedding*.

And that thought made Kaitlyn freeze.

She turned her head and nearly tumbled off the couch in her race to sit up.

"What is it?" Rafe asked, helping her find purchase on the cushion. His hair was disheveled, his shirt half-unbuttoned from where she'd undone it groping his chest. She sat there, gathering her hair up in a ponytail, trying to regain her breath and her sense. "What's wrong?"

"Nothing," she said. "I just—" She halted and closed her eyes. If they were to communicate, she had to stop avoiding hard conversations. "Yes, something is wrong." She faced him on the couch. "I need to know that this isn't just another opportunity to let ourselves get out of control. That night at the wedding it was a few drinks, the blackout. Now it's the haze of falling asleep together on the couch." She swallowed hard for courage. "I need to know this is for real. Not just a...spur-of-the-moment thing. A thing that's too easy for both of us to do without thinking."

Afraid of his reaction, afraid she may have pushed him too far, she turned away, and ended up staring at her hands in her lap. Her heart was beating wildly, and part of her thought she must be out of her ever-loving mind for stopping something so wonderful.

This was not her strong suit, saying these things, especially with him, but she had to know. Because *she* was all in. She'd known it from the moment he'd looked at her over those ultrasound images.

Out of the corner of her eye, she saw him sitting there, bent forward, his long fingers tented together in a steeple between his legs.

"You want the truth from me? I'll give it to you." He paused, and she swore she held her breath the entire time, afraid to inhale. He turned on the couch and faced her. "You haven't called me a coward, but that's the word I would use for myself. Because you're right, it's very easy to start kissing you without thinking. I used the wedding and the blackout and any other excuse I could to justify being with you, but the truth is—the *truth* is—being with you scares me more than going into a burning building."

She couldn't stop herself from reaching up to touch his cheek, gently tracing the outline of one brow and then the other with her thumb, smoothing out the tension. Then she dropped her hand and smiled. "Well, you've been in some pretty dangerous situations before," she said in a low voice, "but you've always come back out."

He looked at her, wide-eyed. She thought about saying more, but it suddenly occurred to her that none of what she would say would matter. What mattered was what he believed himself. She got up from the couch and kissed him softly on the forehead. "Think about that, fireman," she said over her shoulder as she headed for her room.

* * *

Rafe was glad to work a twenty-four-hour shift starting the next morning. Unfortunately, it was a slow one, giving him plenty of time alone with his thoughts. Despite being in charge of grocery shopping and preparing dinner for everyone at the station, he couldn't stop thinking of Kaitlyn. Even trying to sit and concentrate on the newest thriller he'd brought to occupy the slow times between calls wasn't working to divert his attention.

Last night, even though he'd only recently realized it himself, he'd been looking to fall into something easy with her without thinking about it. That was exactly what he'd allowed to happen at the wedding. From now on, he wanted things to be different. *He* wanted to be different. If only he could be the kind of man whose past didn't stand in the gateway of his future. His not only stood in the way—it was bricked and mortared over the door. How did he even begin to break it down and push it out of the way?

When Rafe got off his shift early the next morning, he walked over to Rachel's antique shop to pick up the gifts she'd wrapped for the upcoming shelter party. He found her behind the counter, unwrapping a box of antique glassware. She set a finely cut champagne glass on the countertop. "So pretty. They don't make them like that anymore."

The shop looked festive, decorated for the holiday with a tree covered with tinsel and icicles and bubble lights in the corner. Bowls of antique ornaments abounded. A vintage silver aluminum tree sat on a table near the front counter covered with bright green balls.

"So how many years have you and Dad been married?" Rafe asked, taking a seat in an elaborately carved red velvet chair near the front desk. Rachel had pointed out the stack of packages that needed to go to the shelter, donations customers had contributed over the past month or two.

He knew he should come clean with Rachel, tell her that the engagement was fake, but he just couldn't bring himself to do it. Would holding on to a fantasy be the most he'd ever be able to do, or would he have the guts to come clean?

"It'll be seventeen in the spring. My, time has just flown by, hasn't it?" She unwrapped a wineglass and held it up to the light. "Look at these etchings. So pretty. But these glasses need a good bath first. All their beauty is obscured by grime."

Rafe played with a snow globe that showed kids building a snowman in front of a turreted Victorian house. "You two are a great match," he said.

She smiled, looking up at Rafe with a puzzled expression. "He tolerates my love of putting Christmas decorations everywhere there's an empty space, and I tolerate his penchant to want to read every book he runs into. So it's win-win."

"That probably wasn't easy—moving into the house he shared with Mom."

That made her stop unwrapping. She set the latest glass down on the counter and came and sat down across from him on a mid-century-style orange vinyl chair. "No, it wasn't easy, but it was something we did for you kids. To keep you in the only home you knew. So, Rafe, sweetie, why are you here asking me these questions today when you could be—well, when you could be Christmas shopping with Kaitlyn?"

Rafe smiled. "Something *is* on my mind that I'd like to talk to you about."

Rachel sat back and made a big gesture with her hands. "You have all my attention."

"Can I ask you what you thought of Claire?"

Rachel's finely arched brow rose in surprise. "Claire...Stevens?"

"Yeah. I wondered what your impression was of her...of us. From way back then. What kind of couple were we?"

"You were a very sweet couple from what I remember." She spoke carefully and, he thought, cautiously. "Very young."

Rafe nodded. "We met the first day of college."

Rachel tapped the arm of the chair thoughtfully, like she was remembering as she spoke. "I'm sure Claire taught you a lot about how to love someone. You went through a very important time of your life with her. You two grew up together. Became adults together."

Rafe nodded. "Kaitlyn's a lot different than Claire."

"How so?" Rachel asked, fiddling with a glass bowl of vintage Christmas ornaments that someone had sprayed fake snow on many years ago.

Rafe chuckled. "Claire was quiet. Agreeable. Sweet."

"Kaitlyn's sweet."

"She *is* sweet," he said with a wry grin. "But she's not beyond calling me out on some things."

As soon as Rachel gave him a look, he knew she was going to take Kaitlyn's side on that one. "We all need someone who will tell us the truth when we need it."

"Kaitlyn's very independent—to a fault. She feels like she has to do everything on her own. I keep wanting to protect her, but she's one of the strongest people I know. Sometimes I wish she'd let me do more things for her. Honestly, it was a lot easier to do that for Claire." But in the end, he'd failed Claire. The sudden pain of remembering stabbed him in the gut.

What if he failed Kaitlyn too? Maybe someone like him didn't deserve another chance.

"Kaitlyn took over her grandfather's business at such a young age," Rachel said. "I think she's got big plans for it. So being strong and independent are, for the most part, great qualities that have helped her succeed."

"Yes, but she always puts herself last. I mean, she won't even buy herself a new coat because she's so worried about saving up money for her niece to get to college. And she sneaks cookies to all those elderly guys who come and eat there every day. She's sweet and really fun and...pretty amazing."

"Oh, Rafe." Rachel's eyes were watering up.

Rafe looked up in a panic. "Did I say something sad? I didn't mean to make you cry, Rach. Geez."

Rachel swiped at her eyes. "It's just...do you realize how you sound?"

"A little crazy, I guess."

"No, honey." She reached forward and patted his knee. "Like a man in love."

What? No. That couldn't be what he was feeling.

"I always said that we lost a big part of you in that accident. This is the first time in a long time that I've heard you sound—happy. Like that sweet boy I knew a long time ago."

He looked Rachel dead in the eyes and said exactly what he was thinking. "I can't go back to being the carefree person I was before the accident. Too much has happened."

She leaned forward and grabbed his hands. "Rafe, sadly, you had to learn at a very young age that life can be unexplainably cruel, first with your mother dying and then your fiancée. It's no wonder you have hesitations about loving someone again. And as for going back to being carefree—you're older and wiser now. You wouldn't *want* to go back to the way you were before."

Rafe cracked a smile. "Well, maybe just a little more carefree wouldn't hurt." They sat there together in silence for a little while. When he spoke again, he changed his tone to serious. "Rach, we hit the jackpot getting you as a mom." He got up and hugged her. "I love you."

"I love you too," she said, squeezing him right back. "And I want you *so badly* to be happy." She hugged him hard on the *so badly* part. "Don't be afraid to be happy, okay?"

Katie *did* make him happy. The fact that they were having a baby scared the bejesus out of him, but he couldn't deny that the thought of the baby made him happy too. But he was afraid that if he reached out for all that happiness, it would all disappear in an instant, just as it had before. What if he just couldn't take that risk?

Chapter 17

♥

When Kaitlyn showed up at the vet clinic with Jazz's usual coffee order that morning, she found the vet nervously tapping her fingers on the reception desk.

"Hi, Jazz," Kaitlyn said. "I brought you some cinnamon rolls—hot out of the oven." She gave a little chuckle. "And I brought one for me too." She held up the bag between them and shook it. "All you have to do is let me see that adorable puppy again."

"Oh," Jazz said, flashing her a worried look instead of her usual smile. "About the puppy..."

Kaitlyn, who was pulling a cinnamon roll out of the bag, paused. "Did something happen to him?"

"No, but I really need the space for a sick animal who needs to come in today. The Stevensons' Great Dane has congestive heart failure."

Kaitlyn sat down on one of the chairs near the desk. "Oh, I'm sorry to hear that."

Jazz sighed and paced in front of the desk. "I've had a ton of folks flocking from everywhere around to see this dog because they want a cute puppy to put under the Christmas tree. I just don't trust giving this dog to strangers right before the holiday." She glanced at a chart on the counter. "Do you know the Grays? They're coming in this morning to look at him. If I don't place him today, he's got to go to the pound. Maybe I shouldn't have been so picky. I just hate it when people think of dogs as Christmas toys."

"I'm sorry, I don't know the Grays," Kaitlyn said. "But have a cinnamon roll," Kaitlyn offered. "Maybe it will help you think."

After they ate the rolls, Kaitlyn followed Jazz to the back room. As soon as the puppy saw them coming, he head-butted the bars and barked, scrambling up on his hind legs. When Kaitlyn approached the crate, he nudged her hand so she would pet him, then immediately dropped on his back, paws up in the air, giving her a look that said, *Of course you want to rub my tummy, don't you?* She laughed at his antics. "Oh, you are just an affection hog, aren't you, sweet boy? Yes you are." She complied by giving him a belly scratch.

"He's really cute," she said. But right now she had no apartment, and she could only imagine what Rafe would do if she showed up at his place with a puppy.

That thought would've stopped most sensible people. Kaitlyn couldn't explain why it didn't. Just that she felt positive for the first time in so long over the possibility that her and Rafe's relationship was growing into something else—something wonderful.

What if she *did* bring this puppy home? Maybe it would show Rafe what she already knew—that he was capable of so much love—for his sisters, for his nieces and nephews, for Nonna—and that loving their baby would be just as easy.

Kaitlyn paused the petting. Where did *that* thought come from? The idea of giving this dog to Rafe to help him understand that he wasn't as broken as he thought was a really crazy idea... but also a very interesting one.

"Berners are amazing family dogs," Jazz said. "They're sweet and loyal and gentle with kids." She bent down next to Kaitlyn, who had to sit back on her heels because her stomach, while still not very noticeable, was nonetheless getting too big for her to squat comfortably. "Your baby and this dog could grow up together."

That would be too cute. But then Kaitlyn imagined herself in her tiny apartment with a baby and a huge dog who was tearing circles around the place because Rafe had said *No. Way.*

That made her shudder. She'd be out of her mind to take it. "I'm sorry, Jazz, I just can't—"

Just then the door opened and Bob Harden, the clinic's administrative assistant, popped his head in. "Dr. Drake, is it okay to send the Grays back?" He said hi to Kaitlyn and handed Jazz a file. "They're previous dog owners and they already have a fenced-in yard."

Jazz exchanged a hopeful glance with Kaitlyn as a woman walked in, accompanied by three children, the oldest of whom couldn't have been more than seven.

The kids immediately ran over to the cage. The dog jumped up and gave them an enthusiastic greeting.

Kaitlyn told herself she should go now. The family seemed nice, and Jazz's problem would be solved.

A nagging feeling in her gut kept her feet planted to the tile floor. The feeling that Rafe had been the one to rescue this dog. Maybe that wasn't a random act in the universe. Maybe it really *was* up to her to make something crazy happen because…because sometimes you just had to take a leap. And maybe this dog would rescue Rafe right back.

"It's a purebred, right?" the woman asked. The baby, who couldn't have been more than one and a half, stuck her hands between the bars, and the puppy licked them vigorously. The four-year-old, who was sucking a candy cane, dropped it into the crate, and the dog promptly started licking it too.

The woman made no move to snag the candy cane. "Whoops," Jazz said politely, reaching over and pulling it out of the crate herself.

"We wanted a Pomapoo," the woman said. "Or a Yorkipoo. Or a Maltipoo. Or a teacup pig. Something we could dress up in little outfits. And that could fit in my purse when we go to soccer games."

Kaitlyn was about to say that this dog would fit into a purse for about a day before it outgrew it when one of the kids yanked on her sister's braids and a tussle started. But the mom was more interested in asking more questions about whether the puppy was a purebred.

"Oh, excuse me," Jazz said, glancing at her buzzing phone. "It's the clinic. Kaitlyn, you wouldn't mind answering a few questions while I get this, would you?"

"I'd be happy to," Kaitlyn said, but a sudden sense of orneriness began to overtake her.

"So how big do these dogs get?" the woman asked.

"This dog is going to be *huge*," Kaitlyn said. "See how big his paws are? And look at the muscular legs." Something egged her on to keep going. "And muddy. Very muddy. And the shedding! Wow. We're talking hair by the *handfuls*." Kaitlyn couldn't seem to stop. "They need *tons* of exercise. Probably *miles* every day. Are you by chance a runner?"

"How huge?" the woman asked, frowning.

"*At least* a hundred pounds," Kaitlyn said.

"Okay, kids," the woman said, gathering up her children, "this puppy's taken, but we're going to go look at better ones, okay?"

Jazz walked in a little later to find Kaitlyn alone, kneeling in front of the cage, stroking the top of the puppy's head with one finger. "Didn't work out, huh?" Jazz asked as she opened the cage and placed the dog in Kaitlyn's arms.

"Jazz, I'm so sorry," Kaitlyn said, accepting the puppy. "I discouraged them because *I* want him. *I* want to take him home." She cuddled the dog and kissed it on the forehead. In response, the puppy snuggled against her head and batted her hair playfully with its paw.

"I was so hoping you'd say that," Jazz said.

"You knew I wanted him all along, didn't you?"

Jazz shrugged, giving Kaitlyn a knowing look. "Maybe."

She wanted this dog. If Rafe didn't, well...she'd

make do. She envisioned herself having dog sitters on speed dial right along with babysitters, because that was probably what it was going to take if she had to raise this dog alone.

Jazz, grinning widely, said, "He'll be a terrific companion to a baby. And a fantastic family dog. I'm excited." She walked over and scratched the dog behind the ears. "You're one lucky pup."

Kaitlyn filled out some paperwork and wrote a donation check to help pay for the dog's care over the past few days, then walked out of the vet's office carrying her dog.

As she stepped outside, she looked at her new little buddy and said, "You can thank me later for this—if we're both still alive after Rafe finds out."

The dog responded with a giant lick directly over her lips and nose, which made her giggle. "Okay, well, I'm glad you're grateful for the save."

Kaitlyn just hoped Rafe would feel the same way.

* * *

Kaitlyn stopped to buy a crate and a leash and some dog supplies on her way back to Rafe's house. She held off on the baby gates she knew they'd need to eventually fence off Rafe's big open kitchen from the rest of the house. As she set up the crate in the laundry room, she hoped Rafe would feel the same way as she did about this little dog—that it was a new, high-energy, happy bundle of love—and she couldn't help but see the parallel with what seemed to be growing between them.

At least, that's what she thought until the pup peed on the floor and zoomed around the kitchen clacking its little toenails on Rafe's newly sanded hardwood floors. She began to understand what Jazz had meant when she'd said Bernese Mountain dogs needed lots of room to run around. A vision of Rafe's tidy yard littered with large plastic toys like picnic tables and toddler trikes, the lawn dotted with divots and furrows from where the dog was digging, suddenly popped into her head, making her shudder.

At one point the puppy got tangled up in its feet and went sliding on its belly across the floor, which was one of the cutest things she'd ever seen and made her laugh out loud, dashing her doubts.

She would just explain to Rafe that she'd acted on a conviction that this dog belonged to her—and to him. *Them.* If there was a *them.* Which felt like—maybe there was. Or could be. And from the way her stomach flipped and a giddiness spread through her like warm molasses, she truly thought it was possible.

And hopefully he'd feel the exact same way.

As Kaitlyn closed the laundry room door where the puppy had finally conked out after what had seemed like hours of playing, she walked into the kitchen, slid her apron over her head, and pulled out ingredients for tonight's recipe adventure.

She plugged in the tree and turned on a radio station that played 24-7 Christmas tunes. That helped her to not feel so alone in the nice new kitchen, which was silent except for the intermittent humming of the big fridge and the intermittent *tick-tick-tick* of the double ovens as they heated up. She pulled up a stool to the counter, took out her notebooks, and began to plot out tonight's experiment, where she'd decided to try different types of chocolate.

As she got to work, the kitchen doorknob rattled. She'd been so deep in concentration that the noise made her jump.

"It's me—Rafe," came a voice.

He was covered with snow—big flakes on his jacket, on his hair, on his too-long-for-a-man eyelashes. Fresh winter air flooded the warm kitchen, but seeing him again filled her with instant heat.

"Hey," he said, taking in the scattered cookbooks, the coating of flour on the island, and the general mess everywhere.

"Hey," she said, their gazes instantly locking in a way that made her fumble her wooden spoon.

"It's sort of late to be baking," he said, approaching the island.

She shrugged. "Five more days before the recipe is due," she said, suddenly having trouble talking.

Rafe rolled up his sleeves and walked over to where she was mixing a bowl of dough.

"Did you have a nice day off?" she asked.

He shrugged. "I slept a little. But then I went and did some research."

"Research?"

"Yes," he said, his mouth curving upward, "about Christmas cookie recipes. I was thinking that maybe we could figure this thing out together."

Together? That hit her like lightning. Did he mean

together, as in them *being* together, or was he just talking about baking cookies?

* * *

Rafe dumped the contents of a lunch-sized paper bag on the island. Four chocolate bars slid out. He hoped that Kaitlyn would be impressed that he did his homework. "I stopped at the import store," he said. "This is an extra dark chocolate with eighty-five percent cocoa." He squinted as he read the fine print on the bar. "It says the ingredients come from Swiss alpine meadows."

"Wow," she said, smiling. "Exotic." She was looking at him like she couldn't believe he'd gone to the import store. He hoped that was just the beginning of many surprises he had to show her, and he wasn't just thinking about chocolate.

He reached into the bag again, pulling out another. "*Super* dark chocolate—ninety-nine percent cacao. That's not the same as cocoa, is it?"

"No."

He reached in a third time. "This one is German milk chocolate. And here's a German dark. And finally..." He pulled out the last bar with a little sweep of his hand. "Hershey's. That's for you to eat, because it might not be suitable for a fancy cookie, but it's classic, and not to be underestimated. So let's get to work."

"Thanks for the Hershey's," she said, not wasting any time in snagging it up and ripping it open. "My favorite."

"I've been thinking a lot," he said, as she broke off a piece of the chocolate and handed it to him.

"About chocolate?" She'd already taken a bite, but she suddenly stopped chewing.

"That's part of it, yes. We'll talk later. But for right now—I'm here to help. What can I do?"

"Oh." She seemed surprised again. "Well, you can melt the chocolate. And while the cookies are baking, maybe we can work on the dishes. How's that?"

"I'll get right on it."

"But you don't have to—"

"I want to," he said, meeting her questioning gaze. "Will you let me help? I promise not to screw things up. Too much."

She smiled. "Okay, I'd love your help."

"Great," he said. Thank goodness, she was finally going to let him do something.

"But Rafe, I have to tell you something," she added, causing him to turn around on his way to the microwave. "I hope you won't be upset but—"

Just then a loud yip emanated from the direction of the laundry room. Rafe halted in his tracks. The faint ticking of the oven suddenly seemed very loud as he and Kaitlyn stared at each other across the kitchen. He shot her an incredulous look. "You didn't."

She squeezed her eyes shut. "I did." She rushed onward. "But I can explain."

The dog yipped again, this time followed by a little whimper.

"Jazz needed the space at her clinic for a sick dog," she said, talking as fast as she could, "and she had all these families who wanted a Christmas puppy, but no one she could trust. Then this family came in who wanted one of those fancy poo dogs and the woman wanted to dress it up and carry it around in her purse and I ... I just ..."

Rafe was already in the laundry room flicking on the light. And there was the puppy, tangled up in a towel, blinking its eyes. It looked tiny and a little disoriented. On seeing Rafe, it jumped up and batted the bars of the crate, the white dot on the end of its tail a blur as it wagged back and forth.

Rafe squatted before the puppy. It licked his finger and gave him a baleful look.

Aw, geez.

Rafe turned to Kaitlyn. "First there was the baby announcement. Then there was Nonna getting sick and the fake engagement, which we still haven't set people straight on. Then there was the asbestos."

"Look, you don't have to say any more," she said. "I'll leave just as soon as—"

"Will you let me finish?" Rafe said. His life was changing faster than he could keep track of. But if all those changes brought him closer to Kaitlyn, he could handle them all. "The point is, life has sort of turned itself on its ear lately. But ... I kind of like it." He stood up and faced her. She was clinging to the washing machine. "Babies and puppies should grow up together."

"Yes. You're right." She nodded and let out a huge sigh. "That's exactly what I was thinking."

He tipped his head toward the crate. "So does the little guy have to go outside?"

"Jazz told me to be sure to take him out every time he wakes up from a nap."

Rafe clipped the leash onto the dog's collar. "I'll do it. You get back to baking." He didn't mention that it was going to be a long winter, potty training a puppy in the dead of winter. "Did you give him a name?"

"Of course not," she said, smiling. "I was waiting for you."

Chapter 18

♥

Something was just...different about Rafe. He was true to his word, melting chocolate and taste testing and helping Kaitlyn mix more batches of dough. He not only took the dog news in stride; he seemed to really be happy about it. After their couch make-out session the other night, Kaitlyn couldn't help wondering what conclusion he'd come to within the past few days about *them*.

After they'd just pulled four full baking sheets out of the oven, Rafe glanced at the recipe she'd been using. "What's this?" he asked, his arm grazing hers. The graze felt intentional, but Kaitlyn found him concentrating intently on the handwritten recipe before him on the countertop.

"It's another chocolate cookie recipe of my grandfather's—not the snowcap one," she said. "I thought I'd use similar proportions of the main ingredients."

"No, I mean...why the sideways handwriting?" As

Rafe pointed out her grandfather's faded script, written in pencil in the margin, his arm touched hers again.

Kaitlyn picked up the yellowed bit of paper. "Oh, he used to do that—write ideas for new recipes on any scrap of paper he had lying around." She smiled fondly at the memory of her grandfather sitting down at a table in the Bean, pencil in hand. "He used to listen to radio cooking shows while he worked, and he was always jotting down recipes."

"You looked all through the recipes your mom gave you, right?"

"Yes. Definitely," she said. "Several times."

"But did you read all the sideways notes?"

Kaitlyn gave him a *You've got to be kidding me* look. "There are hundreds of recipes in that box."

He shrugged. "Just an idea." For a heartbeat, his gaze flicked up at her, a move that caused her every muscle to freeze in place. Then he reached over and carefully swiped his thumb next to her lips. His eyes filled with heat, and she knew him too well to not understand the look. Her heart dropped, the plunge as terrifying as the sudden downward spiral of a rollercoaster ride.

"Stop that," she said, managing to step back, her voice sounding snagged up in her throat.

"Stop what?" he asked innocently.

"Are you flirting with me?" she said. "Because this is very serious business. I'm *working*. And I'm never going to finish these cookies if we—"

"That's not flirting," he said, shaking his head vehemently.

"Yes it is. All that arm grazing and chocolate tasting and...and I don't like the way you're looking...at my lips."

"Maybe I'm looking at your lips because you still have a speck of chocolate right there." He pointed with his index finger and she quickly rubbed at it with her hand.

"Did I get it?" she asked.

He stepped closer and examined the spot closely. "I'm not sure. Let me check." Then he bent his head and kissed her—a light, quick kiss—before stepping back. Examining her closely, he said, "No, it's definitely still there." Then he dipped his head again. This time he cupped a hand softly around her neck, threading his fingers through her hair and bringing their lips together slowly and deliberately in a way that felt exactly right. He tugged her against him, tasting her, kissing her thoroughly, stealing her breath away, making her dizzy and trembling. She stood on tiptoe, straining to kiss him, resting a hand on his chest, where his heart beat steadily and strongly under her fingertips.

Slowly, he moved his mouth near her ear and whispered, "Now *that's* flirting."

* * *

Kisses led to more kisses. Kaitlyn's stomach seemed to fill with a liquid warmth that diffused all through her limbs, melting her knees, causing her entire world to tilt and sway. Her hands brushed against the masculine coating of hair on his forearms, the taut muscle, the surprising softness of his skin.

He made a little noise of pleasure in his throat as he ran his hands down her back and pulled her close. She felt safe and dangerous all at once, wanting to be cautious but unable to resist the inescapable pull he had on her heart.

He lifted her up and set her on the island, pushing measuring cups and spatulas and bowls aside. Then he stood in front of her, between her knees, resting his hands on the counter on either side of her. His breathing was a bit ragged, and he took a few slow, deep inhalations, as if he was trying to get his rate back to normal. The smell of cookies baking filled up the warm kitchen. "I don't want to stop, Katie, but I need to tell you a few things."

"Good things or bad things?" she asked, trying hard to concentrate. She rubbed her fingers over her kiss-swollen lips. How could he want to talk when she was still drunk on those kisses?

"I'll let you decide. First of all, I lied," he said.

"About what?" Her heart seemed to stop beating and she held her breath, waiting for him to continue. Lied? That sounded...ominous.

He exhaled deeply. "The night of the wedding."

"Oh." All her muscles tensed, and she feared the worst about why he was bringing this up *now*, but the expression in his eyes was soft and gentle, reminding her of the way he'd looked at her before he'd kissed her the other night on the couch or in the middle of the tree lot before their tree fell.

Somehow, that took away her fear. Clearly, he needed to tell her something. "Go on," she said.

"I'm a pretty big guy," he said, rubbing his neck nervously. "It takes a lot more booze than what I had to make me forget things."

"Forget...things?" Images from that night flashed through her mind like quick scenes from a movie trailer. Running through the drenching rain. Rafe fumbling with the key, and the two of them ending up breathless and panting against the door of his cabin as he kissed her neck, his warm, masculine body pressing up against her. The sudden plunge into darkness as the electricity failed. His lips finding hers in the velvet darkness, her every sense on high alert, every touch twice as intense in the pitch blackness.

"The thing is, I remember everything." He paused, letting that settle. At that moment, she couldn't have looked away if the commissioner of the recipe contest herself had showed up at the door. "I remember the dress you wore. It was blue like your eyes. And I remember thinking I'd never seen such a pure blue. Like the sky above the lake on a hot July day. And I remember how I'd been wanting to kiss you for weeks. No, make that *months*. And how you felt in my arms when we danced, and how much I wanted you but how I couldn't say anything. I could only show you. And once I had you in my arms, I couldn't let you go."

Her mouth dropped open. *How she felt in his arms? Wanted her for months?* Tears swelled behind her eyes. She was vaguely aware that he'd taken up her hands.

"I'm trying to tell you that I can't stop thinking about you. I can't stop thinking about *us*. I've felt that way for a long time. I just...I just didn't let myself go there, if that makes any sense. And what you said the other night—about my job being dangerous—this feels more dangerous. *You* feel more dangerous to me."

"What about the woman with the selfies?" she asked. "Jade or Jewel or whatever her name was."

"I told you about her to push you away." Rafe's gaze didn't falter, nor did his firm but gentle hold on her hands. "I haven't been with anyone since the wedding. I don't *want* to be with anyone else. I want *you*."

Tears blurred the kitchen surrounding them, the bright island lights. "I want you too, Rafe." She'd always wanted him. No matter how often she'd tried to talk herself out of it. She always would.

"I'm not sure I can be who you need me to be." The honesty in his eyes brought more tears to her own. "But I want to try. You *make* me want to try, Katie."

Her heart was full, yet she had no words. She touched his cheek with her palm. Felt the coarseness of his beard stubble, and the warmth. The roughness and the smoothness. In that moment, she swore she would take him, every part of him, all the joy and pain and happiness all rolled together into one complicated man.

A man she loved.

Her eyes were stinging, and her throat was clogged with emotion, and suddenly she recalled the woman she used to be, what seemed like a long time ago. Back then, she hadn't understood anything but her attraction to him—this tall, dark, incessantly charming guy who disarmed her at every turn and made her heart flutter and her knees go weak with just a look.

Or maybe she had sensed more than she knew. Maybe she'd always known there was more beneath the surface.

She'd grown up so much since then. And so had he. This—right now—was the first time they'd both made a step together based on honesty, not just attraction. And it overwhelmed her in every way.

He stood in front of her, his hands on either side of her legs, very near. One side of his mouth quirked up. "Scary, huh?"

She nodded slowly. Swallowed hard past a sudden lump in her throat. "But real."

"I feel like I should crack a joke."

"I don't want a joke right now." She rested her hands on his shoulders. "All I want is you."

* * *

Kaitlyn recalled the first time they'd made love, when they'd come together impulsively, frenetically, in a crazed rush of heat. This time their eyes were wide open. With the bright kitchen lights above them, it couldn't have been otherwise.

He stepped closer and took her face in his hands. She felt the warmth of his fingers, the mild scrape of his callouses against her skin. "I want to make love with you," he said. "I want to start a new chapter in our lives."

She reached up and took his hands. "Take me to bed now, Rafe," she whispered.

He did just that, picking her up and carrying her into his bedroom and setting her down on his bed. Then he got up, walked over to his dresser, and took something out of a drawer.

"The night of the wedding, you forgot these." He held up a tiny scrap of lace with a blue bow. Her *undies*. She grabbed for them, but he held them out of reach. "See the blue bow? I was thinking you wore these because they matched your dress. The dress with the high front and the cut-out circles in the back. You have a really sexy back."

A hot wave of heat rolled through her. "Rafe, give me those back now, please."

"Hush," he said, continuing to hold them out of reach. "When I took these off of you, my hands were shaking. Not because I was drunk. Or so excited to finally touch you that I could barely think, which was true too, but mostly because I wanted you so badly, even though I couldn't admit that to myself. When the lights finally came on, your face was flushed and your eyes were lit up and you—you just had this look that I will remember forever."

He lowered the undies and sat next to her on the bed. "Such a hardworking, practical woman, who gets up at four thirty every morning to open her grandpa's café. Yet she wears the most filmy, lacy underwear with a tiny satin bow. That is the sexiest thing *I've* ever seen."

The honesty of his words touched her deeply. She swallowed hard and swiped again for the undies. But this time he brought them to his face and sniffed them.

"Rafe, stop!" Her whole body was flushing at his antics.

"They smelled like your perfume and like your taste.

And I want to taste you again, Kaitlyn. This time with the lights on."

His words were honest. Heartfelt and erotic and outrageous. It was a very Rafe thing to do—but it was so much more.

"Oh, heck," she said, swiping tears and laughing at the same time. "Keep them if you like them so much. I have lots more."

Slowly, he lay down next to her, side by side, resting his hand on her hip. She met his gaze honestly and unafraid. Sucked in a breath. Felt the heat from his hand seep right through her skin. How many times had she imagined this—this moment between them when they were staring straight at each other and knowing exactly where this was going to lead? For the first time ever, it felt as if neither of them was holding anything back.

With one quick, assured movement, he tugged her against him. All at once, she hit rock-hard muscle, soft flannel, and the masculine scrape of his cheek. The dark look in his eyes was one she was certain she'd seen in her dreams—an unabashed look of pure desire that curled her toes. Except this time, it was real. *He* was real.

"Can I kiss you?" he asked in a whisper. "Can I make love to you?"

"Yes," she whispered, getting lost in the tender way he looked at her. Surely this man, who believed so firmly that he could not love, was unaware of the power of his feeling for his family, his friends, and— just maybe—for her too. Thoughts fled as his mouth met hers, their bodies flush, his big arms holding her tight against him. He kissed her insistently, deeply, and she kissed him back with everything she had.

"You feel so good," he murmured near her ear. The low timbre of his voice and the soft feel of his breath against her skin made her shudder.

"You too," she said, her arms curving around his neck, her fingers threading through the thick layers of shorn hair at his nape. And oh, how she loved the feel of him, the taut, flexing muscle, the coarse, dark silk of his hair, and the heady, familiar scent that was soap and winter air and Rafe.

Despite all they'd weathered in the past month, all the uncertainty and stress, everything about him was reassuring and strong, making hope and possibility burst from inside her.

Their tongues met, and his kisses became more urgent. A moan released low and deep from her throat, and he kissed it away.

"I want you to know I got checked and all's well," he said. "I just want you to know I would never jeopardize you or the baby. But if you want I can still use a condom."

She nodded. "I'm good too. And it's not necessary."

She traced the thick line of his brows, unable to really believe what was happening between them. Then she reached up and pulled his head down, kissing him. And oh, he kissed perfectly, thoroughly, wonderfully, making her dizzy and weak with want.

Rafe untucked her shirt and ran his hand along her waist, rubbing his thumb gently over the skin of her back. She shrugged off her shirt and helped him remove his, thrilled to see his chiseled chest, firefighter muscles rippling all over.

He put his hands on her waist—and looked down. Ran his fingers lightly over the barely there fullness of her lower abdomen and held them there. "You can hardly tell what's going on in there," he whispered.

She put her hand over his. He tilted up her face with his hand and covered her mouth with his, and then she was lost, swept away by him in every way.

Somehow her bra hit the floor, and he was touching her breasts, feeling the weight of them in his hands, kneading their now-exquisitely sensitive tips. Then he dropped his head and took a nipple in his mouth, tugging and using his tongue in ways that sent waves of pleasure through her. Her hands clutched the smooth, taut muscles of his back, her hands fluttering over him as sensation rolled over her in waves.

She unzipped his fly, freed his length, and wrapped her hand around him. This time *he* moaned, deep and long, a sound of pure pleasure. He shrugged off his pants and boxers and climbed over her, kissing her deeply while his finger played along the outline of her undies. He placed kisses on her neck, tracing a path to her earlobe, which he pretend-bit. Unrelenting in his explorations, he dipped into her wetness, using his clever fingers, whispering in her ear as she shuddered uncontrollably, each stroke driving her closer to the edge.

He whispered more to her, telling her how beautiful she was, how he loved the changes in her body. She loved the feel of him, the hard-flexing muscle, the long, beautiful length of him.

She was stroking him, learning what he liked, while he circled her swollen flesh. All her muscles pulsed and tightened. Her legs fell open, and all she could feel was the voluminous building of a wave about to shatter as she surrendered to his touch.

"Let go and come," he whispered. "Just come."

"No," she said, struggling to resist, her breaths coming rapidly. She tugged on him, indicating that she wanted him inside of her.

He understood what she wanted, positioning himself above her and looking into her eyes, saying nothing with his mouth but everything with his eyes as he entered her slowly and deliberately, filling her with his length. She cried out as he pushed to the hilt, their bodies fully joined, her intimate muscles clenching him tightly.

"Everything okay?" he asked. "Too much?"

"Wonderful," she said, wrapping her legs around him tightly as they began a rhythm, every stroke propelling her to a place where there was only Rafe, his body moving over her and in her, his lean muscle, his beautiful, expressive eyes so full of...joy. She could only call it that. It was no more and no less.

They came together, each crying out, in a burst of light and heat and happiness.

Her hands curled around the muscles of Rafe's arms as he finally lay still, panting, his elbows propped on the bed on the sides of her head. She felt them tense and flex as he held himself above her.

He smoothed back her hair, kissed her forehead. "I think I like helping you in the kitchen," he said, a wicked smile lighting his face. "You're more delicious than a chocolate snow cookie," he said.

"Snow*cap* cookie," she managed, feeling weak and shaky, and wonderful and bowled over and—she'd never say it out loud, but—happy. So, so happy.

"That too," he said with a laugh, gathering her to him.

* * *

Hours later, Kaitlyn stirred from a light sleep. They'd made love several times throughout the night, so it wasn't completely unexpected to find Rafe awake next to her.

"You're not staring at me again, are you?" She covered her eyes with her arm. "That has to stop."

"I can't help it," he said, kissing her on the forehead. "I love having you in my bed."

She wrapped her arms around him and snuggled close. "Well, I like being in your bed."

He placed his hand lightly on her hip, rubbing his thumb in slow circles.

"What is it?" she asked. "What are you thinking?"

He dove under the covers, half uncovering them, and placed his hands on her abdomen. "Can I—can I do this?" he asked, poking his head up.

"Do what?" she asked, imagining any number of things.

"Say…hi."

"Say hi?" What in the world…

"To the baby."

She bit her lip as tenderness enveloped her. "Of course you can," she said, her voice wavering. She touched the top of his head and rested her hand on his shoulders as he traced the contours of her abdomen.

"Hi, baby," he whispered, then kissed her belly. Words caught in her throat, tears welled up, and she could not speak.

He looked up at her then, and something passed between them. Something intimate and soul-shattering that caused her entire body to tremble. As he came to lie next to her, he gave her a look of such tenderness, such gentleness, that she was completely overcome. She reached up a shaky hand to smooth down his hair, but he intercepted her by turning his head and kissing her palm. He kissed her knuckles one by one, never taking his eyes off her. Then he drew her in and kissed her on the mouth deeply and slowly. Her body melted against his as she succumbed to his touch, the magnificent feel of his chest against hers, the tender, reverent way he caressed her.

She believed him. She trusted him. She *loved* him.

Much later, Kaitlyn finally lay, content, happy, and sated, enveloped in Rafe's warmth, his body curved around hers, their legs tangled under the down comforter. She didn't want to sleep. Instead she wanted to stay awake and savor the sensation of being wrapped up in him for as long as possible. But despite her wishes, she fell asleep anyway. Sometime later, she heard him stir and sit up, pushing off from the bed.

"What are you doing?" she asked. The clock said 4:15. It was almost time to begin her day.

"I'm going to let the puppy out." He kissed her shoulder, then turned to leave the bed. Even half-awake, she fought the desire to reel him back in, keep him in bed with her.

"It's almost time to get up for work," he whispered. "Sleep a little extra."

He kissed her forehead and covered her with the comforter. She was vaguely aware of him slipping on his shirt and pants and padding down the hall. Then she heard the sink water running. It dawned on her that he was washing the dishes.

That realization struck her straight in the heart. She smiled in an uncontrollable way. Sleepy, satisfied, and warm, she rolled over and for once let someone else take care of things.

Chapter 19

♥

Rafe couldn't help feeling like it was already Christmas, even though it was just another ordinary day. He found himself humming holiday tunes and attacking his chore list with gusto. By noon, he'd done two loads of laundry and gone to the hardware store to look at paint chips. He'd exhausted the puppy playing ball and also tug-of-war on two separate occasions with his favorite socks, which he'd accidentally left in the laundry room. Turns out stealing socks and running away with them was the puppy's new favorite game. As Rafe tossed the wet, chewed-up socks, he couldn't help chuckling.

Kaitlyn, the puppy, the baby…he was building a new life. A life that still seemed too good to be true.

Because of Kaitlyn, he was taking a chance again. He was *living* again.

And he pretty much decided he didn't ever want to see his house without Kaitlyn in it.

That afternoon, Rafe walked into the Bean with a

bunch of paint strips laid out in the shape of a fan. "Hey, beautiful," he said, as Kaitlyn was wiping down tables. "Got a second?"

"Hey, handsome," she shot right back. "What's up?"

"Can you give these a look?" He sat down at a table and she leaned over him to see. He liked the sensation of her hand resting on his shoulder. If she wasn't at work, he would've pulled her right into his lap and kissed her silly. It was hard, controlling himself until later when they could be alone.

"Paint samples?" she asked. "What needs painting?"

He nodded, taking in her familiar vanilla and cinnamon and coffee scent. "The spare room. I thought we could turn it into the baby's room."

"Wait a minute," Kaitlyn said, looking a bit puzzled. "I thought we were turning *my* bedroom into the baby's room. Remember the track lighting, the asbestos crisis?"

He reached up, grabbed her hand, and kissed it. "Maybe that was all a ploy to get you to stay with me." She frowned, so he said, "You know I'm kidding, right?"

"Yes, but I've only been at your place for two days. Plus we've got a new puppy." She smiled at that and spread her arms wide. "Give it a few days—you might be taking back your offer real soon."

"You don't understand," he said.

"Yes, I do." She lowered her voice. "We only made love one night. Everything's new and fresh and wonderful. We don't need to make any sudden—"

He covered her hand with his, which made her stop

talking and look at him. He couldn't seem to stop smiling.

"What?" she asked, smiling too.

He dropped his voice. "I like how you said that. *Make love.*" He squeezed her hand and noticed the adorable way she blushed. "Look, I—I pretty much know that I never want you to leave my bed—or my house—ever again."

As soon as that was out of his mouth, he realized what he'd said. It had slipped out, for better or for worse. She met his words with a skeptical look, which disarmed him. And made him want to prove to her—by his actions, not just talk—that he'd meant it. "Speaking of which, when are you done here?"

"Not anytime soon. There are only a few days left to get my recipe into the cookie contest. I need to think about my final strategy."

"You've been on your feet all day. Maybe you should take a break."

Hazel and Logan came out from the back. "Hey, Rafe," Hazel said with a little wave before addressing Kaitlyn. "We were wondering if we could bake for you tonight. We're done with homework and we know how pressed you are for time. We want to help."

Kaitlyn looked surprised and pleased. "Actually, I'd love some help." She pulled a couple of pieces of paper out of her apron pocket. "I've got two more variations to try. If you can mix up these batches, maybe I can scour that box of recipes one more time."

Hazel took the papers and said, "Great. We'll get started." As the two teenagers walked back to the kitchen, Rafe could hear the sounds of laughter and pans being taken down and Christmas tunes being cranked up.

Rafe raised an eyebrow. "Are you sure you want two teenagers in your kitchen?"

"She wants to help," she said, a touch of pride filling her voice. "Maybe this contest won't be a total loss after all."

The clanging of pots and pans and more giggling ensued.

"If that version of Hazel is the only thing I get out of this contest," Kaitlyn said, her voice full of feeling, "it will be worth it."

"So you're okay with not winning?" He was pretty much sure that wasn't the case.

"I'm not giving up," she said. "Just appreciating that some things are more valuable than winning." She grinned broadly. "But winning would be nice too."

Rafe laughed. "There's the woman I know."

"I'm going to get back to work. Can I get you anything?"

"I want to help too." He didn't like her standing all day, and he knew she'd never quit until she got this recipe right. "I've got to stop in at Nonna's, and then I've got to go let out our little friend. And then I'm great to help mix a batch of dough or do more dishes, whatever you need." He stood and got ready to go.

"Rafe," she said, giving him a solemn look.

"What is it?" he asked.

"It means a lot, just your being here."

He didn't say it, but it meant a lot to him too.

* * *

When Rafe returned an hour later with the puppy in tow, he was hit with the heady scent of baking cookies. All the overhead fluorescent lights were on in the kitchen and Springsteen's "Santa Claus Is Comin' to Town" was blasting. As he took a peek into the kitchen, he saw Hazel with a big streak of flour across her cheek laughing and flicking flour at Logan. They might've been actually filling a couple of cookie sheets with cookies too, but there was such a mess everywhere, he wasn't sure.

Kaitlyn was sitting at an old wooden table backed up against the far wall of the kitchen—she often used it as her desk—riffling through the big box of recipes. Four stacks of paper clippings sat in front of the box.

Hazel came up to the counter just as Rafe was taking a seat. "Hi, Rafe. Aunt Kate's been like that for the past hour. We've been making all kinds of racket and she hasn't even looked up. Want me to get her for you?"

"Let her be for now." One glance at the hurricane in the kitchen made him think he'd have no difficulty occupying his time while he was waiting for her to finish up.

"How about some coffee—and taste test our cookies?" Hazel asked. "We made three batches. Except we might have forgotten the baking powder on the second batch. Or baking soda, I forget which. But the third one might be normal. You can be the first to try it."

"Gee...thanks," he said, flashing her a smile, even if he was a little nervous about being the guinea pig for scary taste testing. "It's nice of you to help your aunt," he said. Because...it was. And he wanted Hazel to know that.

Hazel shrugged. "She deserves to win." While she turned and poured Rafe a coffee, Logan walked up to the counter with a plate full of cookies.

The thought of tasting yet another chocolate cookie...honestly, it was losing its appeal, even if no ingredients were forgotten. But if Kaitlyn wasn't giving up, he wasn't going to either. He gestured with his hand. "Pass them over."

The two teenagers and Rafe all took bites.

Hazel's eyes teared up a little.

"What's the matter, Hazel?" Logan asked.

"Taste it and you'll know," she said in a whisper.

Rafe bit into it and yes—he got it. It was...meh.

He could tell by the expression on Logan's face that he felt the same way.

Hazel put down the cookie and crossed her arms. "It's no use." She flicked her gaze to Kaitlyn. "I don't know how she does it—being so cheerful day after day. Working like this."

Logan wrapped an arm around her shoulders. "We can't give up."

Rafe force-swallowed the cookie. "Logan is right. We can't show her that we think this might be impossible. We've got to support her. That's...that's being a family."

Suddenly a scream emanated from the back.

The puppy startled awake under the table and began barking.

Rafe's heart lurched in his chest. His usual adrenaline response to a crisis, normally so automatic and so controlled, made him trip over his own feet and then on the puppy's leash as he scraped back his chair and ran around the counter to the back room.

Kaitlyn was standing in the middle of the stainless-steel kitchen. Her bright yellow top was the only flash of color in the otherwise neutral space. She was jumping up and down waving a paper clipping. As soon as she saw him, she catapulted herself into his arms.

A million things went through his mind, mostly the primary causes of pregnancy emergencies. "Look, Rafe," Kaitlyn said. "Look at this!" She waved a yellowed piece of lined paper in front of his face. "Are you okay?"

He felt like he'd just had a heart attack, but other than that, he still had a pulse. "Yeah, sure. Are you?"

She squeezed him tightly. "I'm *amazing*. Take a look!"

Amazing? He started breathing again, tried to get his heart to stop pounding in his ears and blocking out his ability to think.

She was *fine*. The baby was *fine*.

Everything was okay.

Somehow, he managed to grasp the piece of paper and focus on it. "'Grandma's orange cream cheese Jell-O in a horseshoe mold,'" he read. That title didn't even have the word *chocolate* in it. He looked at her, puzzled.

"Turn it sideways," she said, clapping her hands. "*Sideways*. Just like you said." She jumped up and down while he rotated the clipping ninety degrees. There, in the margins, were some pencil scrawlings. Faint and very easy to miss.

"I didn't see it the first three times I went through the box. But then I examined the fronts and backs of every single piece of paper. It took me *hours*. But I did it! I found it!" She was smiling from ear to ear, her eyes lit up with happiness.

He squinted at the faded writing. *Chocolate, flour, cocoa powder, butter*... He glanced from the paper to her glowing face, knowing exactly what he was looking at.

He carefully set down the paper and rested his hands on her shoulders. "You did it, Katie," he whispered, his voice all choked up. He grabbed her and lifted her up and twirled her around the kitchen until she grabbed onto his back for dear life, laughing and pounding on his back. "Congratulations," he said. "Now you're on your way."

"Whether I win with this or not, I found it, Rafe! A piece of my grandpa, of my childhood. I'm really excited about that. And I can't wait to try this recipe!"

He was thrilled for her. Even more than that, he was relieved everything was okay. Because the first thing he'd thought was... No, he didn't even want to think where his mind had gone.

"I knew this recipe was too important for my grandfather not to leave a record of it somewhere." She looked up at him with determination in her eyes. "I can win this, Rafe. I know I can!"

He planted a kiss on her neck. "I know you can too. But then, I always knew you could."

Dimly, he became aware that the two teenagers were watching them. Logan had his arm around Hazel, and Hazel had tears in her eyes.

Kaitlyn walked over and placed a hand on each of their arms. "I want to thank both of you for all your help. This was a team effort. You two freed me up so I could look through that box one last time." She hugged Hazel tight and whispered, "Thank you." Then she insisted they go home because it was getting late on a school night.

When they left, Kaitlyn looked around at the disastrous-looking kitchen.

Rafe rolled up his sleeves. "Let's get this job done."

Kaitlyn held him back. "No, I don't think so," she said, a faint smile on her lips.

"I'm not saving this mess for you to clean up in the morning. Those kids may have helped, but I think they used every single dish and pot and pan that you own."

"Rafe, I love that you want to help me, but... not tonight. I feel like doing something else now."

He lifted a brow. The *something else* that came immediately to his mind sounded awesome, but he didn't want to make assumptions. "Something else?"

"Yeah. Something with you. Something we can do together."

The puppy batted its paws against her calves. Kaitlyn reached down and picked it up.

"Come here, sweet boy," Kaitlyn said. "Let's go home."

Rafe put his arm around her and grinned, scratching the puppy behind the ears. "Let's go home."

* * *

The ride to the house seemed to take hours. But once they arrived, Rafe probably broke some kind of speed record tucking the dog into his crate. He met Kaitlyn as she was plugging in the tree and dimming all the lights.

"What do you want to do now?" he asked, leaning on the back of the couch and levelling his gaze at her.

He knew exactly what *he* wanted to do.

And so, apparently, did she, because a second later she was in his arms, wrapping herself around him and dropping enthusiastic kisses on his mouth and face and neck.

They fell onto the couch tangled up and laughing, but soon the kisses took over. Rafe paused long enough to gather her face in his hands and plant a quick kiss on her nose. "I'm so glad you found the recipe," he whispered.

Her hands slid gently up his arms, a move that sent an unexpected shiver through him. "I thought it was lost forever," she said, her eyes wide and blue and melting something deep inside of him.

I thought you *were lost forever*, he thought but didn't dare say out loud. Instead, he kissed her again.

She surely must have felt his passion, his excitement at being with her, his happiness for her. As she unbuttoned his shirt and ran her hands over his chest and tugged on his jeans, her motions turned frantic.

"Hey," he whispered, trying to pull back a little. "Keep that up and this is going to be over really fast."

She kissed him again, and breathlessly, she said, "I don't care. I want you so badly."

"I want you too, Katie." Somehow, his voice cracked. He'd never meant anything as much. "More than I've ever wanted anyone."

The feel of her skin against his was so overpowering he had to catch his breath. He saw something flicker in her eyes, and he knew she understood that had taken him a lot to say. He felt their connection, the honesty borne from years of friendship, her generous and giving spirit accepting him, loving him whether or not he deserved to be loved.

He knew her so well, yet she was driving him wild, stripping him of all his defenses, and he could no longer hide the feelings that were overtaking him. Maybe she sensed how emotional he was, because she silenced him with a kiss, and wrapped her arms around his neck.

With one quick move, he rolled them over so that she was beneath him and helped her strip away her clothes.

He licked at her nipple, laved it with his tongue until she arched beneath his touch and little moans and sighs escaped her throat. When her breathing quickened and her hands clasped and unclasped on his back, he touched her intimately, stroking her and playing with her wet, swollen flesh. "Katie, you're so beautiful," he whispered. What had he done to deserve this, to deserve her? *Nothing. Not a thing.* That thought humbled him and made him want to do everything in his power to please her, to show her what she meant to him.

"Rafe," she said, fighting through waves of pleasure to speak, but he would not stop. "Rafe, I— Oh, what are you doing to me?"

He could have said the same. He kissed away the

soft little sounds she made, watched as she fell apart in his arms. Then he entered her, and being inside her, her body wrapped tightly around his, her arms stroking softly up and down his back, her saying his name on a shuddering whisper, filled him with a joy so powerful he could not contain it.

She grabbed his butt and tugged him even closer. "I want all of you, Rafe. Everything." She wrapped herself around him, both of them clinging to each other with a need he'd never experienced before.

He started to shudder, a fine trembling he could not control. He could not stop himself, could not stop the rhythm or the pleasure as it hit him in relentless waves.

"Rafe, I-I'm coming again," she whispered.

He felt her muscles contract around him, and that was all he needed to finally let go. A long, guttural moan escaped him as he shuddered one final time.

They came together, him calling out her name on a guttural sigh.

As the world slowly came back into Rafe's consciousness, what he noticed was the quiet—in the room, and the peacefulness within him of holding Katie in his arms. For a long time afterward, they lay there together, wrapped up in each other, enjoying being together in the glow of the Christmas lights.

* * *

They might have been just a little noisy, because a little while later, Kaitlyn sat in the laundry room in her flannel pj's with Santa heads on them and the reindeer robe her mom bought her and her reindeer slippers, which a very wide-awake puppy was chewing on. She pulled the puppy away from the stuffed antlers and lowered him into her lap, where he put his head down and snuggled into the folds of her robe.

They sat there like that, her leaning against the dryer, drinking a glass of milk and aimlessly rubbing the puppy's head as he began to doze. In her other hand, she held the recipe.

As she hung out with the puppy, she took ten photos of the recipe *just in case*, including one with Rafe's phone, and memorized it too. She wasn't taking any chances of losing it now.

"So *that's* what Grandpa did," she told the puppy, whose eyelids lifted sleepily at the sound of her voice. "And you'll never guess what the secret ingredient is—coffee! That makes complete sense!"

The giant lick Kaitlyn got on her fingers told her he probably didn't care.

In a few minutes, Rafe walked in, wearing scrub bottoms, his feet and chest bare, little droplets of water from the shower still on his shoulders and smelling like her bodywash that she left in his bathroom.

She couldn't help smiling a little. Mostly because she was ecstatic—about finding the recipe, of course, but also because she couldn't believe what was happening between them. She couldn't believe things had gone back to—no, had *surpassed*—the easy friendship they'd had before, and what had developed in its place was something she couldn't even put into words.

As Rafe set down the dog's water bowl, she reached

into the dryer and handed him a clean towel to line the bottom of the crate. He smoothed out the towel and shut the door and sat down next to her, stretching out his long legs beside her. She leaned into his strong body. He took a swig of her milk and wrapped his arm around her. They sat like that, watching the puppy's deep, even breathing, the picture of peace and calm.

"What is it about sleeping babies?" Kaitlyn said. "So stinking cute."

"You know what Nonna says," Rafe said. "'If babies didn't tug at our heartstrings when they were asleep, no one would want to take care of them.'"

"Well, good thing you were cute then, because Nonna told me you were a handful."

Rafe chuckled. "I was a cute baby. Far cuter than my sisters." He examined the now-sleeping puppy. "Now that the recipe's found, we have other important things to do."

"Like what?"

"Give this little guy a name."

"I've been thinking about that," she said. "Some dogs look like their name, like Snowball or Spot or Fluffy."

"He doesn't look like any of those," he said with a grin. "He might look like Trouble."

"That's like a self-fulfilling prophecy. Better to go with Happy or Angel if you're going to take that route." She thought for a minute. "We could do a theme. Like, you Langdon kids are all named after angels."

"Themes are hard. How about keeping it simple?" Rafe said. "Maybe something masculine, like Bear or Gunner? Moe, Harley, Duke?"

Kaitlyn turned and pretended to look all over his chest and even peered around his back. Which was quite a treat, actually. All those lean, defined hills of muscle.

"What are you doing?"

"Looking for your Hells Angels tattoo."

"Ha ha," Rafe said. "I suppose you have a better idea?"

"Sure. Sunny, Sparkle, Rainbow. Unicorn. Those were Julia's suggestions."

"I don't think I could live it down if I showed up at the station with a dog named *Sparkle*."

"How about Christmas Miracle?" Kaitlyn said. "It *was* sort of a miracle, how you found him. And no one knows a thing about where he came from."

"*You're* a Christmas miracle," he blurted.

Chapter 20

♥

He could tell Kaitlyn was biting her lip, biting back laughter. "What did you just say?"

"Um, I heard that in a movie once," he backpedaled. "Maybe that one where a bell rings every time an angel gets their wings."

She scanned his face carefully, trying to figure him out. "You're insane." Her phone rang just then, and it was his sister Sara congratulating her on finding the recipe. Apparently Hazel had told Rachel who'd seen Gabby at the grocery store who'd called Sara... the joys of small-town living.

Rafe took that opportunity to tuck the dog into his crate and escape. As he stood in the darkened hallway, he could see her laughing on the phone and talking animatedly.

She was everything he'd been waiting for. She *was* his Christmas miracle. She'd opened his heart again in a way he would never have thought possible.

But he couldn't say any of that. He was afraid to say

it, because what if it jinxed everything? So he decided if he couldn't tell her, he would just have to show her.

As soon as Kaitlyn finished her call, Rafe walked back into the laundry room. She was standing next to the dryer reading the recipe again on her phone for the hundredth time. "I bet your neck is sore, looking through that recipe box for hours like that."

"Well, now that you mention it," she said, flexing her neck and rubbing her hand alongside of it, "it *is* a little sore."

He took her phone out of her hand and set it on the dryer. "I could take a look, if you want. I give a mean neck massage."

"Oh, okay," she said, using her now-free hands to wrap around his waist. He moved the hood of her reindeer robe aside and rubbed with his hands along the base of her neck.

He gave a little tug on the robe until it loosened up a little more. "How's this feel?" he asked, making his way along her clavicle. "Good?"

"My back needs it too," she said, gesturing over her shoulder.

As he massaged between her shoulder blades, her hands meandered to the drawstring on his scrubs, untying it, tucking her hands inside.

"I give pretty good massages too," she said, kneading his butt.

"I—I like that," he said, smiling. "A lot."

She looked up at him, and a feeling he could only name as fierce overcame him. It tightened his chest, constricted his throat, and made him kiss her passionately, swooping her up to him so quickly a laugh and a *whoops* escaped her lips.

Behind her, the puppy stirred.

She put a hand over her mouth. "I didn't mean to be loud," she said.

"If that's loud, I really don't think that's a problem." He smiled and bent his head to kiss her again.

She turned her head again toward the puppy. "I don't think we should be doing this here," she said.

Rafe turned to check out the dog in the crate, still fast asleep. "You mean in front of the dog?"

"Yeah. He's a baby. He might wake up and be...confused."

"I have a solution for that." Rafe flipped off the light switch. Then he scooped her up and carried her down the hall to the bedroom.

* * *

They were in bed talking and laughing when suddenly, from down the hall, they heard yips and barks. "Oh no," Rafe said, sitting up.

Lying beside him, Kaitlyn ran her hand slowly up and down his back. "Well, you've gone and done it," she said, her voice a little shaky. "Awakened our poor nameless puppy."

"You are so noisy," he said, giving her a mischievous look as he climbed out of bed.

"You are so the baby of the family," she said, smacking him playfully on the butt. "Such a troublemaker."

"Okay. It was my fault. Next time don't be so..."

"So what?"

So...everything he ever wanted? He'd barely touched her, and yet he could hardly control himself around her. *Houston, he had a problem.* He smoothed her hair back from her face. "So driving me wild with everything you do."

"I didn't do anything, remember? I just relaxed and let you do all the work."

"That's the kind of work I want to do every day," he said, tugging on his scrub pants.

He took one more look at her, beautiful and spent, kissed her on the forehead, and ran out of the room, returning a minute later with the puppy, which he deposited on the bed. Certain it was playtime, the puppy hopped around the comforter, rolling and jumping and attacking the corner of the comforter and tugging it with his teeth.

"The books say not to let the dog up on the bed," she said matter-of-factly.

"Oh, sorry," Rafe said. "I didn't even think about that. Our dog used to sleep in my bed," he said.

"Well then, we're going to need a bigger bed, because this dog is going to weigh as much as me, and I need a lot of room."

The ball of fur scrambled over to Kaitlyn and suddenly tumbled, landing with feet suspended in the air. She giggled and rubbed his stomach.

"That dog is in love with you already," he said. He got it, he totally did.

"I love him too," she said. She glanced up and blushed. "Can't help myself."

Just then the puppy sprang off the bed and ran over to a laundry basket in the corner of the room where he proceeded to tug on a sock that was hanging over the edge.

Kaitlyn ran over to grab the sock, but the dog, sensing a game, ran just out of her reach.

"Hey, not another sock," Rafe said. He nearly grabbed it, but the dog tore out of the bedroom and off down the hall.

"Come here, you little bandit," Rafe said. Suddenly he halted midrun. For a heartbeat, he and Kaitlyn stared at one another.

"Bandit," Kaitlyn whispered, her eyes wide.

"Stealer of socks," Rafe said. He laughed, shook his head, then took off after the dog.

When he got the puppy settled again, Rafe climbed back into bed. Kaitlyn lay down next to him, her hand drifting to his chest.

He put his hand over hers.

"Are you okay?" she asked a minute later, when he was almost asleep.

He glanced over at her. "More than okay," he said. "You?"

She flashed him a grin and nodded, then rested her head on his chest.

As Rafe put an arm around her and held her close, he felt shaky all over, tenderness flooding over him in waves that he could not control. A tide of feeling was engulfing him, towing him under, pulling him out to sea, and he let go, rolling with the amazing flow.

* * *

In the middle of the night, Rafe awakened to find Kaitlyn gone from the bed. He raked his hand over her empty spot, still warm from her body. His eyes fluttered open, and dimly, he became aware that the bathroom light was on. He heard the sound of more light switches flipping, of drawers being opened and shut. He got out of bed, an acid feeling in the pit of his stomach already signaling to him that something was amiss.

He found her in the living room, lifting up the cushions, scattering them everywhere as she searched for something.

"What are you looking for?" he asked.

"I need my phone," she said, her voice cracking.

"I'll help you look for it." She was icy pale, and her hands were shaking.

He touched her arm. "What is it? What's wrong? Are you okay?" But he knew deep inside something wasn't right. He saw the panic etched on her face.

She stifled a sob. "I'm bleeding. I—have to call the doctor."

Bleeding?

No.

He ran to the kitchen island and handed her his cell phone, his own hand visibly shaking.

"Let me help you."

"It—it's okay," she said, already tapping her phone. "I can do it."

She hit the contact number she needed and spoke to the answering service. "Hi. I'm Kaitlyn Barnes, and

I'm a patient—I'm pregnant, and I just noticed some— I'm bleeding. No, not a lot, but more than—more than spots. No, no cramping. Yes. Yes, I can. I'll be right there." She hung up the phone. "They told me to go down to the ER. They're going to do an ultrasound to see if... to see if..." As her voice trailed off, Rafe realized he was just standing there, paralyzed, terrified out of his mind.

He dealt with medical emergencies every day, but it was as if his entire encyclopedia of knowledge left him and he could not think. Could something be really wrong? Could she be about to lose the baby? Yes. Could it be something else, something not awful? Yes, that was possible too, but his mind was fixated on everything terrible.

He mentally shook himself into action and wrapped his arms around her. He forced himself to be calm, but for the life of him, he couldn't think of the right words to say. Afraid to reassure, afraid to imagine the worst, he settled on, "One step at a time. Can I help you find clothes?"

She was crying, tears streaking down her face. "Yes, please," she said, surprisingly calm. He followed her into the spare bedroom. "I just need some yoga pants and a sweater," she said. "Any kind of decent clothes."

He made her sit down while he rummaged through her clothes, at a loss, but he did find the yoga pants. And a bunch of underwear, but he just turned the whole bag over to her rather than go through that.

"You don't have to come," she said. He stopped everything, the words making him wince. She looked at him through tear-streaked eyes. "Rafe," she said, her hand clutching his wrist. Her voice was gravelly and practically a whisper. "I—didn't mean that. I'm scared to death. If things are—bad, I'm not sure I can keep it together by myself."

"Of course I'm coming with you," he growled. "I want to be with you." It was all he could say for now.

Five minutes later they were out the door.

Chapter 21

♥

The ER was bustling at three in the morning. The staff had hung tinsel and Christmas lights from the nurses' station, and the long counter was filled with gift boxes of Christmas cookies, candy, and other goodies. As Kaitlyn sat down in a wheelchair and let herself be wheeled to an exam room, Rafe stayed by her side, nodding to several paramedics, the charge nurse, and a few ER docs he knew from bringing in patients over the years. Rafe looked worried and uncomfortable but Kaitlyn was glad that the staff knew him, glad he knew the doctors and nurses personally.

A woman in a white coat who wore a stethoscope around her neck approached them. "Hey, Rafe," she said, before turning her attention to Kaitlyn. "I'm Amira Miruwani," she said, "one of the ER docs." She smiled kindly at Kaitlyn and gave her arm a reassuring squeeze. "I'll be in to see you as soon as I can." That left them to do one thing—wait.

"She's a good doctor," Rafe said.

Kaitlyn nodded. "I'm calling my mom to go over and check on the puppy. Is that okay with you? I don't want him to be crying and no one to be there."

Rafe ran his hands through his hair, which made it stick up at odd angles. "I can call one of my sisters instead so you don't have to bother your mom."

"She's usually up early. You would just have to tell her how to get into the house."

In the exam room, fifteen minutes felt like fifteen hours.

"Rafe, it's going to be okay," she found herself saying. "No matter what happens, we'll get through this." She'd said *we'll* on purpose. Because after tonight, there was a *we*, wasn't there?

She was trying to be strong for him, but she could see how upset he was. He paced the small room, clenching his hands into fists. She motioned to the chair beside the exam table. "Come sit with me?"

She wanted him to be near her, to hold her hand. To comfort her with his presence. But she wanted to be a calming influence for him too.

"I'm going to ask what's taking so long," he said, walking over to the door.

"You've already asked *three times*," she said in a coarse whisper.

Rafe glanced nervously at his watch. "I just don't understand why they can't hurry up."

"There's nothing they can do if—if I'm losing the baby. It's too...early." Her eyes filled with tears. Across the room, Rafe's face went white as the walls. She'd never felt so helpless in her life. To help herself or him.

Finally Dr. Miruwani came in with the portable ultrasound machine, asking questions as she set up. "Okay, sweetheart," she said, patting Kaitlyn's arm, a gesture that had a surprisingly calming effect. "Take a deep breath. You too, Rafe," she said over her shoulder. "Now, I'm just going to ask you a couple of questions. Are you passing clots? Do you feel light-headed? Do you have pain or cramping?"

No, no, and no. Dr. Miruwani did an abdominal exam and a pelvic exam.

"We had sex earlier," Kaitlyn said. "Could that have done something?" One glance at Rafe showed him to be deathly pale.

"First of all, your cervical exam was normal. There's no external evidence that you're miscarrying the baby. And to answer your question, no, having sex could not have caused this problem. But I'm going to do an ultrasound right now. We'll see if we can hear the baby's heartbeat and maybe find out what else is going on."

Rafe stood next to Kaitlyn's bed as the typical black-and-white fuzz appeared on the screen. And something else too. A rapid, regular *whooshing* sound, a heartbeat under water, that pounded out loud and clear.

Kaitlyn still held her breath, waiting for Dr. Miruwani to speak.

"Oh, that's a good sign," the doctor said, breathing a sigh of relief. "That's a great, strong heartbeat." She pointed to the screen, where they saw, clear as day, the outline of the baby, hands and feet moving as actively as when she'd first seen it.

Hi, baby, she said silently. *Be okay. Please, please be okay, so your daddy can be okay too.*

Out of the corner of her eye, she could see Rafe staring at the screen. She saw him swallow, his jaw taut. She had no idea what he was thinking, just that he looked like he was ready to bolt.

Her eyes blurred as the doctor continued to point out things, reinforcing again that the baby was just fine. But her fear was that Rafe was not.

"The placenta is in a good location," the doctor continued, "and there are no abnormalities there. But I do see a blood clot between the bag of waters and the wall of the uterus. What we call a subchorionic hematoma. That's the likely source of your bleeding."

"What does that mean?" Kaitlyn asked. She really couldn't picture whatever it was the doctor was pointing to.

"In most cases, no one knows why these bleeds occur, but they tend to resolve spontaneously without problem. You should have a follow-up ultrasound in a week. And no sex for now."

At the mention of sex again, Rafe cringed.

"Once it's resolved, you're free to resume sexual activity," she continued, making Rafe turn the color of the sharps container on the wall. "There is a slightly increased risk of miscarriage with this condition, but most of these resolve without difficulty. We tend not to put patients on bed rest for this, but my advice would be to at least take tomorrow off and limit the time you spend on your feet."

"Thanks, Doctor," Rafe said, shaking her hand before she excused herself from the room. "That's great news," he said, briefly catching Kaitlyn's gaze. She tried to connect with him across the room, but he busied himself gathering their coats and papers.

He came and stood by the exam table, exhaling deeply. "I'm really glad the baby is okay."

"Me too." She reached out for his hand—it was a natural instinct. He didn't step away, but he didn't hold it either. He didn't hold *her*. That's when she knew. "Rafe," she said. *Come back to me.* She tried to meet his eyes, but he would not look at her.

"I should get the car," he said.

"Okay," she said. "Good idea." He seemed to be fading away from her, going to some unreachable place, and she didn't know how to get him to stay.

"You're going to take today off, aren't you?" he continued as he headed toward the door. "Rest. And maybe you should take more time off than that. Until we're sure everything's okay."

She forced a smile. "I'll make sure to follow the doctor's orders," she said.

He'd put on his jacket and was pushing open the exam room door when she stopped him.

"Rafe."

He half turned toward her. "Yes?"

A thousand things that she wanted—no, *needed*—to say came to her lips. Things like *I need you, right here, by my side*.

"Oh, never mind," she ended up saying. "You'd better go get the car."

Rafe wasted no time leaving. This time, she wasn't

staying silent because she was afraid to say things, or afraid to confront him. It was because she wasn't going to guilt him into being there for her. As much as she'd believed loving him would heal him, she saw now that it wasn't enough.

* * *

Rafe was shaking. He somehow managed to get them home, take care of the dog, and ask Kaitlyn if she needed anything.

He took a shower, but it didn't calm his nerves or give him any clarity. He seemed to know only one thing—*he couldn't do this*.

He hadn't been able to be there for Kaitlyn tonight when she most needed him. He'd tried but he hadn't been able to hide from her that something was wrong. He'd seen the disappointment reflected in her eyes.

He got out of the shower and walked over to the bed where she was stretched out asleep, still with her clothes on. He should've helped her get her pj's on and made sure she was comfortable.

Instead he was all tangled up inside his own head, terrified for her, terrified for the baby. He walked over to the closet and pulled a thick blanket from the shelf and covered her, making sure to tuck it carefully around her feet. That's when he noticed she'd been holding a wad of Kleenex when she'd fallen asleep.

She'd fallen asleep crying. Because of him.

"I'm sorry, Katie," he whispered.

This past week had made him think he could handle

a relationship, but tonight had taught him he clearly could not. He couldn't love someone—*two* someones— just to risk losing them again.

* * *

Rafe was relieved to spend the next twenty-four hours at work. He texted Kaitlyn several times to ask how she was doing, and each time her reply was short. Okay. Doing fine. The next night was Rafe's night to spend with his grandmother, and he had to admit he was glad not to have to face Kaitlyn at home.

"How's Kaitlyn feeling?" Nonna asked. Rafe was making them some hot cocoa the old-fashioned way, from scratch, the way she'd taught him years ago, with milk and cocoa and sugar in an old cast-iron pan on the stove.

"She's doing fine. She took yesterday off to rest."

"That's good. Maybe she should take the rest of the week off too. She's on her feet a lot."

He nodded. Guilt pummeled him because he knew he was avoiding Kaitlyn at a time when she was probably frightened too, even though the doctor had been very reassuring. He certainly continued to feel freaked out, and he told himself it was probably better for Kaitlyn not to be around him when he was like this. But it felt like yet another way he'd fallen short.

Rafe carried their mugs into the living room while Nonna sat on her old floral sofa. A small artificial Christmas tree that they'd put up a few weeks ago and helped decorate with all her favorite ornaments sat on a table in the corner. It was surrounded by a crocheted tree skirt with tassels. Nonna moved a sizeable afghan that she was in the middle of crocheting and sat down. "What's on your mind?" she asked, patting the seat beside her.

He sat down, knowing he could never hide things from his grandmother. She always seemed to know when something wasn't right, from the time he'd accidentally broken the neighbor's window with a baseball to the first time a girl broke his heart. He wished his troubles now were that simple. "Nonna, I'm glad you're feeling better. And I would never want to hurt you or make you feel stressed out." He needed to tell her that their engagement wasn't real. He was tired of lying to her, to his entire family, to himself.

Nonna sat back with her cup of cocoa and eyeballed him in that way of hers that was half-suspicious and half-understanding. Like she knew he was about to say something she didn't want to hear.

He wished he could keep on with the lie just so he wouldn't hurt her. But this time, things weren't going to get better, and holding off telling her wasn't going to do anyone any good.

He set down his mug on the coffee table and turned to his grandmother. He felt her disappointment in him even before he uttered a word, something he'd always been determined to avoid at all costs. But this time, he couldn't help his failings. He just had to confess them. "Kaitlyn and I . . . we've been friends for a long time."

"You two remind me so much of your grandfather and me. We grew up together, you know."

Rafe nodded, thankful for the stall.

"You know the story about how my father sent me away to America to get me away from the Jewish boy I loved. That was heartbreaking. I never thought I'd get over it. Especially when I found out I was pregnant."

"Nonna, I would never leave Kaitlyn alone to raise our baby," Rafe said.

"Of course you wouldn't," she said. "But listen, there's a point. Jacob, the boy I loved, joined the merchant marine and ended up falling in love with another girl. It was your grandfather, Alphonse, who came all the way to America for me. To ask me to marry him."

He'd heard the story, but he didn't know the details. "As a friend?"

"Of course not. He loved me all along. But I was still in love with Jacob." She sighed. "See, your grandfather figured it out before I did. He *knew* we were right together. That we would always love and care for one another, and that we understood each other like no one else. That's how it is when you're best friends with someone. They know your deepest secrets, and they still love you."

She grabbed his arm like she did whenever she needed him to listen to what she was saying. "Alphonse was the kindest man I knew. I had a lucky life. And I ended up with the right man. But it was only because I had to learn to move on from heartbreak. And when I did, my life became what it was meant to be—full of love and family and joy. You can have that too."

Rafe let out a big breath. "Nonna, I don't think I can get over what happened in the past." That had been hard to say. But it was true.

She reached over and patted him on the cheek. "You see, that's exactly what I said too. But that's the surprising thing about love. It does the impossible." She sat back and looked at him. "It breaks my heart to see you suffer. You're a good boy, Rafe. But you're trapped in a bad place. Fight your way out of it."

His grandmother loved him. But she couldn't fix him. "Thanks, Nonna. I appreciate your concern for me. Now, how about if we watch an episode of that emergency room show?"

"The one where you tell me if it's really like that at the hospital? I love that show."

Nonna fell asleep after ten minutes, leaving Rafe to stare at the screen without seeing anything. He got her message loud and clear. Love had healed Nonna, but it would not work for him. He had too many hang-ups and failings. Kaitlyn deserved a whole lot better.

He picked up his phone to text Kaitlyn again. How are you feeling?

His answer was a thumbs-up emoji. No words.

Great. Wanted to let you know I picked up another shift for someone so I won't be home again tomorrow.

Okay, came the answer.

And then, before she could add anything more—or worse say nothing more at all—he sent her one final text:

We need to come clean about this fake engagement.

Chapter 22

♥

Kaitlyn plopped down a giant hunk of chocolate cookie dough on the island in the Bean. It landed on the metal surface with a big thunk. She pounded down the dough and flattened it out, then tore off little balls and threw those onto the island too.

She was *angry baking*.

This was the last batch of chocolate dough she was going to make for a *long* time. She just had to test the amount of baking powder because she couldn't tell if her grandfather's *t* on the paper was little *t* for teaspoon or big *T* for tablespoon. All the other quantities—the chocolate, the cocoa powder, the butter and fat—were all decided.

And she'd modified the secret ingredient, using a special espresso blend she'd mixed herself. Just this one last batch for testing, then she'd have the recipe ready to submit for the contest.

But while the cookie recipe was coming along well, the rest of her life was falling apart. How could Rafe want to call off the fake engagement? *By text.* How many times had she told Hazel not to trust any guy who breaks up with her by text?

Wait...could you even call off a fake engagement? She'd been too shocked to respond to his text about breaking off the engagement, but she wasn't shocked anymore. Now she was just angry.

She pulled out another giant batch of cookie dough from the fridge and tossed it onto the island, pretending it was Rafe. Or at least her anger toward Rafe. She punched and poked at it a little. Sadly, that did not make her feel any better.

How could she have believed that their playing house was real? How could she have believed they could all live happily ever after, her and Rafe and the puppy and their baby?

That thought made her cry.

She'd totally let down her guard. She'd let him into her heart. Stupid, stupid her.

Rafe *had* managed to open his heart, she knew it. She'd *felt* it. But her pregnancy scare had made him slam it shut again. He'd been scarce for days, leaving her alone in his house with the dog. She couldn't even go home to her apartment.

And now...this. Wanting to tell everyone the truth.

She swiped away her tears. This was it. He'd tried, but his memories were too painful, his fear too great. She was back to square one.

No. No, she wasn't. Things weren't all bad. She had the recipe. Hazel was doing really well. She had a puppy who was going to be a wonderful dog and companion for her baby.

And she'd really, really tried to show Rafe how good their life could be together. That's what hurt the most. Because the two of them together had been so good. How could he not see that?

She heard the side door creak open and Hazel walk in. "Hey, Aunt Kate," she said. "Whatcha doing?"

Kaitlyn rallied for Hazel's sake, wiping away her tears with her apron before Hazel could see. "Hey, sweetie. I'm baking my very last batch of cookies before I submit the recipe to the contest."

Hazel sat down and snatched a ball of raw cookie dough, taking a bite. "Delicious," she said. "So anyway, there was this contest at school that my business entrepreneurship class teacher kind of made me enter."

"What a mean teacher," Kaitlyn said, smiling.

"I know, right?" Hazel said, laughing. "It was a fashion design contest. You had to enter a piece with the theme of color and nature. I entered a dress that had all the colors of the sunset. I guess I was inspired after the weekend at the lake." She picked away at another bit of cookie dough. "Anyway, I won."

Kaitlyn stopped rolling dough into cookies and looked at her. "Did you just say 'I won'?"

Hazel looked up and smiled. So widely it reminded Kaitlyn suddenly of when Hazel was a little kid and Kaitlyn used to take her down the street for chocolate ice cream, and Hazel would smile from ear to ear from pure pleasure, even as it dripped down her chin and all over her clothes. *That* was the kind of smile she wore now. And it was glorious.

Kaitlyn walked around the counter, wiping her

hands on a paper towel before hugging Hazel. "Oh, honey. I'm so proud of you."

"I know," Hazel said. "Because I won."

"Nope," Kaitlyn said, swiping at her eyes and drawing back to look her niece in the eye.

"Because I'm not stealing stuff anymore?" She stared at the floor, and Kaitlyn gently tipped Hazel's chin back up.

"No—I mean, yes, but beyond that. You're pursuing your dreams. So you won't have to rely on anyone else for them to come true."

Hazel seemed to puzzle over this, a fine line creasing her brow. "But you have Rafe. You guys are going to get married and you're going to rely on him."

"Well, I think when you marry someone, you do rely on one another. But it's important to be your own person first—and keep being your own person." Kaitlyn didn't want to lie. Especially since it was all going to come out anyway, and Hazel would only feel betrayed if Kaitlyn kept the secret. It had taken a long time to regain her trust, and she didn't want to jeopardize that. But she didn't want to spoil Hazel's moment with her sadness. "Look, Hazel, the bottom line is, I'm so proud of you. You made a life here—a really good one. You turned things around. And I couldn't be more proud."

"I never felt like I belonged anywhere. But here...I feel like things are turning around." She didn't sound sarcastic or cynical, just honest. And hopeful.

"Your hard work turned them around, sweetie." She gave Hazel another squeeze. "Keep up the good work.

If I wasn't so full from tasting chocolate cookies, I'd suggest we get some ice cream."

Hazel laughed and held her stomach. "I love you, Aunt Kate, but I *am* getting really sick of chocolate cookie dough. Rain check?"

"Rain check," Kaitlyn said, offering a fist bump.

Just then Gabby flew through the door. "Hey, are you still baking those cookies? Geez! Wrap it up, we're all heading over to Nonna's tonight."

"Right now?" Kaitlyn asked. "Is something wrong?"

"Nonna's been doing great, but ever since Rafe stayed with her the other night, she's been a little blue. We thought we'd go over there and bake her favorite— well, *our* favorite—Christmas cookies. Want to come?"

"Sounds like something we all need," Kaitlyn said. She meant it—she loved making Christmas cookies, as long as they weren't chocolate snowcaps. As soon as she agreed to go, she realized Rafe was probably going to be there too. She really didn't feel like baking Christmas cookies with him. And had he told Nonna about them? Was that why she was sad?

Kaitlyn shoved her very last two batches of cookies into the oven. "See you over there, Gabs," she said. Maybe it would be good to be with the family. And sooner or later, she'd have to face Rafe anyway. "I'll bring all these along too. I need a final focus group of taste testers."

"See you over there, Aunt Kate," Hazel said, tagging along with Gabby.

This should be fun. Baking cookies and telling everyone they weren't engaged. She couldn't wait.

* * *

Rafe walked into Nonna's living room to find her hugging Hazel. The last few days had been exhausting—he'd worked a twenty-four-hour shift, gone home in the morning and slept, then he'd worked that entire night for a local ambulance company. Normally he didn't schedule himself so tight…all this avoiding Kaitlyn was exhausting him.

That's why the last thing he'd wanted to do was bake cookies, even if it was to cheer Nonna up. Especially with Kaitlyn there. But Gabby wouldn't take no for an answer. At least he and Kaitlyn would be able to set the record straight before the holiday so the lie wouldn't continue over Christmas.

"Congratulations about the contest, sweetie," Nonna said. "That's wonderful news. I'm so glad that old sewing machine came in handy."

"Thanks, Nonna," Hazel said, looking pleased.

"I found a whole other bag of material bolts and odds and ends in my attic," Nonna continued. "You're welcome to it. And you can come and sew in my sewing room any time you want." She gave Hazel another big hug. "It's so much better to make things than steal them, isn't it?"

"Nonna," Kaitlyn said quickly, coming over just in time to see Hazel's horrified look. She gave Hazel a reassuring smile and a squeeze. "We sure are proud of Hazel," she said, waving a plate of chocolate cookies in front of Nonna. "Would you taste one of these and tell me what you think? It's my grandfather's recipe and I need the opinion of an expert baker."

Kaitlyn. Rafe's heart lurched at the sound of her voice. Seeing her filled him with a confusing mix of excitement and guilt. And he missed her. Yet he was happy for her—happy for the recipe, happy for Hazel. And he loved how she'd included his grandmother. This was what Kaitlyn did. Make everyone feel special and wanted.

Nonna took the cookie, but she didn't immediately take a bite. She inspected both sides first. "Hmmm," she said. "Perfectly baked." She felt the weight of it in her palm. "Nice and hefty but not dense." Then she took a dainty bite and rolled it around on her tongue.

"Rose, you should've been a sommelier," Rafe's dad said, smiling. "What's the verdict?"

Rafe could tell even from across the room that Kaitlyn seemed to be holding her breath.

Nonna appeared ready to pronounce her verdict. "The coating on the outside is not too crisp. And the inside is chewy and a little bit cakey. The chocolatey taste is all over, but I also taste something rich—like melted bits of it. And"—she held up the cookie—"is there coffee in here?"

Kaitlyn threw up her hands. *"That's* the secret ingredient. But Nonna—*how does it taste?"*

Nonna set the cookie down on a napkin. The entire room went quiet. Nonna walked over to Kaitlyn and broke out into a huge smile. "I think you've got yourself a winner, honey."

"Well, there you have it," Sara said to Kaitlyn. "Nonna has spoken."

"Go forth and *enter that contest,"* Gabby said.

Everyone cheered and hugged Kaitlyn. Rafe went to hug her too, but they sort of knocked into one another and she ended up awkwardly bashing her nose into his chest. Her hair smelled really good. It reminded him of when she'd gotten out of the shower and put on those flannel pj's and that silly reindeer robe and...

"Rafe?" his dad said. "Can I talk to you for a minute?"

Everyone was chattering about the cookies, how good they were, and how Gabby had brought over six balls of sugar cookie dough that were ready to be rolled out.

"Sure." Rafe followed his dad into·Nonna's living room, but he didn't stop there. Instead, he walked outside onto the little covered porch.

"Have a seat, son," he said.

Rafe's heart began to pound. His dad's tone was very serious. In fact, he hadn't seen him this serious since Rafe told him he'd decided not to go to med school.

Rafe sat on the porch swing, bare now of cushions. His dad sat for a moment but was soon up and pacing the porch, clearing his throat and swiping at his eyes.

"Geez, Dad," he finally said. "Are you okay?"

His dad clapped him on the back and took a deep breath. "Son, I can't tell you how proud you've made me." His voice even cracked a little, causing even more guilt to seep into Rafe's bones. If his dad only knew what he was really like, he wouldn't say any such thing.

"Dad—"

His dad held out a hand to stop him. "Let me finish. I'm very proud of the man you've become, Rafe. I know life dealt you a hard blow, but I'm overjoyed to see you've overcome it. I—I don't talk much about losing your mother but I—it was hard. I always like to think she had something to do with sending Rachel to our family. The point being, love comes to us in different ways. And living on after tragedy strikes is hard but worth it."

His dad walked to the porch railing and looked out over Nonna's cozy little street, full of old clapboard houses, picket fences, and tidy little yards. Christmas lights were getting turned on and someone was out walking their dog.

"I proposed to your mother right here on this porch." He glanced up, and Rafe could see his dad was somewhere else, remembering.

"I had planned something a little better at a fancy restaurant, but I got so excited I couldn't wait. I was just bursting to ask her."

"I never heard that story before." His dad had always struck him as logical and regimented. The spontaneity in the story surprised him. "So what happened?"

"Well, look down. What do you see?"

Rafe followed his dad's gaze to the painted wood-slatted floor. He knew it well, because last summer he'd resanded and repainted it for Nonna. "The flooring?"

His dad nodded. "Your mother jumped into my arms and the ring flew out of her hand and..."

"No," Rafe said in disbelief. "It didn't."

His dad nodded and pointed at his feet. "It fell right through that crack between the slats."

"So then what did you do?"

"Well, she told me I had to go down there and get it, and I told her I'd never find it in the dark. But she said after three years of dating all through my residency, Nonna wouldn't believe we were really engaged unless she saw the ring on her finger."

"So you crawled under there and found it, right?"

"With a flashlight. I've never seen so many spiderwebs in my life." He chuckled at the memory. "Your mom had a way with humor, just like you. I know she's looking down on us, so proud of you too."

A lump formed in Rafe's throat. What would his mother think of him now?

His dad reached into his pants pocket and pulled out a little box. Rafe knew exactly what it was. Nonna had shown it to him before, and he knew his dad had been saving it for him. This time, tears pricked behind Rafe's eyes.

He had to come clean. He couldn't accept his mother's engagement ring when there was no engagement, when he couldn't even bring himself to go back to his house and talk with Kaitlyn. "Dad, I—"

His dad motioned toward the box. "Just open it."

Rafe didn't want to, knowing seeing it would only remind him even more of all his faults. But the expectant look on his father's face had him cracking the box open.

The ring was a simple diamond solitaire, round cut, with a gold band.

"Of course," his dad said, "times have changed, so you might want to mount it differently or surround it with tiny diamonds like they do now, or make it a white gold band..."

"It's beautiful, Dad," Rafe said. And it was—simple and elegant, just like Kaitlyn. Remorse swept through him, to have his dad put such faith in him, to say he was proud.

He didn't deserve any of that. But the least he could do was tell his father the truth. "Dad—"

"Hey, Doc," Colton said, sticking his head out the door. "We brought down the other...thing. Everyone wants you two to come in now."

"We'll be right in, Colt," Rafe's dad said. He turned to Rafe. "You chose a great woman. She's brought out the best in you. I love you, son." He hugged him and gave him a slap on the back. "We'd better get inside. It's cold out here."

"Thanks, Dad. I love you too." Rafe pocketed the ring and followed his dad inside, where they found everyone already gathered around the living room waiting for them. The little tree was lit, and someone had put Frank Sinatra Christmas songs on, and the place smelled like baking cookies. It was a setup for a great family holiday. There was an empty spot next to Kaitlyn on the couch, which Rachel urged him into. As he sat down, Kaitlyn subtly moved over so their bodies wouldn't touch. He tried to make eye contact, but she was busy laughing at something Gabby had said.

Rafe's dad looked excited and pleased as he carried a large, heavy object wrapped in Christmas paper over to Kaitlyn and set it at her feet.

"What is it?" She turned to him, trepidation in her voice.

"Open it and find out," he said. She looked radiant,

and he felt a stab of longing for her. And a lead weight of regret for messing everything up between them.

"All righty. Here goes." She tore the last paper away to reveal a solid oak cradle. "Oh, it's beautiful," she said, running her hand along the smooth surface. Examining the rockers.

Rafe swallowed the lump in his throat. "My grandfather made it for my mom when she was a baby. We all used it." He stood to give his dad a hand clasp and hug. "Thanks, Dad."

"Your mom would want you to have it," he said. "So would your grandfather."

"What about the girls?" Rafe looked around at his sisters.

"We already used it for Michael and Julia," Evie said, "and now it's *your* baby's turn, Rafe."

Sara looked at Gabby, who gave a nod. Then Sara said, "Dad asked us and we all thought you should have it."

He hugged his sisters and sat back down next to Kaitlyn. His throat was tight and all he could think of was that one day there'd be a baby sleeping in this beautiful, sturdy cradle that his grandfather had made—*his* baby. If only he could be more worthy of that baby and this woman.

"It's stunning," Kaitlyn said, and as he looked over at her, he saw that she was crying.

He went to put his hand over hers, but she subtly moved it away. "I'm okay," she said. Of course she was.

Nonna stood up, holding a paper-wrapped bundle. "Now I have something for you." She handed it to

Gabby, who was sitting next to her on the couch. "Will you be a dear and pass that over to Kaitlyn?"

"Maybe Rafe should unwrap this one," Kaitlyn said, once she held the soft package.

"No, you," Nonna said. "You do it. I made it while I was convalescing in the hospital."

It was a crocheted baby blanket, done in pastel hues with a very soft, fuzzy yarn. "Ooh, Nonna," Kaitlyn exclaimed, holding it up for everyone to see. "This is gorgeous."

Rafe felt the blanket. "Really soft. Thanks, Nonna."

"I wanted to make it pink, but Rachel discouraged me." She held up a hand. "Even though I *am* always right in my baby predictions."

"This feels like a baby shower. Thank you so much," Kaitlyn said, swiping at her eyes.

"It's not a baby shower," Rachel said. "Because I'm planning a shower for all three of you couples. So if you all aren't registered, get on that."

Registered? He exchanged glances with Kaitlyn. She looked a little hesitant, and like so many other times, it seemed he could tell what she was thinking. His stomach was churning as he bent forward. "I can't do it now," he whispered. "I can't tell them the truth." How could he, after his dad had given him his mom's ring and the heirloom cradle?

"I agree," she said, shaking her head. "Not today."

He couldn't help the feeling of relief that washed over him, even though he had no right to feel it. He stood up and addressed his family. "I wanted to say thank you all so much for welcoming our baby," Rafe said. "We couldn't be happier."

Kaitlyn spoke too, still maintaining her distance. "We're thrilled," she said, smiling a little too widely, although no one would pick up on that but him. "Thanks, everybody!"

Then Gabby jumped up to take cookies out of the oven, and the women headed in to decorate them while the guys all got beers and turned on a game, promising to wash all the dishes as long as they didn't have to decorate any cookies.

Before Kaitlyn could head to the kitchen he stopped her. "I got the report from the asbestos inspector today," he said. "Your apartment's been cleared as safe."

"You mean I could go back and live there?"

"Yes. One more inspector has to do a walk-through in the morning, then you're good to go. But—but you don't have to leave my place." He didn't want her to feel pressed to leave, no matter how awkward things were between them right now. "I mean, it's good for Bandit to have a yard for potty training and—" His words sounded so lame. Was he really using the dog as an excuse to have her stay?

She heaved a big sigh of relief. "No, no, that's terrific news about my apartment. I'll move my stuff out first thing in the morning."

He scanned her face. She looked glad to be done with him. He should be relieved that she was leaving too, but instead he felt out of breath, unable to suck in air, as if someone had just punched him in the gut.

"Come on, Kaitlyn," Gabby called from the kitchen. "You're the only one who knows how to ice these professionally."

"Coming," she called to Gabby. To Rafe, she said, "Thanks for letting me know," giving him a smile that never reached her eyes. "See you later."

Kaitlyn went to join the women. Rafe went to the fridge to get a beer and paused by the kitchen door on his way out. His sisters and Rachel were sitting at the kitchen island, mixing different colors of icing. Kaitlyn laughed hard and loud at something Sara said. Rachel poured Nonna and herself a glass of wine while Evie said she was too full of cookies to drink, and Rachel joked that they were saving a ton of money on wine because no one could drink any.

Rafe was filled with a strange mix of regret and longing despite knowing that he'd failed Kaitlyn in every important way. But he couldn't change who he was. He couldn't be the man she needed.

Just then Kaitlyn glanced up and caught him looking at her. He took a swig of his beer and looked quickly away. Then he walked back into the living room to hang out with the guys.

Chapter 23

♥

The next day, Rafe was home, trying to decide if he wanted to replace the leaky showerhead in his bathroom. Or rather, he was trying to convince himself to get started on the project. He needed a project to get his mind off Kaitlyn leaving. Everything in his house had been cleaned up, with no traces of her remaining except for her packed bags, sitting in a neat row near his front door, and the very faint scent of some kind of holiday bodywash that smelled like peppermint.

He read through the showerhead instructions for the fiftieth time, then finally set them down and stood up, pacing the length of his house. Kitchen, family room, hallway. And back again.

He should be glad she was leaving. Things were awkward between them, and he'd managed to avoid her for most of the week. This was what he wanted... wasn't it?

Just then Kaitlyn walked in, taking off her boots and leaving them near the front door.

"Hi," she said, pressing her lips together. "I didn't know you were going to be here."

"Just got home. I see you're all packed." He'd tried to sound casual, but his voice was laced with regret. Yes, regret. He *hated* looking at those suitcases. He was suddenly overcome with a crazy urge to grab them up, unzip them, and empty them all over the floor so she couldn't leave.

He rubbed his temple. What was he thinking?

"I just have to grab some stuff out of the bathroom," she said. "And Bandit."

Not the puppy. But of course she was taking him too.

She walked into the laundry room to get the dog. But she must've forgotten to secure the gate behind her, because Bandit came tearing out of the laundry room and headed straight down the hall.

They both chased him into the bedroom, where he wasted no time hopping onto the bed and burrowing under the covers.

Kaitlyn began lifting layers of bedding. "Where did he go?"

"Hey, Bandit," Rafe called. "Get over here."

"Don't use a gruff tone," she said. "You'll scare him and he'll burrow down even more."

"That wasn't a gruff tone," Rafe said. Was it?

She held up Bandit's leash, ready to clip it to his collar at a moment's notice. But still no dog.

As they stood there waiting for the dog to surface, Rafe filled the silence by asking, "How are you feeling?"

"Great. I have a follow-up in a couple of days."

"You shouldn't have cleaned."

"It wasn't a problem," she said. "I just tidied up a little."

"Still." Didn't she work enough all day? She didn't need to be cleaning here too.

"You don't have to act so concerned," she said, peeling back bedding layers to get to the puppy, which they could see as a wiggling pot roast–sized lump in the middle of the bed.

"I *am* concerned." Were they really arguing over being concerned? Great. This was a new low point.

She frowned at that. She finally found the dog, scooped him up, and snapped on his leash. "Okay, buddy. Time to go home."

Rafe winced. Home? *This* was her home.

He ran to catch up with her as she headed out. "You know, you don't have to go."

In the front hall, she turned around for a brief moment. "Yes, I do," she said quietly and with an air of determination that almost killed him. "You *know* why I do."

"Stay a minute. Maybe we could—have some tea."

She looked at him like he was crazy. Because he hated tea. And that sounded really lame.

"I have a lot to do before the shelter party tonight," she said, the puppy wiggling in her arms. "There are still some presents to be wrapped for the kids, and I promised to bring Bandit."

"I've got to get my Santa suit ready," he said. He'd finally agreed to do it and that should've sounded upbeat, but it came out the opposite. "Katie," he said, stopping her with his voice. "Maybe we could—talk." There. He'd said it. He wanted to talk. *Needed* to talk.

She looked him over for a heartbeat. But then she turned away to tuck some of Bandit's toys into her bag. "What good would it do, Rafe? We've talked *a lot*," she said softly. She didn't sound angry, only sad, and that skewered him. He'd known that he'd let her down, but now he saw it clearly in her face, heard it in her voice. "You can only give someone what you can give. I understand that. I'm not angry with you. I just need someone who can weather the storms, you know? It's not your fault. I knew how you felt about commitment from the beginning. I just thought..." She lifted her shoulders in a sad little shrug "...we might be able to overcome it." With that, she set the dog down on the floor and slung a bag over her shoulder. "Goodbye, Rafe. I'll see you at the party tonight."

Then she walked out his door for good.

* * *

When Kaitlyn entered her apartment later that day, she found that Rafe had dropped off her suitcases, the broken-down dog crate, and a baby gate for Bandit and left them sitting in front of her door. She stood there for the longest time, unable to open the door, unwilling to go back to the way things were in her life pre-Rafe. But she had a squirming puppy in her hands and the shelter Christmas party to get to, and she couldn't waste time on *what if*s.

There were just so many of them.

"Okay, Bandit," she said, setting him down to scramble around on the wooden floors. "This is your new place. What do you think?" She rolled her suitcases in, and then she stopped in her tracks.

The apartment was spotless. There was no trace of the things she'd left scattered about—clothing, mail, dishes. Her shoes were lined up neatly in a plastic boot tray—a sure sign of Rafe's doing. The puppy immediately grabbed a shoe and ran, indicating that his sock fetish had now spread to include shoes, but at the moment she was tearing up too much to care. Finally she walked over to the window. The new caulking was neat and tidy, and Rafe had installed new blinds on the windows. Nice, fashionable blinds that actually worked.

And then there was the baby's room. The track lighting was done, the holes in the ceiling gone, and in the corner was the cradle. In the cradle sat a little stuffed dog—one that looked exactly like Bandit.

She sat down on the couch. Bandit immediately hopped onto her lap and settled in. She gave him a few pats and picked up her phone. She had an hour before she had to be at the shelter. She wondered if Rafe was already there, practicing his Santa act. He'd be great in the role, and she'd have to steel her heart against the sight of him laughing and charming the kids.

She wondered if he'd try to get her to talk again tonight. But after she'd pushed him away, there was no guarantee that he'd try again. Yet he'd gotten her apartment ready for their child. What did it all mean?

"Yoo-hoo," came a voice at her door. Kaitlyn turned to see her mom walking in with a couple of grocery bags. The puppy darted off her lap and ran to give her an enthusiastic greeting.

Her mom made her way over to the couch, setting down her bags on the kitchen counter. "I stopped by to see if I could help you unpack, and...oh dear. You look terrible."

"I don't look terrible," Kaitlyn said, folding her arms, a move that took her back to her teenage years.

"What's wrong?" her mom asked, lowering herself onto the couch. "You want to talk about it?"

Kaitlyn suddenly found tears dripping down her cheeks as she spilled everything she'd held in for so long. "The engagement's not real, Mom. It was something we did for Nonna in the hospital."

The confusion on her mom's face made her feel even worse. "I'm sorry," she continued. "We kept trying to find a time to tell the truth, but things kept happening...and, for a while, things were really good and we thought...I thought..." She finished on a sob.

Her mom passed her a tissue box that was sitting on an end table. "But...the puppy. You two bought a puppy together. And a tree. A tree! How..."

"When I had that scare, he just...withdrew. He said he couldn't handle losing someone he loved again."

Her mom looked around the apartment. "But he somehow found time to do all this?"

"For the baby." She tried to sound matter-of-fact, but her voice cracked on the word *baby*. Because she wanted him to have done it for her too.

Her mom frowned deeply. "Kaitlyn, Rafe loves you."

"Rafe *tries* to love me, but he's too...damaged. But he tried to talk to me today, and I pushed him away."

"He may have freaked out about your scare. But he didn't leave, did he?"

"Mom, I need someone who's going to be there for me. You should have seen him in the hospital. He barely held it together."

"Because he loves you. Because he's afraid to lose you." She let that sink in before continuing. "You know, I raised you to be independent because I was *not* independent when I got pregnant. I married your father because I was frightened that I wouldn't survive on my own with a child. I wasn't done with my degree and I had no job. I was basically terrified. Getting married seemed like the most reasonable solution for everyone, but it wasn't. And all that made me determined that I would raise strong, independent women."

"You did, Mom." Kaitlyn thought of something else. "And you're a strong, independent woman too."

"Well, thank you," she said, waving the compliment away, "but that doesn't change the fact that I screwed up in forcing all this independence talk down your throat."

Kaitlyn jerked up her head.

"You've accomplished so much, and I'm very proud of your accomplishments. But you're not me. And Rafe is definitely not your father. You two love each other. But sometimes you can use your independence to push people away—to keep from getting hurt. Marriage is give and take. No one's perfect. Rafe is trying to tell you he loves you."

"How do you know that?"

"I may not have found true love, but I can see when

two people have it. I see it in the way he looks at you when you share a private joke. The way you two finish each other's sentences. The way you look at each other when you don't think the other one's looking. I don't believe this is insurmountable. I don't believe he's damaged for life. But if you let your pride keep you from hearing him out, you'll never know, will you?"

"Hey, what's going on?" Hazel asked, walking in and unbuttoning her coat. She was wearing a fancy curly scarf made of sparkly green-and-blue variegated yarn, and her plain navy knit cap had blue and green feathers tucked into the side.

"Hazel, I have to tell you something," Kaitlyn said, as Hazel sat down on the couch. "Rafe and I aren't really engaged. That was something we did for Nonna when she was sick and the whole thing got out of control. I'm sorry I didn't tell you sooner."

"Wait, but...you and Rafe..." She frowned, trying to puzzle it all out.

"Aren't together," Kaitlyn finished. Hazel had to see that she was just as fallible as everyone else. Maybe more so.

"Oh," Hazel said quietly. "I'm so sorry. I hope you two can work it out because Rafe is cool. And hot. But...whatever happens, you're going to be a great mom."

"I haven't exactly been a great example for you."

"Actually," Hazel said, fishing into her coat pocket, "you've been a great example." She pulled out a piece of paper folded in fours, which she carefully unfolded.

Hazel held the paper in her lap. "I watched you pour

your heart out into this cookie contest, putting in long hours even after you worked all day. You never gave up. And you didn't give up on me either." She passed the paper to Kaitlyn.

Kaitlyn took the paper but didn't look at it, pleased for a lot of reasons. That Hazel was a lot different than when she first came. That she appeared to have left her life of crime behind. That she was sweet and special. And Kaitlyn didn't really care what the paper was. She only hoped that Hazel had somehow managed to pass her math class.

The paper turned out to be an acceptance letter. To the Fashion Institute of Technology, in New York City.

"Hazel, I . . . this is amazing." Kaitlyn was speechless. She glanced from the paper to Hazel's gleaming eyes. "You got in early admission to FIT? This is incredible!"

Hazel grinned from ear to ear and clapped her hands. "I didn't want to say anything because I never thought it would happen but . . . it happened. Thanks to you, Aunt Kate. And Gram."

"Sweetheart," Kaitlyn's mother said, "you're . . . amazing. I'm so proud."

"Oh, honey," Kaitlyn said. "I'm so proud too. This is the best news ever."

"Oh, I almost forgot," Hazel said. She pulled out a tiny package and handed it to Kaitlyn. "For the baby."

Kaitlyn opened it to find a pair of tiny crocheted baby booties. They were a soft beige with a tiny crocheted flower on each one.

"They're made of organic cotton, and they come in

four colors right now, and they're flying like hotcakes off of my Etsy site."

"How did you learn to make these?" Kaitlyn's mother asked.

"Nonna taught me. And these are going to help pay for some of my college expenses."

They were all hugging and crying in the middle of the living room when Bandit ran in with the ear of the stuffed dog in his mouth and deposited it at Kaitlyn's feet.

"Thanks, Bandit," she said, petting his back and picking up the stuffed toy. He looked very pleased at his good deed.

"That dog is a little heart stealer," Kaitlyn's mother said.

Just like Rafe. Rafe had stolen her heart a long time ago, before she even understood anything about love. Before she'd understood that love meant accepting people's imperfections and always striving to be better. She wanted to do better. She'd pushed him away, and she wondered if it was too late for another chance.

* * *

The women's shelter was housed in an old Tudor mansion on the other side of downtown. At five o'clock on the Friday before Christmas, it was teeming with firefighters, cops, and their families, all of whom had spearheaded a big effort to round up toys and make a fun evening for the kids. Rachel was playing Christmas carols on the piano, Jazz had brought some therapy dogs, firefighters had come early to assemble bikes and other big toys for the kids, and Lou's had just delivered fifty boxes of pizza.

Kids and dogs were running everywhere, a big group of seniors from a retirement community had come to do things like make balloon animals and play games with the kids, and a big chorus of "Santa Claus Is Comin' to Town" started up as the excitement built for the kids to see Santa.

Kaitlyn felt a tug on her pants leg. "Excuse me, but can we have another cookie?" asked two adorable twin girls who looked to be around four as they stopped to pet Bandit. "Of course," Kaitlyn said as she walked over to a table to grab a tray and bring it down to their eye level. On it were a bunch of snowcap cookies she'd baked and frozen over the past few weeks (only the good batches, of course).

"Can the puppy have one?" one of them asked, giggling as the dog licked at her fingers.

"Oh, I'm sorry, but dogs aren't allowed to have chocolate," Kaitlyn said.

"Is Santa on the way?" asked the other, biting into a cookie.

"Yeah, because we've been waiting for a whole year," the other one said.

"That's a long time to be good, isn't it?" Kaitlyn said, and the girls nodded vehemently. "He'll be here very soon," Kaitlyn said. "Don't stop being good," she called, as they skipped away.

Bandit was a big hit with the kids, which made Kaitlyn feel a little better, but she kept looking around for

Rafe. She wanted to take him up on his offer to talk, tea or no tea. The problem was, it was a half hour before Santa was supposed to show up and ... still no Rafe.

Nonna drained her glass of eggnog and came up to Kaitlyn. "This is the best eggnog I've ever had. But where's Santa Claus?"

"Good question," Kaitlyn said. "I'd better go find out."

In the kitchen, Gabby and Sara were helping bring out boxes of pizza, and they had no idea where Rafe was either. She ran into Colton just coming through the door from outside.

"Colt!" she called. "Can you text Rafe? I left my phone in my car, and he's still not here. Have you seen him?"

Colton checked his phone. "No, nothing." He sent off a quick text. "Maybe he fell asleep?" A frown shaded his brows. "It's not like him to be late for anything."

As she waited for Colton to call Rafe, a strange chill ran through her—an eerie premonition of worry, which she tried to shrug off. It was probably that she was on edge and upset anyway. She'd been looking for him around every corner.

"Evan's out on patrol," Colton said, punching in Rafe's number for the second time. "Rafe's not picking up. I'm going to have Evan run over to Rafe's house and see if he fell asleep."

"Okay," Kaitlyn said. She walked over to visit with Cade and Ava, who were watching over Bandit, but returned a minute later, unable to wait any longer. "Any word?" she asked.

"Evan's just coming on duty. He's going to ride by Rafe's house as soon as he can." He gave Kaitlyn a compassionate look. "Hey, you're starting to act like a worrywart like Rafe. He's fine. Everyone oversleeps once in their life."

Still, she couldn't shake off her concern.

Colton ended up having to put on the Santa suit. As he walked out of the bathroom and into the kitchen, it was apparent the legs were a bit too long on him, because Rafe was so tall.

"Let's put more stuffing on your belly," Sara said, playfully squeezing the rounded lump. "That might help."

Colton sent her a look that said he wasn't quite sure about being rotund and jolly.

She kissed him on the cheek. "I love you whether you have a squishy belly or not," she said.

"Hey, Chief, I think you're getting lax on the push-ups," Cade said, just to get his goat.

Colton mumbled something like, "Where's Rafe? I'm going to kill him for this," but he was smiling as he said it.

While Colton was assuming the role, Kaitlyn held the puppy and allowed the kids to gently pet him, something they did with a happy sense of awe and a surprising sense of order. Bandit was on his best behavior until a small child asked Kaitlyn if he had time to go to the bathroom before Santa came. Distracted, Kaitlyn must have loosened her hold on the puppy, who jumped up in the flash of a second and stole a slice of pizza right out of another child's hands.

"That's why he's called Bandit!" one of the kids said, and that made everyone else laugh.

Cade, who was close by, quickly stepped in with a plate of cookies to avoid any tears, and everyone ended up laughing more as the rambunctious little puppy continued to charm.

Colton came out with a deep *ho-ho-ho*, which made all the kids scream in anticipation. He visited with every single child and joked around with many of them.

"He's a great Santa," Kaitlyn said to Sara. "I'm really impressed."

"Even if his pants *are* a little long," Gabby said.

"See, Kaitlyn," Sara said, beaming at her husband as he made a child giggle. "Once these guys fall in love, they love completely."

That comment just about tore Kaitlyn's heart out. She thought about how she'd passed off Rafe's efforts to talk with her, and the foreboding feeling that she'd managed to push down came surging back up again.

Everyone had their fill of pizza and cookies, and the guys helped install batteries in all the toys, some of which had flashing lights and made a lot of noise, adding to the happy chaos. Colton was just taking off the Santa suit when his phone rang.

Kaitlyn, keyed into Colton's reactions, watched his smile drop and his brows knit down in worry.

"What? What is it?" she asked, grabbing his arm. Because she knew something was wrong, down to her bones. She just *knew*.

Colt pocketed his phone and took hold of Kaitlyn's shoulders, a move he'd surely meant to be reassuring but which helped freak her out more. "There's a fire in the farm machinery warehouse on the highway between here and Clydesburg. It started small but then the adjacent buildings caught. And Rafe is inside."

"Colton, no," Kaitlyn said. The world suddenly went mute, like she had water stuck in her ears. She was vaguely aware of Cade relieving her of the dog's leash. Sara and Gabby immediately flocked to her side.

"Rafe knows what he's doing," Colton said, keeping a hand on her shoulder. "He'll be fine."

Kaitlyn let out a sob, then covered her mouth, not wanting to make a scene in front of the kids.

"It's okay, honey," Gabby said. "Rafe will be fine." But she was crying too.

"I want to go there," Kaitlyn said. "I'm going there now."

An arm came around her shoulder. "We're all going," Dr. Langdon said. "I'll drive."

Chapter 24

♥

Randy!" Rafe yelled his buddy's name into his radio but got no answer. Through a weird twist of fate, Rafe found himself suited up in his turnout gear in the middle of a burning warehouse instead of in a Santa suit at the shelter kids' Christmas party. The mutual aid call for the four-alarm fire had gone out to all the surrounding counties just as Rafe had been driving to the party. He'd had just enough time to pull into the station and ride the engine with the Angel Falls crew.

As he made his way through a wall of thick black smoke, the irony wasn't lost on him that he probably got exactly the evening he deserved. He knew he'd screwed up with Kaitlyn. But his only goal now was to do his job, get out of here alive, and make things right. And to do that, he had to block everything else out of his mind.

Visibility was worse than a whiteout snowstorm. Except this was blackout, and he could barely see farther than the tip of his nose. The fire had already eaten through most of the wall in front of them and was now savaging the left half of the building. Their job had been to take a hose line in together through a doorway to attack the south end of the building. But where was Randy?

Rafe followed the hose line, taking care to stay as far away as he could from the tall shelving units loaded with boxes and parts for farm machinery. "Come on, buddy," he said into his radio. "You still owe me a beer from crawling under that porch a few weeks ago."

Rafe couldn't help but think about how much his life had changed since then—for the better, in a hundred different ways he couldn't begin to describe, all because of Kaitlyn. He couldn't think of that now—of *her*. Or how he'd screwed it all up.

A loud, piercing noise sounded over the roar of the fire and made Rafe curse. It was the alarm device on an air pack, *Randy's* air pack, and it was a sound of dread, because it meant he was definitely down. With a mixture of fear and apprehension, Rafe followed the sound to where his buddy lay slumped on the floor. Machinery parts that had crashed down from nearby shelving units were scattered all around him. His helmet was knocked off, indicating that something had likely hit him on the head.

Rafe's heart sank as he saw that Randy's mask had gotten knocked off too. How long had he been without his mask? "No," he said, refusing to believe the worst. He bent low over his friend's face, listening for breath, looking for chest movement. "Hey, you ugly mutt," he said, sighing in relief when he saw him breathe, "you'd better not die on me, you hear?" He carefully replaced his friend's mask, found his helmet a few feet away, and put that back on too.

A loud clatter made Rafe look up just in time to see the huge shelves shifting, chunks of burning debris and drywall falling, scalding hot sparks bursting like fireworks. With horror, Rafe watched a ceiling beam split and tumble down toward them, taking with it more pieces of red-hot drywall. Summoning all his strength, he shoved Randy and himself out of the way, just as the beam crashed down.

With a sudden blow, Rafe was thrown flat on the ground, pain shooting through his leg. Twisting his body, he realized his right foot was pinned under the massive beam, which had fallen across the doorway, blocking their way out. He yanked and pulled and pushed, using his other leg as leverage, but his foot wouldn't budge.

Randy, thank God, was lying a good distance from the fallen beam. But now luck was not on Rafe's side. Pinned and separated from help, he saw fire advancing from the south wall. Things were not looking good.

Rafe tugged hard, struggling to release his foot. This could not be the end. He wasn't going to die here never having told Kaitlyn how he felt. He couldn't leave her wondering if he ever loved her.

For all that time, he'd held back. Never admitted his feelings to himself or to her. Even when she was leaving his house this morning, he could have told her what was in his heart. Even when she was angry and pushing him away, he could have said he loved her, but he'd been too afraid.

And now he would never have the chance.

The irony, he realized now, was that all this time he'd kept her at arm's length, afraid to fall, afraid to love. But the truth was, he already did.

It was too late to try to protect himself because he loved her with all his heart. And he loved their baby.

He wanted that life—that life with her in it every single day. With their baby. And the puppy. With more babies and more dogs. He wanted it all. He did not want to die without ever telling her how much he loved her and their child.

The ceiling above them cracked and groaned, more evidence of the warehouse giving its final death knell. He was running out of time.

He pulled again at his boot. Yanked harder, with all his muscle, all his might, thinking of Kaitlyn, of everything he still needed to say. And then he prayed.

It just wasn't enough.

With one hand, he pulled his ax out of its scabbard. He hacked over and over, trying to free up enough of the beam so he could pull his foot out. Then he tugged on his foot again, but no give.

He loosened his laces and worked his foot back and forth, over and over. Finally, it gave and came free, sending him tumbling backward from the force.

Rafe scrambled to his feet knowing he had no margin for error. The warehouse had windows, but where were they? He grabbed Randy's air pack straps and dragged him away from the fallen beam, in the opposite direction of the door, praying he was right. A straight shot. He knew where he had to go. What he had to do to get out.

Please, God, help me find the window.

He hit a wall and groped frantically. He felt wall, more wall, and then finally...finally the texture of smooth, thin glass.

Chunks of ceiling were starting to rain down around them like fireballs. Rafe used his ax to shatter the glass and hack at the sharp shards. Lifting Randy into a fireman's carry around his shoulders, clutching Randy's arm to his chest, he half climbed, half tumbled out of the window, onto grass and snow, Randy tumbling with him. Rafe righted himself and, limping, dragged his buddy away from the collapsing building, the fire and smoke, the danger.

Suddenly there were hands, so many hands, grabbing Randy, grabbing him. Then he was carried out and away and lifted onto a stretcher. The paramedics were helping him out of his coat, his pants, his one good boot, placing a mask on him, and doing something to his foot, which was suddenly beginning to hurt like hell.

All he knew was he was alive. Maggie McDougal, Jon's wife from the Tap, was on duty and tending to him, and he grabbed her by the arm. Yanking off his mask, he asked her if Randy was all right. She glanced over her shoulder at the other team of paramedics working on Randy. "He hit his head pretty badly, but he's alive and breathing," she said as she replaced Rafe's mask. "That's all I know right now."

He grasped Maggie's arm again. "I need Kaitlyn."

"She's here, big guy," she said, sounding a little teary, patting Rafe's arm. "She's right here."

Maggie affixed an IV bag to the pole near his head and stepped aside. Suddenly Kaitlyn was beside him, a panicked look in her eyes that he hoped he'd never see again. And he swore that he'd do everything in his power to make that happen. She barreled into his arms and clung to him. He pulled off his O2 again and wrapped his arms around her.

"Katie," he said, holding her tightly, burying his face in her hair. "Katie."

"Rafe," she said, spilling tears onto his T-shirt. When he pulled back, he saw she had tear streaks all down her face, and her nose was running. And she was the most beautiful woman he'd ever seen.

"I love you," he said, grasping for her, threading his hands in her hair. "I love you," he repeated, pulling back a little, making sure she saw in his eyes that this was for real. "I love our baby. I want our life together." His voice cracked. "And I'm so, so sorry for what I put you through." He could not hold her tightly enough. He smoothed her hair, kissed her forehead, wiped her tears with his thumbs.

"Rafe—I'm sorry I pushed you away. I knew you wanted to say something—I didn't give you a chance."

"Being in that fire made me realize something—that it's too late for me to worry about holding back." He looked deeply into her eyes. "Because I already love you with all my heart. I have for a long time. You're my everything. I'll do whatever it takes to prove to you that I'm here for the long haul."

* * *

Kaitlyn felt like she was dreaming those words. Dreaming this entire night, with all its terror and now, all the relief. She clutched at him, ran her hands up and down his chest to prove to herself he was really okay. "I love you too, Rafe. I've always loved you."

She lowered her lips to his. Rafe curled his hand around her neck and brought her close, kissing her full and hard on the mouth, a kiss full of joy and happiness and the promise of many more to come.

"Okay, lovebirds," Maggie said, slipping his mask back on for the third time. "Time for more vitamin O2, big guy."

"Is he—is he going to be all right?" Kaitlyn asked. She looked up to suddenly find all the Langdons gathered around. Rachel and Dr. Langdon were up front, Dr. Langdon checking Rafe's heart monitor and oxygen saturation and asking Maggie details about his condition. Rachel stood wringing her hands, flanked by Colton and Cade. Sara and Gabby were both bawling. Evie and Joe each held one of Nonna's hands.

"How is he?" Nonna asked.

"His foot's pretty messed up," Gabby said, cracking a smile. "But it looks like the rest of him isn't anymore."

"Thanks, Gabs," Rafe said, pulling off his mask to talk. "Hey, everybody. I'm fine," he said, giving a wave. He *was* fine. The finest he'd been in a very long time. He laced his fingers around Kaitlyn's. "Don't leave, okay?" he murmured, just as Maggie wheeled him to the ambulance.

"Never," she said.

"How's Randy now?" he asked Maggie.

"Conscious and ornery," Maggie said, the corner of her mouth quirking up. "Just like you."

"Thank God," Rafe said, finally leaning back onto the gurney and closing his eyes.

* * *

Kaitlyn closed the blinds at the Bean at eight on Christmas Eve. "I think we're done," she said to Rafe, who was loading the dishwasher and sanitizing the cream pitchers, even though he was limping a little on his bandaged foot.

She peeked through the slats in the blinds. Giant, fat flakes of snow were falling and starting to stick. They couldn't have asked for a more perfect Christmas, even though the snow was just the icing on the cake. "It's beginning to snow. And oh—the FedEx guy's pulling up."

The bell over the door rang, and Larry, her usual FedEx delivery guy, walked in, dusting snow off his jacket.

"Hey, Larry," she said, heading behind the counter. "I still have some coffee left. Want a cup to go?"

"I'd love some," Larry said, stamping the snow off his feet. "I still have a half-dozen deliveries left." He slid an envelope across the counter to Kaitlyn. She placed a handful of cookies in a bag and passed them over the counter with a to-go cup. "Trade you," she said, smiling.

"Thanks," he said, taking the coffee and cookies. "Merry Christmas to you both."

"Merry Christmas, Larry," Rafe said.

Rafe opened the door for Larry and then locked it behind him. Then he flipped off the overhead lights, turning the Bean into a twinkly Christmas wonderland, illuminated by the strings of colored lights that ran over the counters and crisscrossing the old ceiling tiles.

Kaitlyn stood in front of the counter, her arms folded. "It's pretty Christmasy in here," she said.

"We should do something," he said, waggling his eyebrows suggestively.

"Well, the floors *do* need to be swept," she said, biting down on her lip to keep from laughing.

"Um, not what I had in mind," he said, stepping closer.

"How about the counters. We could *definitely* scrub the counters," she said, tapping a finger to her lips in mock consideration.

"I had something a little more romantic in mind."

He kissed her, a slow, wonderful kiss, his lips just grazing hers before he pulled away.

She opened one eye. "Why did you stop?"

"It's more Christmasy at home. What do you say we get out of here, go turn on the tree, and make out on the couch?" He came closer and rested his hands on her hips. Nuzzled her neck until she arched just from the sheer pleasure of it. As she wrapped her arms around his neck, the envelope dropped to the floor.

Rafe bent to pick it up, his eyes suddenly widening as he straightened up to his full height. "Katie, you're not going to believe this." He passed the cardboard envelope over to her. "Open it."

She glanced from Rafe to the envelope and back again before she finally tore it open, using the perforations. The return address read "Famous Cookie Company." She stared at the envelope. Then at him. "It's the contest."

She nearly dropped the envelope. "My hands are shaking," she said, shoving it into his hands. "You open it."

Rafe reached in with his hand, only to pull out another sealed envelope.

"Open it, Rafe," she whispered. She sat there on the counter, shielding her eyes with her hands, holding her breath, waiting for what felt like an eternity for Rafe to read the letter to her.

When she finally got up the courage to look, he was staring at her, breaking into a huge grin. "Well, I'll be."

Kaitlyn tried to see the paper over his shoulder but couldn't. "What? What is it?" Did they send rejection letters by FedEx? She had no idea.

A giant grin lit Rafe's handsome face, nearly making her forget all about the contest. "You won," he said quietly.

"I won?" That wasn't really computing until Rafe picked her up from the counter and twirled her around the café.

"Yep," he said, nodding. His dark eyes shone with excitement. She put a hand over her heart because it felt full to bursting.

"You won it all," Rafe said, opening his arms wide and laughing incredulously. "The money, the pastry classes. The whole contest. The grand fricking prize. Congratulations."

She jumped into his arms and kissed him good and hard.

"You're amazing, you know that?" Rafe said, kissing her back. "You didn't give up—on experimenting or on finding the recipe. Brava for you."

"I hit the jackpot," she said. "But not because of a cookie recipe." Then she kissed him on the lips.

* * *

It didn't take Kaitlyn long to collect her things from her apartment and move them back to Rafe's. Later that night, after they had taken full advantage of making out near the Christmas tree, she entered their bedroom to find Rafe sitting up in bed wearing a plain white T-shirt and scrub pants, his bandaged foot propped up on pillows. He was reading one of those thrillers he was so fond of, which would be the last thing she'd ever read before trying to fall sleep.

The sight of him in his reading glasses unexpectedly bowled her over, making warmth diffuse through her chest and spread everywhere, because surely there was nothing sexier than a big, burly firefighter with reading glasses—and he was all hers.

She lay down next to him and rested her head in the crook of his arm. She couldn't help but notice how perfectly she fit there. A little sigh of contentment escaped her as she settled in next to him. "I can't wait to see my sister tomorrow," she said. "I'm so glad she was able to fly in."

"Hazel seemed excited to see her mom too. It's been a long six months."

Kaitlyn nodded. "I think she's going to be okay."

Rafe half frowned. "What makes you say that?"

"Because she told me she's getting so many orders for her organic baby booties she's going to have to hire out the crocheting. She's even commissioned Nonna to make some."

"Is that right?" he said, absently stroking his arm. "Well, I'm not surprised. Love can turn anybody around."

"I'm just glad she's happy." She looked over at him. "You're really cute when you read, but are you going to be doing that much longer?"

A wry grin lit his face. "Can't stay away from me, can you?"

She gave a pretend huff and crossed her arms. "Well, if you're going to be cocky about it, just keep reading."

"Oh, hey," he said, casually glancing up. "I have something for you."

She immediately sat up. "Is it a surprise?" she asked, rubbing her hands together expectantly.

He shut his book and smiled down at her. "Nah, I wouldn't say so."

"Well, what is it?" she asked.

He reached behind his pillow and handed her a small box. *The* box. The kind of box that made her heart thud crazily in her ears and her hands tremble. She looked at him, wide-eyed. "Rafe, I—"

"Open it," he whispered.

She didn't hesitate. She cracked it open to find a beautiful diamond ring, simple and perfect. "I love it."

"It was my mom's," he said. "You can change the setting any way you want to make it yours, of course."

"It's perfect," she said, tearing up, seeing in his eyes how much this meant to him. "And—I love the simplicity of it. Just the way it is. I feel honored to wear your mom's ring."

Rafe nodded at that, and he too seemed to be fighting back emotion. She kissed him and stroked his face gently with the back of her hand. "I love it. And I love you."

"I think I forgot to ask the question," he said, kissing her back. Looking into her eyes, he asked, "Will you marry me, Kaitlyn?"

"Yes," she said, punctuating her answer with a kiss. "Yes, yes, and yes." And many more kisses followed.

Afterward, he took up his book again, absently stroking her arm while she lay next to him, enjoying being nestled in the crook of his arm and occasionally rotating her fingers so her ring caught the light and sparkled a million different ways.

"Next Christmas is going to be a lot different," she mused. "The baby will be here, the puppy will be *big*...and maybe we'll invite Hazel and Nikki to stay with us. Would that be okay with you?"

"What's a couple more with all the rest of the chaos?"

Rafe pulled off his glasses and focused his gaze on her. She felt flooded with love, and in that moment, she knew two things.

One, that she truly loved this man, with her whole heart and soul. That what she'd felt in the beginning in her blind crush was nothing compared to what she felt now that she truly knew him. The second was that Rafe was hers, completely and fully hers. The funny, joking Rafe was back, just the way he was when they were friends... except now they were more. So much more.

"I don't know about you, but I'm really looking forward to all of that," he said.

"All of what?" she asked.

"To all of it, Katie. All of...life. To doing it all with you." He turned—a little awkwardly because of his foot—to wrap both his arms around her. Then he kissed her forehead.

"How's your foot feeling?" she asked.

"It's hurting a little."

"Oh no," she said. "Poor thing."

He grimaced. "Yeah, it's pretty painful." He paused and gave her a deeply meaningful look. "I think I might need a kiss."

She climbed on top of him and pulled the edges of his T-shirt up, sliding her hands up the warm, sculpted muscles of his chest. "I can think of something else that might help you forget the pain," she said.

"I can't wait," he said, settling his hands on her hips.

But instead of kissing him, she wiggled out of his grasp, climbed off the bed, and ran out of the room, returning with a present.

"Merry Christmas," she said. "It's just something little."

He opened it to find the photo of them kissing at the falls, backlit by white twinkling lights, the angel statue behind them, making a heart with its wings.

He propped the photo up on the nightstand. "That was the night of our first date."

She rested a hand on her belly. "What do you mean?"

"What I mean is, it was the first night we *chose* to go on a date, we didn't just let things happen. That's what I'll always think of when I see this."

"I also enjoyed our first pre-date," she said, making air quotes for *pre-date*.

"We've known each other for twenty years. What's a pre-date?"

She shot him a poignant look.

"Oh, wait." She saw the second he got what she meant. "You mean . . . the wedding?"

She nodded. "We can re-create that. Like, we can turn out the lights and pretend it's a blackout."

"You're on," he said. "Except we might have to be a little creative with my foot all wrapped up."

"I can do creative," she said.

"Oh, I almost forgot," he said, reaching under the bed. "I have something else for you too."

She flashed her ring finger. "Isn't this enough for one day?"

"Hey, it's Christmas. This is a Christmas present." He twisted his back a little to lift a big rectangular box from under the bed.

She frowned. "But my present wasn't—"

He placed a finger on her lips and looked lovingly into her eyes, which made her think that he was the only thing she wanted, would ever want. Him. Just him.

"You gave me everything for Christmas, Katie," he said. "I know you hate accepting gifts. But it's something I really want you to have. And to use every day, not just for special occasions. All right?"

It seemed important to him, so she sighed and said, "I love it already, because you seemed to put so much thought into it." Then she tore into it.

It was the gorgeous camel-colored coat. Wrapped in an elegant nest of tissue paper that even smelled wonderful, like lavender. She climbed off the bed and unfolded it, running her hands up and down its gorgeous, soft length, then sat next to him on the bed. "I love it," she said, rubbing her chin against the soft furry collar. "I'm thrilled you want me to have it."

"Try it on," he said.

She ran into the bathroom and came back with it on. And she just might've left her pj's on the bathroom floor, but she didn't tell him that.

"What do you think?" she asked, climbing over him and leaning down low so that she was very near—close enough to see the tiny crinkles around his eyes, the fullness of his lips, the strength of his stubbled jaw, and the extreme tenderness in his eyes.

"I love it," he whispered, tucking a strand of hair behind her ear, running his fingertips down her cheek, and wrapping his hand around her neck to draw her even closer.

"I need some help with the buttons," she said, and of course, being a gentleman, he complied, unfastening them and peeling back one side of the coat.

"Wow. Oh, wow," he said, settling his hands on her hips. "Merry Christmas to me."

Kaitlyn laughed as he drew her in for a kiss. She sat up and ran her hand along the fine, soft material of the coat. "I really love it," she said, as his hands strayed over her warm skin, leaving a trail of tingles everywhere, splaying across her abdomen where their baby grew.

"But Rafe," she said, her voice cracking a little as he moved again to kiss her, "all I really ever wanted for Christmas was you."

He gave a soft chuckle. "Merry Christmas, Katie. I love you."

The expensive coat hit the floor with a soft thud.

And then they made it the best Christmas of all.

Epilogue

♥

One Year Later

Rafe's voice awakened Kaitlyn from a sound sleep. "Katie, wake up," he said. Something nudged her on the shoulder. Rafe's hand. "Am I late for work?" she asked, rolling over, away from the bathroom light, which Rafe had just flicked on. The cool air from the bedroom invaded the cozy heat under the covers, and she drew them back up around her shoulders.

"Merry Christmas," he said, bending down to kiss her cheek, smoothing her hair back. "I let you sleep for as long as I could." Kaitlyn opened her eyes to gray light streaming in the windows—a Christmas morning dawn.

Kaitlyn, smiling at his kisses, finally sat up in bed. Rafe sat next to her, handing her a cup of coffee. Now that they were married, there was no need to set the alarm-clock coffee maker. *He* was often her coffee maker now. And he made it just the way she liked it.

"I let you sleep in," Rafe said, the cries of a fussy baby in the background. "We had cereal and peaches except now she wants milk."

"Thank you for letting me sleep. I'll be right there," she said. After Kaitlyn used the bathroom, she walked into the living room to find Rafe standing in front of the Christmas tree, their seven-month-old daughter in his arms. Bandit was asleep on the tree skirt. Rafe wore flannel pj pants and a white T-shirt, and he was barefoot, his thick dark hair still tussled from sleep. The sheer masculinity of his tall form holding the tiny baby made her pause in her rush. But hearing him talk to their baby daughter made her heart melt.

"Your mama was wearing a blue dress. Just about the shade of your bunny sleeper there, princess. And she was the prettiest woman at the whole wedding, yes she was."

Intrigued, Kaitlyn paused.

"So then I asked her to dance, and as soon as I held her in my arms and took her hand in mine, I knew I would never be able to let her go. And oh, I really tried. But she was all wrapped around my heart, right from the start. Just like you are." He kissed their child on her little blond head.

"Ba!" Baby Rose said, reaching toward all the shiny ornaments on the tree. Many of which had Rafe's grade-school face glued to Popsicle sticks and Styrofoam cups. "Bababababa!"

He cupped the back of the baby's head and turned around. When he saw Kaitlyn, his face flushed a little.

"Rafe," Kaitlyn said, busted for listening in.

"Kaitlyn." The corners of his mouth turned up in a little smile. "I didn't hear you. I was just telling Rose the G-rated story of the night she came into being." Baby

Rose saw her mama and tilted her whole body toward her, starting up a bunch of jabbering and waving her arms. Rafe laughed. "I tried to hold her off but she's *hungry*. And she's clearly excited to see you."

Kaitlyn kissed her daughter's sweet head and smiled. "That's because I have breakfast, don't I?" Kaitlyn sat down on the couch and unbuttoned her pj top and unhitched her nursing bra.

She held her hands out for her daughter. "Come here, little one." She put the baby to her breast and let out a sigh when the baby began nursing. Rafe came and sat next to her, stroking Rose's downy head as she nursed.

They heard the tinkling of dog tags as Bandit got up and walked into the kitchen. The sounds of him lapping up water came through loud and clear. Then they heard another noise.

"What was that?" Kaitlyn asked.

"That sounded like the high chair scraping the floor," Rafe said.

Before Rafe could get up from the couch, the dog trotted back in with the baby's bib in his mouth. Pleased as can be, he deposited it solidly on Rafe's lap.

"Good dog," Rafe said, rubbing Bandit's head. He bent low to examine the dog, who'd grown quite a lot in the past year. "Are those peaches in your fur?"

Kaitlyn snorted. "Guess it's your turn to clean up," she said with a smug smile. "Since I'm...occupied."

He tossed his head back and laughed. Then he sat back and wrapped his arms around her and Rose. "You've filled up my whole life, Katie, in ways I never could've imagined," he said, looking at her in a way she never would have dreamed was possible just a year earlier. "You and Rose and our crazy dog are my life, and I wouldn't want it any other way."

"Oh, Rafe," she said, trying not to cry but failing. "You and the baby are everything to me. I love you so much. I love our life together."

He stroked her hair and kissed the top of her head. "I love our life together too." She always knew he'd had the capacity to love, but she'd had no idea how much. Once Rafe opened his heart, he'd opened it wide as the sky. And that had made her own heart full to bursting.

The baby nursed on the other side and nodded off to sleep and Kaitlyn took her back to her crib. Suddenly Rafe was behind her, silently taking hold of her hands and leading her to their bedroom.

"Merry Christmas, Kaitlyn," he said, flashing a twinkle in his eye that he always got when he wanted to...

"Um, don't we have to get ready for brunch at Nonna's?" she asked, already melting inside at his touch.

"We can be a little late," Rafe said, guiding her to the bed and unbuttoning her pj top. "We can blame it on the baby."

"Good excuse."

He kissed her neck, finding the sweet spot that she loved.

"Well, maybe we *can* be a little late," she said, arching her neck so he could kiss her more thoroughly.

* * *

Nonna's dining room on Christmas day was full of noise, family, and laughter, the kind Rafe remembered from all the Christmases of his childhood. Cade was chasing Michael and Julia into the living room with a Darth Vader mask on yelling, "I am your father!," making the kids scream with delight. Three babies sat in a row in high chairs while Gabby took photos and videos of their every move. Rafe positioned Gabby's fancy tripod behind her, setting up his 35mm camera for a family photo.

Sara was trying to wipe spilled mashed peas off the floor, but Bandit and Champ, Colton and Sara's dog, had gotten there first—followed quickly by Rocket, of course, never to be outdone by the younger dogs.

"Bandit!" Rafe called in a voice of authority. The dog looked up at him with a guilty expression and then promptly resumed licking up the peas.

"Nice job training that puppy," Colton said, slapping Rafe on the back. "Hope you do a better job with the kid." To which Rafe gave him a look.

Sara passed over to Colton a crying baby whose angelic face was filled with peas. "Hold Luke for a sec, would you?" she said, running into the kitchen, probably for more paper towels. The baby promptly rubbed his face on Colton's shoulder.

"Oh no," Colton said, which made his son laugh.

Sara ran back and swiped at the baby's mouth with a wet paper towel. "You think Daddy's funny covered in peas, don't you?" she said to the baby, who laughed even more.

"Next time *I'll* get the paper towels," Colt said.

"You smell bad," Sara said, laughing and wrinkling up her nose.

"Who, me?" Colton said innocently. "'Eau de pea'?"

"No, *Luke* smells bad," she said, laughing. "I think that's why he's crying."

"I'll change him," Colton said, then dropped his voice. "After I change my own shirt."

"Peas is a good look on you," Rafe said. "Very Christmasy."

Rafe walked over to his daughter, who was enjoying *her* peas, which Nonna was feeding her as well as Mia, Gabby and Cade's daughter.

"I'm so glad you named Mia after Mom," Sara said to Gabby.

"Right," Kaitlyn said. "Because if she was a boy, she would've been named Harlan Coben Marshall, right, Cade?"

"Well," Cade said, cleaning up his daughter, "I'm glad you and Rafe settled on Rose instead of Raphaela."

"I love that you named the baby after Nonna," Rachel said. "Rose is a lovely name."

"I don't know why you people think this parenting business is so hard," Nonna said, taking off Rose's bib. "It's easy. Right, little girls?"

When Colton returned with a better-smelling Luke, Gabby said, "Will you put him in Nonna's lap, Colton? I'd love to get a picture of all three babies with Nonna."

Colton complied. Next to Gabby, Evie was helping Julia take a picture with an iPad.

"Bet you're glad you're done with this baby phase, aren't you?" Kaitlyn asked Evie.

"Actually," Joe said, wrapping his arm around his wife and clearing his throat, "We have some news."

"Oh my gosh," Gabby said.

"Evie! You just went back to work full-time!" Sara said.

"I know, but since Kaitlyn just hired a partner...I guess I can figure work-life balance out too."

"We'll figure it out together," Joe said, squeezing his wife's hand.

"Congratulations, sis," Rafe said, giving Evie a hug. "Good thing you're pregnant because I don't think we have enough babies around here."

"We *don't* have enough babies around here," Rachel said. "Another grandbaby! How wonderful. We are so blessed."

Rafe's dad chuckled. "Does this mean we're going to babysit another afternoon a week? I thought I slowed down so I could play more golf."

"I'm always happy to babysit." Rachel poked him playfully in the side. "And you are too."

Everyone congratulated Evie and Joe.

Rafe went with Kaitlyn to go visit with Nikki, their mom, and Nonna, who were all sitting on the couch with balls of yarn in their laps and holding crochet needles.

"What are you all doing?" Rafe asked.

"Hazel needs more inventory," Nikki said, winking at Hazel.

Hazel smiled at her mom. "Crochet faster," she said, gesturing to her to speed up.

"I think she's going to be a businesswoman, like you." Nikki got up and linked one arm with Kaitlyn's and the other with Rafe's.

"Thanks for letting me stay at your old place. It's perfect. And it's so wonderful to be here for the holiday. And..." She teared up. "Thank you both for saving my daughter."

Kaitlyn hugged her sister. "She taught me a thing or two too," Kaitlyn said. "She taught me that you don't have to be perfect to help somebody else."

"Hazel has a big heart," Rafe said. "She just needed a little encouragement."

"She's doing so well at FIT," Nikki said. "I feel like I have my daughter back."

"Maybe you should come back to Angel Falls too," Kaitlyn said. "We miss you."

"Hey, guys," Gabby said, gathering everyone. "Time for a family picture." She tapped Kaitlyn's mom on the shoulder. "That means you too, Mrs. B. Everybody stand by the fireplace."

It took a while to get everyone positioned. "Merry Christmas, Kaitlyn," Rafe whispered quietly while they were waiting, wrapping his arm around her, a little apart from the crowd. He kissed his baby daughter on the head. "And you too, Rosie-Posie."

"It's a great Christmas," Kaitlyn said. "It's a little crazy in here today—dogs, spilled peas, crocheters."

"The happiest chaos ever," Rafe said, and he meant it. His heart was full.

"Maybe you should help Gabby," Kaitlyn said.

"Great idea." Rafe left his spot, took the iPad from

Julia, set it on the table, and motioned for her to join the others. Then he adjusted his camera one more time until the timer started beeping.

"Can I hold the baby?" Hazel asked at the last minute, holding out her hands for Rose, who gave Hazel a toothless grin.

"Hurry up, Rafe," Nonna said as she went to take her place next to Kaitlyn. As she passed him, she dropped her voice. "Thank goodness everyone's smiling today. I wouldn't want to have to fall into the Christmas tree again."

Rafe jerked his head up, but Nonna's face was as blank as could be. Wait a minute—what? A face plant on purpose? His gaze locked with Kaitlyn's. She looked as shocked as he did, but then she gave a little shrug and a smile, because Nonna was... Nonna.

"Smile, family," Rafe said with a sigh. "Say 'more grandchildren,' Rachel. Say 'one semester of college down,' Hazie." Then he ran as fast as he could to get into the picture, standing next to Kaitlyn and wrapping his arm around her tight. He almost tripped over one of the dogs, who ran at the last minute to get in on the action too.

There weren't any angels in the background, or coins to toss into the falls. He wasn't big on believing in luck, but he did believe in the unbreakable bonds of his family, the loved ones here and the ones who had passed on. And he believed in the power of love. Which made him feel like the luckiest man alive.

"Love you, sweetheart," he whispered.

"So much," she said back, blowing him a kiss before she smiled for the camera.

KAITLYN'S CHOCOLATE SNOWCAP COOKIES

- 4 ounces bittersweet or semisweet chocolate pieces
- 1 cup flour
- ½ cup cocoa powder
- 3 teaspoons instant espresso (optional)
- 2 teaspoons baking powder
- ⅛ teaspoon salt (optional)
- 4 tablespoons (½ stick) unsalted butter
- 1 cup light brown sugar
- 2 eggs
- ½ teaspoon vanilla
- 2 tablespoons milk
- confectioners' sugar for rolling cookies (at least a cup)

Preheat oven to 350 degrees.

Using a Pyrex or other heat-safe bowl, heat the chocolate pieces in a microwave at 30-second intervals until nearly melted. (Go slowly and don't overdo this because the chocolate keeps melting even after it's out of the microwave.) Let the chocolate cool while you're mixing the rest of the dough.

In a medium bowl, mix the dry ingredients (flour, cocoa powder, espresso, baking powder, salt).

In a large bowl, cream the butter and brown sugar with an electric mixer until well blended. Beat in the eggs, one at a time, add the vanilla and then the cooled chocolate. Gradually add the dry ingredients and the milk and beat with the mixer on low until just combined. Flatten the dough and place it in a plastic bag. Seal well and freeze for an hour.

Line two baking sheets with parchment paper or baking mats. Use a small cookie scoop to scoop out dough and drop each doughball into a bowl of confectioners' sugar (I used a bread pan—it held a bunch of doughballs). Roll each dough piece into a 1-inch ball and then recoat with the confectioners' sugar. Let the doughballs sit in the sugar until they are ready to bake.

Place cookies on baking sheets 2 inches apart and bake for 12 to 14 minutes until the cookies have spread a bit and the coating has cracked. Let the cookies sit on the baking sheets for about 10 minutes before moving them to a cooling rack.

Enjoy the chocolatey, melty goodness and think of Rafe and Kaitlyn!!

Miranda's Tips

* Between the cocoa, chocolate, and espresso, this recipe has enough caffeine to start your car, so please be careful with your heart! There is a decaf espresso product you can use if you still like that coffee flavor without the added caffeine! Also, the bittersweet chocolate I used (65% cacao) has more caffeine than Nestle Toll House semi-sweet morsels (47% cacao).

† I used bittersweet chocolate chips with 65 percent cacao for a richer taste (and because it's

what my grocery store had), but use what you prefer.

‡ This dough is very soft. Before rolling the doughballs, I flattened the dough, I plopped it into a gallon plastic bag, flattened and sealed it, and *froze* it for an hour. If you do that, I suggest letting the dough sit for 5 to 10 minutes after you take it out of the freezer so you can work with it. (Alternatively, other recipes stated that you can *refrigerate* the dough anywhere from an hour to overnight.)

** Using a cookie scoop is a great idea because it makes the doughballs uniform. Dropping them immediately into the powdered sugar before rolling them into perfect ball shapes is another great idea or else your hands get coated with sticky brown dough. ☺

About the Author

Miranda Liasson loves to write stories about everyday people who find love despite themselves, because there's nothing like a great love story. And if there are a few laughs along the way, even better! She's a Romance Writers of America Golden Heart winner and an Amazon bestselling author whose heartwarming and humorous small-town romances have won accolades such as the National Readers' Choice Award and the Gayle Wilson Award of Excellence and have been *Harlequin Junkie* and Night Owl Reviews Top Picks.

She lives in the Midwest with her husband and three kids in a charming old neighborhood that is the inspiration for many of the homes in her books.

Miranda loves to hear from readers! Find her at:

MirandaLiasson.com
Facebook.com/MirandaLiassonAuthor
Instagram: @MirandaLiasson
Twitter: @MirandaLiasson

For more information on new releases and other news, sign up for her newsletter at mirandaliasson.com/#mailing -list.

DON'T MISS A MOMENT OF LIFE IN ANGEL FALLS!

Christmas on Mistletoe Lane

Annie Rains

Christmas is coming to the North Carolina mountains, and the air is fresh and crisp and filled with promise. After the devastating loss of her job in the big city, inheriting her grandparents' charming bed-and-breakfast in the small town of Sweetwater Springs was just the new lease on life she needed. Only it comes with a catch—and a handsome and completely infuriating one at that. Now co-owner of the B&B with Mitch Hargrove with two months to make the inn a success, Kaitlyn is faced with a real challenge. With the holiday fast approaching and a grand reopening looming, will Mitch and Kaitlyn realize the true gift they've been given?

FOREVER
New York Boston

For Ralphie, Doc, and Lydia. May your dreams in life be as big as your hearts.

Acknowledgments

No book is ever written alone. There are so many people who come together to make a book come alive. First, I want to thank my family for making sure I have the time I need to put my stories on paper. Sonny, you win the "Best Husband Award" for spending an entire day touring bed and breakfasts with me as research for this book. And to my mother-in-law, Annette, for watching the kids during said research. Thank you to my parents for always encouraging my love of writing. Your support means everything to me, and I love you all to pieces!

Thank you to my editor, Alex Logan, for believing in this project and pulling me aboard the Grand Central / Forever team. Working on this book together has been a dream come true for me. I'm still pinching myself! A huge thanks to the entire Forever team for everything that goes on behind the scenes! I would also like to thank my agent, Sarah Younger, for your tireless work in finding this book its perfect home. I am so honored to be a part of your team and NYLA!

Thanks to my wonderful critique partner, Rachel Lacey. Your advice is worth its weight in gold, as is your friendship. Also to the #TeamSarah ladies and my #GirlsWriteNight gals. You all inspire me so much! Thank you for everything (to include ideas, support, and friendship).

A huge thank-you goes out to my readers group for offering up ALL the Christmas ideas to incorporate into this book. Thank you to all my readers for spending time in my stories and falling in love with my characters. Every review, message, and line of encouragement means so much! Xoxoxo.

CHAPTER ONE

*K*aitlyn Russo twisted the key in her hand but the front door to the Sweetwater B&B didn't budge.

"Great. Just great," she muttered under her breath, which floated away in a little white puff of air. Shivering and wishing she'd worn a heavier coat, she turned the key again, pressing her full weight into the door as she did. This time it flung open and promptly dumped her on the pinewood floor inside. Dust flumed under her nostrils. With a cough, she looked up and inspected her grandparents' old bed and breakfast.

Scratch that. *Her* bed and breakfast.

She climbed to her feet, grabbed her luggage, and then closed the front door to bar the wintry cold. Turning on the light in the front room, she surveyed the homey design with high wood-beamed ceilings, a detail that, as an interior designer, she'd always loved. The furniture was a tasteful blend of antique and contemporary. This place was exactly how she remembered it from her infrequent childhood visits, minus the dust mites.

Nothing a little hard work couldn't fix.

But first she had plans to meet with the lawyer handling her grandmother's estate. He'd be arriving sometime in the next half hour. When she'd spoken to Mr. Garrison by phone earlier, he'd mentioned something about another person in Mable's will. Kaitlyn couldn't imagine who that would be. Other than her parents, who'd inherited various other family heirlooms, her grandmother didn't have any living family. The Russos were a dwindling clan—all the more reason to keep their legacy alive.

From the corner of her eye, Kaitlyn saw movement in the window. Then a dark figure filled the space behind the curtain. Something told her this wasn't Mr. Garrison. Lawyers tended to be civilized people who knocked on doors. Maybe a squatter had been camping out here since her Grandma Mable's passing last month.

The shadow slipped out of sight. A moment later, she heard a shuffling sound behind the front door.

Terror sliced straight down her middle, and her heart kicked into a choppy staccato. She dashed to the fireplace and lifted one of the long metal pokers used to move hot coals. It could second as a lethal weapon if necessary.

Like it had for her, the front door didn't release immediately. *Why, oh why, didn't I lock it after myself?* If she were still in New York, she would have.

The intruder gave the door a firm push, and it swung open, crashing against the wall behind it and making Kaitlyn scream.

Standing before her was a broad-shouldered man with dark eyes, wavy, overgrown hair, and a close-trimmed beard. He was dressed in a nice pair of jeans and a weathered leather jacket. Her gaze fell to his brown mountain boots. Definitely not homeless, she decided.

She held the fire poker up like a sword. "Don't come any closer," she warned with a shaky voice.

"Are you planning to use that on me?" His voice, in contrast to hers, was deep and gruff. And if she wasn't mistaken, there was a little humor threading through it.

Was he teasing her? Because while, yes, he was larger than her, *she* was the one holding a pointy metal death stick. "I might," she said, wishing there wasn't a warm, tingly awareness settling low in her belly, competing with the fear still coursing through her veins. Rugged good looks had never been a more accurate description. This guy had it down to an art form.

He held up his hands in surrender. "So, you're little Katie Russo?"

She cocked her head to one side. "How do you know that?"

"Mable spoke of you often."

Kaitlyn lowered the metal poker just a notch. "She did?" she asked, keeping her eyes pinned on him.

"Your grandfather too—when he was alive."

Grandpa Henry had died several years earlier, leaving Grandma Mable to run the Sweetwater Bed and Breakfast alone. They'd been the only two people in the world to call her Katie, and her mom had always been vocal about her objections, preferring the formal name Kaitlyn instead.

"My name's not Katie. It's Kaitlyn. And you could've read that on my luggage there by your feet." She'd met her fair share of con men living in the city. Guys who could conjure a name with only a pair of initials. "A simple inquiry into this place could've told you who my grandparents were."

The man stepped forward and offered his hand. Kaitlyn didn't move to shake it.

"I'm Mitch Hargrove. I grew up around the corner. Mable and Henry used to take care of me after school while my mom worked. They kept me supplied with milk and cookies and helped with my homework."

That sounded exactly like something her grandparents would do.

"In exchange, I did odd jobs for them here at the inn during the school year. During the summers, my mom and I RV'd with my aunt, much to Mable's disappointment. She always said she wanted to introduce us."

He continued to hold his hand out to Kaitlyn. "Guess Mable finally got her wish. She always was a stubborn one."

Reluctantly, Kaitlyn returned the rod to its place on the hearth and slipped her hand in his. Rough, calloused skin dragged across her palm as they shook. "I think I remember my grandmother speaking of you. She had a photo of you on her nightstand." Kaitlyn was only able to come for a brief visit once each summer, the trip sandwiched between various camps her parents had enrolled her in. Each year, the photo on her grandmother's nightstand was updated with a more recent version of the boy with the magic eyes. That's how Kaitlyn had thought of him back then. Dark, magic eyes that seemed to jump out of the frame. In all honesty, the boy in that picture was her first crush.

And now he was standing in front of her.

Pinning her gaze to his, she recognized those eyes, changed only by a shimmer of something that resembled sadness. "I'm so sorry for your loss," she said quietly.

"You're family. I'm just"—he shrugged—"the neighbor boy. I'm supposed to be offering my condolences to you," he said.

Kaitlyn swallowed thickly. Mitch was almost a foot taller than her, which required her to look up at him. "Thank you.

So, did you break into the B and B to introduce yourself?" she asked.

"Jacob asked me to meet him tonight. Since I already have a key, he told me to come inside and wait where it's warm."

"Jacob Garrison, the estate lawyer? Why would he want to meet you here?"

"Seems Mable left half this place to me." Mitch's gaze roamed around the front room as he said it.

Kaitlyn shook her head, feeling breathless with panic. "No. You must be mistaken. *I* inherited this B and B."

His gaze dropped to hers. Mistaken, but *holy moly hot*. Her cheeks flushed, and she looked away, reminding herself of her resolution on the drive down Interstate 95. This was a fresh start for her, an opportunity, and she wasn't going to blow it.

"All I know is what I was told," Mitch said.

As if on cue, someone knocked on the front door.

Mitch held up a hand, signaling her to stay where she was. "Wouldn't want you to threaten Mr. Garrison with that fire poker," he teased.

Kaitlyn watched as he opened the door to an older man with salt-and-pepper hair and a dark-gray suit buried under a heavy coat.

Despite the cold, the man smiled warmly from the porch. "Hey, Mitch. Good to see you."

"You too, Jacob."

They shook hands, and then Mitch gestured the man inside, closing the door behind them.

"Mr. Garrison, I presume," Kaitlyn said, stepping forward and shaking the older man's hand.

"That I am. Nice to finally meet you, Ms. Russo. Your grandparents spoke of you often over the years."

"Please, call me Kaitlyn. Thank you so much for coming. I know it's late." She'd offered to meet Mr. Garrison tomorrow at his office but he'd insisted on seeing her as soon as she arrived in town. He'd apparently asked Mitch to come as well. And that little tidbit wasn't sitting well with Kaitlyn at the moment.

"No problem at all. I'm on my way home, actually," Mr. Garrison said.

"Well, let's sit and get to business, shall we?" She moved toward the room's high-backed Victorian couch and sat down. "I would offer you a warm drink but I just arrived myself. I'm not sure what's in the cupboards."

"Oh, I'm fine." Mr. Garrison sat next to her and laid a briefcase on the coffee table in front of them. She watched as he pulled out a file. Hopefully, it would set things straight. *She* was the owner of the Sweetwater B&B, and only her.

Mitch sat in a matching antique chair off to the side and leaned forward, propping his elbows on his knees. His chest was thick and broad like a linebacker's, although his appearance made her think of a man who'd emerged from a mountain cabin rather than a football field.

Kaitlyn pulled her gaze back to Mr. Garrison. What if she'd misunderstood on the phone? What if this place wasn't hers after all? She'd purchased a used car and had moved out of her pint-sized apartment in New York City, taking everything she owned with her. She had no home or job to return to because she didn't plan on going back. It'd been a rash decision, yes, but she hadn't really had another viable option. This was it, her only lifeline, and she'd latched on with all the grit and determination that had once made her an up-and-coming interior designer.

"So." Mr. Garrison clapped his hands together. "Congratulations, you two. Looks like you'll be business partners."

Kaitlyn straightened. "I'm sorry. What?"

"Mable left you half of the Sweetwater B and B," he told her and then looked at Mitch. "And you the other half. I'm sure you know the Russos thought of you as a grandson, Mitch. They were very proud of your service as a military police officer."

Kaitlyn's eyes darted between the two men. "Excuse me, Mr. Garrison, but I was under the impression that *I* was the new owner."

"You are. Along with Mr. Hargrove." Mr. Garrison pointed at the papers in front of him. "Says so right here. Under one condition that your grandmother spelled out in no uncertain terms."

Kaitlyn's head was spinning. "Condition?" she asked.

Mr. Garrison nodded. "That's right. The condition is that you and Mr. Hargrove must run this place together for the first two months after signing these documents." Mr. Garrison settled his glasses up on his long, narrow nose as he read. "Both parties must stay in Sweetwater Springs and run the Sweetwater Bed and Breakfast on Mistletoe Lane as a fully functioning inn for exactly two months from the date of signature. If either party declines, the bed and breakfast is forfeited for both parties and turned over to charity."

"What?" Kaitlyn sat up straight, panic gripping her as it had when she'd thought Mitch was an intruder. And he was. She did not want him here, claiming half of what she'd thought was solely hers.

"No way I'm staying in Sweetwater Springs for two months," Mitch said flatly. "I love Mable but charity can have this place."

Kaitlyn shot him a scornful look. "This was my grandparents' business. We can't just let it go."

"I hate to break it to you but this place has been declining for years," Mitch said. "Mable rarely had a full inn. Any charity we offered it to likely wouldn't even take it. A bed and breakfast requires time and money. I say we save ourselves the trouble and forfeit now."

"We are *not* forfeiting," Kaitlyn snapped between gritted teeth. She didn't care how big or attractive Mitch Hargrove was—and he *was* big and attractive—she'd lost too many fights lately. She was fighting for this B&B with every ounce of strength she had. "Is there any way to get around the legal terms?" she asked. "So I can run the B and B and Mr. Hargrove can go on his merry way?" Which would be best for everyone. The sooner, the better.

Mr. Garrison frowned. "I'm afraid not. The will is detailed. Mable was insistent that you two work here together. Leaving the inn to the both of you was her final attempt to revive this old place."

Mr. Garrison angled himself to look at Kaitlyn. "Mable was proud of how creative you are. She said you could turn menial things into magic." He turned back to Mitch. "And she said you could fix just about anything. Between the two of you, she was adamant that the Sweetwater Bed and Breakfast could be transformed back into the jewel it once was. Her words, not mine. Two months. That was Mable's terms, and she asked me to make sure that's what happened."

Mr. Garrison's gaze flitted between them. "She knew it would take the talents of both of you combined."

Kaitlyn stared at Mitch. She'd liked him a whole lot better when she'd thought he might be trying to kill her.

"So," Mr. Garrison said on an inhale, "do you accept or not?"

"No," Mitch barked at the same time that she said, "Yes."

Kaitlyn folded her arms across her chest. How dare he

even consider refusing her grandmother's final wish. "We're not giving up on this B and B."

"Do you have money for repairs? Money to keep the lights and heat on for guests? This inn is a money pit. We'd be fools to go into business together." Mitch shook his head. "And I don't know about you but I have a life to get back to. Two months of trying to avoid the inevitable isn't in my plans."

"I have a life," Kaitlyn shot back. Albeit one that seemed to be in shambles lately. Apparently, Grandma Mable had been struggling too. How had Kaitlyn not known her grandmother was under so much financial strain? Not that Kaitlyn could've helped. All she'd really had of value when she'd driven down from New York to the North Carolina mountains was hope, and even that was dwindling fast.

* * *

Mitch was having a hard time listening to Mr. Garrison. Partly because he was too distracted by little Katie Russo all grown up. She was gorgeous, yeah, but also feisty enough to threaten a six-foot-one former marine with a poker stick. He could've disarmed her faster than she could bat those long eyelashes of hers, if he'd wanted to. He'd enjoyed watching her think she had the upper hand though. He'd enjoyed watching her, period.

"The B and B doesn't make a profit?" Kaitlyn asked as Mr. Garrison laid out the paperwork.

"Not in recent years, no," Mr. Garrison said apologetically.

Mitch already knew this. He'd always visited Mable whenever he'd come off a deployment and returned to Sweetwater to see his mom. Since Henry's death, Mable had been struggling financially. She'd never seemed undone by it though. She was a strong woman, didn't give up easily, and was as stubborn as the valley here is deep. Mable was always expecting a surge of new business. Always hoping the Sweetwater Bed and Breakfast would return to its glory days.

"This business belonged to my grandparents. It means something. At least to me."

Mitch swallowed, remembering how he'd sat in this very room after school. As a teen, he'd worked behind the scenes at the bed and breakfast on weekends too. Mable had taught him to cook fancy breakfasts and fold napkins just so. Henry had taught him to care for the landscaping. There weren't a lot of good memories locked up in this town for Mitch but the Russos and the Sweetwater B&B were some of them.

He turned to Mr. Garrison. "So, you're telling me that in order for Katie to keep this place, I have to stay in Sweetwater Springs?"

"Kaitlyn," the woman in question snapped.

"That's correct," Mr. Garrison said.

"And if I leave?"

"Then she loses the business as well."

Mitch rubbed a hand over his forehead. *Thanks a lot, Mable.* He couldn't stay in Sweetwater Springs— wouldn't—and she'd known that. The last few times he'd come to visit, he'd mentioned that he wasn't reenlisting in the corps. Mable had known he would have time available. But she'd also known he was planning on taking a contract job running security in Northern Virginia. He knew quite a few ex-military who'd done the same kind of work after getting out. The job offered good money. Too good to pass up. *This* would complicate things.

"Two months?" he clarified.

"Two months. And what a perfect time. You'll be home for the holidays, Mitch," Mr. Garrison said, as if that was a selling point.

Mitch hadn't been home for the holidays since he'd joined the military when he was eighteen years old. There was a reason for that. One that made the stipulations of Mable's will feel more like a death sentence than a vacation.

"How you go about running things isn't specified," Mr. Garrison continued. "After the two months are up, we'll complete the paperwork and the bed and breakfast is yours to sell or do with as you choose."

"Please," Kaitlyn said, turning to Mitch, her brown eyes wide and hopeful.

He didn't know this woman from a stranger off the street. He didn't owe her anything. But he did owe Mable and Henry. They'd practically raised him while his mom worked two jobs. Mable and Henry had stood by him after the accident too. He'd never forget their loyalty. "I'm not making any decisions tonight," Mitch finally said. Especially not a decision that would cost him the next two months of his life.

"Of course. The clock doesn't start until you sign the preliminary paperwork though," Mr. Garrison advised.

Mitch nodded, catching the look of disappointment in Kaitlyn's eyes. He couldn't help that. This deal was a lot to ask.

The lawyer closed his briefcase and stood. "Just give me a call when you two make your decision."

"We will." Kaitlyn followed him to the door. "Thank you for coming."

"Of course. Anything for Mable."

That should've been Mitch's immediate answer too. Anything for sweet, caring, kind Mable Russo.

Anything but this.

CHAPTER TWO

"Look, it's been a long day," Mitch said, turning to face Kaitlyn, who stood only a few feet away. "Neither of us were expecting this…*complication*. Let's get some rest and revisit how we'll handle things in the morning."

She hugged her arms around herself, lifting tired, beautiful eyes to meet his. "Yeah, you're right. The drive from New York was exhausting. We can meet back here first thing and look over the papers Mr. Garrison left us."

"Meet back here?" Mitch didn't like the sound of that. Since he was 50 percent owner, he thought he would at least get a room at the B&B.

"Well, you're not staying here. This is where I'll be sleeping."

"It's a bed and breakfast. It's meant to house more than one person," he said.

"Yes, when it's open, but we're not open. *Yet.*"

An argument rose in his throat and settled on the tip of his tongue. Then his gaze caught on the poker stick resting against the wall behind her. He'd unintentionally scared her when he'd gotten here. Understandable, considering he was a stranger who appeared to be breaking and entering. As much as Mable had told him about her, she obviously hadn't told Kaitlyn much about him. A young, single, beautiful woman had every reason to be wary of a strange man staying under the same roof.

"Fine," he said, wishing he wasn't such a nice guy, because he didn't want to impose on his mom. He hadn't even told her he was coming to town. His mom, being the workaholic she was, would've insisted on cleaning and cooking and driving him absolutely nuts with all her doting. She had enough to do without taking care of him. "I'll sleep somewhere else tonight and be back at seven a.m. tomorrow."

Kaitlyn's jaw went lax. "Seven? Isn't that a little early?"

He smiled. "Get used to it. If you're set on running this place, Mable was up at four thirty every morning cooking breakfast for her guests." He got a little satisfaction as the realization dawned on his would-be business partner's face. He guessed she hadn't thought that far ahead. It didn't seem like she'd thought about this at all.

Gesturing behind him at the door, he said, "I'll see you tomorrow. *Bright and early.*"

* * *

Kaitlyn dragged her tired body and suitcase past the wooden staircase and headed down the long hallway to her left. She remembered that her grandmother had always stayed in the downstairs bedroom near the kitchen and laundry area. The three rooms were blocked by a swinging door and made separate living quarters, which, even on their own, were much larger than her city apartment had been.

What Kaitlyn didn't remember is her grandmother waking so early to cook breakfast. Then again, like a good hostess, her grandmother had the first meal of the day ready when she'd stayed over. Kaitlyn was none the wiser about when or how it'd been prepared.

Four thirty? Well, if that's what she had to do, so be it. This was a new life for her. A godsend. At least that's what she'd thought on the drive down. Now doubt niggled in the dusty recesses of her mind, not unlike the inn's unkempt corners. This place was run-down, and she'd already spent a good portion of her savings on a used Ford Taurus to get here.

With a sigh, she dropped her luggage on the bedroom floor. The room was spacious with a king-size bed on one side fitted with a handmade quilt that Grandma Mable had likely made herself. An antique dresser sat along the wall and a rocking chair invited Kaitlyn to sit and possibly cry her eyes out later. Right now, she bent to unzip her suitcase and search for her favorite pair of flannel pajamas. As she sifted through her belongings, her cell phone rang against her hip. She pulled it from her pocket to her ear.

"Well?" her best friend Josie said in lieu of a hello. Josie still lived and worked in New York. "How is it?"

Kaitlyn climbed into the wooden rocker and clutched the phone to her ear. "It's awful. I mean, the inn itself is gorgeous but it needs work. And according to my new co-owner, this place can't even cover its own power and heating bills."

"I'm sorry—what?" Josie asked on the other end of the line.

Kaitlyn sighed. "Apparently, I'm not even the full owner. Grandma Mable left this place to me and the guy who grew up down the street." The image of the large, sexy man that

Kaitlyn had spent the last hour with came to mind. "According to the will, Mitch and I have to run the bed and breakfast together for two months or we both forfeit to charity."

"Whoa. That's an unusual scenario," Josie said.

Indeed it was. "After the time is up, we can do as we like with the B and B, and since Mitch doesn't seem to care about staying, I plan to take out a loan and buy him out."

"There you go. That's perfect."

Kaitlyn pressed her head back against the rocker and closed her eyes, grateful to shut out at least one of her senses. "Except he hasn't said yes to the agreement. Also, since the business isn't turning a profit, there's no way the bank will give me a loan to buy him out. I thought this place would be my fresh start." Those tears threatened behind her eyes. She swallowed hard, refusing to let them through.

"Well, if this is really what you want, you can't give up," Josie said in the determined spirit that was her hallmark. "You have to make it a success."

Kaitlyn opened her eyes. "As much as I want to, I'm not sure that's even possible."

Josie hummed thoughtfully into the receiver for a long moment. "Maybe it is. I think I have an idea."

Kaitlyn resisted the hope springing up in her chest. Josie was the queen of good ideas. That's how she'd become such a successful magazine editor, managing the lifestyle section of *Loving Life* magazine. Josie had interned with the magazine fresh out of college and had immediately started impressing those around her, moving up the ranks.

"*Loving Life* is doing a December cover story on the most romantic holiday getaways in America. I wrote the article myself so I can add in one more spot, if I want. In fact, I gamble to say that Sweetwater Springs, North Carolina, might be *the* most romantic holiday retreat in America. And the Sweetwater Bed and Breakfast is the perfect place for couples, new and old, to stay while they discover the magic there."

"That would be a lie, Josie. Didn't you take some kind of journalistic oath or something? This place is hardly the most romantic, and it's nowhere near ready for business. The holidays are just around the corner."

"You just said you only have two months to make this happen. You don't have time to think like that. Besides, I owe you. Whether you think so or not, I'm the reason you ever got a gig with Bradley Foster. That makes me partly responsible for—"

"I don't want to talk about that," Kaitlyn said quickly, cutting her friend off. In fact, Kaitlyn would be happy to never hear celebrity extraordinaire Bradley Foster's name again. "That wasn't your fault. You couldn't have known."

A slight pause hung between them.

"Even so," Josie finally continued, "if running that B and B is really what you have your heart set on, you can turn that place into whatever you want. It really can be the most romantic holiday retreat in America. And as my best friend, you better not make me a liar, because I'm adding Sweetwater Springs to my article tonight. The magazine goes into circulation a couple of weeks before each new month, so you better get your partner to agree and then get busy."

* * *

Mitch cut his headlights before he pulled into his mom's driveway. She was early to rise and super early to bed so he guessed she'd already be asleep. He'd considered calling one of his buddies in town for a place to stay but his mom lived around the corner from Mistletoe Lane, where the Sweetwater Bed and Breakfast was located, so this seemed most practical.

He grabbed his overnight bag—leaving the rest of his belongings in the cab of his truck—and headed up the front porch steps. There was a spare key in the flowerpot off to the side. It wasn't a wise hiding location but he couldn't convince Gina Hargrove of that. His mom was as stubborn as Mable had been. That was maybe one reason they'd been such great friends.

He quietly let himself in and headed straight to the guest room down the hall. Shutting the bedroom door behind him, he stripped off his shirt and lay back on the twin-size bed of his youth, staring up at the ceiling. He couldn't stay here. That was a fact. The money from the contract security job was double what he'd made as a police officer in the corps. Not only that, he had a past in Sweetwater Springs. One he'd rather not relive.

The choice was clear. When he met back with Kaitlyn Russo in the morning, he'd just tell her there was no way he could make this arrangement work. It would break her heart since she was obviously determined to reopen Mable and Henry's B&B but one day she'd thank him. The inn was a lost cause. There was no resuscitating it. Turning the deal down would be doing her a favor.

* * *

The aroma of freshly brewed coffee stirred Mitch to life early the next morning. He followed the scent down the hall and into the kitchen.

"Hey, Mom."

His mother nearly dropped her mug of coffee as she whirled to look at him. "Where did you come from?"

"Sorry. Didn't mean to scare you," he said, immediately thinking of Kaitlyn and her poker stick from last night. "I got to town late."

"I didn't even know you were coming." She set her mug down and pulled him in for a tight hug. "It's so good to lay eyes on you. I was beginning to worry. You got out of the military a month ago. Where have you been?"

"Around," he said. He had tried to get back for Mable's funeral but he'd still had one week left to serve, and his request was denied. "I'm fine. You know that."

"I don't know it unless you pick up the phone to tell me so," she said in a voice reminiscent of the one she'd regularly used on him growing up. He'd had a few rebellious years that were no doubt the cause of her initial few gray hairs. Now, at fifty years old, Gina Hargrove had a head full of solid gray hair that she wore past her shoulders. She could probably attribute all of it to him, he thought.

He walked over, grabbed a mug from the cabinet, and poured himself a cup of coffee. "Busy day ahead?" he asked.

She took a seat at the small table off to the side of the kitchen. "No more than usual. I need to clean the Mallorys' house today and then the Lances' after that."

Mitch's hand tightened around the mug. "I wish you wouldn't work so hard." She didn't need to. He made sure of that, sending money home from every paycheck he got.

"Hard work never killed anyone." She continued to sip. "Soon as I pay this house off, I might slow down. You know, after Laura Brown retired, she found out she didn't have enough money to live off. She lost her home and had to move in with her son and daughter-in-law. If that happened to me, where would I go? You don't even have a place to live right now."

"That won't happen to you," he said. With his looming

contract job in the works, he'd be even better able to ensure that her needs were met. His gaze dropped from his mother's bloodshot eyes to her shaking hands. "What's that about?" He gestured as he stepped toward her.

She settled her hands down on the table. "Just tired. These old things are resisting any kind of work after cleaning up the debris and leaves around the Dennys' rosebushes yesterday. That stuff will harbor pests if you don't."

"Yard work? I thought you stuck to cleaning houses."

"Well, they asked me to help. What am I supposed to say? No?"

"Yeah. That's exactly what you say."

"It's fine." She waved a hand.

It wasn't fine with him though. Looking at her closer, he noticed she looked pale and tired.

"So, tell me why you're here," she said, changing the subject.

"Can't a guy visit his mother?"

She narrowed her eyes.

"Fine. I need to handle a few things at the Sweetwater Bed and Breakfast."

"Really? It's been closed since Mable passed away last month."

"I know, but her granddaughter is in town working on the place."

"To reopen it?" his mother asked, pulling her coffee mug toward her again.

"Doubtful." Because he wasn't going to fulfill his end of the will's stipulations. He guessed Kaitlyn might be able to take out a loan and buy it from whatever charity it was left to when all was said and done. That was an option if she was as headstrong as she appeared to be.

He took one more long sip of coffee and set his mug

down. "Actually, I've got to get over there pretty soon. Mind if I use the shower?"

"Of course not. This is your home and always will be," his mom said warmly.

He kissed her temple and looked down at her shaky hands once more. Something in his gut tightened.

"And when you get home tonight, I'll cook you something tasty for dinner," she said. "We'll talk some more. It'll be nice."

He pointed a finger. "You're not going to cook me dinner after working all day. I'll cook for you."

"I'm not one of your marines. Put that finger away." She rolled her blue-gray eyes.

He was tempted to laugh at her stubbornness. Instead, he shook his head and headed down the hall to the shower.

After a quick rinse, he dressed and drove his truck to the century-old inn at the end of Mistletoe Lane. It was a large two-story Victorian home with navy blue shutters. The wraparound porch featured several wooden swings for guests to sit and enjoy the mountain air and scenery. In Mitch's mind, the view was the best part. From this location, the mountains dipped and rose over his cozy hometown nestled deep in the valley. He'd always thought they seemed to encase and protect Sweetwater Springs. But that was before the car accident. He'd been an inexperienced driver on the icy mountain roads that night and more than *his* life had veered off course.

All in a blink of an eye. In a single heartbeat. Life had swerved left and had never made itself right again.

His cell phone rang beside him as he parked in the B&B's driveway. It was still early in the civilian world but not in the military.

"Yeah?" he said, cutting the engine.

"Mitch. Hey, man. This is Jim Smalley."

Relief flooded Mitch at the sound of the man's voice on the other end of the line. It was his contact with the security firm in Virginia. Jim was supposed to call when everything was lined up. The sooner, the better. "Jim," Mitch said, feeling a smile lift through his cheeks. This was the perfect excuse to give Kaitlyn for why he couldn't stay.

"Bad news," Jim said, cutting to the chase. "There's a hang-up with the funding for the job."

Mitch's smile fell like a stack of heavy bricks. "How long?"

"Probably not until right after the new year."

"I see." Today was October twenty-ninth. What was Mitch supposed to do until January?

"I'll give you a call when I know more but I wanted to give you a heads-up. That's how these contracts go sometimes. The job is yours when it opens, but I understand if you need to find something else."

"No. I'll wait," Mitch said. "Thanks for calling, Jim."

"Sure thing. I'll be in touch."

Mitch disconnected the call and sighed. If he didn't know better, he'd guess the infamous Meddling Mable was sabotaging his plans from heaven. Well, she must know that he was just as stubborn as she was.

"Still not staying, Mable," he said under his breath in case she was listening. Then he glanced at his watch. It was earlier than the time he'd agreed upon with Kaitlyn. Well, maybe having someone knock on her door at this early hour would serve as a wake-up call. Once Kaitlyn realized the reality of the situation, she could go back to wherever she'd been holed up all these years. New York, he thought he remembered Mable telling him. The delay in his contract job didn't change his mind about staying in this town one bit. He'd been wise with his money over the years, not just sending some to his mom but also putting a portion away in savings. Two months without a paycheck—if it came to that—wouldn't break him. Two months of staying in his hometown, however, just might.

Climbing the porch steps, he felt a wave of sentimentality about the fact that Mable would never again greet him at the door with a plate of freshly baked chocolate chip cookies. Even as a grown man, she'd met him with a batch—and he'd never resisted. For one, Mable Russo was a hard woman to say no to. Two, he'd always believed her cookies had some secret ingredient that made a person feel better just by taking a bite. He could use some of Mable's cookies right about now.

He rang the doorbell and waited. It took several minutes, which he assumed meant Kaitlyn was still asleep. Then the door opened, and she surprised him, dressed in a peach-colored sweater and fitted jeans with her dark hair pulled neatly into a ponytail. She definitely hadn't just dragged herself out of bed.

"Hi," she said, holding a plate of chocolate chip cookies. "Sorry it took me a minute. Had to get these out of the oven." A smile bloomed on her fresh face. No sign of pillow creases in sight.

He looked between her and the plate, the scent of chocolate and butter circulating under his nose, mixed with something acutely female.

"Grandma Mable didn't have much in the cupboards. She did have the ingredients for cookies though. Except for the milk and eggs, but I stopped on the way into town for those staples last night."

Mitch's mouth watered.

"I thought this could be our breakfast. I have coffee too, if you want some."

It was hard to be anything but agreeable when she was offering him caffeine and sugar. He gave a quick nod and stepped inside after her. The front room seemed less dusty than it had the night before. The floors shined beneath his boots too. "Looks like you've been hard at work."

She glanced over her shoulder as she led him toward the kitchen. "It was a late night for me. I couldn't sleep. Too excited."

"Yeah? About what?" Certainly not about this place. She'd cleaned, sure, but there was still a laundry list of things to be done. The inside of the house was livable, albeit dusty and in need of minor repairs. The outside had lost its curb appeal though. And most importantly, the place hadn't drawn in real guests for a while. With the ski resorts that had popped up in the neighboring town of Wild Blossom Bluffs, Sweetwater Springs wasn't as appealing to tourists. There was nothing here to grab their attention.

"About being here, of course." She set the plate down on the granite countertop—one of the few updates to the bed and breakfast in recent years—and gestured toward a stool. "Sit and I'll get you a cup of coffee."

"What's so special about here?" Mitch asked, watching as she poured him a cup.

She shrugged a shoulder, sliding his mug in front of him. "It's gorgeous, for one. I remember thinking Sweetwater Springs was a magical place as a kid."

"Mable thought so too." Mitch chuckled as he pulled the black coffee to his mouth. Bitter and smooth, just like he liked it. "And when I was a kid, I believed her."

"Not anymore?" She sat on the stool across from him.

He met her eyes and hesitated. "Nah. Same as Santa Claus. The beard has been snatched, so to speak."

She frowned. When she did, he noticed the plumpness

of her pink lips. He pulled his gaze away and stared down into the black abyss of his coffee instead. He wasn't here for attraction. He was here to put an end to whatever well-intended but naive thoughts the Russos' granddaughter had running through her mind. They could struggle for two months and then admit defeat—because this place was hopeless—or they could walk away now.

And he was voting for the latter.

CHAPTER THREE

*K*aitlyn's heart had been racing ever since her conversation with Josie last night. If *Loving Life* magazine promoted the town and her B&B, then surely people would come. Maybe a lot of people. She'd almost argued with Josie when she'd made the suggestion. She couldn't let Josie put her and the magazine's reputation on the line.

But if I can pull this off…

Kaitlyn looked at Mitch, who was sampling one of her cookies. She hadn't been thrilled about him being here last night but if she was going to do this, she was glad there was somebody here to help her. Josie said the magazine would be going into distribution sometime in the next two weeks. After that, the Sweetwater B&B needed to be ready for business. The thought of hosting happy couples was terrifying. And electrifying.

The town itself was already living up to the claim. It was cozy and had so much to offer. There was a charming downtown area with quaint shops and good restaurants, and she couldn't wait to try them. The town was enclosed in a mountain valley, and there was a park with hiking trails that passed natural hot springs and led to some of the best lookouts in the area. The stage was already set. Sweetwater Springs just needed a hook to draw people in, and this was it.

"So," Kaitlyn said, leaning over the counter. Mitch met her gaze, and her mouth immediately went dry. She'd never noticed it in his childhood photographs but his eyes were brown and green with a hint of blue too. They were like the stained-glass windows of the Trinity Church in New York. She'd made a point of walking by it every day, even though she knew a shortcut that would get her to the subway faster. Part of her had wanted to live in those stained-glass windows. And now Mitch's eyes held the same appeal.

She swallowed and dropped her gaze for just a second. "So," she said again, clearing her throat. If he was going to be her business partner, and she fully intended to convince him to be, she needed neutral feelings toward him. "I have a plan to make this work."

Mitch chewed on a bite of cookie as he watched her. "You mean you haven't come to your senses yet?"

A frown tugged at the corners of her mouth. "Meaning do I want to walk away? No. And you're not walking away either. If my plan works, we can have this place booked solid with a waiting list running into the new year."

He chuckled softly. *Was he laughing at her?*

"I'm serious. My best friend, Josie, is the executive editor for the lifestyle section in *Loving Life* magazine." If he recognized the name of the periodical, it didn't show. "It's one of the biggest, most widely read magazines in the country. Josie is about to run a feature on the most romantic holiday getaways in the country. Some couples like to have a little private time before they're bombarded with family events."

He nodded. "Okay. What does this have to do with anything?"

Kaitlyn ignored the irritation in his voice. "Well, I was talking to her last night and she offered to put Sweetwater Springs on the list. Not just on the list, she offered to put it at the top of the list." A swell of excitement ballooned in her chest. The idea was genius. It would work. She knew it would.

Mitch's face held no expression. "Has she been here before?"

"No, but she hasn't gone to all the other places on the list either. That's what Google is for. You can research pretty much everything about a place, to the point you almost feel like you've been there. Even this old B and B is online."

"Yeah, but the website showcases how it was ten years ago." He glanced around the kitchen to make his point.

Yes, the cabinets were old, and the color of the walls was tired but she could fix that. And although her parents had never been big on celebrating the holidays, decorating was her specialty. She held out her hands and realized they were shaking. Mitch's laser-sharp eyes noticed too. *So what?* This meant a lot to her. She didn't care if he knew she was nervous. "If this B and B is promoted in *Loving Life*, it'll bring customers. Customers bring in money. Then the bank will approve me for a loan to buy you out at the end of the two months."

He narrowed his stained-glass eyes. She needed him to buy into the plan. There was no backing out once they got started. Turning the B&B on its head and transforming it into a romantic holiday haven wouldn't be easy. But it was doable.

"It's a lie," he finally said.

"It's not a lie. Sweetwater Springs *is* romantic. I've always thought so. And there aren't that many repairs to be done here. Not really. I'm sure my grandmother has a tree and other festive décor. I'll find it."

His mouth was set in a grim line.

It was hard to take him seriously with a cookie crumb lodged in the corner of his mouth though. She focused on that as she pressed on. "Look, my grandparents must've meant something to you if Grandma Mable put you in the will."

"Mable and Henry meant a lot to me. But running a bed and breakfast isn't my dream. I'm not cut out for greeting strangers and making them feel welcome. And I'm certainly not jolly old Saint Nick."

Obviously. "Great. Then you'll get a payday and leave at the end of the agreement, which if we signed today, would fall on Christmas Eve." She pointed to a calendar she'd conveniently laid on the counter. "See, that makes eight full weeks, which according to the fine print of the contract, defines two months. Then it's a merry Christmas for both of us." She watched him run a hand through his overgrown dark locks as he seemed to consider what she was telling him. Her fingers suddenly itched to run through his hair too. She'd never been attracted to a man with a beard before. Not until now.

His jaw ticked on one side as he studied her. Then he lifted a finger and wiped his mouth, removing the crumb. "*If* I agree, I don't want to be front and center. I'll handle repairs, anything you need while I'm here, but this place is yours. You can buy me out at the end of the agreement. Even though I don't think you'll be anywhere near ready to do that by Christmas Eve."

"We'll see." She reached for a list she'd been working on last night. "I started writing down the things that need to be done. These are the jobs I think are better suited for you."

Most of the items she'd written down were small. The chimney needed to be swept. Lightbulbs and air filters needed to be changed. A fuse had blown for one of the rooms upstairs and there was no electricity running to it. One of the biggest repairs she'd listed was that there was no hot water in the house. She'd discovered that this morning after enduring an ice-cold shower, which she still hadn't managed to warm up from.

Mitch took a long moment scrutinizing the to-do list. "Fine. I'll get started on this today," he finally said.

"Does that mean you'll stay?"

He hesitated, and it almost looked painful for him to nod even though physically she suspected he was in tip-top condition. "I'll call Mr. Garrison and tell him it's a go."

She squealed in excitement and, unable to help herself, ran around the kitchen island and threw her arms around his neck. "Thank you, thank you, thank you!"

After her brain caught up with her body, she realized her chest was pressed up against the hard mass of his muscled body. And *oh, heavens*. He smelled divine, like pine trees and honey and alpha man. Her body buzzed with awareness.

Squelching it, she pulled away.

Mitch was staring at her, and if she wasn't mistaken, his kaleidoscope eyes had gotten darker.

She swallowed, wondering if he could also hear the boom of her heart in her chest. Just from that brief physical touch—which she would be sure to avoid from now on.

Taking the list, he stood.

"Sorry. I just got excited." She offered her hand for him to shake. "Partners?"

He slipped his warm, calloused hand in hers. More physical touch. *Crap.* "For the two months. Then I'm leaving," he clarified.

"Understood."

* * *

Three hours later, Kaitlyn collapsed on the sofa in the main room. She'd cleaned until she was breathless and sore, and she'd barely made a dent in the long list of to-dos she'd assigned herself. Pressing her head back into the couch cushion, she closed her eyes for a moment. Perhaps she could hire someone else to help her. Except she didn't have money for that.

Maybe she could ask her parents for help. But they hadn't even approved of her coming here in the first place. Running a B&B was career suicide, her mother had told her on the phone as she'd packed. And then again on the drive down Interstate 95.

Kaitlyn had gone to the New York School of Interior Design. She'd worked her butt off for the last couple of years building a solid reputation in her field. Little did her mom know that Kaitlyn's career was already dead in the water though, thanks to Hollywood's favorite action hero, Bradley Foster.

Kaitlyn scanned the long list of things that still needed to be done before the article released in two weeks, resisting the sudden fear climbing through her like unwanted vines. This was just the cleaning. To make good on Josie's promise, the inn needed to be merry and romantic too. That was the fun part. Maybe she could browse Pinterest for ideas.

As she considered her options, her cell phone rang on the coffee table.

Kaitlyn gave a quick glance at the caller ID and answered on the second ring. "Hey, lady."

"All right, the December magazine has gone to press. Your neck and mine are on the line so I hope you're prepared to make this happen."

Kaitlyn's mouth dropped open. "We just talked last night. It's not even been twenty-four hours."

"Maybe in your world, but in mine, time moves fast. No rest for the weary, blah, blah, blah. Please tell me your partner is in."

Kaitlyn warmed just at Mitch's mention. It was an unconscious, physical reaction. *What is wrong with me?* "He said yes."

"Perfect!"

"Yes, it is." Kaitlyn stood and walked to the mantel above the fireplace where several framed pictures were displayed. Her gaze paused on a photo of her grandparents standing in front of the B&B, the pride on their faces clear. A grand-opening sign hung behind them. Kaitlyn had always favored her father, who'd obviously gotten his looks from Mable. All three had the same dark hair and large, brown eyes. The same straight nose.

Kaitlyn regretted that she hadn't spent enough time with her grandparents to really know who they were. Not that she'd had any say in the matter as a child. Her parents preferred to spend their vacation time at fancy resorts and on cruises. Once Kaitlyn was in college, she'd always stayed in the city and spent her Christmases with friends who didn't have anywhere to go, or she'd gone home with Josie. Because Kaitlyn had spent so little time here, coming to see her grandparents for the holidays just didn't feel natural. Even so, she wished she'd come anyway.

Josie cleared her throat on the other end of the line.

"Listen to this. The Sweetwater Bed and Breakfast in Sweetwater Springs just might be *the* most romantic holiday retreat in America. How could an inn with an address on Mistletoe Lane be anything less? Each of the large, airy rooms, named after a few of America's favorite romantic couples, features a breathtaking view of the North Carolina mountains. Stay in, snuggle, and read by the fire. Or take a walk under a blanket of twinkling stars. Make a wish on one and watch it come true as you live out your most romantic fantasies this Christmas season."

The breath caught in Kaitlyn's chest. "Is that what you wrote?"

"Something like that. I pulled a late night on your behalf. I described the town and then I pitched the bed and breakfast hard. I was praying the website was up to date."

Kaitlyn cringed. As Mitch had already pointed out, the website was slightly behind the times. "The rooms aren't named after romantic couples but that's a genius idea."

"I thought so too, especially since you're such a romantic-movie buff."

"You're a closet buff," Kaitlyn accused.

"I only watch them with you, and only for the popcorn and soda you provide."

Kaitlyn laughed, suddenly sad that she and Josie wouldn't be having any of those girls' nights in, watching movies and stuffing themselves silly, anytime soon.

"Now go make it happen. I, on the flip side, need to get started on articles for the January issue of *Loving Life*."

"Or you could try sleep for a change," Kaitlyn suggested.

"In broad daylight? You must be crazy."

After they hung up, Kaitlyn went to retrieve her list from the coffee table. She grabbed a pen and added, "Update website." She'd loved what Josie had written about the B&B. It made her want to come and visit this place herself. And she couldn't wait to name the rooms. The interior designer in her already had the wheels spinning. The first room could be named after *Anne of Green Gables*. Anne Shirley and Gilbert Blythe were the first fictional characters to ever make her heart skip a beat. The room could be done in a multitude of pasture greens with antique furniture from the early 1900s.

Yes. A smile molded her lips. This was exactly the kind of work that had thrilled her in interior design school. This was going to be amazing. She was going to transform this inn into everything the feature article Josie wrote had promised. In two very long, sleepless weeks.

* * *

Mitch had been plugging away at the list that Kaitlyn had given him over the last few days. There were just a couple of items left to do but those would wait until tomorrow. Right now, he needed to check on his mom, who'd looked exhausted when he'd left her early this morning.

He packed up his toolbox that he kept in the cab of his truck and gave Kaitlyn a wave on the way out, forgoing talking to her because, one, he was tired, and two, he'd been keeping his head down, focusing on his work—or trying to—instead of allowing himself to get distracted by her. She was definitely distracting. The way she walked. The way she twirled her hair around her index finger when she was lost in thought. Her every little mannerism was driving him insane. How the heck was he supposed to work with her for two months?

Climbing in his truck, he drove to the stop sign at the end of Mistletoe Lane, turned the corner, and pulled into his mom's driveway, letting out a deep sigh of relief when he cut the engine. His mother drove him crazy too but in a completely different way. No doubt she was inside preparing dinner just like she'd done every night since he'd arrived, even though he'd insisted she didn't need to.

He climbed out of his truck and headed up the porch steps. "Mom?" he called as he stepped inside.

The TV was blaring as he entered. He was doubly accosted by a thin veil of smoke in the air. "Mom?" he said, adrenaline firing through his veins. Like a hound dog on a scent, he followed the smoke to the kitchen just as the alarm started shrieking on the wall overhead. There were two items on the stove top, one of which was bubbling over and spilling onto the hot surface with a sharp sizzle. He grabbed the handle to remove it and then jerked back as the heated metal stung his palm. "Mom?"

The smoke detector continued to wail in his ear. *Where the hell is she?* He grabbed a dishtowel and pushed the overrunning pot to the back of the stove. Then he turned the stove's dials off on the back panel. Finally, the alarm silenced.

As he walked briskly back through the empty living room, he scanned the surroundings for his mom. He followed the hallway down to her room and paused at the sight of her lying across the bed. "Mom!"

She wasn't moving. Not at first. She began to stir as he grabbed one of her shoulders and gave an urgent shake. The smoke detector must have been loud enough to alert the neighbors. How had she napped through it?

Her eyes fluttered open. "Oh, Mitch, you're home," she said groggily.

"What's wrong?" he asked, giving her an assessing once-over.

She grimaced and scratched the side of her cheek. "Nothing. I guess I dozed off. I was just—" Her eyes widened. "The stove! I have food cooking on the st—"

"Already turned it off," he said, concern tightening his chest. "Mom, the smoke detector was going off, and you didn't wake up."

Her brows pinched above red, tired eyes. "Really?" She sat up, moving slowly for a woman who never slowed down.

"Are you feeling okay?"

"Oh, I'm fine." She laughed softly as if to think otherwise was silly. "It was just a long day between the two houses I cleaned. I only intended to rest for a minute."

Mitch didn't like what he was hearing. He remembered being so tired when he was in boot camp that he would practically pass out as soon as his head hit the pillow. A grenade could've gone off and he wouldn't have woken, as tired as he was. He didn't like to think that this was how his mom was living these days. He knew she was serious when she cleaned houses. She scrubbed the floors and cabinets by hand, vacuumed, dusted. It was the reason everyone in Sweetwater Springs wanted to hire her. "The house could've caught fire," he said.

"Oh, I would've woken up eventually." She patted his knee as he sat beside her on the bed. "Don't worry about me. Are you hungry?" she asked, flipping the subject.

"Do you ever stop?"

She shook her head. "It's not often that my only son comes home to visit. I love cooking for you."

"Not tonight." He got up, walked over to the headboard of her bed, and propped up several pillows. Then he pointed. "You're sitting right here and having dinner in bed tonight."

Her mouth fell open to protest.

"No arguing. I'm serving you here, and I'll eat beside you."

She chuckled softly. "Okay. That sounds nice."

"Good." He watched her climb under the covers and sit up against the pillows. Then he went back to the kitchen and got to work finishing their meal. But he wasn't hungry anymore. Instead, worry sat heavily in his stomach. His mom was one of the strongest people he knew. She was always caring for others and evidently neglecting herself in the process. While he was here, he'd change all that, he promised himself. At least that was one good thing to come out of this situation with the bed and breakfast. If he and Kaitlyn really could revive the place and she did buy out his half, then perhaps he could pay off his mom's mortgage. He'd continue to send her money too, of course, and her days of working to the point of exhaustion would be over.

"Here we go," Mitch said, carrying their dinner plates into the bedroom a few minutes later.

"You really are the best son a mom could have." She secured her plate of baked chicken, brown rice, and green beans on her lap.

He took the spot next to her.

"It's burnt," she commented as she stabbed her fork into the dry chicken breast. "My fault."

"I like it burnt."

She snorted. "Liar. But I love you for it. You've been here a few days already. How long are you staying this time?"

He swallowed the bite of chicken he was chewing. It tasted more like cardboard than actual food. It struggled to go down almost as much as his next words struggled to come up. "I'll be staying longer than expected."

"How long?" she probed.

"Two months."

His mom whipped her head to the side. "You'll be home for Thanksgiving and Christmas!"

Not by choice. "I have some things to take care of."

Her smile engulfed her face. "Well, this is reason to celebrate. Maybe we should open the bottle of champagne I keep in the refrigerator."

Mitch laughed unexpectedly. It felt good in comparison to the stress he'd been shouldering just being in Sweetwater Springs. "No. After dinner, you're going to sleep while I clean up the kitchen." He popped another bite of extra-crispy chicken into his mouth and chewed.

She was quiet for a moment. "Well, if you're staying for any amount of time, you should know that Brian Everson is—"

Mitch held up a hand, every muscle in his body suddenly tense. "Stop right there." He had a rule. He didn't talk about the Everson family. He kept his distance out of respect and a promise he'd made when he was eighteen years old. Shutting the door on any information about the Everson family was for his own sanity. He was a fixer but no matter how hard he tried, he'd never be able to fix what had happened to Brian in the accident.

CHAPTER FOUR

Kaitlyn lay across the couch and yawned. She wasn't ready to head to bed just yet. Not when there was so much to do. She pulled her sketchbook toward her and stared down at the basic layout of the house. It was two stories with the main entrance opening into a formal living room. To the right was the sitting room, where she was now, and to the left was a dining area. The B&B had five guest rooms upstairs and living quarters for the host on the first floor.

Most curious was the first-floor ballroom. What had her grandparents done with a ballroom? She never remembered seeing it when she'd come to visit as a child but those were very brief trips hallmarked by smiley face pancakes, piggyback rides, and Grandpa Henry reading her books by the fireplace.

Kaitlyn drew a question mark in the box on the inn's layout that represented the ballroom. She'd keep that room closed off for now. Any guests that came to visit didn't need to go there. All they needed were their own rooms, which she'd already started preparing. The rooms didn't feel quite as romantic as she wanted them to yet. Grandma Mable had made them cozy enough but Kaitlyn wanted to make each one unique and unforgettable. She envisioned guests wanting to come again to experience a different room.

With another yawn, she traded her sketchbook for her laptop and settled it over her thighs. Then she opened a browser and searched for romantic interior designs on Pinterest. She'd always gained inspiration from what others had done before her. "Why reinvent the wheel?" one of her professors had liked to ask in college. "Just redecorate it." Kaitlyn liked that philosophy. She'd loved everything about interior design school. Being there had only solidified her desire to create beauty in her environment.

Scrolling down the Pinterest search page, she looked for something that would catch her eye and then froze when she came across a design she'd done for Bradley Foster. With her design firm, she'd worked for lots of important people in New York—mayors, athletes, newscasters, business executives. But Bradley was her first celebrity job. Designing a room for him had been a dream come true. A step in the right direction for her career, or so she'd thought.

A sick feeling slithered through her stomach as she stared at his image. Being an action movie hero, he didn't lack for muscles. He had dark hair and eyes that could intimidate any bad guy on-screen and make any female with one good eye swoon. Heck, his good looks aside, the man's voice had enough appeal to attract the opposite sex from one end of the world to the other.

Below his photograph was a picture of a majestic-looking living room that Kaitlyn had helped design. Most clients didn't get involved with the details of the work but Bradley had. He was always there, and at first, it was exciting. Then there was a moment when she'd thought Bradley might try to kiss her while working on that front room pictured on the computer screen, but she'd diverted his attention. She wasn't romantically interested in Bradley Foster, world-famous movie star or not. For one, he was married with kids. He was just getting carried away from being in such close quarters, she'd reasoned, making excuses for him and putting it out of her mind. But his advances had only escalated after that. He'd hired her for another job, and she'd agreed because it was the opportunity of a lifetime. How could she possibly say no to Bradley Foster?

Kaitlyn closed her laptop with a huff. She was done with this walk down memory lane. She needed every bit of her energy—physical, mental, and emotional—to get the Sweetwater Bed and Breakfast up to par on a nickel-and-dime budget. And that meant not letting herself get sidetracked by thinking about her ex-client.

Or by drooling over Mitch.

* * *

Christmas music floated through the overhead speakers at the local hardware store as Mitch headed inside. Really? It was barely November. Plus, there was no need to put shoppers in a gift-buying frame of mind here. All he needed was a chimney brush and some pipe extensions to check off yet another item on Kaitlyn's to-do list.

On his way through the aisles, he also grabbed a couple of large tarps to cover the living room, a pair of goggles, and a face mask to keep him from inhaling any smut or ash.

As he was heading to the checkout, he heard someone call his name.

"Last-Ditch Mitch!"

A groan settled deep in his throat. He hated that nickname. Turning, he saw Tucker Locklear grinning at him. Looking at his longtime friend, Mitch wouldn't know that the last couple of years had been rough on him, losing his wife Renee. The only clue was the dark telltale shadows under Tuck's eyes that even his Cherokee Indian complexion couldn't hide.

"Hey, man. I thought the lighting in here was playing tricks on me," Tuck said as he approached.

Mitch shook his head and then Tuck's hand. "No, I'm home for a while."

"Yeah? How long?" Tuck was a physical therapist now, which was fitting because, as an adrenaline junkie, Tuck knew injuries and how to treat them. He'd likely strained or broken every muscle and bone in his body over the years.

"I'm helping the Russos' granddaughter fix up the B and B for business."

Tuck's brow lowered. "Really? I thought that place was closed now that Mable has passed. I'm sorry about that, by the way. I know you thought a lot of her."

"Thanks." Mitch folded his arms at his chest, applying pressure to the ache there. He did miss Mable, more than he wanted to let on. Henry too. That old couple had been as good as family to him. "I actually inherited half the business," Mitch confided. He hadn't even told his own mother yet. If he wasn't careful, she'd find out from someone in town before he got to tell her himself. That wouldn't be ideal for either of them.

"Wow. That's great, man. So you're going to run a bed and breakfast now that you're out of the corps? Is that the plan?"

"Not a chance," Mitch said without hesitation. "Can you see me baking cookies and playing nice with difficult guests?"

"I don't know." Tuck shrugged a shoulder. "Your museles are a tad oversized and maybe a little intimidating but you're nothing but a big bear, in my opinion. I think you'd be good at it."

Mitch narrowed his eyes. "Not happening."

Tuck grinned wide. "So, at least a couple weeks, huh?"

"Something like that."

"Great. I'll call Alex and set up a night for us all to catch up. Maybe a case of beer over at the bluffs for old times' sake."

"That's still illegal," Mitch pointed out.

"True. And since you and Alex are both law enforcement now, I guess we'll just knock a few back at the Tipsy Tavern."

Mitch nodded. He and Alex had always wanted to be police officers growing up. They'd both been junior cadets in high school and had planned to attend police academy together. After the accident though, Mitch had needed the quick ticket out of Sweetwater Springs that the military recruiter had offered him. He'd achieved his dream of working in law enforcement by becoming a military police officer while Alex had stayed local.

"Did you hear that Skip runs the tavern these days? His Uncle Jake retired and handed over the reins," Tuck continued, oblivious to Mitch's mental sidetrack.

"Skip Mazer runs a bar?" Mitch asked, blinking his old friend back into focus. One Christmas tune in the background switched out for another as Tuck slapped a hand on his back.

"See what happens when you stay away too long? Everything changes."

Not everything.

"I'll bring you up to speed when we go out." Tuck started

to walk away and then jabbed a finger in Mitch's direction. "I have your number, and you better answer. I can get Alex to put out an APB on you if you don't."

"Hanging out sounds good. I'll answer," Mitch promised, offering a wave and continuing toward the checkout again. A night of drinks with his old friends would be fun, he told himself. Catching up on the goings-on in Sweetwater Springs would also be good. There was never a risk of running into one of the Eversons at the tavern. Most of them were too good to hang out with the locals. At least that was Mitch's perception. Except for his former classmate Brian Everson, who'd always been a nice guy.

Mitch got in line and shifted back and forth on his feet, trying not to let the guilt settle in around him like it usually did when he thought about Brian. The sweet holiday music compounded his agitation and chipped away at his patience as he waited in line. *Bah humbug.*

After finally purchasing his items, he climbed into his truck and drove to the B&B, where Kaitlyn was on a ladder leaning against the large wraparound front porch. She was at least ten feet off the ground.

Cursing under his breath, he pushed open the driver's side door and headed over. "What do you think you're doing?" he barked.

She whipped her head around to face him and squeaked as she momentarily lost her balance. Her body swayed in the air.

Mitch's reflexes were primed. He took off running toward her and anchored the ladder as it shifted.

"You scared me to death!" she accused, white-knuckling the ladder's rungs.

"Well, you shouldn't be up there. Especially when there's no one here to help if you get in trouble."

"I was doing just fine until you shouted at me, thank you very much."

He closed his eyes and took a steadying breath. One hard-headed female wasn't enough in his life, apparently. Now he had both his mom *and* Kaitlyn Russo to deal with. "Please come down," he said, tempering his frustration.

"I'm not done yet."

"Done doing what?"

"There are a bunch of branches on the roof of the veranda."

He followed her gaze and noticed that the second-story windows were open too. Wreaths now hung on each one. He imagined her dangling out the windows to hang them. A low growl emitted from his throat. "There are a dozen things to take care of and you decide to hang Christmas wreaths? It's still two months away."

"I found the box of wreaths when I was in the storage building getting the ladder," she explained. "And it's only seven weeks away. Christmas will be here before you know it."

He could only pray that was true as his hands anchored the ladder. Because the sooner the holiday got here, the sooner he could leave.

He looked back up where he had the perfect view of her perfect backside. A surge of unruly, unwanted attraction curled through him.

"You can let go. I'm not going to fall, you know. Unless you start yelling at me again." She glared down at him.

He hesitated before stepping away. "I didn't yell. I was concerned. Now, please come down. I'll get the branches myself." His shoulders relaxed as she started to do as he asked. She traveled down two rungs and then missed the third and her body went into free fall—straight into his ready arms.

He gripped her against him. "I got you," he said, noticing how wide her brown eyes had become. And how delicious she smelled, like a rose garden in bloom. "If I hadn't been here, you'd be laid up on the couch for the rest of the week."

"I don't have time for that." She didn't move to get out of his hold on her though. Not immediately. Resting against his chest, her face was dangerously close to his. They spoke in quiet voices because they were only inches apart. Close enough to lean in and kiss her, if he wanted to. And yeah, there was some foolish part of him that thought that was an excellent idea.

"How do the wreaths look?" she asked.

His gaze shifted momentarily. "Like you could've broken your neck putting them up."

She smiled, and that spoke to the foolish part of him that desperately wanted to taste those lips. Therefore, the only reasonable thing to do was put her down and take a step back, which he did, quickly and efficiently.

"The front of the house is the first thing people see when they pass by," she explained. "First impressions are everything."

"How about this? From here on out, you take care of the inside of the house, and I'll manage things out here," he said.

"Okay. There are plenty more things to do in the guest rooms. But I might need your help with a few of them."

"You got it. And next time you decide to climb up on the roof, don't." Not unless he was here to catch her, because he wouldn't mind holding her in his arms again. What the hell was wrong with him?

He watched her stubborn chin tip up and fully expected those plump lips of hers to spout off something smart.

Instead, she whirled on her heel, turning her back to him. "Don't fall," she called back to him. But her tone of voice made him wonder if she wouldn't mind seeing him bust his butt.

Mitch worked steadily until dark and then stepped inside to say good night. He purposefully walked with heavy feet on the hardwood floors to make his presence known. Kaitlyn had proved to be a little jumpy since he'd met her. Granted, her first impression of him had been to think he was an intruder. But every time he'd rounded a corner over the last week, she'd seemed to stiffen.

She turned to acknowledge him. "Hey."

She had soft music streaming in from an old-time radio off to the side of the room. Thankfully, not Christmas tunes. A few of the tarps he'd gotten earlier were scattered on the floor along with a couple cans of paint.

"I found the paint and brushes in the laundry room closet. What do you think of the color?"

His gaze settled on the soft yellow of the walls. "It looks great. You did all this while I was outside?" he asked, winning a smile from her.

"It still needs a second coat but it's amazing what a difference a little paint can make."

"Seems so."

"I also named a few of the guest rooms while I worked."

He lifted a brow. "Have you been sniffing the paint too?"

She laughed. "All the guest rooms are going to be named after a famous couple in books or the movies. The whole room will have a theme to match."

"I think that's a great idea. Who do you have so far?"

She set her paintbrush in the roller tray and wiped her hands on the apron she was wearing. Then she ticked off her responses on her fingers. "I'm starting with my favorites. Anne of Green Gables and Gilbert Blythe. Scarlett and Rhett."

"Good ones," he said.

"Those are both books that were made into movies, so two birds with one stone. I was thinking Scarlett and Rhett's room could have a Deep South décor. There is actually some Civil War–era furniture here that I can relocate to that room."

"I'll help you with moving furniture," he said, enjoying how her whole face lit up as she talked about her ideas. Her passion was evident. "Any other couples?" he asked.

"Just one more right now." She pulled her lower lip between her teeth. "Baby and Johnny."

He shook his head, trying to figure out who she was talking about.

She gave him a look of total disbelief. "Oh, come on. From *Dirty Dancing*."

"Oh, right." He nodded. "Let me guess. That room will have a sixties vibe."

She grinned. "Wouldn't that be fun?"

"It would."

"Any other suggestions for me?"

He scratched his chin beneath his beard. "I prefer action movies," he said, noting how her smile wilted just slightly. He guessed she stuck strictly to romance. "Also nonfiction books. The books I read don't really talk about well-known couples. How about I handle the repairs and you do all the decorating, including naming the guest rooms?"

She nodded, smiling easily again. "Seems like we make a good team."

He was usually more of a solo kind of guy. As an MP, he'd never had a partner, unless one counted his police dog, which he did. Scout was retired a few months before Mitch got out of the corps. The lucky canine now lived with a nice civilian family, hopefully spending his days chewing bones and barking at birds.

"Yeah," Mitch said, knowing he should say his goodbye and walk out the front door. Instead, he stared at Kaitlyn for a moment longer. She was marked with paint and beaming with creative energy. Seeing her in her element unhinged something inside him. There was nothing more attractive than a woman having fun. It made him want to stay and have fun with her.

Bad idea.

He cleared his throat. "Okay, well, I'll see you in the morning. Don't climb any tall ladders while I'm gone," he teased, and then grinned as her mouth dipped into a playful frown.

"I won't. And come hungry. I'll have breakfast and coffee waiting for you."

"You don't have to do that."

"I figure I better get used to serving others. I'll practice on you."

When she put it that way, it was hard for him to say no.

* * *

Kaitlyn had been up since five thirty. She'd grabbed a few groceries the day before, hoping they'd last a week, but she'd already burned the toast, twice, and was on her second batch of scrambled eggs because the first batch had been a disgusting mush.

She glanced at the clock above the stove. Mitch would be here any minute. She pulled a cast-iron frying pan to one of the vacant burners and began placing sliced bacon inside.

"You're supposed to wait until it's hot first," a voice said, coming up behind her.

She jumped and whirled in one simultaneous motion

while also pulling a hand to her chest. "You snuck up on me!" she snapped, suddenly buzzing with adrenaline.

Mitch stopped for a moment, giving her an unreadable expression, and then stepped beside her. "You should lock the doors."

"I did last night but I guess I left it unlocked when I went out to get the newspaper this morning."

He surveyed her breakfast display. "You didn't cook the eggs long enough. It helps to add a little milk if you want them fluffy. Maybe put in some shredded cheese for flavor too. Did you add salt?"

She pressed her lips together. "I grew up with two working parents. They were always in a rush so breakfast was usually a Pop-Tart on the way to school."

The corner of his mouth twitched. "I would've given my right arm for a Pop-Tart. They were too expensive. Our neighbors had chickens and gave us eggs in exchange for my mom doing odd jobs for them. So that's what we had every morning."

He took a commanding step closer, causing her to move aside. Then he began lifting the bacon off the pan and placing it on a napkin. He adjusted the dial from high to medium heat.

She watched him work, taking mental notes and trying not to let her emotions get in the way. So she wasn't a fantastic cook—yet. She'd learn. She'd do whatever it took. How hard could cooking for a house full of guests be?

"Eggs, bacon, what else?" he asked, grabbing a mixing bowl from one of the cabinets. He expertly cracked several eggs with one hand.

"What do you mean *what else*?"

"Well, if I were a guest, this wouldn't be enough. You usually want a starch as well. Mable was famous for her made-from-scratch biscuits but I don't expect you to tackle that."

Kaitlyn shoved her hands on her hips. "Why not?"

"No offense. Mable used to say it took her the better part of a decade to get them right. It's not fancy but you could serve grits."

Kaitlyn wrinkled her nose, which made him chuckle. It was a reserved, quiet sound that reverberated through her. She liked it and suddenly longed to hear it again.

"You are definitely not from the South, are you?" He splashed some milk with the egg yolks and beat them with a wire whisk that he'd located in a drawer beside the stove.

She was amazed at his cooking skills. A man who knew his way around a kitchen was a definite turn-on. And a woman who didn't...probably not so much.

"Did my grandmother teach you how to cook?" she asked.

He looked almost apologetic as he nodded. "Yep. She ran the gamut with her meals. Sometimes she offered up a simple country sampler breakfast like this one. Other times, she treated guests to gourmet omelets and pastries. She was a talented chef."

"And you know how to make her famous made-from-scratch biscuits?"

"I'll teach you," he said. "Mable tended to exaggerate. It only took me a couple years to master her biscuits." He winked in Kaitlyn's direction.

Her insides turned mushier than her eggs. "Hopefully it won't take me that long to master them." She needed to learn fast, before the guests started making reservations and Mitch left. "I'm expecting customers to start booking after next week. Josie told me that the magazine hits stands and mailboxes a couple weeks before each new month."

She stepped aside and watched as Mitch took over preparing the bacon and eggs. Then he set a saucepan of water to boil and retrieved a cream-colored bag from the pantry. "You can't move south and not love grits. I'll make them, and you'll wonder where you've been all your life."

She folded her arms across her chest, watching him work. "I've been in New York having my food delivered. I have all my favorite places on speed dial."

"Well, today is the day you'll learn the art of making breakfast, the most important meal of the day," he said, measuring out the contents of the bag of grits.

Twenty minutes later, they sat down together at one of the dining room tables with full plates. The aroma wafted under her nose and made her mouth water. So did the man in front of her. She'd been snuffing out little fires in her belly ever since he'd entered her kitchen this morning. Ever since he'd walked into the B&B a week ago.

She picked up her fork and stabbed at a fluffy lump of perfectly golden eggs. "Long jog this morning?" she asked, making small talk. There was something about that strong, silent alpha vibe Mitch had going that made her uncharacteristically nervous. She could usually talk to anyone. But the man sitting across the table had her stomach fluttering and her tongue leaden.

"Only about seven miles."

She choked on the lump of eggs that she'd just forked into her mouth.

Everything in Mitch seemed to stiffen as he watched her. She held up a hand to ward him off, guessing he was about two seconds away from hopping over the table and performing the Heimlich. And while the thought of his arms wrapped around her again was appealing, having her breakfast fly across the room in front of him was not.

"I'm fine," she choked out. She took a drink from her glass of orange juice. "Just surprised that you jogged so far."

"You wouldn't believe how good it feels when you're done. Better than sex."

She started to choke again. "You...did not just say that," she said on a laugh.

A smile crept through his angled features. "Sorry. I'm used to being around a bunch of marines, I guess."

"Well, if you're going to be helping me with the B and B, you can't talk to the guests like they're marines."

"I'll just try not to talk to them at all. I'm good at flying under the radar."

She raised both brows. "I've noticed. You've been sneaking up on me ever since we met." She bit into a piece of salty bacon, chewed, and swallowed. "You said your mom still lives in town?"

He nodded while continuing to eat. "Yep."

"What about your dad?"

His fork paused momentarily. "He died when I was nine."

Her heart broke a little for him. "I'm sorry. That must've been hard for you."

"It was. And watching my mom work two jobs to make sure we had what we needed was hard too."

"Is that why you're so set on leaving again?" She regretted asking as soon as the question had come out of her mouth. It was none of her business why he wanted to leave. He'd agreed to the stipulations of the will, and that's all she needed to know.

"It's more complicated than that," he said after a long moment. "Sweetwater Springs represents my past. Not my future."

"I see."

"My turn to ask questions," he said, locking her gaze and holding it captive.

"Okay."

"Who hurt you?"

She nearly choked again. "Excuse me?"

"Every time I walk into the room, you stiffen. Why?"

Her heart was beating fast now. Thanks to Bradley Foster, she was jumpy. He hadn't gotten what he'd wanted but he'd still taken something from her. Her trust. "No one. I'm fine," she lied, pulling her gaze to her plate. But she had every intention of making that lie a truth. Her nerves would eventually settle. Her memories of Bradley's hands on her would soon fade—hopefully.

Mitch didn't speak again until she looked back up at him. "You don't have to worry about me," he said in a quiet voice, his eyes steady and sincere.

She nodded. "I know."

"A friend of mine says I'm just a big bear." The hard angles of his face softened as he smiled.

Her insides turned to mushy eggs again. "Well, I'll try not to poke you."

One of his eyebrows shot up, and heat flooded her cheeks. That comment had unintentionally sounded sexual. The entire vibe between her and Mitch was unintentionally sexual, and that's what she had to worry most about with him. He was temporary, and she wasn't looking for a relationship. It wasn't the right time in her life to get romantically involved. She had a life to reconstruct, one room at a time.

CHAPTER FIVE

On a late Friday afternoon, three weeks into the contract, Kaitlyn checked off yet another to-do item on her dwindling list of things to be done. Mitch had been taking care of the outside of the house all day. She'd barely laid eyes on him since breakfast when he'd given her another cooking lesson. This one on Grandma Mable's famous made-from-scratch biscuits.

She glanced around the large, open front room of the B&B. In less than a month's time, it had transformed from dusty and shabby to a warm and welcoming home. She'd left a lot of things the same but she'd added her own flair to the place. Her bachelor's degree in interior design had to be good for something now that she'd lost her dream job.

Gah, she'd been such an idiot to think Bradley Foster had seen something in her that the other newbie designers didn't have. Yeah, he'd seen something, all right, but it hadn't been talent. That should have been clear as his excuses to have her come over had increased. His advances had become more blatant every time she went. Why had she been a fool to keep going to his place alone? Why hadn't she listened to her gut before things had gotten so out of hand?

A chill ran up her spine. Bradley had been harder to push off that last night. There'd been an arrogance about the way he'd leaned over her, touching her even after she'd told him she wasn't comfortable.

Sexual harassment, for sure. Would it have turned into more? She didn't know.

"Who do you think you are? You're nobody," he'd gritted out as he'd pawed her like a cat on its scratching post. "You don't deserve to be here. The only reason you're here is because I wanted it. Working for someone like me will look good on your résumé. You owe me for pulling you ahead."

"Stop." She'd tried to yank her wrist out of his grasp as his other hand crept higher on her thigh. "Bradley, stop!" she said a little more forcefully.

Did I say it forcefully enough?

Then she'd heard the downstairs door slam. He'd pulled back just for a moment, and she'd swung away from him. But not before shoving a knee between his legs—hard.

His shriek had been loud and high-pitched—unworthy of his action hero persona on-screen.

"You're right. I don't deserve this job. I deserve better." She'd marched past the cleaning crew, trembling and praying to God he didn't chase after her. Then she'd taken a cab straight to the police station to file a report. She doubted it'd done any good though. There were no witnesses, and a hand up her skirt was as far as Bradley had gotten. When she'd gone to work the next day, her boss had summoned her to his office. Bradley had called to complain. He'd said that Kaitlyn had made an inappropriate and unwanted advance toward him. She'd also assaulted him with her knee to his groin, and he was threatening to press charges.

Kaitlyn had tried to explain what had happened. *She* was the victim, not Bradley Foster. But her longtime boss had fired her anyway. Her career with one of the leading design firms in New York was over.

Kaitlyn blinked, realizing her eyes were stinging. A tear slipped down her cheek. *Crap.*

Then the front door opened, and Mitch stepped inside.

She could feel his gaze assessing her as she quickly wiped the tear away. "Hey. I was just, um, cleaning. All the dust in here seems to be stirring up my allergies." She kept her gaze hidden, hoping he'd buy her excuse even though the house was spotless these days.

He nodded. "I thought I'd get to work fixing the front door. It's still catching a little bit."

"Um-hmm." She pulled her sketchbook to her and pretended to make herself busy, though the page was blank and her pencil lead broken. She'd never been good at lying, and even if she were, she doubted she could pull anything over on Mitch.

He graciously pulled his gaze from her and looked around the room. "Looks like you found more of Mable's Christmas decorations."

Kaitlyn looked up and watched him assess what she'd done. "Hopefully there's not a rule about waiting until after Thanksgiving here."

"Not according to Mable. She was as bad as the stores, playing 'Jingle Bells' before Halloween."

Kaitlyn smiled at this. Thanksgiving was next Thursday so she wasn't quite that bad. And she'd never had a house and several boxes' worth of decorations to put out. This was new, and it challenged the interior designer in her.

"You've been busy."

"So have you. We've barely stopped working over the last few weeks, and it's paid off, I'd say. The magazine will be floating around the country anytime now. Then I expect the phone to start ringing off the hook." She looked over at the old-fashioned phone on the table by the wall. It was silent just as it had been all day. No matter if the December issue of *Loving Life* wasn't out yet, the B&B was in the phone listings. People could happen upon it and book reservations anytime.

Mitch was watching her again. She probably looked a mess. "You know what? This place is ready," he said.

She shook her head. "No. There are still a few things left to do."

"Maybe, but everyone deserves a break." He stepped closer. "You haven't explored the town since you've been here. When the guests arrive, how are you supposed to direct them where to shop or eat?"

"I've been to Sweetwater Springs before," she said.

"Not recently. Go get dressed. I'm taking you out."

"You don't have to. I'm sure that's not how you want to spend your afternoon."

"And you'd be right about that. I hate sightseeing almost as much as I hate shopping."

She cocked her head to one side. "Then why are you offering to take me out to do just that?"

"Because I know you'll love it."

* * *

What am I doing? All Mitch knew was he'd walked into the B&B and Kaitlyn had been in tears. She'd been working too hard. Blue circles underscored her brown eyes, telling him she wasn't sleeping. How could she when she'd spent the last couple of weeks cleaning and decorating so that she could revive this old inn in such a short time? He could suffer through a couple hours of exploring downtown if it'd help her relax.

She didn't move an inch.

"Might want to wear a heavy coat," he advised. "Once the sun goes down, it's freezing in the valley this time of year. I have spare clothes in the truck. I'll clean up and change in one of the guest bathrooms." He wasn't taking no for an answer.

"Mitch, really, I'm fine. You agreed to help me fix up this place, nothing else."

He walked over and sat down on the edge of the couch. He'd been working outdoors all day and didn't want to dirty anything up. "Okay. Have it your way. It was a bad idea. I was kind of looking forward to the homemade fudge though."

She turned to look at him.

This was going to be easy. He almost felt guilty about manipulating her. "Triple chocolate. Dawanda makes it better than anyone I know. I used to crave it on deployments, where the most you could hope for was a MoonPie from someone's care package."

"That's a shame."

"Dawanda's Fudge Shop is one of my favorite stores downtown. It's right next to a little gift shop my mom enjoys going into. You know, the kind where you're afraid to move because you might break something?" He looked at Kaitlyn, whose big brown eyes were narrowed.

"Do you really think I'm that easy?" she asked.

He shifted his gaze. "I'm not sure what you're talking about."

"You *do* think I'm that easy," she said, surprise lifting her voice. She let out a small laugh. "You actually think the mention of chocolate and knickknacks is going to make me race down the hall to get dressed and go out with you." She chuckled harder.

Well, this was one way to make her feel better. Apparently, he'd made a fool of himself, and she thought it was hilarious. Watching her catch her breath, he decided he'd be a fool for her any day of the week.

She looked at him seriously. "Thank you," she finally said. "I needed that. You know, you're pretty adorable when you try to do something sweet."

The *s* word made him twitch a little bit. "I'm not sweet."

"It's okay. I won't tell anyone." She grinned and punched a soft fist into his shoulder. "It'll only take me a few minutes to get changed. You can put on fresh clothes in the Elizabeth Bennet and Darcy room."

"Thought you just called me out on my BS."

She nodded. "I did. And to pay you back, I'm going to enjoy watching you suffer as we go into every single store downtown."

* * *

After getting cleaned up, Mitch drove Kaitlyn to the town square. They parked and strolled along a strip of shops that hugged Silver Lake. He'd been right about the weather. The windchill was already in the upper twenties, even with the sun at their backs. Since she hadn't heeded his warning about a heavy coat, he leaned in and wrapped his arm around her as they made their way along the boardwalk.

"For warmth," he said, hoping to convince himself as well.

"I never would have guessed you were so sweet."

"Not sweet, just trying to help."

She laughed. "Does the word *funny* offend you too? Because I also find you pretty funny. Why do you hide it under a serious, macho shell?"

"I'm a marine," he told her as if that were any justification.

"Were a marine," she corrected. "Or is it 'once a marine, always a marine'?"

He considered his answer. He'd enjoyed being a military police officer, but he'd always known he wasn't a lifer. He'd only joined because he'd needed to leave town and wanted to help his mom financially. Now that he had job experience and highly sought-after skills, he could continue to help her as a civilian. "I guess I'll always have a little marine in me. And a little cop." He tugged her over to keep her from stepping on a broken piece of sidewalk.

She looked up and started to say something.

"Don't call me any of those cutesy words," he warned, only half joking, "or no fudge for you."

"Grouch," she teased.

"That's better."

* * *

The air was a mixture of the surrounding evergreens and Mitch. Two of Kaitlyn's new favorite scents.

"Fudge first, right?" he asked, his arm still draped around her.

"I'm curious about the best fudge I've never tasted. You know New York boasts just about the best of everything. You can't walk a full block without seeing a sign promoting something that's either the best in the world or at least world famous."

"I've never been to New York," he confessed.

She was surprised. "Everyone's been to the Big Apple."

"I've pretty much been everywhere else in the world though. And I can say with all confidence that Dawanda's fudge puts everyone else's to shame." He stopped walking in front of a glass storefront. "Forewarning," he said before pulling the door open, "Dawanda also likes to do complimentary cappuccino readings."

Kaitlyn lifted her face so she could get a good look at him. Was he kidding? "I've never heard of cappuccino readings before."

He laughed—a full-on, sincere chuckle. "Well, there's one thing Sweetwater Springs has over New York. Maybe you can send some of your guests in Dawanda's direction once they start arriving."

The way he said *your guests*, referring to the B&B's customers, didn't go unnoticed. She and Mitch were just having a good time this evening and nothing more.

They walked into the fudge shop and were greeted by a woman in her mid to late fifties with short red hair that formed tousled waves atop her head. She had lipstick color to match. Bright-blue eyes complemented her fair skin and vibrant hair and lips.

"Mitch!" the woman squealed, clapping her hands in front of her. "You're home!" She came running around the counter, a tiny fireball shooting toward them.

"Just for a little while," he said.

The sprite of a woman gave him a huge hug. "That's what you say, but I told you"—she pulled back and pointed a finger at him—"one of these days you'll come home, and some young thing will steal your heart and make you stay. The cappuccino never lies." The woman, who Kaitlyn guessed was Dawanda, turned and looked at her. "Or maybe you've

already found her. Who is this?" Dawanda pulled her hands
away from Mitch and offered a hand to Kaitlyn to shake.
"I'm Dawanda. You're new in town."

"Yes. Just arrived three weeks ago. I'm Kaitlyn Russo."

Acknowledgment registered in Dawanda's expression.
"You're Mable and Henry's granddaughter." The store
owner's eyes colored with sadness. "I'm so sorry about your
grandmother. Mable spoke of you often. She was so proud
of her granddaughter working in the big city. She used to tell
me about some of your clients. Big names too!"

Kaitlyn lowered her gaze for just a second, thinking of
the biggest name she'd worked with. The one who'd sunk
her career.

"Kaitlyn inherited the Russos' bed and breakfast," Mitch
told Dawanda.

"Oh, how wonderful. So you'll be fixing it up?" the shop
owner asked.

Kaitlyn gestured between herself and Mitch. "Mitch and
I both inherited it, actually. We're fixing it up together."

"But I'll be selling my half and heading out as soon as
possible," he clarified. "I have a security job lined up in
Northern Virginia."

Dawanda's red lips tugged into a frown. "There are security jobs here. I know for a fact that the police department is
shorthanded. What's Virginia have that Sweetwater Springs
doesn't?"

"Certainly not the best fudge I've ever tasted," he said.

"They certainly don't. *I* have the best fudge." Dawanda
winked at Kaitlyn. "Would you like to try some, sweetie?"

"I'd love to."

Kaitlyn and Mitch followed Dawanda to a table along the
side of the wall and sat down.

"How about a sampler?" Mitch said.

"A sampler plate coming right up." Dawanda disappeared, leaving them alone.

"Dawanda did one of these cappuccino readings on you?" Kaitlyn asked.

He shook his head and looked down at his clasped hands on the table. If she wasn't mistaken, he looked a little embarrassed. "She did. But I'm not giving you any of the details."

"Oh, come on. Something about a girl stealing your heart away?"

He met her gaze and stole her breath. "I don't believe in fortunes, especially ones that come out of a coffee mug." The corner of his mouth quirked softly.

She giggled in response. "Does she believe in them?"

"Who? Dawanda? Oh, definitely. Don't try to convince her it's just foam. I love Dawanda though. I've been coming to this place since I was a kid. Dad used to bring me here. My mom couldn't much afford to take me out after he died. Dawanda always insisted on giving me a free treat when we came to town though. It meant a lot."

"I'm sure."

"Here you go!" Dawanda set a plate of fudge squares in front of them. "No fighting over them, you two," she said. "And when you're done, you'll have a complimentary cappuccino."

Mitch gave Kaitlyn a look that told her she was in for something she'd never forget, and she couldn't wait. She was enjoying every second of this unexpected outing with Mitch, maybe a little more than she should.

CHAPTER SIX

*M*itch didn't have that much of a sweet tooth but he was enjoying the hell out of his visit to Dawanda's Fudge Shop, thanks in large part to Kaitlyn.

"I think I have a sugar high," she said, laughing at something he'd said.

"One might think you've been drinking Dawanda's equally famous eggnog."

"Eggnog too? I can't wait to try it."

It was good to see Kaitlyn having a good time. That was the whole point of tonight.

She shook her head as her laughter died down. Then her gaze fell on the last piece of fudge on the plate.

"Dawanda said no fighting, remember?" he reminded her.

"I won't have to fight you." She grinned, and a little spark of mischief lit up her brown eyes. "We'll decide who gets the final piece like two civilized adults."

Honestly, he didn't want that last piece but he was intrigued by whatever plan she had up her sleeve. "Okay." He leaned forward on the table, resting his elbows there. "What do you have in mind?"

"A game of chance." Her gaze flicked to the door, where only a handful of people had come and gone since they'd arrived half an hour earlier. "I say the next customer to walk in will be a woman."

"How old?" he asked.

She tapped her chin thoughtfully. "Late twenties. Your turn. Whoever is closest to the actual truth wins the last piece of fudge."

"Okay. I'll guess that the next customer is a man in his fifties. Graying hair."

She rubbed her hands together in front of her. "No way. The man would probably need to be watching his blood sugar."

"Dawanda makes sugar-free fudge." He liked how playful Kaitlyn had become now that she was away from her long to-do list. She seemed relaxed and carefree. And for a moment, he forgot that he was neither of those things as long as he was in Sweetwater Springs.

They both turned to look at the door but no customers walked through. Kaitlyn drummed her fingers on the table and looked at the plate of fudge again. Mitch was just about to surrender it to her when Dawanda buzzed over.

"Okay, you two. Cappuccino time!" She placed a tray with two cups of coffee and a metal pitcher of steaming milk in front of them and then grabbed a chair from a neighboring table and pulled it up to sit beside Kaitlyn. "All right, sweetheart. I'm sure Mitch here has told you about my special skill."

Kaitlyn met Mitch's gaze. "A little bit."

"So you're going to let me read your drink, yes?"

"Umm..." Kaitlyn hedged.

"Ah, come on. Don't be a chicken." Mitch gestured to the mug. "It's all in fun."

Dawanda jerked her head up. "No, it's not. It's serious. I know you don't believe me but you will. One day." She moved her gaze back to Kaitlyn. "So, is the answer yes?"

Lifting a shoulder, Kaitlyn nodded. "Okay, I guess."

"Good." Dawanda set one cup of coffee in front of Kaitlyn and turned the handle until it pointed in Kaitlyn's direction. "We need to make sure the cup knows who it's reading." Then she reached for the pitcher of shiny, white milk and ceremoniously held it up to the mug. "The cappuccino never lies," she said solemnly as she poured directly into the middle of the beverage, making a creamy froth at the top.

Dawanda didn't blink. She kept her blue eyes pinned to the design that formed inside the drink.

When Dawanda had read his cappuccino a couple of years back, she'd predicted he'd fall for someone here in Sweetwater Springs. If that happened, he'd be tempted to stay, and no part of him wanted to do that. But it was all in fun.

"Hmm," Dawanda hummed, leaning over Kaitlyn's mug. Her face was only a few inches from the drink. Not very appetizing.

"What is it?" Kaitlyn asked, looking worried. If Mitch didn't know better, he'd think she actually believed in this unheard-of form of fortune-telling.

"Well, this is very interesting." Dawanda looked up. "It appears that you will be entering into a long-lasting partnership that will change your life. See the door?"

Kaitlyn squinted at the frothy topping in her drink and shook her head. "Not really."

"Right there." Dawanda pointed. "The door is fully open.

That represents a partnership or relationship." Dawanda frowned into the mug. "Well, this is very unusual."

"What?" Kaitlyn leaned forward.

Dawanda lifted her gaze to meet Kaitlyn's. "I can usually read what type of relationship a person is entering into but yours is unclear. I'm not sure if it's a friendship, business arrangement, or maybe something romantic. Could be you'll fall in love in Sweetwater Springs too. Whatever the relationship, it's a good thing for you. I don't see any bad signs here. Embrace the relationship when it comes." A wide lipstick grin spread through Dawanda's high cheekbones.

A timer beeped in the kitchen. Dawanda pushed back from the table and stood. "That's my cue. I have fudge cooking." She lifted a second cup of coffee off the tray, added the milk, and then pushed it in front of Mitch. "Enjoy your drinks and holler if you need anything!" she called as she scuttled away carrying the tray and pitcher of milk with her.

Kaitlyn furrowed her brow as she stared down into her cup of cappuccino. "How in the world did she read anything from this? All I see is coffee and foam."

Mitch chuckled. "Who knows?"

The door to the store dinged behind him.

"Customers," Kaitlyn said, her eyes lighting up.

Mitch hoped for her sake that the description matched what she had guessed. He'd hand over the final piece of fudge to her regardless. Turning, he inspected a blond woman in her late twenties holding the door open as a tan-skinned man entered the shop. Mitch's stomach turned, twisted, and then flopped like a dead fish in his belly. Brian Everson was the last person he wanted to meet here tonight. And the last person he wanted to see him.

Mitch ducked his head, feeling caged in the store suddenly.

"Looks like I win!" Kaitlyn cheered.

He pushed the plate toward her. "All yours. Now let's get out of here."

* * *

The sun had crept down below the mountains, and in turn, the temperature had dropped even further while Kaitlyn was in the knickknack store with Mitch. They'd stepped into the pottery shop after that, and Kaitlyn had found a beautiful piece as a Christmas present for her mom. Not that her parents were likely to be around for the holidays.

Kaitlyn hugged her arms around her body as they retraced their path back to Mitch's truck. He hadn't offered to put his arm around her for warmth this time. He'd been noticeably distant ever since they'd left Dawanda's Fudge Shop, making her wonder if it had anything to do with the cappuccino reading. It wasn't as if Dawanda had said Kaitlyn would enter into a long-lasting relationship of any type with him.

"Thanks for tonight. You were right. This was just what I needed," she said, trying to get Mitch to snap out of his sudden funk.

"I'm glad you had a good time."

"I did." She looked over at Silver Lake and stopped in her tracks. The moon was full tonight and reflected perfectly in the pool of water. "It's so beautiful," she said, her words making white puffs in front of her. Then she looked up at the sky and the twinkling blanket of stars just like Josie had described in her article. This was a different world from her life in the city, where looking up she only saw lights from the neighboring apartment buildings.

"Uh-oh. Looks like you're falling in love."

She shifted her gaze to him, and her heart caught in her throat at another wonderful sight, this one of a beautifully rugged man whom she was starting to like entirely too much. "Excuse me?"

"With Sweetwater Springs," he clarified.

"Oh." Her gaze swept to her feet and back out to Silver Lake. "Maybe I am. There's a lot to love about this place." She looked up at him again. Big mistake. Either she'd taken a step closer or he had. They were standing only a foot apart now. She held her breath. Then he reached up and swept a lock of her hair from her cheek. The tip of his finger caressed her skin as it slid past, sending shivers through her body. And for a moment, she thought he was going to kiss her.

Do I want him to kiss me?

She wasn't looking for anything romantic but if ever there was the perfect moment to share a kiss, it was this one, with the starry sky and illuminating moon, standing by a lake and staring into Mitch's dusky eyes. *Oh, goodness*, she wanted to feel his lips on hers. Needed it almost as much as her next shallow breath.

Did he want to kiss her too?

Without thinking, she flicked her gaze to his mouth. Nothing subtle about that. She might as well have whispered, "*Kiss me. Kiss me now.*"

Hearing her loud and clear, he dipped his head toward her and pressed his mouth to hers. She braced a hand over his muscled chest as she went up on tiptoes and parted her lips, allowing his tongue to sweep inside her mouth. Just like with everything else, he was good at kissing. Very good.

What am I doing? The question was short-circuited by the pure pleasure firing through her. Didn't matter. She'd worry about the repercussions of kissing Mitch later. It'd been a long time since she'd been kissed. And she'd never been kissed quite like this. The feel of his beard tickled her cheek and aroused her from head to toe.

His hand curled behind her neck, a welcome anchor because otherwise she might have just floated up and away into the starry night sky. Maybe she was already floating. That's how she felt. Light and free.

After a long moment, he pulled back. "I'll, uh, take you home."

She looked into his eyes, hoping to read what that kiss had meant. It was so good that it had to mean something. In answer, she saw a coolness in his gaze. Then he turned and started walking again as if nothing special had happened at all.

* * *

Mitch was well practiced in self-control. Or so he thought but Kaitlyn's lips had offered an escape he couldn't resist. After seeing Brian in the fudge shop, he'd needed an escape more than he needed air to breathe. Taking Kaitlyn into his arms had felt as natural as anything he'd ever done.

But kissing her was wrong. He had too many regrets in this town and didn't want to add her to the list. Parking in front of the B&B, he glanced over. There was a look in her eyes. Hope that he might kiss her again? Worry that he would do just that?

He cleared his throat and looked away because the temptation to lean in and taste her once more was too strong. She'd tasted like cappuccino and chocolate. Like heaven in his mind. "I'll, uh, see you in the morning."

"Yeah. Okay." She reached for the door handle.

"Hold on. Let me get that for you." He wasn't necessarily a Southern gentleman but he wasn't a brute either. If you kissed a woman, the least you could do was open the truck door for her.

He ran around and pulled the passenger door open.

"Thanks," she said, stepping down onto the driveway's pavement.

The movement brought her close to him—too close. He could smell her, could practically taste the sweetness of her lips again. His mouth watered in response.

Get it together, Mitch.

He took a step back, feeling awkward and restless and completely out of his element. Kaitlyn's eyes still offered that same escape. Tempting as it was, he needed to bolt. Right about now he was counting his lucky stars she hadn't allowed him a room at the B&B while he stayed in town. Because going inside with her would break his steel willpower. He had no doubt about that. There were limits to the kind of temptations a man could resist, and he was walking the edge of that limit.

"Good night," he said, turning away before his body betrayed him. He climbed into his truck and scolded himself all the way to his mom's house.

"Hey," his mom said, looking up from her recliner when he let himself in.

"What are you doing awake?" She was normally early to bed and started working as soon as her feet hit the floor, usually before the sun came up.

"Can't sleep."

"Not tired?" he asked, unable to imagine how she wouldn't be. He set his keys on the coffee table and took a seat on the couch across from her. There was a book in her lap, he noted. The woman couldn't be idle for a second.

"Oh, I'm tired, all right, but my body doesn't seem to have gotten the message."

Mitch frowned. "When was the last time you had a checkup?"

She shook her head. "I've already told you: I'm not sick. Maybe I should get some vitamins or something."

Mitch leaned forward and propped his elbows on his knees. "What's the worst that could happen if you see a doctor? Huh?"

She looked at him and swallowed. "Oh, I don't know. He could tell me I'm dying." She laughed weakly but neither of them really found it funny. That's what had happened to Mitch's dad. He'd had a lingering cough. Just a cold that wouldn't go away. Everything had been fine until his dad had gone to the doctor and was told otherwise. Then nothing was ever fine again. His dad was diagnosed with stage-four lung cancer and had died six months later.

"That won't happen," Mitch said, reaching out a hand to place on her knee. He squeezed gently. "You need to make sure everything is okay, Mom. Please. For me."

She blew out a breath, patted his hand, and then finally nodded, much to his relief. "Fine, fine. I'll call and make an appointment tomorrow if it'll make you happy."

"It will." He leaned back. "And seeing you get to bed will make me happy too. Just lie in bed and close your eyes. Isn't that what you used to tell me? Fake it until you make it? It always worked when I couldn't sleep."

They both stood.

"What did I do to deserve a son like you?" she asked. She meant it in a good way, he knew, but he'd often asked himself the same question. His mom had endured so much heartache in her life, and some of it had been his doing.

* * *

"You did what?" Josie gasped on the other end of the line.

Since Mitch had dropped her off, Kaitlyn had turned on one of her favorite romantic movies and was halfway through a tall glass of white wine. She was now feeling the buzz tangled with a bunch of unruly hormones and a large dose of confusion. "I kissed him. It was a mistake." Saying so didn't seem right though. Kissing Mitch had felt amazing.

"*Okayyyyy*," Josie said.

Kaitlyn could imagine her friend sitting behind her desk working, even though it was past ten p.m. Josie was always working on her next article or interview or big idea.

"Are you going to kiss him again?" Josie asked.

Kaitlyn sipped more of her wine. "Of course not. We work together, and then he's leaving after Christmas."

"Well, I don't recommend kissing people you work with but kissing men who are leaving is perfect. It takes the pressure off."

"Perfect for you maybe," Kaitlyn said, swirling her wine around the glass in little circles. "I kind of like the idea of getting attached to a man one day."

"Someday, but not right now. Right now, you're building your business. There's no time for anything else. But, just for kicks and giggles, was he a good kisser?" Josie asked.

Kaitlyn rested her head back against the couch cushion, staring at the muted television screen. "The best. He has a beard that's soft and rough. I've never kissed a man with a beard before."

Josie sighed. "Bearded kisses are the best. Did his hands roam while you were kissing? Or did they stay put?"

Kaitlyn thought back. "One of his hands started at the

back of my neck and slid around to my cheek." A shiver ran through her at the memory, and she could almost feel that calloused finger brushing over her skin again.

"I wrote an article on kissing once. When I interned at *Teen Vibe* magazine in college. I think we labeled that the sweet kiss."

Yeah, it was definitely sweet. And sexy too.

"The sweet kiss is a prelude to the let's-get-it-on kiss. Make sure you're wearing your best lingerie next time you plan on kissing him."

Kaitlyn choked on her sip of wine. She didn't plan on kissing Mitch again but the thought of experiencing a let's-get-it-on kiss did things to her.

"So, back to business," Josie said. "Has the phone started ringing yet?"

"Not yet. But the December issue just went out, right?"

"Right. Like I mentioned before, we start circulating a couple weeks ahead of each new month so it should hit mailboxes in the next couple of days. Let me know when people start booking."

"I will. Thank you again. I wouldn't be doing this without your help."

"That's what friends are for. But listen, I need to go. If I don't get this article for the January issue drafted, I might not see my bed tonight."

"You're a machine," Kaitlyn said with a yawn. Bed sounded nice, if she could convince her legs to walk her there. "Good night." She disconnected the call and placed her cell phone on the couch at her side. Then she grabbed the remote and turned the TV off. Standing, she felt her head go fuzzy. Perhaps she'd had a tad too much wine.

She headed toward the hallway and then stopped short when the doorbell rang. She froze for a long moment. Who visited this late? And she didn't know anyone in town except for Mitch, who usually just snuck up on her.

It rang again.

Well, this was a functioning bed and breakfast. She'd updated the website just this morning. Maybe someone had found it online and needed a room. She set her glass of wine down and walked to the door. On an inhale, she pulled it open and offered up a smile.

To a tall, dark-haired man in a leather jacket, tight jeans, and biker boots.

Her heart may have stopped in that moment. He looked like he belonged on a Harley driving down an open highway. And if she had to guess, there was probably a motorcycle in the driveway that wrapped behind the house. She hadn't heard it rumble in but she'd been distracted by her phone call with Josie. "Hi. Um, can I help you?"

"Yeah. I know it's late but I need a room." His voice was deep and smooth. He had pale blue eyes that seemed to pop against his all-black clothing.

A little fear and excitement sliced through her, which was silly. Bikers weren't dangerous or aggressive. But famous movie stars like Bradley Foster weren't supposed to be aggressive either.

"This is a B and B, right?" he asked, when she didn't respond immediately.

"R-right. Yes. Come in." She gestured for him to step through the front door, despite the sudden anxiety prickling inside her.

"So, do you have a room available for me?"

He stepped over the threshold, and she willed herself not to take a step backward. This would be fine. Everything would be fine.

"Of course we do. Like you said, we're a B and B after

all." Only there was no *we*. Mitch was gone for the night. It was just her. "You can stay in the, um, *Dirty Dancing* room."

The biker lifted a pierced brow.

Heat scorched her skin. "That came out wrong." She laughed nervously. "All of the rooms are named after a romantic couple. The *Dirty Dancing* room is named after Baby and Johnny."

And this man oozed Johnny. He was gorgeous and had "bad boy" written all over him but he didn't stir the same kind of rumblings in her belly that Mitch did.

"Cool," he said, and then offered his hand. "My name is Paris." Before she could respond, he nodded. "I know. Not a name fitting for a guy who rides a bike. My folks were romantics. They honeymooned in Paris, and then I came along nine months later."

She smiled, relaxing just a notch. "I love that. I'm Kaitlyn Russo." She offered her hand. "Welcome to the Sweetwater Bed and Breakfast. If you don't mind, can I wait to give you a full tour of the place until morning? It's a little late." And the thought of roaming through the house alone with a sexy biker was a little intimidating after what she'd been through.

"That's fine." Paris pulled a wallet out of his back pocket.

She'd played around with the credit card swipe machine the other day to make sure she was ready. She took his card, walked it over to the machine, and swiped it. After a moment, the information went through without a problem.

Handing it back to him, she said, "Okay, Paris. Let me show you to your room."

She walked with him upstairs to the room at the end of the long hall. She adored the *Dirty Dancing* room. It was simple and reminded her of a hot summer day. The curtains were sheer like Baby's dress in the final scene of the movie. Every time Kaitlyn stepped inside, she heard the beat of that final song play in her head and thought of Baby running across the dance floor and Johnny catching her as she dove like a bird in the air.

Paris set his lone bag down on the floor. "This is great. Thanks."

She nodded and stepped back. No matter how nice he seemed to be, he was a stranger, and she was still unnerved by her recent past. "Um, what time would you like breakfast?"

He shrugged. "Seven or eight, I guess."

"Either of those times will be fine. The dining room is downstairs. It'll be a home-style breakfast, where you serve yourself."

"Sounds good."

She exited the room and headed downstairs. The buzz of the wine was gone now, replaced with a bubbling *uh-oh-what-do-I-do* nervousness coursing through her. When she got to the landing of the stairs, she cast a glance back up to where she'd just left Paris. She'd imagined couples coming to the B&B, two people absorbed in their own love for the other. She was fully prepared for that. She'd never considered that single, gorgeous biker dudes would show up or that she'd be in a house all alone with them. Which would've been completely fine a few months ago. But after her last episode with Bradley...

Not fine. Not fine at all.

She retrieved her cell phone from the couch, sucked in a breath, and dialed. She didn't know what else to do or who else to call.

"Hey." Mitch's deep voice calmed her as soon as she heard it. "Something wrong?" he asked.

"No. Yes. I was wondering if you could do me a favor."

"Sure. What is it?"

Gah. This was more than a little embarrassing to ask. "Can you stay with me tonight?"

CHAPTER SEVEN

After the kiss, Mitch had decided to steer clear of Kaitlyn. They'd gotten too close for comfort tonight, and that wasn't part of the deal. He'd heard the shaky quality of her voice when she'd called just now though. She hadn't sounded like a woman inviting him back for a nightcap. Instead, she'd sounded upset.

He pulled his truck around the back of the house and parked beside an unfamiliar motorcycle. A guest? As he climbed the porch steps, Kaitlyn opened the door.

"Thanks for coming," she said, looking sheepish. "Come on in."

He stepped past her with his overnight bag and watched her lock the door behind him. "Whose bike is that outside?" he asked.

"That's why I called. We have our first guest," she said, offering a wobbly smile.

"Is that the reason you asked me to spend the night with you?"

Her cheeks flushed. "Well, spend the night at the inn. Not...with me." She looked away. "I guess having someone arrive tonight took me off guard. I might need your help cooking breakfast in the morning."

"I usually get here early enough to cook breakfast with you," he said.

"I know." She pulled her lower lip between her teeth. "I'm sorry to pull you away from your mom."

"Don't worry about that. She can take care of herself." Or so she kept telling him. At least she'd agreed to call and make a doctor's appointment tomorrow. "I don't mind staying tonight if it'll make you feel more comfortable. It's not a problem."

Kaitlyn nodded quietly. "Thanks. I was just having a glass of wine before our guest arrived. Want one? Or a beer."

"A beer would be great." He followed her to the kitchen and sat on one of the barstools at the center island, watching as she bent into the refrigerator to retrieve the beer. His eyes unintentionally fixated on her curves from behind. Soft and inviting.

That kiss they'd shared earlier tonight kept playing on a continuous loop in his mind. He'd been nowhere near sleep when she'd called.

Kaitlyn closed the refrigerator, retrieved a glass from the cabinet, and carried the items back.

"You were drinking alone before the new guest arrived?" he asked. "Nightcap or is something bothering you?"

She pushed his can across the counter and poured herself a deep glass of wine. "A little of both, I guess." Her gaze hung on his. Something dark passed across it. He'd gotten good at recognizing the darkness. "If it had been a couple or a single woman, would you have asked me to come over tonight?" he asked.

Averting her gaze, she shook her head. "Probably not."

"There's nothing wrong with a woman not wanting to stay alone in a house with a man she doesn't know. Except now you're sleeping under a roof with two men you don't know."

She looked back up at him. "I know you."

He liked that he'd won her trust. "There's another reason you wanted me to come tonight. You don't have to tell me what it is if you don't want to. I just wanted you to know I understand what it's like to run from things." He reached for his beer and took a drink. "Sometimes it helps to talk to someone." Not that he'd ever talked about the accident that had paralyzed Brian Everson.

"There's not some big secret in my past, if that's what you're thinking."

"But there is something eating away at you. I get that you're excited about inheriting the bed and breakfast but a person doesn't just drop their entire life and move if they're happy where they are. I assume you had a home, friends, a job."

He could almost see her considering whether she was going to open up to him. Fidgeting with her hands around her wineglass, she lifted a shoulder. "Growing up, I used to redecorate my bedroom every couple of months. I've always loved making places feel happy. Or energetic. Sad. It's always kind of fascinated me that you can walk into a room and have your entire mood change." The corner of her mouth twitched in not quite a smile. "So, when I went to college, I knew exactly what I wanted to study. And I always knew exactly which design firm I wanted to work for. Beautiful Designs is the most well-known interior design firm in New York City. They work with some of the richest and most famous in the area. My friend Josie had done an article on the firm's owner. She pulled some strings and got me an interview with him. That's how I found myself working with Bradley Foster."

Mitch blinked. "Bradley Foster, the movie star?"

"That's the one." She looked away as she continued. "I thought Bradley saw something special in me after he looked at my portfolio. Talent. He said he loved my designs. It was a dream come true. Then he started needing me to stay late at his vacation house. I was flattered, I guess, because he turned down the other more experienced designers. He said he only wanted me."

Mitch was already jumping ahead of her story, putting the pieces together, and feeling an angry blaze erupt in his belly on her behalf. "Did he hurt you?" he asked, the muscles tightening uncomfortably in his jaw.

She lifted her gaze to meet his. "No. He was more aggressive the last time I worked with him though. He wouldn't take no for an answer. If not for the interruption of his cleaning crew, I'm not sure he would've stopped. I tried to tell my boss at the design firm the next day but Bradley had already called to complain about my inappropriate behavior. He also threatened to press charges against me for assault."

Mitch lifted a brow questioningly.

"My knee might have bumped him in a sensitive area before I ran out." Her cheeks flushed a deep rose color. "My boss didn't want to believe me, probably because Bradley Foster is one of the business's biggest clients. I was fired, and now my reputation is ruined. Once you've worked for the best, there's only one way to go in New York, and that's down." She reached for her glass and took a sip. "My firm also won't give me glowing references for any other jobs. I'm sunk."

"That's despicable," Mitch ground out.

She released a sincere laugh. "Yeah. I can drink to that."

"Want me to beat Bradley Foster up?"

Kaitlyn eyed him curiously. "Something tells me that's not an empty offer."

"I don't make empty offers." And part of him wanted to get in his truck and drive to New York regardless of what she wanted from him. A guy like Bradley Foster needed to be taught a lesson before he found himself alone with another woman who wouldn't be as lucky as Kaitlyn.

"No. And I wasn't running when I came here. I could've stayed in New York and searched for another job. Or got in the unemployment line. Truthfully, I haven't felt inspired by my work in a long time. For Bradley, I designed a living room and a kitchen. I'd picked the colors and the theme based on his personality, which I got to know a little too well. Before that," she said, frowning, "I'd worked on restrooms and boring boardrooms, where I had zero creative liberty. When I found out that I had inherited this place, it felt like fate. Like at the exact right time, my grandmother had opened an amazing opportunity that I couldn't say no to." She shrugged. "I guess I'll have to get comfortable with having attractive single men staying here with me."

He thought she was talking about him until she gestured upstairs.

"I mean, he's probably a nice guy," she added.

Mitch blinked. She was talking about the new houseguest. Mitch hadn't laid eyes on the guy yet, but apparently he was alone, attractive, and probably a nice guy. That sounded like bad news to Mitch. "I'll stay as long as you need me to," he said, feeling equal parts protective and suddenly jealous.

"Thank you. That means a lot. And you're right. It does help to talk to someone. If you ever need me to return the favor…"

He swallowed and looked down at the beer in his hands. Not a chance. Some burdens weren't meant to be shared.

* * *

Kaitlyn stared at the ceiling in her bedroom. Mitch had the *Beauty and the Beast* room right above her—fitting because he had that beastly, untamed quality about him, and she was itching to run her fingers through his mane.

She squirmed under the heavy quilt on her bed. Her room was the only one in the house that had yet to be named. She guessed that was all right since it wasn't for guests. She didn't need a themed room.

Blinking, she tried to make sense of the shadows along the wall. She'd spent so little time in here that she didn't have the floor plan memorized yet. When she'd been a child, she'd been terrified of the shadows. Now the main thing that scared her was failing.

Okay, the thought of coming face-to-face with Bradley Foster again was a little scary too. She didn't care if she ever saw another of his movies again.

Sitting up in bed, she decided to get a glass of water to quench her post-wine thirst. She slid her feet into a pair of slippers. *Gah.* She was going to town tomorrow to buy something a little more attractive and less old lady–like than flannel pajamas and slippers. And it had absolutely nothing to do with either of the men currently sleeping upstairs.

Doing her best to be quiet, she shuffled across the kitchen floor and swung open a cabinet. Then she grabbed a glass and carried it to the sink.

A soft knock on the wall behind her made her whirl around.

"Hey." Paris was standing at the edge of the kitchen in a black T-shirt and holey pair of jeans. "I didn't mean to scare you."

She appreciated the knock. Mitch usually just appeared out of nowhere, like Casper the sexy ghost. "You didn't. Do you need something?" she asked.

"I thought I'd see if I could get something to drink."

She pulled a hand to her chest. "I'm so sorry. I should've left a glass in your room with bottled water and complimentary beverages. I'm a little new to this B and B host role."

"It's no problem." His smile was slow and easy.

"Have a seat. I'll get you a drink." She grabbed a second glass from the cabinet and then turned to look over her shoulder at her guest. Muscles popped from his fitted undershirt. "Water okay?"

"That's fine. Anything to wet my palate... That sounded strangely inappropriate, didn't it?"

Kaitlyn laughed nervously as she filled the glasses. "Well, *now* it does." She slid his in front of him.

"Thanks." He took the water and drank.

She did too, keeping one cautious eye on him. "So, Paris, what do you do for a living?" she asked, taking the stool across from him.

"Graphic design. I'm self-employed," he said.

Her eyes widened. "Really? That's awesome."

"Yeah, I'm not really one for rules and dress codes. Plus, I can pretty much work from anywhere."

"Will you be working while you're staying here?" she asked.

He nodded. "I have a few projects that need finishing."

"Well, we offer free Wi-Fi. The code is in your welcome

packet upstairs. I'll try to place any other guests who arrive at the other end of the hall so they don't disturb you. If you're planning on staying, that is."

He set his glass on the counter in front of him. "Thought I'd stay through next week if that's all right."

"Of course."

They talked for a few minutes more, and then Paris waved good night and headed back to his room.

That wasn't so bad, Kaitlyn thought. She'd enjoyed talking with Paris and he seemed like a nice enough guy. Tomorrow, she'd tell Mitch he didn't need to stay another night on her account. Not unless he wanted to, which of course, he wouldn't.

* * *

The room Kaitlyn had given him was fitting because Mitch felt like a beast right now. He didn't like this wild, crazy feeling consuming him. First, he hadn't been able to sleep after what Kaitlyn told him about her former client. Mitch wanted to meet that creep in a dark alley, give him an old-fashioned shakedown, and leave him in one of the dumpsters where he belonged. Second, he'd walked up on Kaitlyn and the new guest in the kitchen. They hadn't noticed him, of course, because they were too busy laughing like old friends. And maybe they'd been flirting a little bit too, which left Mitch unnerved. Not that he had any claim to Kaitlyn. One kiss didn't mark her as his. One kiss that never should've happened in the first place. Except now it kept repeating itself in his mind. That was the third reason for his insomnia.

He lay back on the king-size bed in his room. He wouldn't be able to go to sleep until he heard the stairs creak and knew that Mr. Muscle Head was back in his room. Alone.

Mitch blew out a heavy breath. If Kaitlyn wanted to join Muscle Head in his room, she could. She was a grown woman. She'd asked for Mitch's protection tonight though, and he didn't like the idea of another strange man's hands on her body. Or his mouth on her sweet-tasting lips.

The top landing creaked.

Mitch's ears pricked. There was just one set of footsteps heading down to the opposite end of the hall. Muscle Head was alone, and Kaitlyn was still safe and sound, and presumably tucked into her bed alone downstairs.

Mitch massaged a hand over his face because now he was thinking of her alone in her bed. Thinking of all the things he wouldn't mind doing to her in that bed. Stripping off those flannel pajamas that were unreasonably sexy. Touching her soft skin. Giving her another kiss, or two or three.

He cursed under his breath. This just might be one of the longest nights of his life.

* * *

Mitch awoke with a start and looked at the clock on his nightstand. Eight a.m. He'd slept in for the first time in ages. He lay in bed and let last night come streaming back. He was at the Sweetwater B&B. Kaitlyn was downstairs, and there was a guest here that she found hot.

That got him out of bed. He flung his legs over the side and started reaching for his clothes. They didn't know anything about this new guest, and the whole point of Kaitlyn calling him here last night was so she wouldn't have to be alone with the guy.

There was the sound of kitchen clatter downstairs. Mitch pulled on a shirt and some pants and then jammed his feet into a pair of shoes and headed in that direction.

"Hi." She turned and offered him a bright smile as she cleaned up the dining room table. "Paris has already had breakfast," she said. "And I didn't do so bad with those made-from-scratch biscuits on my own."

"Paris?" Mitch asked.

"That's our guest's name. He went back to his room. I have leftovers if you want some."

"I don't have much of an appetite right now." Not after learning that Kaitlyn and Paris had shared a nice breakfast alone. Probably flirting. Mitch hadn't even met this guy yet, and he hated his guts already.

"Okay." She grabbed several items from the table. "Do you mind helping me get those plates to the dishwasher?"

"Sure." He grabbed the dishes and followed her. He'd never been a jealous man, and he didn't like the feeling. She dipped and placed the dirty dishes in the washer and then reached back and retrieved what he was carrying. "Thanks." She straightened. "Guess the room I put you in was satisfactory?"

"Yeah."

"Good to know. Well, don't feel like you have to stay again tonight. It was silly of me to be afraid yesterday." She looked away. "I don't know what I was thinking."

He did. She was thinking of her would-be attacker. A guy unworthy of his fame and fortune.

"I don't mind," Mitch said. "And I think I will stay another night."

"You don't have to—"

"I said I don't mind." He wanted to make sure Paris (and

what the hell kind of name was that?) kept his hands to himself.

"Great. Then you can help make our new guest feel at home. He said he'll be staying through next week."

"Love to," Mitch lied. Making people feel at home wasn't exactly his forte. He was only doing this because he wanted to protect the woman in front of him, he told himself. But that was partially a lie too.

CHAPTER EIGHT

*K*aitlyn pulled the magazine out of the mailbox on Monday and hugged it against her chest. This was it! Josie had only come up with the idea a short while ago and already it had become real. She pulled the magazine away and started reading the cover as she hurried back toward the B&B.

"Walking and reading is a dangerous sport, you know?" Mitch said, sneaking up on her as always. She only jumped a little this time. She guessed that meant she was getting used to his presence. But her breath froze in her lungs when she looked up. She'd never get used to those hot chocolate eyes or that barely there grin buried under a short, sexy beard.

"It's here," she said, unable to contain her enthusiasm. "The article about Sweetwater Springs."

"Oh yeah?" He stepped closer to read over her shoulder.

"America's Most Romantic Holiday Retreats," he read, his breath tickling her ear.

She swallowed and stepped away from the large, beautiful man who was making her heart beat in triple time.

"I'm going to go inside and have a hot apple cider. Want some?"

He gave her a strange, amused look. "Mable was always forcing that stuff on me during the fall and winter months. Not my cup of tea, you might say."

Kaitlyn climbed the steps, aware that each one put her butt at his eye level. She climbed more quickly. "I found my grandmother's secret recipe tucked away in one of her cooking books the other day. It's actually very simple to make. And once I have a cup in hand, I plan to read this article until I have it memorized. Then we're going to finish fulfilling its promise."

"Oh, we are, are we?"

She glanced over her shoulder. His teasing tone matched the look in his eyes. She was glad he wasn't fighting her on this anymore. He'd done everything she'd asked and more, and they already had one satisfied guest. Paris had ventured out this morning to work at Dawanda's Fudge Shop, per her recommendation. "Yes, we are."

A few minutes later, with her cup of hot apple cider and a notepad in hand, she leaned over the article on the kitchen counter. It was mostly a fluff piece, painting a picturesque town, which wasn't an exaggeration by any measure. Sweetwater Springs did have beautiful rolling mountains and natural hot springs that could be found by a simple hike through the pine-filled woods. She hadn't seen the springs yet but they were in the brochures on display at the B&B's front entrance.

Her gaze moved from the article to Mitch's lower half. The rest of him was currently hidden behind the refrigerator. He was fixing a slow leak from a loose water line to the ice maker. She'd checked out his backside before but now she stared unapologetically.

Her cell phone rang beside her, and she jerked upright. She placed it to her ear. "Hello?"

"Well, what do you think? Can Sweetwater Springs and your little B and B live up to the promise?" Josie asked.

"Oh, definitely. The town was never a concern. And Mitch and I have already fixed a mile-long list of things here at the inn. Actually, he fixed most of them and I've done all the decorating." There were only a few little tweaks left to make and the place would be perfect.

Kaitlyn dragged her gaze back to the article. "The only thing I'm missing is the Christmas tree."

"No tree? The perfect holiday getaway demands a tree, Kaye," Josie said. "And not one of those artificial ones."

"Of course it does. I'm sure there's a farm or something around here." But how would she get it back to the B&B in her small car?

Mitch straightened from behind the fridge. "Merry Mountain Farms sells the best trees," he said. "Sorry. Couldn't help overhearing you."

"It's okay. I'm talking to the friend who wrote the article," she told him.

"Oh, he sounds sexy," Josie purred into the receiver. "No wonder you have such a crush on him."

For a moment, heat crawled through Kaitlyn's skin. Until she remembered that Mitch could only hear her half of the conversation and not Josie's. *Thank goodness.* "Merry Mountain Farms. Good to know. I'll try to check it out later this week."

Josie cleared her throat. "Okay. I just wanted an update. The tension between you two can be felt all the way in New York. So please don't let me interrupt you jumping his bones."

Kaitlyn choked. "That's not...I'm not."

"Just keep me updated. I'm expecting a windfall for the B and B."

"I hope so. You can come visit it for yourself anytime, you know."

"Tempting," Josie said. "Maybe I will if I can ever get out from under these deadlines."

After a minute more, they said their goodbyes and disconnected.

Mitch stood and stared at her. Josie was right. The sexual tension could be sliced with a nail file.

"I, uh, need to take off early this afternoon. I'm taking my mom to an appointment in town."

"Oh." Kaitlyn nodded, surprised at the disappointment settling over her. She'd gotten used to having him around all day, and now during the nighttime too. She liked having him here.

"Will you be back tonight?" she asked, trying to keep the hope out of her voice. She grabbed her cup of cider and took a sip.

He nodded. "Yeah. I'll take you to get that Christmas tree if you want."

"Really?"

"Sure. I'm afraid if I don't, I'll find you out in the woods with an axe."

She placed her hands on her hips and feigned insult. "I'm perfectly capable of using one, you know."

"Of course you are. But humor me and let me take you to get a tree anyway."

Kaitlyn had to admit spending time with Mitch was even more exciting than picking out a real live tree. All she'd ever had were the small artificial kind that sat in a corner of her room.

"Who will watch the inn though? I can't just leave this place. We have a guest now."

"My mom used to come by for Mable and Henry all the time," Mitch told her. "She won't mind at all."

Kaitlyn blinked, unable to think of any excuse to say no. Not that she wanted to refuse the invitation. "Wow. Problem solved. I'd love to go tree hunting with you, then."

"Good. It'll be fun." He turned back to the refrigerator and began shimmying it back into its place against the wall.

It wasn't a date, she told herself as she watched, ignoring the flurry of anticipation falling over her like the first winter snow. Definitely not.

* * *

Mitch was glad he'd told his mom he was taking her to her doctor appointment this afternoon. Because the more time he spent with Kaitlyn, the harder it was to keep his hands to himself. And now he'd promised to take her Christmas tree hunting tonight. It was like he lost his mind whenever she was around.

He pulled into his mom's driveway and honked the horn. Her appointment was at 3:30 p.m., and there was no time to meander. She better not have changed her mind, he thought. He'd go inside and carry her to the appointment kicking and screaming like a toddler if he had to.

He relaxed when he saw her open the front door and head out, dressed in a heavy coat and pale-blue knit hat.

"You didn't have to do this, you know?" was the first thing she said upon opening the passenger side door of his truck.

"I know that's what you think but you're wrong. I'm your son, and I do have to do this." He watched her buckle herself in and then reversed back onto the street. "Especially since you're not taking care of yourself." The night she'd passed out on the bed hadn't been a fluke. He'd witnessed her dizzy spells several times since then. There were other symptoms too. She was pale and had a few bruises.

"Who are you to talk? What about that time you sprained your ankle a couple years back and wouldn't go have it checked out?"

"It was a sprain, Mom. I know how to treat a sprain. And a sprain is no big deal." He glanced over and pinned her with a stare. He hoped to God his mom's condition wasn't a big deal either, he thought as he returned his attention to the road.

"So, how's the B and B coming along?" his mother asked, changing the subject.

Mitch blew out a breath. "Good. Kaitlyn got her food-handling license, and the inn passed inspection last week. It already has its first guest too. Speaking of which, I have a favor to ask you." He saw his mom perk up in the seat beside him. She lived to help others.

"Oh?"

"I need to take Kaitlyn to get a tree tonight. Do you think you could watch the inn?" Mitch doubted any medicine the doctor offered today would be as good for her as this request.

"Well, of course I can. I've always loved working at the B and B—you know that." His mom's tone of voice was suddenly upbeat and cheerful.

"Not work," he clarified. "Watch. Feet up. TV on."

His mom didn't argue but she didn't agree either. "Your dad used to take me to get our Christmas trees. Do you like Mable's granddaughter? Is she pretty?"

Mitch groaned as he pulled into the physician's parking lot and cut the engine. "Don't make me regret asking you."

She turned in her seat and pointed a finger at him. "Only

if you promise not to try to go in the examining room with me. I'm a grown woman, Mitch, and there are some things a mother doesn't want her son hearing about her body."

He frowned. "How am I supposed to know what's going on with you if I'm stuck in the waiting room?"

She shrugged. "I guess you'll just have to trust that I'll tell you."

A growl emitted from deep in his throat. He trusted his mom but he didn't put it past her to keep things from him. Judging from the stubborn lift of her chin, he could see he wasn't winning this argument though. "Fine."

He opened his door and got out, meeting her around the back of the truck and walking toward the small doctor's office, which was in a string of other businesses. "But you'll tell me everything." He wasn't asking.

His stern tone of voice and demeanor seemed to be lost on his mother as he held the office door open for her and she walked in ahead of him. "Of course, dear."

* * *

Later that afternoon, Kaitlyn set out a dish of sugar cookies and accommodations for hot tea in the dining room.

"Did you get a lot of work done?" she asked Paris, as he walked in the room to peruse the selection.

"Mostly. Dawanda kept interrupting though."

Kaitlyn giggled to herself. "She didn't serve you a cup of cappuccino, did she?"

"She did. Apparently, my fortune couldn't be read. She said it was the first time that ever happened."

"That's strange."

He shrugged. "I'm not sure I buy into cappuccino readings anyway."

Kaitlyn was surprised that part of her did believe. There was something about how seriously Dawanda took the reading that chased away Kaitlyn's doubts. "Well, I can promise a distraction-free evening for your work if that's what you want."

"Thanks. Mind if I take a couple of cookies up to my room?"

"Of course." She turned as the phone rang on the wall. "Excuse me." The landline phone was the one that guests would use to make reservations. She crossed her fingers at her side in hopes that it was a potential customer and not a telemarketer as she went to answer. "Hello. Sweetwater Bed and Breakfast. How can I assist you?"

"Yes. Hi there. I'm Marvin Krespo," a man's voice drawled. "I was hoping to make a reservation for me and my wife. You got any rooms open?" he asked.

"Yes, of course. When will you be coming?"

"Tomorrow if you have vacancies. My wife doesn't think I'm romantic anymore. She said I need to step up my game or else."

Kaitlyn's mouth fell open. "Um, well."

"I doubt that means she'll leave me, but she likes to withhold my favorite foods and sex when she's in a tiff."

"I see." Kaitlyn cleared her throat. "Well, tomorrow will be fine. We'll have a room prepared for you."

"Great, darling. See you soon."

Kaitlyn hung up and went to retrieve her appointment book nearby. She scribbled in Mr. and Mrs. Krespo's names.

"Will you be needing anything else tonight? Dinner?" Kaitlyn asked as Paris headed toward the stairs with a handful of cookies. She wasn't planning on cooking full meals every night for her guests but since there was just one, she didn't mind.

"No. I thought I'd head out later and explore more of the area."

"Okay. Well, I'm actually heading out myself. Mitch and I are going to pick out a Christmas tree for the inn. His mom will be watching over the place if you need anything."

"I should be fine. Don't worry about me. Enjoy your date," he called before disappearing up the stairs and into his room. Before she had the opportunity to correct him. Getting a tree together was simply part of her arrangement with Mitch. The inn needed one, and she couldn't do this on her own.

Even if it wasn't a romantic arrangement, she still needed to look nice before heading over to Merry Mountain Farms, she decided. She checked her watch. Mitch would be coming back soon. Her heart did a little dance. Stealing a cookie from the tray, she hurried to her room to change.

An hour later, Mitch walked into the inn. Beside him was a slender woman with long, gray hair and a huge smile.

"You must be Kaitlyn Russo. I'd recognize you even if Mitch hadn't told me you'd taken this place over." Mitch's mom wrapped Kaitlyn in a warm hug. "Mable was always showing off the pictures your parents sent her way." The woman pulled away and looked at Kaitlyn. "My, you've grown into such a beautiful young woman."

"Thank you. It's nice to meet you, Ms. Hargrove," Kaitlyn said, almost at a loss for words at the heartfelt greeting. "And thank you so much for agreeing to watch the inn tonight."

"Please, call me Gina. And I'm happy that you gave me something to do."

"As if you sit around twiddling your thumbs all day," Mitch said sarcastically behind her.

Gina rolled her eyes. "If you listen to him, I work myself

nearly into a grave." Her smile fell. "Oh, I'm sorry. That's so insensitive of me, considering your grandmother just died."

Kaitlyn shook her head. "It's fine. Please make yourself at home. We won't be gone long."

"And no cleaning," Mitch bellowed as he ushered Kaitlyn out the front door and into the driveway where his truck was still running. He opened the passenger side door for her and then reappeared in the driver's seat.

"Your mom seems really nice."

He nodded. "Oh, she is. Nice and stubborn, if you ask me."

"Did everything check out at her appointment earlier?" Kaitlyn asked, even more concerned now that she'd met Gina.

Mitch cranked the engine. "Dr. Jacobs ran some labs. We should get results sometime next week. Until then, Dr. Jacobs said for her to rest and take a good multivitamin."

"That's always good advice," Kaitlyn said.

"Assuming Mom actually listens to it." He glanced across the seat as he came to the stop sign at the end of Mistletoe Lane. "Now, what do you say we go pick out a Christmas tree?"

Kaitlyn grinned. "If I didn't know better, I'd say you sound a little excited yourself."

"What can I say? I'm a man. We like to hunt and gather."

Something about that made Kaitlyn's blood heat. He was a man, for sure. Big and strong, doing exactly what he was made to do. And she absolutely was not going to kiss him again tonight. Their kiss at Silver Lake had been a mistake. One that shouldn't happen again.

CHAPTER NINE

"I've never been to a Christmas tree farm before," Kaitlyn said, glancing across the seat at Mitch.

He kept his eyes on the road, following the curves and bends precisely. "I used to go with your grandfather to pick one out," he told her. "Henry always liked to get the biggest one on the lot."

Kaitlyn laughed beside him. The sound was completely angelic. "I regret that I didn't get to spend a lot of time with them but I do remember Grandpa Henry having a fancy for doing things large."

Mitch nodded. "The larger the better. Your grandfather was a very good man."

They talked a little more about Mable and Henry, the inn, and Kaitlyn's continuing plans for improvement as they drove to Merry Mountain Farms on the edge of town. Mitch hadn't been here in years. Not since before his senior year of high school.

He pulled into the lot, which was already crowded and

buzzing with couples and families in search of their own perfect tree this holiday. Christmas music jingled in the air along with the laughter of children as he stepped out. Although it was frigid outside, Mitch's chest grew warm. Once upon a time, he'd loved Christmas more than anything.

"Do you think your truck will hold the biggest Christmas tree in this lot?" Kaitlyn turned to look at him as he walked around the truck to meet her. "Because that's the one I plan to get."

"No Charlie Brown tree?" he asked.

She shook her head. "If that's all I were planning to get, I wouldn't need you, would I?"

He walked beside her up the dirt path that led to the expanse of fir trees ahead. Kaitlyn walked down every path, inspecting each tree. Then, true to her word, she did pick out just about the biggest of the bunch forty-five minutes later.

"That one!" She rubbed her gloved hands together and beamed at him, her soft brown hair flowing underneath her bright-green knit hat.

"You sure?" he asked.

"One hundred percent. That's the one."

Her enthusiasm was contagious. "Okay."

"Last-Ditch Mitch!" He heard a familiar voice call from a few feet away.

Mitch spun to see Tuck and his sister, Halona, with her son, Theo. It seemed Mitch couldn't really go anywhere without running into people in this town. "Hey, looks like you guys had the same idea," Mitch said, inspecting the tree they were carrying. "Did you pick that one out?" he asked Theo, who merely stared at him.

"He's not much of a talker these days," Halona said, a hint of worry wrinkling her brow. "Good to see you, Mitch."

"You too. This is Kaitlyn Russo," he said, introducing Kaitlyn.

"Russo? You're Mable and Henry's granddaughter," Halona said. "They were wonderful people. I'm so sorry about Mable's passing."

"Thank you. How do you know Mitch?" Kaitlyn asked.

"We all went to school together," Tuck informed her.

"And why do you call him Last-Ditch Mitch?"

Mitch cupped a hand to the back of his neck and answered Kaitlyn's question himself. "Because if all else failed, I was always the sucker to call in high school. For a ride or homework. I even got asked to help someone break up with his girlfriend once. I said no to that request."

"Mitch is steadfast and responsible," Tuck explained. "You can ask him for anything, and he'd do it."

"Within reason," Mitch said.

"Well, it was nice to meet you, Kaitlyn," Tuck said. "I'm afraid this tree is heavy, and Theo over here has a bedtime soon." He tipped his head at Mitch. "We still need to get together, buddy."

"Yeah." Mitch shoved his hands in the pockets of his leather jacket. "Sounds good."

Tuck grinned. "See you later, guys! Have fun on your date."

"It's not a date," Mitch corrected, perhaps a tad too surly.

Tuck looked between him and Kaitlyn and then to his nephew, who was still watching them. "Theo, give Mr. Mitch a piece of what's in your pocket to help him out."

The mischievous sparkle in Tuck's eyes made Mitch wonder if he should hold out his hand for what the boy was now offering up. Halona's son was so cute though, that Mitch dutifully opened his palm. Then he blinked at the sprig of mistletoe the child had dispensed.

"Good night, you two!" Tuck called as he and Halona continued forward with their tree and little Theo chased behind them.

Kaitlyn's cheeks were red when he looked up at her. "Mistletoe," she said.

"It grows rampant around these parts this time of year."

She nodded, and he suspected they were both thinking about that kiss at Silver Lake. The kiss that had been way out of line.

He shoved the sprig in his coat pocket and set about cutting down the perfect tree for the inn. It was time to be on their merry way before they ran into someone else. Or before he decided to pull out that mistletoe and make good use of it.

* * *

The doorbell rang at two p.m. the next afternoon. Kaitlyn used her hands to iron out the wrinkles in her shirt and locked her stray hair behind her ears. With a smile, she pulled open the door, expecting to meet the Krespos, who had reservations for today.

Instead of an older couple, however, a very young couple stared back at her.

"Yes?" she asked.

The young man slapped a wiry arm around the girl and pulled her close. "Yeah. We're hoping to get a room here."

Is that a pimple on his cheek? How old are these kids? Do their parents know they're here?

Kaitlyn blinked, speechless for a moment. "Umm. Okay. Well, let me check and see if we have availabilities. Please come in," she said, leading the young couple to the couch.

"I'll be right back." She took off walking down the hall toward the kitchen to find Mitch.

Could she in good conscience rent a room to those two kids? Knowing they were likely to have sex?

"What's wrong?" Mitch asked, standing with a toolbox just outside her bedroom.

"We have more guests," she told him.

"The Krespos?"

"No. They're not here yet. This is a young couple. They look like they might be twenty or possibly younger. They want a room. I can't give them a room, can I?" Her gaze dropped to his toolbox. "What are you doing outside my bedroom?"

"Installing a lock. You shouldn't sleep in a room that doesn't have one. Any one of the guests could stroll in anytime they want."

Including him, she thought, hoping he'd had a hard time going to sleep last night too. After they'd gotten the tree, they'd brought it back here and relieved Mitch's mom from her post. Then Mitch had returned and had a nightcap with her, keeping a safe six feet of distance between them at all times. As if he were scared that coming any closer might lead to something more.

"I'm still not so sure about this Paris character," he continued, as if that explained the lock. "He's overstaying his welcome. This will be the fifth night."

"He's our guest, and he's welcome here as long as he wants. So, what do I do?" She intertwined her fingers in front of her, trying to contain her nervous energy.

"What do you mean?" Mitch asked.

"I can't rent them a room, can I? Isn't there a minimum booking age here? What would Mable have done?"

He tipped his head and looked at her through long, black

eyelashes. It wasn't fair that a man could have such beautiful lashes.

"Are you serious? If the kids are legal age and have money, they can do whatever they want."

"They want to have...*sex*," she said, lowering her voice to a whisper.

The hallway was dimly lit, and Mitch's eyes narrowed, pinning her to where she stood. "Everyone who comes here is probably going to want to have sex, Kaitlyn."

"Not Paris," she said, folding her arms in front of her.

Mitch's jaw ticked. "He might want sex too. Which is why I'm putting a lock on your door."

"Paris and I are *not* having sex," she said, keeping her voice low. She hoped he couldn't see the burn moving up her chest and past her neck.

"A single man who shows up at a bed and breakfast alone is suspect. Your picture is up on the website now. Maybe he saw it and thought he'd come see if he had a shot with you."

"Now *you're* being ridiculous." *And completely adorable.*

"I know guys. There are two main things we think about." He ticked off those things on his fingers. "Food and sex."

She swallowed, knowing she shouldn't ask. "You're a guy. Is that what you're thinking about right now?"

He looked at her long and hard with those dark coffee-stained eyes of his. The ones that made heat swirl in her belly like hot fudge on an ice cream sundae. She melted in the look, and part of her wanted to take his hand, pull him into her bedroom, and test that new lock he was installing. That was the part of her that was a glutton for punishment. The part she was suppressing.

"Mable would've gotten their credit card information and then rented the room to them," he said, avoiding the question. He gestured down the hall to the living room where the young couple was still waiting. "It's not your job to judge or condone other people's sex lives."

"That's not what I'm doing."

He lifted a brow. "They're adults. Give them a room."

She pressed her lips together. Then she sucked in a breath and blew it out. "Fine. But I don't have to like it." She headed down the hall. "Good news. You're in luck," she told the couple and then waited for them to stop French kissing on the couch. The boy with the pimple had roaming hands—one on the girl's butt and one creeping up her miniskirt. Didn't she realize it was twenty degrees outside?

Kaitlyn cleared her throat. "Good news," she said again, a little louder and more cheerful this time.

Finally, the couple came up for air.

"I have availabilities. You'll be staying in the *Pride and Prejudice* room. It's inspired by Elizabeth and Mr. Darcy."

"Who are they?" the girl asked, twisting her expression.

"You know—Jane Austen?" Kaitlyn waited for recognition to cross the couple's features. From the corner of her eye, she noticed Mitch standing off to the side.

"All the rooms here are named after famous couples," Kaitlyn explained. "Scarlett and Rhett, Baby and Johnny, Anne and Gilbert Blythe—my personal favorite."

The couple looked at her as if she were speaking an alien tongue.

"Do you have a Bella and Edward room?" the girl asked.

Now Kaitlyn stared at them as if *they* were the ones from another planet.

"You know, from *Twilight*."

Mitch coughed but Kaitlyn suspected it was really a laugh. She wasn't amused.

"No. I'm afraid we don't have a room named after vampires."

The boy shrugged. "We won't be paying much attention to the decorating anyhow, babe," he told his girlfriend.

Kaitlyn glanced over at Mitch. He was right. It wasn't her job to judge but who came to a bed and breakfast and didn't pay attention to the décor? "Okay. So, how will you be paying for your stay here?"

"Plastic," the overeager boyfriend said, handing her his credit card.

Kaitlyn ran it, secretly hoping it would be declined. When it wasn't, she handed the card back and forced a smile. "Well, let me lead you to your room."

The couple followed her up the stairs.

"I can't wait to get you behind closed doors," the boy said.

The girlfriend moaned. "Me either."

Do they realize I can hear them?

"*Okayyyyyyy.*" Kaitlyn swung open their door. The Elizabeth and Mr. Darcy room deserved so much more than this for its initiation. "Enjoy and let me know if you need anything."

"Yeah, we need a DO NOT DISTURB sign." The boyfriend grinned.

"Trust me. You won't be bothered." Kaitlyn couldn't leave fast enough. Mitch was waiting for her downstairs. When she saw him, she submitted to a total-body shudder.

He laughed again, not bothering to hide it this time.

"I seriously want to call their parents and tell them what's going on."

"They're probably on fall break from the local college. Mable used to get quite a few couples from there."

"And she didn't mind?"

"Oh, your grandmother was old-fashioned and romantic. She minded. She didn't discriminate though."

Kaitlyn folded her arms over her chest. "I'm glad you're here."

"Me too," he said, and the crazy thing was that he sounded like he meant it for once.

"Hey," he said, looking a little shy. He scratched his chin and averted his gaze. "Mom wanted me to ask you if you have plans for Thursday."

Kaitlyn frowned, forgetting momentarily that this was the week of Thanksgiving. "Oh. No. My parents usually go to an expensive restaurant. Mom doesn't really like to cook. I'm not even sure she knows how to turn the oven on." She smiled weakly. "Dad usually wore the apron when I was growing up but he didn't inherit Grandma Mable's talent in the kitchen."

Mitch shifted on his feet. "Mom wanted me to ask you to have Thanksgiving with us. Nothing big. It'll just be me and her." He shrugged. "Feel free to say no. I told her you probably couldn't because of the B and B."

"Right." Kaitlyn nodded. "One of us needs to stay when there's a guest." Disappointment flooded through her. Going to Gina Hargrove's home for Thanksgiving would be wonderful. "Hey, I have an idea. Why don't you invite your mom here? I can't leave unless you or someone else I trust is watching the place. But she can come here." Kaitlyn drew her hands to her chest. "And I'm pretty sure Paris doesn't have any plans. It'd be a shame for him to be all alone."

"Maybe he wants to be alone," Mitch said gruffly. If she didn't know better, she might think he was jealous of their leather-clad guest.

"No one wants to be alone, even if they say they do. Do you think your mom will come?"

Mitch nodded. "I think she'd be thrilled. And she'll insist on taking over your kitchen to do the cooking. She might allow you to help if you ask nicely."

Kaitlyn burst into laughter. "Wow. I was just going to let

the day come and go but now I'm actually excited. This is going to be great. Then maybe after dinner, you and I can decorate that Christmas tree of ours." And yeah, without intending it, there was a flirtatious tone to her voice.

"Thought you were the decorator in this arrangement," he said.

"I am. But you told me, in no uncertain terms, not to get on a ladder without having you around. So you can catch me when I fall."

Her heart melted as he smiled back at her. And then it stuttered to a halting stop. She seriously doubted she'd be falling from a ladder. But falling for the man in front of her wasn't so far-fetched.

* * *

On Thanksgiving morning, while the women had been cooking, Mitch made himself useful getting the outdoor holiday decorations out of the storage building. Kaitlyn had already hung the wreaths in the windows a few weeks ago, but Mable had also been putting out a nativity scene alongside a blowup Santa Claus for as far back as he could remember. After spending an hour or so setting them on display just like he and Henry Russo used to, Mitch headed back inside the house.

The air was thick with spice, butter, and fried things. Mitch had to admit that his mom was an excellent cook. Kaitlyn had been in the kitchen for the last few hours, helping and hopefully doing most of the work. Who was he kidding though? His mom was no doubt bustling around like a darn turkey with its head cut off. Dr. Jacobs's office still hadn't called with results but his mom kept insisting she was fine. Mitch wouldn't believe that until he had proof.

"Hey, Mitch," Paris said, coming out of the sitting room.

"Hey." Mitch's mouth wobbled in not quite a smile. He still didn't trust the guy but his gut was telling him it was for no other reason than Kaitlyn had called Paris attractive that first night. "You able to work down here?" he asked.

Paris glanced back to the sitting room, where he'd likely left his computer. "Hard to concentrate with the smell of delicious food looming."

At this, Mitch gave a sincere laugh.

"I offered to help but the women shooed me away."

"Sounds about right," Mitch said with a nod. Mitch stood there for another awkward second. Paris was a guest here, and as part owner, Mitch was technically a host. He didn't know a thing about hosting though. "Want to watch some football while we wait?"

Paris furrowed his brow. "Nah, man. I don't watch the games."

Mitch felt his whole body relax. "Me neither. That's just what guys do on Thanksgiving, I guess." Mitch couldn't really remember. He'd stayed far from home for the last few Thanksgivings. And Thanksgiving while on shift as an MP meant take-out food at the station and maybe a delicious piece of dessert from one of the wives if he got lucky.

Paris sat down on the front room's couch while Mitch took the high-back chair across from it.

"So, you're a graphic designer?"

"That's right," Paris said. "I do freelance work."

"And you're just traveling up the coast alone?" he asked, not intending the suspicion that coated his words.

"I guess you could say that. I lived in Florida when I was married. Divorced now."

"Sorry to hear that."

"It happens," Paris said. "It's not a whole lot of fun when it does. You ever been married?" he asked Mitch.

Mitch shook his head. He'd never had time to even consider the idea. He'd leaped from high school to the military, from one deployment to another. "No."

"Well, it's a great idea if you find the right one. Otherwise, it's a really *bad* idea." Paris chuckled.

"All right, you two." Mitch's mom came breezing down the hall wearing a food-splattered apron and a huge smile. Kaitlyn followed behind her, looking fresh and beautiful. Mitch breathed a little easier just seeing her face. "Men are allowed to help set the table, so come on." His mom waved a hand, signaling them back.

Fifteen minutes later, they all sat around the table for Thanksgiving dinner and began passing dishes of stuffing, lima beans, rolls, cranberry sauce—you name it. This wasn't so bad. Especially watching how much Kaitlyn seemed to be enjoying herself. That was something to be thankful for.

As expected, his mom quickly zeroed in on the newest person at the table and started peeling off his layers, which Mitch found a welcome distraction. He'd learned a little bit about their guest but it wouldn't hurt to learn more.

"So, what brings you to town, Mr. Montgomery?"

Paris appeared to flush a little at that title, which Mitch found humorous. "You can call me Paris. I'm here to meet up with the Bikers for Santa group at this weekend's Lights on the Lake event."

Kaitlyn straightened. "I've never heard of that. It sounds like fun."

"Oh, it is," Mitch's mom agreed. "The event always kicks off the holiday season with the lighting of the town's Christmas tree. It can't be missed. All the downtown stores stay open late, and they show off their holiday decorations for the first time. There are carolers and fake snow for the kids. The real snow won't come until later in December or early January, of course."

"And there's an Angel Tree in the town square," Paris continued. "That's why the Bikers for Santa are meeting. We'll all pick an angel off. A kid's wish list is on the back of each one, and it's our job to make it come true."

"I think that's a wonderful cause," Kaitlyn said.

Mitch had to agree. Of all the reasons he'd expected to hear for why Paris had chosen to come to Sweetwater Springs, this was not one of them.

Paris shrugged. "I grew up in foster care and had a lot of miserable Christmases. There was only one that was ever worth remembering, and it was here. Seems fitting to be back. I've actually been considering moving here."

"Really?" Kaitlyn asked, stabbing at several lima beans on her plate.

He nodded. "Can't stay at a bed and breakfast forever. I do well with my business but not *that* well." He winked across the table, which put Mitch back on guard.

"Well, there's a sign posted in Alice Hamilton's yard. She has a garage apartment for rent," his mom said.

"Mom, Ms. Hamilton might be looking for someone a little more...conservative." Mitch turned to Paris. "No offense."

"None taken."

"Nonsense. I'll put in a good word," his mom promised. "And I'll bring you over there to introduce you two myself."

Paris nodded. "Thanks. That might work out well."

"It would put you close to the inn," Kaitlyn said. "And I was thinking of hiring a good graphic designer soon to help me with some promotional items."

"I'll help any way I can."

"That's perfect." Mitch's mom shoveled some sweet potato casserole into her mouth and shook her head as she chewed and swallowed. "Things just seem to work out exactly how they should. Just like your grandmother leaving this inn to you, Kaitlyn. I know you're going to love it here."

"I wish I could thank her." Kaitlyn turned to look at Mitch. "Leaving the inn to us was an unexpected gift."

Mitch stiffened. To think he'd naively thought the conversation wouldn't turn to him.

His mom set her fork down and narrowed her gaze. "Us?" she asked. "Is there something you failed to mention to me, Mitchell Douglas Hargrove? *You* and Kaitlyn inherited the B and B?"

He closed his eyes and counted to five before facing her. "Yeah. I've, uh, been meaning to mention that. That's why I came back to Sweetwater Springs."

She clapped her hands together. "To run the Sweetwater B and B?" she said, breathless with excitement. "This is fantastic Thanksgiving news!"

"No, Mom. To sell it."

She blinked.

"The will says that Kaitlyn and I have to run the inn together for two months. Then Kaitlyn can buy me out and run it on her own," he explained. "That puts me here through the holidays, so stop frowning and be happy."

His mom clamped her mouth shut, lifted her fork, and stabbed at a stalk of asparagus. "I am happy you're home. Especially this time of year." She looked up with her smile pinned back in place.

Mitch wasn't fooled though. He knew she wished he'd make Sweetwater Springs home again. He would do just about anything for his mom but that wasn't really in the cards. She must've known it too because she didn't bring the subject back up. Instead, she turned the conversation back to the Lights on the Lake event. "You have to go, dear. Mitch can take you, and I'll watch the B and B. I won't take no for an answer." Her eyes shifted to Mitch's, daring him to break her heart again. "Right, son?"

Kaitlyn was watching him too.

The entire town would be at the lighting of the Christmas tree. Not his idea of a good time. He chewed on his food and his excuses—none of which he thought his mom would accept.

Then the doorbell rang. *Saved by the bell.*

"Maybe that's the Krespos," Kaitlyn said, scooting back from the table.

"Great," Mitch said, following behind her. Instead of an older couple though, she opened the door to two young men wearing ugly Christmas sweaters. One had his arm draped around the other.

"Hi," Kaitlyn said. "Can I help you?"

"Yes. I'm Nate Trapp and this is Chris Trapp. We were hoping to get a room for a couple of nights," the taller one said. "Sorry for the late notice but my mom won't allow us to sleep in the same room even though we're married now."

"Don't worry," Chris told him, "she'll come around. I can tell she likes me."

"Of course she does." Nate shared a look with his husband. "What's not to love?"

Kaitlyn smiled at the couple. "Well, you're in luck. We do have a room for you. And dinner if you're hungry."

Nate held his stomach. "Mom may not want us sharing a bed but she had no issues feeding us."

Kaitlyn laughed. "I'm Kaitlyn Russo." She gestured to Mitch, who was standing behind her. "This is Mitch Hargrove."

"Hey," Mitch said.

"We're the owners here. Come inside. We'll get you settled for your stay."

Mitch took Chris's credit card and scanned it while Kaitlyn showed the couple around downstairs. Then she took them upstairs to their room. A moment later, she came down the steps and met Mitch in the front room.

"What's wrong?" she asked, no doubt seeing the lines of distress on his face.

"I would just prefer if people would make reservations. This could quickly get out of hand."

"Well, like you just told your mom, you want us to make enough money for me to buy you out. A full house is how we're going to make that happen. We'll just have to deal with the chaos." She grabbed his hand and tugged him back toward the dining room. "Now, let's return to our feast before your mom and Paris eat all the food."

Hopefully, they had, which would mean the meal was over. He really didn't want to take the hot seat again and tell his mom he absolutely would not be taking Kaitlyn to the Lights on the Lake event.

CHAPTER TEN

"I don't think I'll be able to eat again until Christmas," Kaitlyn sighed as she loaded the last of the plates into the dishwasher.

"Me neither," Mitch said.

Kaitlyn had insisted that Gina not help with the cleanup, and surprisingly she'd listened and gone home. As Kaitlyn was hugging Gina goodbye and thanking her for all her help with dinner, a newlywed couple, the Jamiesons, walked up the steps. The Trapps hadn't seen the article about the B&B but the Jamiesons told her they had. They'd visited their family in nearby Shadow Ridge earlier and had made the short trip into the valley in hopes of getting a room here.

The inn only had five rooms, which were now occupied by Mitch, Paris, the Trapps, the Jamiesons, and Missy and Joe, aka the horny college couple, who'd gone off to spend their Thanksgiving afternoon in a nontraditional way at the local movie theater.

"Did my mom look okay to you?" Mitch asked as he wrapped tinfoil over the leftovers.

"She seemed just fine. Full of energy and excitement. She's probably in bed resting already, so stop worrying." Kaitlyn laughed softly under her breath. "Your mom is amazing, by the way. I've only known her a few days, and it feels like I've known her forever. She had so many stories about my grandparents to tell." Kaitlyn cleared her throat. "And *other* stories."

She saw him straighten from the corner of her eye.

"Okay. Let's have it. How many embarrassing stories of mine did she tell you while you two were in the kitchen?"

"Only a few," Kaitlyn teased as she closed the dishwasher. "There. All done." As she was wiping her hands on a dishcloth, her cell phone dinged from the counter. She walked over and checked the screen to see a message from Josie waiting for her.

Missing you today. Hoping you've advanced from the sweet kiss to the naughty one. That would give you something to be thankful for.

Kaitlyn tapped the screen quickly in case Mitch decided to look over her shoulder. She usually went to Josie's home for Thanksgiving Day. Her own parents—who hadn't called or left a message, by the way—didn't typically do much. Josie's mom wasn't the most domestic but at least she tried. She usually had a turkey that was as tough as jerky and a series of fancy bowls filled with vegetables that she'd warmed from the can.

Kaitlyn put her phone back down and made a mental note to text Josie back later. Maybe she'd call her parents too. She could tell them about the inn's first holiday event. Not that they'd likely be impressed.

"Okay. Are you ready?" Kaitlyn asked, pushing away her regret and disappointment and turning back to Mitch. It was a day to focus on the good. She didn't need a naughty kiss from Mitch to be thankful. She had this inn, and she'd just enjoyed a five-star meal with her newfound friends. In addition to that, all five guest rooms were occupied.

"Ready for what?" Mitch asked skeptically.

"Well, now that the inn is booking, we definitely need to get that Christmas tree decorated." She led the way to the sitting room where they'd set up the evergreen tree on Monday night. Then she turned on the old-fashioned radio inside an antique cabinet against the wall. She'd already loaded a holiday CD, and all she had to do was push Play to fill the room with soft carols.

With that done, she stepped over to a box of ornaments she'd found a few weeks ago and lifted off the lid. "This is a ton of ornaments. It might take us all night." And despite his frequent surliness, she didn't mind that prospect at all. Kaitlyn had seen a totally different side of him this afternoon. For a short time, he'd been relaxed and doting. The very image of a tad overly protective son. And he'd made sure his mom and Paris had felt welcome here. He'd done the same for the Trapps and Jamiesons when they'd arrived. He could protest that he wasn't cut out for hosting all he wanted but he'd been wonderful today.

Kaitlyn reached for the strings of lights and stood. "First, we have to add these." She plugged one set into a drop cord and retrieved the small ladder that Mitch had placed here earlier in the day.

"I got it." Mitch immediately took it from her and set it up.

He wasn't just overprotective of his mom, it seemed, and that sent gooey warmness trickling through her.

* * *

This was a form of torture somewhere, Mitch thought, watching Kaitlyn climb up the ladder for the millionth time in the last hour to hang another ornament. It wasn't the fact that she wanted to discuss each one in detail. No, it was the curves of her body positioned right in front of him. But he had no choice. What if she fell off the ladder like she had outside the other week? It was his duty to make sure she was safe. So why the hell did he keep secretly wishing she'd misstep and land back into his arms?

"You're awfully quiet," Kaitlyn commented, whirling to face him on the ladder. She was only on the second step, so doing so put her eye to eye with him. "What are you thinking about?"

Things I shouldn't.

"Nothing."

The corner of her mouth quirked as if she knew that was a lie. She turned back to the tree with her ornament and climbed a few steps higher.

He braced the ladder, just in case, as she reached for the spot she'd deemed worthy of the little heart-shaped decoration in her hand. As she reached, one of her legs came out to balance her weight and plowed right between his legs.

Mitch let out an unexpected cry of pain. Which, in turn, sent Kaitlyn spinning on the ladder again.

"I'm so sorry. Did I just…" Her gaze dropped to his hands cupped over his groin as the music sang about chestnuts roasting over an open fire. His nuts weren't in such good shape right now either.

Both of Kaitlyn's hands flew over her mouth. "I didn't mean to do that. I'm so, so sorry. That's twice in a month. First with Bradley, now you. Although Bradley was intentional. Yours was an accident. I'm going to get a reputation if I don't stop."

"Hold on to the rungs," he bit out, forcing his hands up to brace the ladder again.

She shook lightly as she suppressed a giggle. "I wouldn't want to put a crimp in your sex life," she finally said.

"You let me worry about my sex life."

She gave him a curious look and then turned back to the ladder and descended to retrieve another ornament from the box. "I'll tell you if you tell me."

"Tell you what?" he asked.

"About your sex life." She grabbed a candy-cane-shaped ornament and climbed the ladder once more while tossing a mischievous look over her shoulder. "I'll start. I haven't had sex in nine months, and that was with an old boyfriend who came to town. We'd been together before, and we were going through a dry spell. So we decided to be adults about it."

The distraction of the conversation alleviated the pain in his nether region. "Adults about having sex? So you were just satisfying needs?"

She shrugged. "Trying to. He was satisfied, but...Well, let's just say I'd forgotten that he had never been great at satisfying me. It's one of the reasons I wasn't that sorry we broke up in the first place."

She traveled down and then climbed back up as she talked. As if this were just a casual conversation between two people who weren't supposed to be attracted to one another.

"Your turn," she prompted.

He hesitated but fair was fair. She'd just told him her

story so he went ahead with his. "Three months ago. I wasn't out of the marine corps yet. It was just a small break. I came home, drank too much at the Tipsy Tavern, and hooked up with a waitress there."

"A one-night stand." Kaitlyn twisted on the ladder again. "I've never had one of those."

"I wouldn't recommend it. You probably wouldn't find satisfaction in that either."

Her brows drew up. "So you didn't even know her?"

Mitch had a feeling he was going to regret spilling so many details about his last sexual encounter. "I knew her from growing up here. She was younger than me. We were just casual acquaintances, and that's all I'm dishing on that subject. A gentleman doesn't kiss and tell."

Kaitlyn clamped her mouth shut. Then she continued to quietly go about her task for several minutes.

"What's wrong?" Mitch finally asked.

"Just lost in thought. Maybe I should have a one-night stand," she pondered, more to herself than him.

He swallowed. "I don't think a woman like you would enjoy that kind of thing."

"What does that mean, 'a woman like me'?"

"Well, from what I see, you're passionate. You don't do things halfway. If you wanted to find a good man to satisfy all your needs, not just the sexual, I'm sure you could find one without any problem."

She stared at him for a long moment, and for some reason, he had a longing to be that kind of guy.

She took one step down, still facing him, leveling her eyes to his, her mouth to his. Daring him to kiss her again.

Her gaze flicked to his lips. His arms, bracing the ladder still, pinned her body almost to his.

"Not a good idea," he whispered.

"Why not?" Her bottom lip pulled down just slightly.

"Like I said, you deserve more than just some guy who can satisfy the now."

"Do you protect everyone in your life?" she asked.

Heat pulsed in the space between them. "I guess so. I was a marine corps cop after all."

"Since when is kissing a crime?"

He swallowed, wanting more than anything to taste her again. She brought one hand up and curled it behind his neck, tugging softly. It didn't take much to break him. Then his mouth was on hers.

Her hot, wet tongue slid up against his.

Mitch's hands moved to Kaitlyn's waist. His quickly waning willpower kept them from sinking any lower.

"That was the last ornament," she said, when they finally pulled away. "I guess we're done for tonight." Something twinkled in her eye, and it didn't take a cup of Dawanda's cappuccino to read what she was thinking right now. He'd meant what he said though. She deserved a better man.

"Great. I'm pretty tired," he said. Which was a lie. After that kiss, he might not get a wink of sleep tonight.

Disappointment shone in her eyes now. "Yeah. Me too," she said after a long pause. "Thanks for helping."

"That's my job, isn't it?"

"You went above and beyond though. As always. I'm not sure what I'll do after you leave."

"You'll be fine. I have faith in you." And he did. Kaitlyn had proved herself to be steadfast and strong. She was a fighter, and she'd make this bed and breakfast work no matter what obstacles came her way. He admired the heck out of her.

And if conditions were different, maybe...

They cleaned up and headed out of the sitting room.

"Good night, Kaitlyn," Mitch said, forcing his feet to move toward the stairs that led to his room and not to follow her down the hall to hers.

"Mitch?"

"Yeah?"

She pulled her lower lip between her teeth.

Anticipation hung in the air. His willpower was already near its breaking point. If she put into words what she wanted, if she made him make that choice, he wouldn't be able to say no. She could ask him to strip naked and climb Mount Pleasant right now. Or jump into Silver Lake in the dead of winter. His answer would be yes.

"Do you think—"

The doorbell rang behind them.

"Who's that?" he asked as they both turned.

She shrugged. "We really should invest in a CLOSED sign. I don't like people showing up after dark."

He took the lead in answering. Pulling the front door open, he stared back at a short, older couple. The man had a white comb-over. The woman had fluffy bluish-colored hair and sloppy lipstick.

"Good evening. We're the Krespos." The old man smiled. "We meant to come earlier in the week but we're here now. Ready to claim that romantic room you promised us."

Mitch looked at Kaitlyn, who was now standing beside him in the doorway. They'd been resigned to the fact that the Krespos weren't coming.

Her eyes were wide and her skin, which had been flushed and pink when they'd been beside the tree together, was now pale as new-fallen snow.

"The Beauty and the Beast room is available," he said, offering up his own room. "I just need a quick minute to prepare it for you. Please come in. There is water and fruit at the table along the wall if you need refreshment," he told the couple, gesturing them inside. The old man was frail in comparison to his robust wife.

Mitch offered a reassuring glance to Kaitlyn before heading upstairs to pack his things and change the bedsheets. Ten minutes later, he returned downstairs. "All set. The Beauty and the Beast room is yours."

"I'm Beauty, and she's the Beast," Mr. Krespo joked as he stood from the couch.

Mrs. Krespo jabbed an elbow into his ribs with enough force to crack a few. In return, Mr. Krespo moaned in pain.

Kaitlyn turned to Mitch, a slight crease in her brow.

"I'll see them up," he told her.

She nodded. "Thank you."

"No problem." He didn't mind giving up his room but that meant either he had to head to his mom's house tonight—and he didn't like the idea of leaving Kaitlyn alone with so many guests to cater to—or he had to sleep on the couch, which he guessed wasn't exactly good B&B host etiquette. Not that he'd ever been one for etiquette.

He showed Mr. and Mrs. Krespo upstairs to their room and then headed back down the staircase, where Kaitlyn was waiting for him.

"You can sleep in my room," she said, giving him a third option for where to sleep tonight.

"I'm not sure that's the best idea."

"Why not? We're two adults, and I trust you."

He stepped off the bottom stair and walked toward her. "I'm not sure I trust myself," he said quietly, in case other guests were in listening range. "Especially after that kiss."

Her eyes widened, her lips parted, and he wanted nothing more than to keep kissing her.

She took hold of his hand and tugged. "Don't be silly.

You're staying in my room tonight, and I'm not taking no for an answer."

* * *

Kaitlyn sat on the edge of her bed and watched as Mitch pulled out the old air mattress from her grandparents' closet and attempted to blow it up. This was not what she had in mind when she'd dragged him to her room.

She was already in her flannel pajamas featuring multi-colored snowflakes. She wished she had something sexier to wear right about now. Not that she wanted to be sexy and lure Mitch to her bed.

Okay, that was totally what she wanted. When her hormones were in charge, she didn't care if he was forever material or not. She wanted him on top of her, underneath her, all over her. Mitch didn't think she was the type of girl to have a one-night stand but maybe she was.

As if hearing her blaring thoughts, he turned back to look at her. "The pump isn't blowing this thing up. There must be a leak in the mattress somewhere." He continued to try for several more minutes and then shook his head.

"This is a king-size bed. It's big enough for the two of us," Kaitlyn offered. Even if it were a twin-size bed, it'd be big enough for them. In fact, a twin-size would be far better.

"I'll just go to my mom's tonight and return early in the morning to help out."

"Not necessary. I mean, she's probably sleeping, and you'll wake her. She needs her rest, remember?"

Mitch stood just a few feet away. "I can sleep on the floor, then. It's fine."

"Will you just stop?" She pulled back the covers on the

opposite side of the bed. "You're sleeping in my bed with me, and that's final."

"Not a good idea." Those were the same words he'd used at the Christmas tree, right before kissing her. And he'd been wrong. That had been an excellent idea.

"Why?" she asked, feeling the tension between them dial up to crackling.

"You know why, Kaitlyn. Kissing is one thing. Anything more is irresponsible."

"For who? Me or you?"

"Me. Mable didn't leave this place to us for me to take advantage of you."

"Is it taking advantage if it's what we both want?" Sucking in a breath, she reached for the hem of her shirt and pulled it over her head.

"Kaitlyn," he said on a deep groan. She watched his gaze flick down to her white lace bra.

It was a bold move, unlike her for sure, but she was tired of waiting for Mitch, who seemed to have the patience of Job. Her desire bordered on need. She could barely breathe as she waited for him to make his move.

"You're going to have to invite me over there," he finally said in a gruff voice.

"I kind of thought taking my shirt off was an obvious invitation. Being together doesn't have to change things between us, Mitch. It can just be two adults having consensual sex."

Sex had always meant something to her in the past though. Maybe it would now too, but she didn't want to think about that at the moment. Her body needed him. She hadn't been satisfied sexually by a man in a very long time, and she had a feeling Mitch would raise the bar for any man who followed him.

He took the smallest step toward her, his gaze unwavering. Then, detouring, he flipped off the lights and climbed onto the opposite side of the bed with his back turned to her. "It's been a long day," he said. "We're both tired. We should get some sleep."

She blinked, feeling hot tears descend. Snatching up her top, she put it back on and stared once more at the shadow of a man. *Gah. How embarrassing.* She'd offered Mitch sex with no strings attached, and he'd rejected her.

Burrowing under the covers, she hoped sleep would find her fast. By the sound of the heavy breathing beside her, it'd already found her bedmate.

CHAPTER ELEVEN

*M*itch flopped restlessly onto his side as he slept. He was in one of those dream states where he was right on the edge of waking but he couldn't get his eyes to open. And he needed them to open.

He was at a party where he probably shouldn't have been. But when you're seventeen, the things you shouldn't do usually sound like the best ideas. He had a beer in his hand but he didn't intend to drink it. It was all for show. He also had his eyes on the head cheerleader across the room. The night was promising to be one of the best of his life.

Not the worst.

"Last-Ditch Mitch," his buddy Tuck called, grabbing his elbow and pulling his attention away from the blond. "Something's wrong with Tim."

Mitch turned to Tuck, whose black hair was overgrown, making waves that turned in varying directions on his head. "What's wrong?"

"He's sick."

Tim Sampson was always sick. He was one of those kids, chronically pale, thin, catching every virus in the air. If survival of the fittest were in play, Tim would be the first one to die in their group of friends.

"He'll be fine," Mitch said, curling his fingers around his bottle. It'd taken some convincing from his friends to even come tonight but he was glad he did. All the worry that came with being a teenager in a single-parent home had melted away with the crowd, music, and girls.

Tuck gestured at Mitch's drink. "You've barely taken a sip from your beer. I've had a whole one. We all have. You should be the one to drive him home."

Mitch looked at Tuck as if maybe his friend had lost his mind.

"Don't you remember how Tim almost died last year? After eating the bad burgers?" Tuck pressed. "My parents don't know about this party. If we call an ambulance, they'll definitely find out, and I'll be grounded until college."

Mitch started to argue but Tuck raised a good point. Tuck came from a strict home, and having the party here tonight while his parents were away would get Tuck grounded for life. He'd probably never see his friend again.

"He only lives a few minutes away. Drop him home and then you can come back and flirt with Tanya."

Mitch sighed. "Fine. Where's Tim?" He went in the direction that Tuck pointed and nearly had to carry their scrawny classmate to the door. The air was chilly as they stepped outside. Ice had been forming every night lately, and Mitch had to watch his step on the pavement to make sure he and Tim didn't bust their asses as they walked.

With Tim secured in the passenger seat, he got behind the wheel and jabbed the keys in the ignition of his mom's car. She worked for the prestigious Everson family in the daytime and usually let him have the car in the afternoons and evenings to go to his job at the local diner. That's where she thought he was tonight. He felt mildly guilty for lying to her but he deserved to be a normal kid like his friends sometimes too. Right?

He turned on his headlights and took to the winding mountain roads, trying to remember which turn led to Tim's house. "Hey, Tim." He nudged his friend, trying to get his attention. "Tim?"

Tim stirred in the seat beside him.

"Which road do you live on, man?" Mitch reached over and gave his friend's shoulder a harder shake.

"I don't feel so great," Tim moaned. "I think I'm going to barf."

"No, no, no." Mitch glanced across the seat. "Please don't vomit in my mom's car. She'll kill me, dude." And he'd be busted on his lie. He hated disappointing his mom. She was always working so hard.

Tim lurched forward, making a gurgling sound as he did.

No, no, no!

Mitch grabbed an empty fast-food bag from the floor and started to shove it into Tim's lap. Then a sharp squeal shot terror into his lungs. Mitch whipped his head up to look at the road and saw only lights, so blinding that he yanked the steering wheel right, but not before something hit the front of his car, throwing his mom's old Cavalier into a tailspin on a patch of black ice.

The moment seemed suspended in time. One split second seemed to float like one of the snowflakes starting to fall from the sky. A million thoughts raced through his mind.

What is happening?
What did I hit?
Is this the end?

His mom would be so disappointed. So lost without his dad and now him too. How could he do this to her?

The moment broke, and Mitch's head slammed forward into the steering wheel, bouncing off like a rubber ball. Pain, like a lightning bolt, seared his brain. Then Tim's body fell into his lap like a rag doll.

Is he dead?

The car finally came to a slamming halt against the guardrail. Or maybe they'd gone over, had fallen down the mountain, and this was death.

Mitch's eyes cracked open, a splinter of light jabbing into his pupils.

Tim stirred on his lap. Still alive. Still in one piece—hopefully.

Turning, Mitch saw the SUV he'd hit rolled over on the other side of the road. He knew deep in his gut that the accident had been his fault. He had dipped to get a paper bag for Tim, taken one hand off the steering wheel as fate had tossed black ice in his path. Instead of turning into the spin, he'd jerked the wheel. His driver's education teacher had taught him better but that training had gone out the window in his terror.

Mitch focused on the SUV, thinking it looked familiar in the beam of his broken headlights. He knew the person who drove it but in his groggy state he couldn't remember who it was.

Sirens sang in the distance. *Please get here. Please help us.* A passerby had pulled over on the roadside now and was running toward the scene of the accident.

Accident. It was all a terrible, horrible accident. He hadn't intended for any of this to happen. Hopefully everyone would be okay, and he'd just be grounded from now until he went to the police academy next year with Alex.

Watching the SUV, with no sign of life inside, he had a sinking feeling that wouldn't be the case.

* * *

Mitch's eyes flung open. A thin layer of sweat covered his skin. He blinked in the darkness, making sense of his surroundings. He glanced over at the dark figure lying next to him in bed. Kaitlyn. That hadn't been a dream. She was real.

They hadn't had sex but he'd wanted to. All those years of practicing self-control in the marine corps had paid off. Kaitlyn wouldn't be waking up with any regrets related to him this morning. He didn't want her to wake up next to him sweating and shivering like this either.

Careful not to wake her, he got out of bed and pulled some jogging clothes and sneakers out of his bag on the floor. He needed to go work off his pent-up sexual energy and frustration before showering.

After dressing, he slipped out of the bedroom and then the front door. He hopped into his truck and drove to his favorite jogging spot at Evergreen Park. It was still dark out, but he didn't mind. He locked up his truck and started down the path.

Between his interaction with Kaitlyn last night and his nightmare about the accident, he was ready to implode: physically, mentally, and emotionally. He upped his speed, running from the weight of it all, but it stayed steady on his shoulders.

Up ahead he could hear the natural hot springs. The sound called to him as each foot pounded the earth.

Then the image of Kaitlyn's lace lingerie popped into his mind. What was he going to do about her? He didn't have a clue. He hoped it would come to him by the time he got back to the B&B. He had a feeling she still might use that fireplace poker on him if provoked.

Which he might've done last night.

* * *

Kaitlyn rolled over and stared at the empty space beside her in bed. Before nodding off last night, Mitch had turned on his side, away from her, and he went to sleep without a second thought. Then apparently, after she'd finally drifted off, he'd slipped away. He'd rejected her and then decided he didn't even want to stay in the same bed as her.

Jerk.

Blowing out a breath, she sat up on the edge of the bed. The clock read five a.m. She supposed she needed to get up and start preparing to be the happy host for her house full of guests. She headed into the bathroom, showered and dressed, and then dragged herself down the hall to the kitchen. Mitch was nowhere to be seen. A quick glance out the window revealed that his truck was missing too. Maybe he'd gone back to his mom's place. *Gah*—she shouldn't have thrown herself at him last night. What was she thinking?

"Need a hand?"

She jumped and whirled to face Paris. He was dressed in his usual jeans and black T-shirt. She wondered if he owned anything else. "You know how to cook?" she asked.

"I didn't survive this long on cold cereal." He went to the sink, washed his hands, and then started collecting ingredients from the fridge. She had been doing this routine for a couple weeks now, and she was getting good at it. It was nice to have help though.

"You are a godsend, you know," she said as she beat eggs in a bowl.

"I could say the same. I got on my bike and headed down here without planning for a place to stay. I'm glad your inn had a room for me."

"Me too."

She and Paris prepared enough food to feed a dozen people and set the tables just as the first guests started to arrive downstairs. More guests spilled into the dining room a few minutes later and took their seats. Kaitlyn had decorated the tables yesterday, setting floral bouquets inside mason jars at each one, creating a cheerful environment.

Mr. Krespo pulled out a chair for Mrs. Krespo. The old woman eyed him suspiciously. "You're going to pull that out from under me when I go to sit," Mrs. Krespo accused, talking loudly enough for the other guests to hear.

"I would never do that, sweetheart. That's your paranoia and dementia talking."

"I don't have those two things. Are you trying to lock me away so you can find some other hot, young thing to live out the rest of your days with?"

"No, I'm trying to be more romantic. That's what you said you wanted, remember?"

Mrs. Krespo shook her head. "By trying to kill me?"

Mr. Krespo's hands flew up at his sides in surrender. "I give up."

"Want me to do damage control?" Paris offered.

Kaitlyn shook her head. "No, I've got this." She walked over and grabbed the back of the chair that Mr. Krespo had already pulled out. "Why don't you have a seat, Mrs. Krespo, and I'll bring your breakfast?"

Mrs. Krespo gave her a suspicious look too but Kaitlyn had no reason to do the older woman harm. On the contrary, if Kaitlyn harmed Mrs. Krespo, she had a feeling the older woman would go after her for all this place was worth, which still wasn't much.

The older lady sat and frowned at her husband, who took a seat next to her.

"There you go. Why don't you two talk while I get breakfast for you?" Kaitlyn gave a slight nod at Mr. Krespo when he looked up at her. "Maybe talk about what you'd like to do today," she suggested, and then grabbed a nearby brochure. She laid it on the table in front of Mrs. Krespo. "This might give you some ideas. I recommend going downtown and walking along Silver Lake. Dawanda's Fudge Shop sells hot chocolate nearby. You might stop there after your walk."

Before Mrs. Krespo could argue with the suggestion, Kaitlyn walked away to get the serving dishes passed around. Then she sat down with Paris, Chris, and Nate.

"How was your stay last night?" she asked them as she filled her own plate.

"Wonderful. Much better than it would have been at your mom and dad's anyway," Chris said, looking at his partner.

Kaitlyn looked between them. "If you don't mind me asking, why won't your mom let you two share a room, Nate?"

He shrugged. "She's still getting used to the idea that we're not just friends, I guess. We're married now, and there won't be any grandchildren for her."

"Not in the traditional way, at least," Chris said, smearing strawberry jam on his biscuit. "We can adopt," he told Nate. "I love kids."

"Me too." Nate turned back to Kaitlyn. "My mom sometimes takes a while to come around but she usually does. This just means that Chris and I might be booking more nights at your inn over the next couple of years."

"Well, you're always welcome," Kaitlyn told them. "And

if you have any suggestions to make the stay better, please feel free to tell me. I'm still learning the ropes of running a bed and breakfast. This is all very new to me."

Chris shook his head. "I can't think of any recommendations. It's absolutely perfect here."

They continued to make small talk, and then Nate leaned over to Chris and whispered loudly. "Chris, why don't you ask her?"

"Ask me what?" Kaitlyn looked between them.

"Well"—Nate grimaced slightly—"Chris and I can't figure out which one of the guys who work here is your partner."

"Business partner?" she asked.

"No, *partner* partner," Chris said.

The room suddenly went very quiet.

"I mean, you were with the big guy with the beard last night," Nate said.

"That's Mitch," Chris offered and then nodded at Paris. "But you're eating breakfast with him."

Paris started choking on a bite of his biscuit. "I'm just a guest here," he said when he finally swallowed. "Kaitlyn and I are just friends." He looked at her. "Once you've shared a Thanksgiving dinner together, you're officially friends, right?"

Kaitlyn nodded, a little stunned by the Trapps' question. "Yes. We're definitely friends. *Just* friends," she told the group.

"So, the other guy, Mitch, is your boyfriend? I say boyfriend because there's no ring on your finger." Nate nodded at her left hand.

She pulled her hand back from the table. When she'd decided to be the host here, she'd had no idea she would be the object of such speculation. "I'm single, actually. Mitch is also just a, um…um…" She had no clue what Mitch was to her. Maybe they weren't even friends anymore.

"Sex toy?" Mrs. Krespo asked from across the room. "That's how me and Marvin started out too. Sex buddies, and then he knocked me up."

The room filled with gasps. Then Missy and Joe started giggling uncontrollably.

"You laugh," she said, pointing a finger at Joe, "but I sure hope you used protection with her last night, young man, or your good times are over. Once the baby comes along, all the fun is sucked right out of life. No more staying at fancy bed and breakfasts like this one. Not until you're old like me, at least. And by then you're no longer attracted to one another." Mrs. Krespo gave a pointed look at Mr. Krespo, who was busy keeping his head down and nibbling on his bacon.

Awkward.

Kaitlyn made a mental note to offer Mr. Krespo some more tips that might put him back in favor with Mrs. Krespo. He'd told Kaitlyn over the phone that his wife wanted romance. Kaitlyn could certainly help with that.

The front door to the house opened, and Kaitlyn heard heavy footsteps in the living room. Her breath stuttered in her chest.

"You go check on who it is," Paris said. "I can help out here if anyone needs something. That's what friends are for." He winked.

"Thanks." Relieved to distance herself from the conversation, she headed to the front, even though she already knew who was here. The only person who would enter without ringing the doorbell.

"Sounds like everyone is already having breakfast," Mitch said when she rounded the corner and stopped to look at him. He was sweaty and dressed in jogging clothes, and something about that turned her on.

Which also infuriated her. After last night, she didn't want to be attracted to him.

"The guests started coming down early. Paris helped. In fact, I think I can handle things on my own from here on out. You can just come by during the day for the next month to satisfy the conditions of the will."

His gaze was steadfast. "Kaitlyn, I'm trying to be a good guy here."

She folded her arms. "I don't know what you're talking about."

"Good guys don't make plays for a woman when they know they aren't staying."

She shook her head. "If you're so eager to leave, then why did you agree to stay in the first place, Mitch? Why didn't you just go?"

"I couldn't do that to Mable. Or to you."

"I was a stranger. You didn't owe me anything." Tears burned in her eyes. She wasn't going to cry in front of him though. No way, no how.

"Kaitlyn." He took a step closer. "You're upset about last night. I get it."

"Last night was poor judgment on my part. I'm glad you wanted nothing to do with me. I couldn't be happier that you saw me with my shirt off, then rolled over and started snoring."

"That's not what happened, and you know it," he said. "I did want you. I think that was pretty obvious."

The image of his heated gaze on her flicked across her mind. He hadn't turned away immediately when she'd stripped off her top. "What's obvious is that you and I could never work together. I don't know what my grandma was thinking when she set up this arrangement."

"Kaitlyn," he said, reaching for her hand, "it's not that I didn't *want* to have sex with you. Because believe me, I did."

Her body temperature dialed up.

"Ahem."

Both Kaitlyn and Mitch snapped their attention to the corner where a few of the guests stood watching them. Kaitlyn pulled her hand away from Mitch's.

"Hi, guys," Paris said. "Um, sorry for interrupting this, um…"

"Lovers' quarrel," Mrs. Krespo called behind him. "That's what you call this." She seemed to be an expert on everything this morning.

"No." Kaitlyn shook her head but she couldn't explain away what the guests had just witnessed. Mitch had just mentioned her and sex in the same sentence. "We're not lovers," she said before turning and walking toward the kitchen to clean up.

And not being lovers was the problem.

* * *

Mitch ran his forearm across the layer of perspiration on his forehead. He'd worked himself into a sweat setting up spotlights to shine on Mable and Henry's wooden cutouts that he'd put out on Thanksgiving morning. People loved to drive around and look at decorations this time of year. In addition to spotlights, Mable had always insisted the house be strung with lights from top to bottom. Mitch had always helped Henry with the lot while Henry fussed and complained under his breath.

Damn, he missed Henry just as much as he did Mable. Those two made Christmas nice. And they'd always taken

Mitch to the Lights on the Lake event while his mom watched the inn when he was growing up.

After last night, he guessed he didn't have to worry about taking Kaitlyn to the event anymore. As angry as she was, she may never talk to him again.

Done, he carried his ladder back to the shed and retreated to his truck. He needed a shower but he wasn't about to go in the room he and Kaitlyn had shared last night to grab clean clothes or rinse off. He wasn't crazy. He had clothes at his mom's house. She would let him shower there, and he guessed maybe he'd stay the night with his mom too. He supposed he'd be staying the next month with her.

Mitch rounded the corner of Mistletoe Lane and pulled into the driveway of the second house on the right. He got out of the truck and walked up the porch steps of his child-hood home, remembering how he used to race out the front door when his dad drove up from work every evening. He'd idolized the man. His dad was the exact kind of guy he'd hoped to be. The kind he'd never live up to, no matter how hard he tried.

"Mom?" he called, as he stepped inside the house.

"Mitch. What a surprise. I thought you'd be busy with the duties of hosting a bed and breakfast." She walked through the living room in her bathrobe.

"Why aren't you dressed?" he asked. The mother he knew was always dressed before sunup. "Is something wrong?" he asked.

She waved a hand. "Stop treating me like that."

"Like what?"

"Like you're my parent and not the other way around. It's the day after Thanksgiving. I worked hard and ate too much. I'm taking the day off if that's okay with you."

He kissed her temple and sat on the couch, waiting for

her to sit across from him in the recliner. He couldn't help scrutinizing her every movement. "You sure you're okay?"

"Never better." She wiggled back into the chair and looked up at him. "I'm taking the vitamins like Dr. Jacobs told me to, and I'm already feeling much better. I have the energy of a twenty-year-old, in fact."

He pointed a finger. "I know you. Just because you have renewed energy doesn't give you a license to double your workload. Have you gotten your lab results back yet? Maybe we should call and see what the holdup is."

"I'm fine, Mitch. I promise. You, on the other hand, are not," she said. "I can see it on your face. What's going on?"

He leaned forward over his knees and blew out a breath. "I got in a fight with Kaitlyn. I wish I didn't have to stay and fulfill Mable's final wishes. It's time for me to get out of Sweetwater Springs."

His mom was quiet for a long moment. "For such a brave man, which you are, you always seem to be running."

"I'm not running. I just don't belong here. You know that. I'm just idling while I wait for the security job to open up in January."

"You could find temporary employment here until then."

"In Sweetwater Springs?" He grunted. "There's no money to be made here."

"Money? Is that what this is about, Mitchell Douglas?" she said with a scoff. "I don't care about money. And I didn't raise you to care about it either."

"I need to make sure you're provided for."

"You've spent the last ten years making sure I was well taken care of, sending me money that I never asked for." She lifted her chin stubbornly. "How many times do I have to tell you I'm the parent? I support you, not vice versa."

"You lost the job with the Eversons because of me. For

the past decade you've worked twice as hard for half as much, and that's my fault. So sue me if I just want to make sure you're taken care of." And judging by how run-down she looked, he wasn't doing a very good job. "I shouldn't have let you prepare Thanksgiving dinner yesterday."

"Nonsense. I don't need taken care of. All I need is for my son to be happy. And you're not happy."

Happy. Mitch had experienced bouts of that since coming back here, which surprised him. Most of that had to do with Kaitlyn but he'd messed that up just like he had every good thing in his life.

He ran a hand over his head, missing the way his crew cut used to bristle at the touch. Now his marine corps crop was grown out. He'd liked it last night when Kaitlyn's fingers had sifted through his longer hair while they'd kissed beside the tree though. Right before she'd invited him to her bed and taken off her shirt.

He cleared his throat, shaking that thought away. "I'm not staying at the B and B tonight."

"Well, where are you staying, then?" his mom asked.

He thought it was a joke at first but her expression was deadpan. "Here."

She grimaced. "Sorry, honey. I gave the guest room to your aunt Nettie tonight. She's arriving in about an hour. Better late than never for Thanksgiving, right? Which I guess means I need to get up and get dressed."

Mitch furrowed his brow. "Okay, well, I can sleep on the couch."

"I don't think so, dear. You know how Aunt Nettie and I are once we get together. We stay up all hours, watching movies and laughing." His mom shook her head. "I could really use a girls' night with her. You're the one always telling me I need to relax and have fun. This'll do that for me."

Aunt Nettie was his father's sister but she and his mom were as close as if they were blood related. "So I can't stay here?" he clarified. "In the home that you said would always be open to me?"

"It is. Just not while your aunt Nettie is here. I suggest you make up with Kaitlyn before sunset." She shifted and stood back up.

"Seriously? You don't want my help and then refuse to give me a place to stay?" He said it teasingly but his world was being turned upside down right now. Where was he going to stay tonight? Even if he made up with Kaitlyn, the only room available at the inn was her room, in her bed—and that had been a disaster last night. He didn't want to repeat it. And he didn't think he had enough self-control to last another night without giving in to his desire and ravaging Kaitlyn's body.

He got up and headed toward the door.

"Where are you going?" his mom asked.

"To find a place to stay. Not at the B and B. I'll check with Tuck or Alex." And if they couldn't help, he'd get a room at a hotel up the mountain—although they might be full because of the Thanksgiving holiday.

"Just don't run from that beautiful woman too long. She's a jewel. Some other man is liable to snap her up."

Mitch didn't bother acknowledging that comment. First off, he wasn't running. Secondly, Kaitlyn finding another man was exactly what he was afraid of. He wasn't supposed to be interested in or attracted to her. Wasn't supposed to care about her in a way that went beyond a business relationship.

Stepping outside, he took a moment to breathe in the fresh mountain air. There was no place on earth that cleared his lungs so easily. And no place where he felt more claustrophobic either. Fishing his cell phone out of his pocket, he tapped on Alex's contact in his list and thumbed the phone number. Alex had an extra guest room that Mitch had stayed in during past visits to Sweetwater Springs.

"What's up, man?" Alex asked in lieu of a hello.

"Hey, buddy. I need a place to stay tonight," Mitch said.

"Thought you were staying with Mable's granddaughter now," Alex teased.

Word in a small town traveled about as quickly as an echo from Wild Blossom Bluffs. "Not anymore," he said.

"Tuck and I are actually meeting up at the Tipsy Tavern tonight for our own little post–turkey day celebration. Why don't you join us?"

"A drink sounds great, actually," Mitch said, sucking in some more of the cool mountain air. If he could bottle up this stuff and take it with him when he left, he'd be good to go.

"Great," Alex said. "I'll head over there around seven."

"See you then." Mitch hung up and headed back inside. No matter if his mom didn't have a bed for him tonight, he still needed a shower. He'd needed an ice-cold one since last night. Between that and a few drinks with the guys tonight, he planned to get his head on straight before facing Kaitlyn again.

CHAPTER TWELVE

"He'll come back," Paris said, taking a seat beside Kaitlyn on the couch later that evening. She had a design sketchbook in her lap. Even though she would probably never work in New York again, she still liked designing big, beautiful rooms that felt magical when you stepped inside them.

"Who?" she asked.

"Mitch is the reason you're moping, right?"

She leaned back into the couch cushion with a heavy sigh. "Well, you and several other guests heard our argument this morning. You know what happened." She shook her head, still embarrassed over it all. "Rule number one of hosting a bed and breakfast: Don't throw yourself at any of the guests or your business partner. Why didn't my grandmother leave me a rule book for this job?"

Paris chuckled. He was holding a glass of red wine in his hand. Shouldn't a biker drink beer? He was a walking contradiction in her mind. "Life doesn't have rule books, unfortunately."

"Have you found anyone who sparks your interest since your divorce?" she asked, suddenly curious to know more about him.

Paris shrugged. "Not really."

She frowned. "Well, I was happy to hear you might be making Sweetwater Springs your home. I'm new here too so that would be one more friend I'd have in town."

"Who needs romance when you have friends, right?" He bumped his shoulder against hers. "You know what? The best medicine for a broken heart is a night out on the town. That's my experience at least."

"A night out?" she asked.

"Yeah. We should go have drinks," he said, and she was beyond certain he wasn't flirting with her. She had nothing to worry about with Paris.

"I would but I can't leave the inn. A host's job is never done. No more barhopping for me," she said on a laugh.

"Did someone say bar?" Joe asked, bounding off the bottom stair with Missy following close behind him in a short skirt and skintight leggings. "Because I am so in."

Kaitlyn had learned that their prolonged stay was because of their fall break from college. Both of their families lived too far to drive back for the week. And while Kaitlyn had been put off by their behavior at first, she'd grown fond of the young, overly affectionate couple.

She turned to look at them. "The Tipsy Tavern downtown is supposed to be good. Why don't you two go with Paris and check it out?" She narrowed her gaze at the couple. "Wait. Are you at least twenty-one?"

Missy giggled. "I love getting asked that question. I just became legal last month."

"I love being asked too," Kaitlyn said. "Even if it isn't happening as often as I'd like anymore," she whispered to Paris.

He laughed and then nudged her with his elbow. "The Jamiesons told me earlier they were going out for drinks tonight. They asked me to come along. Why don't we all go?"

Kaitlyn hedged. "I'm not sure the Krespos would enjoy that. But I can stay here while the rest of you go have fun. Really, I'm fine."

They all turned toward a sudden commotion that erupted at the top of the stairs as Mrs. Krespo chased her husband with her cane down the open hallway.

The Trapps peeked their heads out of their room to see what the disturbance was.

"Uh-oh," Kaitlyn said, prepared to run interference.

Instead, Paris stood to address the group. "A few of us are going out to a bar tonight. Do you all want to come along?"

"It's okay if you don't," Kaitlyn assured them, knowing the older couple would likely refuse.

"Oh, I'd love to!" Mrs. Krespo said, surprising her.

"Us too," Chris and Nate agreed, heading out of their room.

Paris turned back to Kaitlyn with a mischievous grin. "Looks like a group event. I'll call a taxi van. No need for a DD. Just a good time."

A good time. Right. Going to a bar with two horny college kids, a mysterious biker, a gay couple, newlyweds, and an old lady with a cane and a husband who loved her as much as he seemed to fear her. What was the worst that could happen?

* * *

An hour later, Kaitlyn walked into the Tipsy Tavern with Paris, Mr. and Mrs. Krespo (canes and attitude included), the

Jamiesons, Chris and Nate Trapp, and the young college love-birds. Maybe this would be a regular activity at the B&B, she considered. Friday nights at the tavern. *Yeah.* She liked the idea.

Paris pointed at a long table with a booth lining the wall toward the back of the tavern. "We'll all fit over there. Not that we'll be sitting. That dance floor looks tempting."

"I'm not much of a dancer," she called over her shoulder, unsure if Paris could even hear her over the cacophony of music, laughter, and glasses clinking on the scarred wooden tables. She looked back to make sure the Krespos were okay. Mrs. Krespo whacked her cane back and forth, scooting people to the side in a not-so-subtle way.

Kaitlyn choked on a laugh. It was hilarious and a bit concerning. She reached the back table and plopped down in a seat.

"Oh, no you don't." Chris shook his head. "Dance first, drink later."

"I think it goes the other way around. I need drinks to make me dance. And maybe not even then." She signaled the waitress who was walking by.

"Need a drink?" the twentysomething blond asked. She was tall, thin, and beautiful in an obvious kind of way.

Kaitlyn remembered Mitch saying he'd had a one-night stand with a waitress here a few months back. She sized the waitress up with a smile, wondering if this was the one. "Yes, anything strong that you have on tap, please."

"Coming right up." The waitress headed off.

"Are you checking her out?" Nate plopped down in the space next to Kaitlyn.

"Yes. Actually, I was. But not for the reason you're thinking. Someone I know had a fling with a waitress here. Just wondering if it was her."

"You are as see-through as that woman's dress over there." He gestured to the dance floor and a woman who looked naked at first glance. "Would that someone happen to be Mitch?" he asked. "And are you jealous?"

Chris snuggled in beside Nate, leaning over to listen. "She has good reason to be jealous. I hate everyone in your past," he told Nate. "Even the ones I like I still hate."

Nate grinned. "Must be love," he told his husband.

"Oh, no." Kaitlyn shook her head. "Mitch and I aren't... We don't have that kind of relationship. We just, well, we might have kissed. But only twice."

"You're not telling us anything we don't know. The whole house is buzzing about that fight this morning and what happened last night." Chris bounced his eyebrows.

Kaitlyn sighed and looked around. The Jamiesons were seated at the bar. The Krespos had moved to the dance floor along with the college kids. By the looks of it, Mr. Krespo still had quite a few moves. Mrs. Krespo was actually smiling as she tried to keep up with him.

Kaitlyn turned back to Chris, Nate, and Paris. "Unfortunately, nothing happened last night, and that's the problem." She covered her face with both hands. There was nothing like complete honesty with friends—kind of—to humble you.

A drink was set in front of her. She lifted her head, thanked the waitress—whom they were all watching with interest now—and took a healthy sip.

"So you made a move on him?" Nate asked.

She bit her lower lip, weighing how much detail to disclose. "He's been giving me mixed signals since we became business partners. He looks at me with those eyes and talks to me in that voice. I thought he was feeling the vibe between us too."

"You sure you weren't imagining it?" Paris asked.

She swallowed, remembering the night she'd gone downtown with Mitch. She hadn't imagined the heat between them. "Mitch kissed me. But maybe"—she shook her head—"maybe he didn't want to take it any further. Maybe that part was just me." She shook her head again. "This is so embarrassing. I'll never be able to look at him again."

"Hate to break it to you, sweetheart," Paris said.

She looked at him curiously. "What?"

Gesturing, Paris pointed across the room.

Kaitlyn's heart sunk and did a little somersault at the same time. Her heart was evidently just as confused as she was at the sight of Mitch Hargrove.

* * *

Mitch was halfway through his first beer and having a decent time with the guys. He'd laughed more than a few times, and it'd felt good. *He* had felt good until he'd overheard a commotion going on behind him. He turned around to see a little old lady with a walking cane parting the crowd like Moses with the Red Sea.

What is Mrs. Krespo doing here?

Scanning the room, he noticed the entire gang of B&B guests weaving through the bar. Then he spotted Kaitlyn and his heart stalled for a second. What was it about that woman that made her so damn hard to resist? Why did he want her so badly? And why did the sight of her alongside Paris make him want to go punch a hole in the wall?

He wasn't eighteen anymore. He might've done that over a girl back then but now he was marine strong with an iron cast will.

"Earth to Mitch."

Mitch turned toward Alex's and Tuck's raised brows. "Sorry. Mr. and Mrs. Krespo are here."

Tuck and Alex followed where his gaze had just been.

"Who?" Alex scrunched his face. "I know everyone in this town, and I've never seen them before."

"They're staying at the Sweetwater B and B."

"Right. That article in *Loving Life* magazine is drawing a small crowd to the area. That's good for commerce but it'll make the department busier. I'll have to hire more officers if the tourists keep coming in. I'm shorthanded as it is."

"Looks like the host is here too," Tuck said. "Kaitlyn seems awfully friendly with that Harley Davidson model."

Mitch frowned. "That's Paris. He's in town for some kind of Santa thing."

"Bikers for Santa," Alex said with a nod. "They're meeting up at the Lights on the Lake event this weekend."

"Yeah," Mitch said with a nod.

"Since I'm short-staffed, I'll be working the event myself," Alex said.

"You expecting trouble with the carolers?"

Alex frowned. "Janice Murphy spiked the eggnog last year."

Tuck laughed out loud. "That was the best. I'll be there with my nephew, Theo. Halona is keeping her flower shop open late for customers that night."

"You going?" Alex asked.

Mitch gave his head a shake. "As much as I'd hate to miss the drunk caroling, I don't think so."

"You have to. It's the town's biggest event," Tuck pressed.

"Exactly," Mitch answered. Attending Sweetwater's biggest event was akin to skinny-dipping in a lake full of piranhas. At least in Mitch's mind.

"Hey, guys." A waitress stepped up to the table.

Mitch inwardly groaned, recognizing the voice before he even looked up. "Hi, Nadine."

"Long time since you've been at one of my tables, Mitch," she said. "I've missed you."

Mitch briefly looked at his friends, which was a mistake. He hadn't told them about his one-night stand with Nadine the last time he was home but these guys missed nothing.

"Sounds like your lucky night," Alex told Nadine. "Maybe you can take a break and Mitch here can sweep you across the dance floor."

"I don't dance," Mitch said through gritted teeth. If he put his hands on Nadine, she'd expect another night together. Despite what everyone said, one-night stands came with strings attached, which was why he'd turned away from Kaitlyn last night.

The image of Kaitlyn's bare skin against white lace flashed in his mind for the millionth time today. Given a second chance, he wasn't sure he'd be able to resist her again.

"Well, if you change your mind..." Nadine winked. "I've got customers to attend to. See you, guys."

"She's pretty," Tuck said, pulling from his beer and watching Nadine sashay off.

"Well, you take her home then," Mitch grumbled.

Tuck shook his head. "Not my type."

"You've barely dated since Renee. Maybe taking Nadine for a spin on the dance floor or out to dinner sometime would help get you back out there," Alex suggested.

Tuck frowned grimly, and his eyes dulled. "Maybe I don't want to get back out there. I'm good."

Just like with Mable's passing, Mitch had been unable to get leave from the corps when Renee had died from cancer two summers ago. Neither of them had been blood relatives. He'd thought a lot of Renee though. She and Tuck had started dating in high school. Mitch hated to think about his friends not getting the happy ending they deserved. He couldn't imagine what Tuck had gone through or how he was even functional enough to be here tonight. Life went on, Mitch guessed. People did the best they could with the cards they were dealt.

"If you don't go break in on that dance, there's a chance that Kaitlyn and Paris might go home together tonight," Alex said, pulling Mitch from his thoughts.

Mitch turned to look back at the dance floor. The music was fast paced, and Kaitlyn was swaying back and forth in front of Paris. There wasn't a good chance that they'd go home together tonight; it was definite. They were both staying at the Sweetwater B&B. Whether they returned to the same bed, though, was over Mitch's dead body.

He set his beer down and pushed back from the table.

"Yeah, buddy!" Alex shook a fist in the air. "Go get her."

Kaitlyn wasn't his to get. He just didn't want her to get hurt—all the more reason he should skip breaking up the happy couple and head to the men's restroom instead.

He continued forward until he was standing somewhat awkwardly in front of a dancing Kaitlyn and Paris. Everyone was moving to the beat except him.

"Oh," Kaitlyn said, finally noticing his presence. Her smile quickly fell. He guessed she was recalling that she was still ticked off at him about last night.

"Hey, Mitch," Paris said, freezing to a halt. "What's going on, man?"

The muscles of Mitch's jaw bunched. "I'm cutting in. That's what."

* * *

Kaitlyn wrapped her arms around Paris's neck and pulled him to her. "I don't think so," she said.

Is he serious right now?

Mitch had rejected her last night but he didn't want her dancing with Paris?

Paris grabbed hold of Kaitlyn's arms and gently loosened them. "Actually, I have to visit the men's room. She's all yours, buddy." He winked at Kaitlyn, which she took as an apology, but he'd be hearing from her about this later. They'd only known each other a week but they were supposed to have each other's backs. Friends didn't let friends dance with burly, sexy, off-limits men.

"Kaitlyn?" Mitch said. As he did, the music transitioned from a fast, upbeat tune to something slow and romantic. The lights dimmed, reminding her of a middle school dance. She'd never liked those. They were awkward, and she'd spent most of her time holding up the wall and avoiding eye contact because she was too nervous to approach any of the boys. And the cute guys never asked her to dance. Instead it was always the sweaty ones with an overeager smile.

Mitch was the cute guy tonight. The cute guy was asking her to dance, and she couldn't say no. Not to him, no matter how much she wanted to.

"Fine. But just so you know, this doesn't mean I like you." In fact, she was doing her damnedest to hate him. But he was right when he'd told her earlier that he was one of the good guys. He'd proven that time and time again.

Mitch anchored his big hands on her waist and pulled her body toward him.

Her arms dutifully went to his shoulders but she didn't make eye contact. She clamped her mouth shut and didn't say a word. If they were going to talk, he was going to have to be the one to start the conversation.

"Kaitlyn?"

Reflexively, her gaze went to his. *Traitorous gaze.* "What do you want from me, Mitch?" she asked on a sigh. "Last night you acted like you wanted nothing to do with me. Fine. You got it. But now you're here asking me to dance and looking at me with those puppy dog eyes, and it's just confusing. Make up your mind. You either want me or you don't."

"I don't want to want you, but..."

She swallowed thickly. "But?"

"But I do, and I'm not sure what to do about that."

"You probably didn't hesitate with that waitress when you took her home a few months back."

"No," he admitted, his expression unreadable. "And I regret that. I had too much to drink that night, and I'd just gotten off my last deployment. I had a lot going on in my head. Nadine was just a Band-Aid for the crap I didn't want to deal with. The same way you wanted me to be your Band-Aid last night."

Her eyes widened. She considered arguing that point but wondered if maybe it was true. Was she just trying to use him last night? "Well, what's wrong with Band-Aids? If I want you and you want me, then what's wrong with just going with it? It doesn't have to *mean* anything."

His mouth was set in a flat line. Not a frown, but not a smile either. She studied the growth of hair that surrounded his lips, remembering how soft it'd felt when they'd kissed. Full-force tingles rushed over her. She was still mad. Still wanted to hate him. Still wanted to take him back to her bedroom and use him as the fuel to her sexual fantasies for the next year. Screw the consequences—she wanted to live in the moment. She wanted to be whisked away from all the crap of the recent months.

Her arms tightened around him. Even as the song ended and transitioned to something more upbeat, she didn't pull away.

And neither did he. Their bodies were stuck to each other like magnets.

"Why did you ask me to dance if you don't want me?"

His gaze lowered, and their mouths were dangerously close to one another. Close enough to kiss a third time.

"Aren't you listening? I never said I didn't want you."

Those tingles combusted into flames.

"My turn," a high-pitched voice said as the waitress who served Kaitlyn earlier stepped up beside them. "Thought you weren't up for dancing, Mitch, but it looks like you changed your mind." Her gaze slid to Kaitlyn for a millisecond and then back to him. "The beer on tap here will do that to you, I guess."

Kaitlyn debated whether she was going to allow this to happen. Before she had a chance to decide, Mitch shook his head.

"I'm sorry, Nadine, but not tonight. I'm actually on my way out."

Nadine's gaze slid from him and back to Kaitlyn. "I see. Some other time, then," she said, looking disappointed.

He nodded. "Would you mind calling a cab for the group over there when they're ready to go?"

She shrugged. "Sure. I never let anyone leave this bar if they've had too much to drink anyway."

"Thanks. Have a great night, Nadine." Mitch grabbed Kaitlyn's hand and then started leading her toward the door.

"I can't leave," Kaitlyn said, even though her body was begging to differ. Going anywhere alone with Mitch right now was a terribly fantastic idea.

"The guests will be fine. Paris will make sure they all get back in one piece. I trust him that much."

"You just don't trust him to be alone with me?"

Mitch stared at her with heated brown eyes. "I don't want any other man to be alone with you. You can text Paris from my truck."

"Where are we going?" she asked—not that she cared.

There was a sudden urgency in his movements as he pulled her toward the exit. "To settle this thing between us once and for all."

CHAPTER THIRTEEN

Mitch was quiet as he steered the truck along the curvy road, revisiting the memories that flashed through his mind only briefly. Kaitlyn was beside him, no doubt wondering where he was taking her. Her silence told him she was nervous. Or still mad, although the anger had definitely melted away by the end of their dance. This attraction between them was building every time they were together. It was too strong to resist, and he was tired of trying.

The road turned again, and pain seared through his heart the way it always did at this spot. "This is where I crashed my truck when I was seventeen." He kept his gaze forward. Instead of speeding up as he sometimes did, he lifted his foot off the gas and slowed the truck, taking in the natural beauty of what was an awful place for him.

Kaitlyn gasped softly. "Were you hurt?"

"It depends on what you mean by hurt. I'm still alive but the accident hurt someone else." He hated being responsible for Brian Everson's disability. "It paralyzed a guy I went to high school with."

Her hands flew to her mouth. Mitch couldn't bear to look at her though. He hated himself for that one mistake. How could he ever expect anyone else to feel differently?

He pulled the truck to a stop at Majestic Point, a favorite lookout for sightseers. Putting the truck in park, he gripped the steering wheel as if his life depended on it. "I never should have been on the roads that night. I was young and stupid, and the domino effect of my poor choices ruined lives. Mine. My mom's. Brian Everson's."

She placed a hand on his forearm. "You didn't mean to."

"Intent doesn't matter." He finally looked at her. "Brian was training for the Olympics. My actions took that away from him. He'll never walk because I decided to go to a party. If he and his family never want to see my face in this town again"—which was what they'd told him in no uncertain terms in the accident's aftermath—"then that's the least I can do for them."

"I'm not sure what to say. Mitch, I'm so sorry."

"I walked away from that accident with barely a scratch," he said.

Kaitlyn's eyes were glistening as she listened. In the dark, they sparkled like Silver Lake under a star-filled sky.

"It wasn't your fault. Bad things happen sometimes. You can't blame yourself."

Even though that's exactly what he'd been doing ever since that fateful night. He didn't know how *not* to carry this blame. And the Everson family certainly blamed him.

"This is why you don't like Sweetwater Springs." She turned her face to look out the front windshield. From this spot, they had a perfect view of Mount Pleasant, cast in the light of a waxing moon.

"I joined the marines so I could escape and provide for my mom. She'd worked for the Eversons at the time. They fired her. She lost her benefits and had to work several jobs just to make enough to pay the bills." His mom had been working herself to exhaustion ever since.

He soaked in Kaitlyn's face and the softness there. "If things were different, kissing you would be easy, Kaitlyn."

Kissing her was already way too easy.

She leaned across the seat.

"What are you doing?" he asked in a gruff voice.

"Kissing me doesn't have to mean anything. Sometimes people just need a Band-Aid," she said, reminding him of his own words. "Kiss me, Mitch."

"Haven't you heard anything I just told you?"

"Every word," she whispered. "And it only matters to me because it's part of who you are. I'm not worried about yesterday or tomorrow. All I care about is tonight, and tonight I want to be with you."

Who is this woman? She was beautiful, strong, amazing, and yeah, he wanted to kiss her more than he wanted his life right now. Crossing the rest of the distance, he gave in, fully this time, shutting off his mind, which would no doubt object. Their lips met and opened to each other, and with her kiss, he swore she reached into his very soul.

Her arms wrapped around him, holding him, pulling him in. "Let's get a room," she whispered, pulling back as his hands continued to roam lower on her waist. Now that he'd started, he couldn't stop touching her this time.

"I know a place. Recently under new ownership, actually. I hear it's supposed to be one of the most romantic places to spend the holidays."

She grinned and then kissed his lips again. "Sounds perfect. Take me there."

* * *

The B&B was quiet as they entered. Either the guests were still at the Tipsy Tavern or all were in bed sleeping. Mitch didn't really care as long as they didn't stop what was about to happen between Kaitlyn and him. He was tired of fighting their attraction. All he wanted to do was rip Kaitlyn's clothes off and explore every inch of her.

Taking her hand, he tugged her down the hall into the room they'd shared last night and locked the door behind them. Then he kissed her, grabbing hold of the hem of her shirt at the same time. He lifted it over her head and tossed it across the room. Assisting him with the mission, she reached behind herself and unclasped her bra.

His gaze fell on her breasts, soft and round in the dim cast of moonlight streaming through the window. His hand followed, squeezing one softly, and then harder as she moaned, driving him insane.

"Please tell me you have a condom," she half whispered, half moaned.

He did. In his wallet. It crossed his mind that he could stop what was about to happen by telling her he didn't. That's what he needed to do. It was a ready excuse that would leave no hard feelings between them. But he'd been taken to the edge of his willpower, and it was now shattered. "I have protection," he said.

Then, kissing her all the way, he led her to the bed, shedding clothes in their wake and letting the moment take them wherever it wanted. Fear prickled in the back of his mind as he let himself go. Some lines couldn't be uncrossed. Just like crossing lanes and hitting a classmate. Or signing on the dotted line that committed your next four years to the marines. Somehow having sex with Kaitlyn felt like one of those lines that couldn't be uncrossed, and yet he wouldn't, *couldn't*, stop himself this time.

* * *

Kaitlyn eased into wakefulness, not letting go of sleep too quickly. She'd just been having the best dream. A sleepy smile crossed her face as her eyes fluttered open to see Mitch sleeping beside her.

Not a dream. Last night had been real, and it had surpassed all her past experiences with a man—not that she'd been with many. She watched him for a moment as he slept. He was a tough alpha male, and he was sleeping like a baby.

"Stop staring at me," he growled quietly and then cracked open an eye to look at her. The corner of his mouth turned up.

"I didn't know you were awake." Or that he could see through his eyelids. This was a man of many talents.

His hand reached under the covers and caressed her arm, the touch sending her body into full need.

She could spend a million nights like the one she'd just had.

"Oh no!" She sat up in bed and turned to the clock on her nightstand. "I have to make breakfast. The guests." Those ooey-gooey feelings that had been flooding her were now a flurry of panic.

"I'll go get takeout." Mitch tugged on her arm, attempting to pull her in for a kiss.

She stopped just short of his lips. "Takeout? Don't the guests expect something...more? I mean, it's called a bed and breakfast. I'm supposed to supply both of those things."

He leaned in and finally kissed her. Then he pulled away and started to dress. "I suspect the guests are all experiencing a bit of a hangover from last night. All they'll need is hot coffee and lots of it."

She watched him yank on a pair of jeans. He was still bare chested, and her fingers itched to slide over the smooth contours of his muscled abs. "No takeout." Tearing her gaze from him, which was no easy feat, she got up and hurried to her dresser. She chose a pair of jeans and a long-sleeved I LOVE NEW YORK T-shirt. "You make the bacon, and I'll make the eggs and grits. I have frozen biscuits in the freezer. Not Grandma Mable's recipe but those'll have to do."

"Your choice."

She went to the bathroom and then hurried down the hall and into the kitchen where she began bustling around on autopilot.

"You've really gotten this routine down," Mitch observed a few minutes later. "Mable would've been proud."

Kaitlyn grinned up at him. "I'm kind of proud of myself. I wasn't sure I'd be able to pull this off. But I am. I wish…" She shook her head. What was the point of wishing for something that wasn't going to happen?

"What?"

"It's just…my parents thought I was crazy to leave New York and come here. I wish they could see this place now and how I've got it all handled."

"So show them," he said. "Invite them here to be your guests."

She considered the idea. "We just reopened. I'm not sure it's ready yet."

He flipped the slices of bacon to their other sides. "You just said you weren't sure you'd pull this off but you are. You have guests and they're plenty satisfied with their stay here. You're ready."

You're. This was still her endeavor, not his. Last night had meant a lot but it hadn't changed the end game.

"I'll think about it. Thank you."

"What for?"

"Listening. It's one of the many things you're good at." She winked at him.

"You too." There was a serious note in his voice despite her air of flirtation. He'd shared things with her last night that she suspected he didn't talk about very often. Somehow that felt even more intimate than what they'd done in bed afterward. This had been more than a one-night stand—even if it had only been for the one night.

She fetched the bag of corn grits from the pantry and laid it on the counter. The water was already boiling. All she needed to do was add some substance and stir.

"Ho, ho, hoooooooo!"

Kaitlyn exchanged a glance with Mitch and then hurried toward the dining room to find Santa Claus standing among the other guests. Except Santa was tall, thin, and had pale-blue eyes like Paris. He was also wearing all black except for his bright-red Santa hat and white fluffy beard.

"I guess today is the big day?" Kaitlyn asked.

"Tonight actually. I'm heading down to the Sweetwater Café to meet some fellow bikers this morning though."

"So you're not staying for breakfast?"

He shook his head, his beard scraping low on his chest. "The café is offering us free breakfasts if we dress up."

"That's nice of them," Kaitlyn said.

"You're a crappy excuse for a Santa," Mrs. Krespo bellowed from one of the tables. "Though I can see why Mommy was caught kissing Santa under the mistletoe if he looked like you."

Kaitlyn pressed her lips together to keep from laughing.

"Afterward, I'm checking out the garage apartment for rent down the road. Do you think it'll help if I wear my hat and beard?" Paris asked.

Kaitlyn tilted her head. "Maybe. Although I'll be sad to see one of my favorite guests leave if you do rent that place."

"Your nightly rate is reasonable to a point," he said. "After two weeks, it'd be unreasonable for me to stay. I'll see you all later." He headed out the door, and a few minutes later, she heard the sound of his motorcycle roaring out of the driveway.

Kaitlyn walked over to the Krespos' table. "Sleep well?" she asked.

Mr. Krespo gave her a sheepish smile. "Very well," he said.

"No kissing and telling, Marvin," Mrs. Krespo muttered, reaching for her coffee cup. "Kaitlyn doesn't need to know you got lucky last night."

Mr. Krespo's face turned beet red. "I didn't tell her that, Evie."

"Well, you might as well have." Mrs. Krespo gave her husband an assessing look. "I haven't danced in years. I forgot how good of a dancer you were. It did things to me."

Kaitlyn nearly fell over in her shock that the older woman was being civil, even flirting with her husband.

"Maybe I should take you dancing more often," Mr. Krespo said with a small grin.

"Maybe you should," Mrs. Krespo agreed, her stiff demeanor softening as she smiled at him.

Well, wonders never ceased. The bed and breakfast was already bringing couples closer.

"All right, everyone. Who's hungry?" Mitch asked, coming into the dining area with his hands full of food.

Kaitlyn whirled, finding herself surprised a second time

this morning. The Mitch Hargrove she'd come to know was standoffish with guests. He didn't make grand entrances. Instead, he usually snuck up on people.

She watched as he set the dishes at the center of one of the tables and began serving the guests with a smile on his face. He also made easy chitchat, which Kaitlyn had never seen him do here. After a moment, he looked up at her.

Right. She was just standing there, equal parts stunned and charmed by this new side of Mitch.

* * *

Christmas was exactly one month from today. Mitch was halfway home with his commitment and suddenly trying to throw a wrench in things by sleeping with Kaitlyn.

Not that he could bring himself to regret even one moment.

The prospect of one more month with her didn't sound so bad if it went like last night. The prospect of another month in Sweetwater Springs going stir-crazy in this inn, however...

He'd already checked off everything on Kaitlyn's to-do list. He'd power washed the outdoor Jacuzzi this afternoon and then showered the grime off and spent time online perusing places to rent in Northern Virginia. That was it. Now what was he supposed to do for another month?

Kaitlyn came breezing into the room where he'd been sitting and staring at the blinking lights of the tree. "What do you think?" she asked, doing a little twirl in front of him.

He hesitated. "Is this some kind of trick question?" She was wearing a bright-red turtleneck with a pair of fitted blue jeans. A crystal snowflake necklace added just a little cheer to what she was wearing.

"Your mom and aunt Nettie are here," she said as if that explained her question. It only raised more in his mind.

"Why?" he asked.

"To watch the inn for us."

He furrowed his brow. "Again, why?"

Kaitlyn placed her hands on her hips. "So you and I can go to the Lights on the Lake event, remember?"

Mitch tensed. "I don't remember agreeing to that."

"Mitchell Douglas Hargrove," his mom said, walking into the sitting room. She paused from lecturing him to admire the tree. "Oh, how lovely!" she said. "Isn't that pretty, Nettie?" she asked his aunt, who'd stepped into the room as well.

"It really is," Nettie said. "So bright and colorful! You two must have worked so hard." She turned to look at him. "Hello, my favorite nephew."

"Your only nephew," Mitch said, suddenly feeling like a hostage in this room of women.

"Kaitlyn is new in town," his mom continued, "and she deserves to go. I raised you to be a gentleman, which means you're taking her."

That didn't sound like a request.

Mitch massaged his temple where a headache was forming. The entire town would be there. Including the Eversons. "Mom, you're supposed to be taking it easy," he reminded her. "Not minding the inn for us."

"I'll have you know that Dr. Jacobs's office called this afternoon."

Mitch swallowed. "And?"

"And aside from being a little low on my iron level, I'm as healthy as a horse. Those were Dr. Jacobs's exact words."

"Low on iron?" Mitch asked, scrutinizing his mom's appearance. A rosiness had replaced the pallor of her skin over the last week. She was almost glowing, part of which he knew was because she was happy to have him home.

"Dr. Jacobs said I have anemia," his mom said, "which can cause a whole host of problems. It accounts for me being so tired and weak all of a sudden. Dr. Jacobs said to take an extra iron supplement along with my multivitamin and to come back to see her next month."

"Well, that's wonderful news!" Kaitlyn said.

"It certainly is," Nettie agreed.

Mitch narrowed his eyes. "Is Dr. Jacobs sure?"

"Very. She also told me to tell you to stop worrying and to have a little fun. Doctor's orders. Now get moving. You're taking Kaitlyn out tonight, and we're watching the inn."

There was no arguing with his mom once she'd made up her mind on something.

Mitch turned to Kaitlyn. "Wouldn't you prefer if I took you to a nice restaurant?" Because it wasn't Kaitlyn he had a problem with.

Kaitlyn opened her mouth to speak but his mom held up a hand. "She would prefer to go to the one town event that everyone will be talking about until next year's Lights on the Lake. Mable would've insisted on it."

How could Mitch argue with a dead woman? "Fine," he finally said.

"Are you sure?" Kaitlyn's forehead wrinkled. "If you don't want to, I'm sure I can get a ride over with Paris."

"On the back of his bike?" Mitch ground out, hating that idea even more. "I said I'd take you."

"It'd be his pleasure," his mom said, narrowing her eyes at him.

Pleasure was taking Kaitlyn back to the bedroom. Not walking into what felt most certainly like enemy lines.

* * *

The moon was on a slow rise in the nearly December sky. Music floated above the crowd.

"I know why you were hesitant to come," Kaitlyn said, reaching for his hand.

Surprising himself, he took her hand as if it were as natural as holing up and hiding himself from the world. He was also surprised that being out and about didn't bother him as much as he'd expected. He had a large dog-eared hat covering his head and a full beard on his face. In such a thick crowd, no one would likely even recognize him. He'd been worried for nothing. "I'm glad I came."

Engines roared from somewhere in the distance.

"Sounds like the Bikers for Santa." Kaitlyn squeezed his hand excitedly. "I'm going to pull an angel off the tree too. It's for a good cause."

Mitch nodded. "Mable and Henry always did. They were my Santa as well, although I didn't know that for a long time. Mom couldn't afford to buy me a lot."

Kaitlyn's hand squeezed tighter as they continued down the row of stores, all lit up and decorated, enticing shoppers to come inside and let the holiday shopping begin. Now that Mable was gone, there were only two people on Mitch's list to buy for this year. Make that three. He wanted to get Kaitlyn a little something too.

"Hey, aren't those the Trapps?" Kaitlyn asked, pointing across the busy street.

Mitch followed her gaze to the two young men standing with an older couple. "Yeah. Those must be Nate's parents."

"Hmm. Well, being the good hosts we are, we should go say hello," Kaitlyn suggested.

He wasn't in the mood for socializing but he didn't want to argue. "Sure."

Kaitlyn stepped slightly ahead of him as they approached. "Fancy seeing you guys here," she called out, gaining their attention. "I didn't know you two were coming tonight."

"Kaitlyn." Nate went in for a hug, and then Chris did as well. After that, they shook Mitch's hand. "Paris convinced us to come. Then we roped Mom and Dad into coming along too." Nate turned back to his parents. "Mom, Dad, this is Kaitlyn and Mitch. They run the Sweetwater Bed and Breakfast. Kaitlyn and Mitch, this is Tina and Jim, my doting parents."

Mitch shook their hands, very aware of Tina's disapproving look.

"Thank you for giving the boys a place to stay but I really wish they would have spent the holidays at our home. That's where they belong, not with strangers," the woman said.

"Mom," Nate warned, "you know why we didn't stay with you. We aren't discussing that here." Nate's tone and demeanor were relaxed. "We're together tonight, and we're going to have fun."

Tina shook her head. "It's just that Christmas is coming, and I don't want you staying at some cold inn when you have a perfectly good home."

"With all due respect, Mrs. Trapp," Chris said, putting an arm around Nate's shoulders, "Kaitlyn and Mitch's bed and breakfast is anything but cold. It's warm and cozy. They've taken very good care of us."

"Thank you," Kaitlyn said.

Mitch looked over at her and could tell she was working hard not to say whatever was on her mind. He also knew she'd eventually say it.

"Nate and Chris have been such a delightful couple to

have," Kaitlyn said after a moment. "We gave them one of my favorite rooms at the inn."

"Together, I gather?" Tina asked, making no attempt to hide her disapproval.

"Of course. I agree that family belongs at home for the holidays but a married couple belongs in the same room."

Mitch noticed the worried glance between Nate and Chris.

"You are so lucky that your son found someone to love," Kaitlyn continued, keeping her smile steady even though her tone was pointed. "Not everyone does. It's something to celebrate. Don't make Nate choose between you and his husband. It's not fair. And if you do, it'll likely work in my favor," Kaitlyn said, "and I'll see Nate and Chris at the Sweetwater B and B more often over the coming years."

Tina frowned and then looked at her husband, who kept his head low. Mitch guessed Jim didn't mind the couple sharing a room. Kaitlyn was right. Tina's behavior would eventually put a wedge between her and her son if she didn't change her rules.

"It was so nice to meet you," Kaitlyn said, offering her hand to Jim first and then Tina. Tina hesitated before taking it. Mitch shook the couple's hands as well. Then they said their goodbyes, and Kaitlyn promised Nate and Chris a delicious breakfast in the morning.

"Kaitlyn Russo is not someone to mess with," Mitch teased as they continued down the sidewalk.

She gave a sidelong glance at him. "Or she never learned when to keep her mouth shut."

"Nah. Nate's mom needed to hear that. You did a good thing. I'm impressed." Mitch reached for her hand again as they walked. It felt natural. Family belonged at home. Married people belonged in the same room. And he belonged here, with Kaitlyn.

Where did that come from?

Before he could analyze his thoughts, Kaitlyn pointed.

"Oh wow, look! Carolers!" She tugged him toward a group of festively dressed singers. Kaitlyn and Mitch blended in with the crowd and watched for several songs. He'd spent many a Christmas at this very event when he was growing up. Somehow, he'd never appreciated it until now when he'd stayed away for so long and missed so many years.

A strong hand slapped his back, sending Mitch into a cough that he quickly suppressed to avoid drawing attention from the onlookers.

"Hey, man," Alex said with a laugh. He was dressed in his full police uniform tonight. "You must be Kaitlyn," he said, offering his hand to her.

Kaitlyn dropped Mitch's hand to shake with Alex.

Alex looked at Mitch and lifted his brows. "No wonder you didn't need a place to stay last night," he said just loud enough for Mitch to hear.

Mitch shook his head. "You'll always be a jerk. Some things never change," he said in the most affectionate of ways.

"Having fun tonight, Kaitlyn?" Alex asked, ignoring him.

"Oh, definitely. This is amazing. I can't wait to see the Angel Tree. I've heard so much about it."

"It's my favorite part of this shindig. The Sweetwater Springs Police Department adopts quite a few kids each year. Make sure you check out the cake walk too. The ladies in town make dozens to give away. I'm sure your guests would love some cake tomorrow."

"Good idea. Thank you." She hugged her arms around her body instead of reaching for Mitch's hand again.

Mitch shoved his own hands in his pockets and then

turned as Alex's radio buzzed to life at his hip. From his years as a military police officer, Mitch was attuned to the sound. Adrenaline suddenly zipped through his veins. He missed the sound of a call. Missed racing toward a scene.

"B and E at Dawanda's Fudge Shop on Main Street," someone reported through the radio.

Alex cursed softly. "I've got to go, you two. There's been another B and E. This is two in a week's time."

"I'm going with you," Mitch said.

Alex narrowed his eyes. "You're not SSPD."

"No, but you're short-staffed. I'm not letting you go into a B and E without backup."

"What about Kaitlyn?"

Mitch had almost forgotten about his date.

"Go. It's fine," Kaitlyn urged. "I'll stay a little longer and then get a cab ride home. Or maybe Paris can give me that ride after all."

Mitch's teeth ground together but he nodded anyway. "You sure?"

"Positive. Go help Dawanda. I'll see you later tonight."

CHAPTER FOURTEEN

Mitch rode shotgun in Alex's police SUV, zipping down the familiar streets of Sweetwater toward Dawanda's Fudge Shop. As soon as Alex cut the engine, Mitch hopped out and followed him. As they stepped up on the curb, Mitch glanced in the shop window. No sign of anyone other than Dawanda sitting at one of the tables with her head in her hands. She looked up as a bell overhead announced their entrance.

"You okay?" Alex asked immediately, looking past her and around the store. "Anyone else here?"

"No. But the jackass left with everything in the register."

Mitch wasn't sure he'd ever seen Dawanda without a smile on her face. He didn't like it. "Did you recognize the intruder?"

Alex glanced over. "Let me ask the questions, okay?"

"Yeah. Sorry." Mitch ran a hand through his overgrown hair.

"Did you recognize the intruder?" Alex repeated, turning back to Dawanda.

"No. He had on a mask. I thought I recognized the voice but I don't know. It all happened so fast. He said if I didn't give him the money, I'd be sorry."

"Did he have a gun?" Mitch cut in, forgetting that he was supposed to stay quiet.

Alex shot him another dour look.

"No. Maybe. I'm not really sure. He kept his hands in his pockets the whole time."

"I see. Did he come in through the front of the store or the back?" Alex continued.

"The back, while I was making the fudge...Oh, darn it. I burned the fudge," Dawanda whined. "That makes me even madder!" She shot out of her chair and went to the kitchen.

As she did, Mitch headed to check the back door. It was unlocked and cracked open. He was careful not to touch anything as he glanced outside. No one in sight, which meant the thief wasn't a fool and didn't have a death wish, because Mitch had a mind to knock the guy's lights out if given a chance. Mitch wasn't part of the Sweetwater PD so he didn't have any rules to abide by.

"All clear," he said several minutes later as he returned to the front of the store.

Alex was leaning forward and getting a statement from Dawanda, who'd returned from the kitchen. "Any other details you can give us?" Alex asked her.

"I would if I could."

"Well, sometimes details come back after you've had a chance to relax. If you think of anything tonight or tomorrow, here's my cell phone number." Alex handed her a business card.

"Might want to keep the back door locked," Mitch added.

"I always do," she said.

Mitch furrowed his brow and turned to Alex. "There was no sign of forced entry. Looks like the perp just walked right in."

Alex looked at Dawanda. "Maybe you forgot to lock it this time."

"Would've been the first time that's ever happened." She rubbed her temple. "I think I'll just close up early tonight. There's no serving fudge after something like this. Or doing cappuccino readings." She winked at Mitch, even though her expression was still troubled. "Unless, of course, you're up for one, Chief Baker. I haven't had the pleasure of peeking into your future yet." Her face lit up just a bit as she looked at Alex hopefully.

Mitch did his best to contain a grin. "Yeah, buddy. It's your turn."

"Another day. Right now, I'm determined to catch our thief. This makes two in this area. I'm guessing another one of these stores will be hit next."

Dawanda's mouth dropped open. "I'll call the ladies and tell them to keep protection." Her eyes twinkled mischievously. "And by protection, I mean weapons."

Alex cleared his throat. If he was fazed by the comment, it didn't show. "I don't want a bunch of store owners packing guns down here, Dawanda. That can make things worse. I'll just have my officers patrol the area more frequently."

"Thought you were shorthanded at the station," she said.

Alex's gaze narrowed. "How'd you know that?"

"I know a lot of things, Chief Baker. People talk, especially when you offer them caffeine and sugar."

Mitch was already regretting what he was about to offer. "I'm in town through Christmas Eve. I can help." *What the hell am I doing?* Keeping a low profile at the bed and breakfast was one thing. Riding around the town as part of the SSPD was another.

Alex looked at him with interest. "Thought you were busy with the B and B."

"I have time, and you know I have the experience. Besides, I want to see this perp behind bars as badly as anyone. No one messes with Dawanda and gets away with it."

* * *

Gina Hargrove was right. Lights on the Lake was an event that should not be missed. The Angel Tree towered next to the lake like a beacon of hope to onlookers. Its light reflected perfectly in the pool of water. It was a sight to be seen. So was the cluster of bikers wearing Santa hats across the way.

Kaitlyn spotted Paris and waved. She didn't want to bother him for a ride though. He was in his element, and she wasn't ready to go back to the inn just yet. Coming from New York, she was used to getting lost in a crowd. In some way, being one of many was comforting. She headed toward a small park along the lake where a snow machine was set up for the kids and took a seat on one of the benches to watch them squeal with delight. The song "I'll Be Home for Christmas" filled the air around her.

She was home, she thought. She just wished the people she loved could be here with her for the holidays. Maybe Mitch was right. She should invite her parents to the inn to spend Christmas with her. There was a chance they'd say yes, although slim.

"Kaitlyn?" A woman stepped up to the bench and smiled brightly. She was dressed warmly in a coat and brightly colored knit hat that complemented her tanned complexion.

"Hi, Halona. I thought you would be working at the flower shop tonight."

Halona took a seat on the bench next to Kaitlyn and gestured toward Theo, who was playing in the snow with his uncle Tuck. "I closed early and headed over to join in the fun. I never miss Lights on the Lake. It's one of my favorite events of the season."

"I can see why. It's gorgeous," Kaitlyn said. Then she held up her laminated paper angel. "And for a good cause. I picked a six-year-old girl who wants a baby doll."

Halona held up a similar angel. "Nine-year-old boy who wants Nerf guns."

Kaitlyn laughed.

"Are you here all alone?" Halona asked.

"I was with Mitch but he left with Alex to go on a police call."

Halona furrowed her brow. "Oh my. I hope the eggnog wasn't spiked again. That stirred quite a ruckus last year."

"So I hear." Kaitlyn hugged her arms around her body for warmth as she watched Halona's son make snowballs, one after another, and pitch them at his uncle mercilessly.

"How's the bed and breakfast coming along?" Halona asked.

"Fine. Mitch and I have things running smoothly now, knock on wood." Kaitlyn knocked her fist along the wooden bench seat. "We've had several guests already, and reservations are booking up for next month. The article about the town in *Loving Life* magazine has helped."

"I've even seen an uptick in business at the flower shop," Halona told her, "which I have to say is nice because Theo's wish list gets more extensive each year."

The two women continued talking like old friends until

Theo came running over and stared at his mom with hopeful eyes. He didn't say a word though.

"Is it time for hot chocolate?" Halona asked as if reading some secret signal that Kaitlyn wasn't privy to. He nodded happily.

Halona turned to Kaitlyn. "Want to join us?"

Kaitlyn shook her head. "Thanks, but I better get back to the inn. Mitch's mom and aunt are watching the place tonight. I don't want to take advantage."

Halona stood. "That makes sense. Well, let me know if you ever need flower arrangements. I'll give you the friends-and-family discount."

Kaitlyn was touched. Her friends and family from New York might not be here with her for the holidays but she had one more person she could call a friend in Sweetwater. "Thanks. You guys have fun. Bye, Theo. Bye, Tuck."

"Keep Mitch in line, will you?" Tuck called back, taking his nephew's hand.

"That's easier said than done." Kaitlyn grinned as she watched them walk away, and then she stood and looked around. She still had the cab company's number programmed into her phone from her trip to the Tipsy Tavern. She decided to go ahead and start walking toward the parking lot before calling. Sometimes cabs parked there, waiting for customers.

Instead of seeing a cab when she got to the parking lot, Kaitlyn saw a dwindling collection of motorcycles. And one familiar-looking biker.

"Ho, ho, hoooooo. Where's Mitch?" Paris asked as she approached.

"He's playing cop," she said with a shrug.

Paris removed his helmet and extended it to her. "Hop on Santa's sleigh, then. I'll take you home."

She hesitated. Perhaps a cab ride was a better choice.

Only there didn't seem to be any in sight. Taking the helmet, she slipped it over her head. Paris moved the stuffed polar bear he had riding shotgun, and she straddled the bike behind him. Strangely enough, straddling a sexy guy like Paris did nothing for her. The only man she hoped to wrap her legs around tonight was Mitch.

The bike roared to life, and she hugged her arms around Paris's midsection. "I've never ridden on a motorcycle before," she warned.

He glanced over his shoulder with interest. "There's only one rule. Hold on tight," he said before zipping out of the parking lot and down the dim mountain roads.

* * *

Kaitlyn awoke just after midnight to someone entering her room. She recognized the shadow and the woodsy smell of pine.

"Hey," she whispered, rolling over to look at Mitch.

"I hope I'm not being presumptuous. I can always sleep on the couch," he said.

She reached for him, and he stepped toward her. "I was hoping you'd come to my bed." She yawned and propped her elbows up behind her, raising her upper body off the mattress. "How'd it go? Is Dawanda okay?" she asked, her thoughts circling back to earlier in the night.

"Yes. I'll fill you in at breakfast. There's no need to worry."

"Good. Now take those clothes off. Or am I being presumptuous?" she asked, nibbling her lower lip and biting back a mischievous grin.

"Not at all." He lifted his shirt over his head and tossed it to the floor.

Indeed, this was the only man who lit her up these days. Brighter than the Angel Tree at Silver Lake.

* * *

"Do I get an honorary badge?" Mitch asked Alex the next morning, as he walked into the Sweetwater Police Station. He already knew Alex would insist on a background check just for procedural reasons. Mitch was more than qualified to work here though. For a month. That was all he could offer. After that, he was moving on.

"We have the plastic kind we give to the kids when they come to visit," a uniformed woman said from behind the desk.

Mitch gave her a closer look and realized he recognized her. "Tammy?"

"The one and only. Hey there, stranger." The African American woman smiled back at him. She'd graduated from high school with Mitch, Alex, and Tuck. Tuck's sister, Halona, had been a year behind them all. It must've been ten years since he'd seen Tammy but she still looked the same. "You joining the force?" she asked.

Mitch gave a small nod. "Temporarily."

"Wonderful. Give the chief hell," Tammy said with a cheerful laugh.

"Will do."

"Hey," Alex said, looking somewhat intimidating, "I'm not above locking up any hell-raisers in the jail for a night or two. In fact," he said, turning to Mitch, "next time you need a place to crash, I've got a cell with your name on it." He lifted a hand and waved at Tammy. "See you after all the crime fighting."

"Don't forget to stop at Debbie's Donuts," Tammy teased.

"And bring me back one of the chocolate ones with rainbow sprinkles."

Alex rolled his eyes. "She thinks all I do is sip coffee and chat with the locals," he said, leading Mitch to an SUV with the SSPD logo in the parking lot. He clicked a button on his keychain, unlocking it, and then they both got inside. "Some days, she's right, but I'll never admit to it."

Mitch chuckled as Alex started the vehicle and pulled out of the parking lot. "I never would've expected Tammy to work at the station. She was quite the rule breaker in school."

"Yeah, well, life is full of surprises. For example, I'm surprised you offered to help out at the station. Don't get me wrong—I'm glad you did. We could use a good man right now. The holidays are a busy time around here."

"It's a win-win for us both, I guess. Another month locked away at the inn would be my undoing." And Kaitlyn might be his undoing in a completely different way. "After Christmas, I'm heading out as planned though. You might want to start interviewing officers now."

"Like it's that easy," Alex said with a head shake as he pulled up to a stoplight and waited for some pedestrians to cross. "I'll take as much help as you can offer." He glanced over. "I'll take having one of my best friends around as long as I can too. We've missed you, buddy."

The light turned green, and Alex refocused his attention on the road. Mitch was grateful because it gave him a second to swallow past his pesky emotion.

He cleared his throat. "So, tell me the truth. How is Tuck doing these days?"

Alex hesitated for a long moment. "I think he's doing okay. It was hard for him right after Renee died. He kept to himself a lot. Over the last six or so months though, he's started coming back out with me to the tavern. We've been hiking and climbing. He moved out of his old place with Renee. I think he's making a real effort to move on with his life."

"Where did he move to?" Mitch asked. He knew the town inside and out.

"A cottage on Blueberry Creek. It's oversized for just one man but you know how Tuck likes to commune with nature."

Mitch chuckled, remembering their friend's various selection of wildlife pets growing up. "Didn't he have a pet squirrel for a while?"

"That was better than the pet skunk that lasted a day." Both men started laughing like the kids they'd once been.

"We avoided him for a week after that fiasco," Mitch managed to choke out through shortened breaths of amusement.

Life hadn't been all bad here. It was easier to tell himself it was, but when he came home, the realization was like a sledgehammer to his system. Even though he and his mom had struggled financially after his father's death, life had been idyllic in this cozy mountain town. He never would've left if not for the accident.

"So, what's the deal between you and Kaitlyn?" Alex asked a moment later. "For a man who insists that he's not staying, you two were looking awfully cozy last night at Lights on the Lake."

They'd been awfully cozy last night in bed too, Mitch thought. And again this morning. "We have our own arrangement going."

"You know what they say about mixing business with pleasure."

Mitch turned to look at his friend and new boss. "She knows it's only temporary. Same as you."

"Doesn't mean I won't try to change your mind." Alex looked over briefly before returning his eyes to the road. "I'm guessing she's thinking the same."

* * *

Kaitlyn felt sentimental watching her first guests leave on Monday morning. She'd grown fond of all of them over the last few days. Even the Krespos, who'd spent most of yesterday in the bedroom. When they'd finally emerged, both had a glow and a smile on their faces. Then after breakfast, she'd helped them carry their belongings to their car.

"You might see us again," Mr. Krespo had said through his rolled-down window.

"You're welcome anytime." Kaitlyn meant it even though Mrs. Krespo hadn't been the easiest guest.

Now it was Chris and Nate's turn to depart.

"Thank you so much for staying at the inn," she told the couple.

"Thanks for having us. It's been an absolutely wonderful stay," Nate said. "And thank you for what you said to my mom."

Chris shook his head. "I still can't believe she called and invited us to come back for Christmas. And promised us a room together."

Kaitlyn's mouth fell open. "You're kidding."

"Nope." Nate chuckled softly. "She promised not to say a word about it too. She said we were grown men, and she wouldn't interfere. You got through to her, Kaitlyn."

"I only told her the truth. I'm so happy for you two but I'm a little sad this means you probably won't be needing a room here again."

Chris wrapped an arm around Nate. "I was thinking we could come back for our one-year anniversary. We certainly can't stay at your parents' for that occasion."

Nate grinned. "I love the idea."

"Me too." Kaitlyn watched them get into their car and waved as they drove away. She heaved a heavy sigh as she walked back inside the inn. She was expecting two more couples this afternoon. She needed to clean and prepare the now-empty rooms for whoever came next.

A little excitement buzzed through her. It was so much fun meeting new people and also unexpectedly fulfilling. She'd made a difference in the Trapps' life. She even felt like she'd helped the Krespos regain a little spark for one another.

Humming cheerfully, she headed to the laundry room to retrieve some cleaning supplies and then tromped upstairs to clean Mr. and Mrs. Krespo's room first. An hour later, she entered the room where Nate and Chris had stayed and paused at the small wrapped gift sitting on the edge of the bed.

"Oh no," she said, walking up to it and picking it up. She'd have to call and let them know they'd forgotten something. She paused when she saw her name on the tag.

To Kaitlyn

She sat on the bed's edge and peeled off the shiny Christmas paper slowly. Then she lifted the lid off a gift box. Inside were a beautiful ornament and a card. Kaitlyn removed the ornament first. It was in the shape of a house that could've been the inn. It appeared to be hand-carved and painted with great detail. She guessed they'd probably purchased it on Saturday night at one of the downtown shops. She couldn't wait to hang it on the tree downstairs. Next, she opened the card and read as tears welled in her eyes.

Thank you for being our home away from home.
Love, the Trapps.

CHAPTER FIFTEEN

Over the next two weeks, Kaitlyn ate, breathed, and loved every second of her newfound life. Including the part where she shared a bed with a surly ex-marine.

Kaitlyn lay back on her bed now for just a moment. Her memory lapped over the sex she and Mitch had early this morning before he'd left to go to the station. It was the kind of sex where you wonder if you're still asleep. She'd been in the middle of a dream when he'd woken her. Her eyes had cracked open just enough to see him giving her that heart-melting smile of his. Then they closed again, and she'd writhed and moaned at all the things he'd done to her under those covers.

Even now, her face flushed. As much as she'd like to, she couldn't lie on her bed and think about him for the rest of the day though. There were things to be done, always, and people to catch up with.

She tapped the screen of her cell phone and pulled it to her ear, waiting for her best friend's voice to answer.

"Finally!" Josie said. "I was beginning to wonder if you'd fallen off one of those mountain cliffs and died."

Kaitlyn stared up at the ceiling fan above her. "More like died and gone to heaven. I love it here."

"So, it's booking up?" Josie asked.

Kaitlyn could hear the tapping of Josie's computer in the background. The woman could carry on a conversation and write her next article at the same time practically. "It hasn't slowed down for a second. I don't even know what day it is half the time because guests are coming and going continually."

"Rich people and retirees don't keep to weekend trips."

"I've noticed. But we've had couples celebrating their anniversaries too. And people staying here on business trips instead of getting a hotel room. I already have a waiting list started. It's reaching into the New Year."

"That's awesome. How long before you buy out the other guy and it's all yours?"

Kaitlyn's breath and excitement stilled in her chest. That was the plan, the goal, but she wasn't looking forward to saying goodbye. With the success of the B&B came the termination of her business relationship with Mitch. But what about the other relationship they were swept up in? "Um, well, I'm not sure. He says he's not in a hurry to be bought out, so..." Kaitlyn absently traced imaginary hearts on her quilt as she spoke. "We're making steady income now so I'm sure it's just a matter of time."

"And how long until you start sleeping with him?" Josie asked.

Kaitlyn choked on a gasp. It took her a moment before she could even answer. "No holds barred, huh?"

Josie laughed. "None. Last we spoke, you kissed him and liked it. Soooooo?"

"I'm pleading the Fifth."

Josie gasped on the other end of the line. "You slept with him already and didn't tell me? I thought we were best friends."

"We are." And Kaitlyn had always called Josie immediately after sleeping with a guy. Josie was her go-to person. Always. But sleeping with Mitch was different. If she told Josie, she knew she'd have to explore how she felt about him, because that's what they did. Only, Kaitlyn wasn't sure how she felt about Mitch.

Or she was and it was a little terrifying.

She pressed the heel of her palm to her forehead. "I'm in over my head this time, Jo."

"You really like him, don't you?"

Kaitlyn swallowed. "He's sexy. He can fix things and cook just about anything. He's a great listener and..." She shook her head. "He's a tough ex-marine who's secretly funny and sweet." And he could make her toes curl with pleasure. Josie didn't need that little detail though.

"Wow." It wasn't often that Josie was reduced to one word.

"So you can see my predicament."

"Yeah," Josie finally said. "This is why I bury myself in work. I'm too busy for my own drama. Let me know how this story ends. I'm rooting for him to fall madly in love with you."

"About as likely as you coming to Sweetwater Springs for a visit," Kaitlyn said hopefully.

Josie chuckled into the receiver. "I'm not planning a trip just yet. I have fires to put out here in New York. Speaking of which..." She grew quiet on the other end of the line.

"Yes?" Kaitlyn's stomach tightened the way it did when

she felt the subject turning in a direction she wasn't going to like. It was in Josie's tone of voice. The slight hesitation. The way her pitch lowered.

Goose bumps fleshed up on Kaitlyn's skin. She braced herself for impact. "What is it?"

"Well, there's a little buzz online that Bradley Foster got handsy with one of his leading actresses—that's all. She posted on social media yesterday but it was taken down quickly. I guess Bradley didn't like being outed publicly."

"Well, good for her. Someone needs to out that sleazeball."

"Agreed."

Kaitlyn sat up now, nausea rolling through her stomach. She hated to hear even the mention of Bradley Foster's name.

"One of these days, he's going to get what's coming to him," Josie said.

"I should've kneed him between the legs so hard he couldn't function to force himself on another woman again," Kaitlyn said, which made Josie laugh.

"Then you'd be in jail right now instead of at a beautiful B and B."

"True."

The bedroom door opened, and Mitch walked in. When he looked at her, concern etched itself in his features. Kaitlyn realized her eyes were stinging, not from tears but from anger. Bradley used his celebrity status and power to take advantage of people. To hurt people. She'd admired him, and he'd betrayed her trust by pushing himself on her and then lying about what really happened.

"Sorry," Mitch said. "I knocked but you weren't answering."

Kaitlyn shook her head. "It's okay. I guess I didn't hear you."

Josie cleared her throat on the other end of the line. "Listen, Kaye. Don't worry about that jerk. Just focus on Mitch and figure out how to keep him around a little longer. Anything that makes you smile is a good thing. You deserve happy—remember that. And Bradley and your old boss deserve a bad case of the crabs."

Kaitlyn burst into laughter. Josie was always good for that. "Thanks. I'll talk to you soon."

"You better."

They said their goodbyes and disconnected the call. Then Kaitlyn tossed her cell phone on the nightstand.

Mitch sat down on the bed next to her, the weight of his body tipping her toward him. Not that she planned on going anywhere else right now. Sharing space with him felt entirely too good, like a warm blanket on a cold, snowy night, which was a perfect analogy for her life right now. In some way, she felt like she'd been left out in the cold with the situation in New York. Then Mitch had come along and made her feel safe again. Wanted again.

"Everything okay?" he asked.

"In Sweetwater, yes. Meanwhile in New York, Bradley Foster is groping one of his leading ladies." She only hoped they kicked harder than she did. Or packed a mean punch. Maybe Mace too.

Mitch's body tensed beside hers. She had no doubt that, if she asked him to, he'd drive up the East Coast and make Bradley regret he ever met her.

He reached for her hand and gave it a gentle squeeze, his rough skin brushing against hers. Almost like magic, her worries fell away with just that touch. Mitch seemed to have that effect on her.

That was just one more reason she was glad he was around.

* * *

Since the Lights on the Lake event, there'd been three more robberies downtown. The robberies were small—chump change, really—and Mitch didn't quite get the point of the thefts. One incident had been the tip jar at the Sweetwater Café. A tip jar couldn't have held more than twenty bucks. It didn't make sense that someone would risk taking it and getting caught.

Mitch pulled his police cruiser to the curb in front of Dawanda's store and stepped out to go check on her. He also planned to nab a piece of her peanut butter fudge while he was at it.

Dawanda came barreling out from behind the counter as soon as he walked in, a smile on her face and her vibrant-colored hair poking into the air like an erupting volcano. "My favorite protector. Did you bring your friend?" she asked hopefully.

"Alex?" Mitch asked, remembering that she'd wanted to read his fortune in the cappuccino.

"No. Your lady friend. Kaitlyn."

Mitch shook his head. "No. Just me this time. Sorry to disappoint."

"You never disappoint." She had to reach up to pat his back and then pointed to a chair. "Sit. I'll get you some fudge and coffee to go. I know this street is much safer now that you're on the job."

"Temporarily," Mitch clarified. He didn't want anybody getting the idea that he was staying.

"Right. Right." She headed back behind the counter.

A few minutes later, she laid a white paper bag of fresh fudge and a foam cup of coffee on the table in front of him.

Mitch shifted to pull out his wallet. "How much do I owe you?"

"I don't charge knights in shining armor." She shoved her hands on her little hips like he'd insulted her.

"Well, I'm not taking this for free."

"Not free. In exchange, you keep me and my store safe and bring that girl of yours back sometime." She pushed the paper bag toward him in a not-so-subtle gesture.

"You are a stubborn woman, Dawanda." Which seemed to be a theme in his life right now.

"The best ones are." She winked and made a shooing motion as more customers entered the store. "Now, if you don't mind, I have paying customers to attend to," she teased.

"Thanks." He picked up the bag as he stood and then walked back to the cruiser on the curb.

"Officer! Officer!" someone called just as he reached his car door.

Mitch whirled to see a woman wearing a heavy jacket and knit scarf wrapped loosely around her neck. He knew exactly who she was the moment he saw her face, drawn tight with distress. She was apparently so upset that she had no idea who he was, however. "What's wrong?" he asked, bracing himself for her to recognize him at any second and start beating him with her purse.

"My nephew!" The woman's hands clasped the side of her face. "I can't believe I did that. I stepped out of my car just for a second to drop my Christmas cards in the post office collection box. I only stepped a foot away from the car."

Mitch's adrenaline dialed up. "What happened?"

The woman—Brian Everson's youngest sister—rubbed her temple and then pointed to a silver car a few spaces up. It was parked just shy of a large blue mail collection drop-off. "He's locked inside the car. I left my keys in the ignition…So stupid!" Tears started spilling down her cheeks.

Mitch touched her arm just briefly, then took off toward the car to assess the situation. Sure enough, there was a wide-eyed little boy, who couldn't have been older than three, sitting in a child's car seat in the back. Mitch futilely pulled on the passenger door's handle. His gaze darted to the locks on the driver's side. All secured.

He turned back to Brian's sister. What was her name again? He tried to remember. It started with a *p. Priscilla? Pamela?* She was the youngest of the five Everson children. Mitch thought she'd been in the same grade as Tuck's sister, Halona. "It's okay. Do you have a spare key hidden anywhere on the car?"

She shook her head. Then the toddler in the back seat, possibly seeing how upset his aunt was, decided to start wailing loudly.

Mitch gestured back to his police cruiser. "I need to get a tool. I'll be right back." A moment later, he returned with a three-foot-long rod called a BigEasy, used for just this purpose.

He turned back to the woman. *Penelope.* Yeah, that was her name. Penelope—Penny—Everson. No doubt she hated him as much as her parents did. "I'll be careful but there's a possibility this might damage your car," he warned.

She nodded hurriedly as the toddler screamed louder. "Please, I just want him to be safe."

"Okay." Mitch worked quickly, and a moment later, he opened the passenger side door. He pressed the automatic unlock button for the back seat, and Penny Everson whipped open the door and went to her nephew.

"I'm so sorry. I'm so, so, so sorry," he heard her tell the boy. She released him from his restraint and pulled him to her.

Mitch was about to turn and head quietly back to his

car—and get as far out of Dodge from any member of the Everson family as he could—until Penny called him.

"Officer?"

Mitch turned reluctantly.

She wiped a hand under her mascara-smudged eyes and offered a grateful smile. "Thank you so much. I don't know what I would have done if you weren't here." She patted the child's back as he calmed and melted into her shoulder. "I'm not usually so careless. It's just, the holidays and...It doesn't matter. There's no excuse. I made a mistake, and it could've been much worse if not for you." Tears sprung in her bright-green eyes.

"It happens," Mitch said. He knew all too well about making mistakes. "Just enjoy the rest of your afternoon. And your holiday."

She nodded as her eyes narrowed in. Her grateful smile was still set in place. "You look so familiar." Her gaze dropped to his name badge. "Hargrove."

He watched his last name register. That smile slipped, and confusion twisted her features. No doubt because Mitch wasn't supposed to be here. He'd made a promise to the Everson family that he would stay away, except for brief visits to see his mom, of course. But he wouldn't make his home here. That was the deal.

He was keeping his promise. He didn't plan on staying, even though wearing a police officer's uniform contradicted that.

Penny was still staring at him, gripping the boy now as if she were trying to keep him safe, possibly from Mitch instead of a locked car now. Or was that just Mitch's imagination?

The hero that Dawanda and even Penny made him out to be scattered like dandelion fluff in the wind.

What could Mitch say? *Don't worry. This isn't how it looks. I won't be here long.*

"Thank you again," she said, briskly this time. Then she turned from him and started loading the boy back into her vehicle.

Mitch turned as well and slunk back to his car, reminded once more why he couldn't get comfortable in his hometown.

* * *

Laundry had never been one of her favorite chores, and yet it was never done here. There were always linens to wash. Towels. Tablecloths. Not to mention her own clothes.

Kaitlyn leaned against the front of the washing machine that she'd just loaded with sheets from the guests who'd just checked out, hesitating a little to go back out into the main rooms where she'd have to socialize. Her phone sang "Carol of the Bells" behind her. Turning, she checked the screen, already knowing who it was. The ringtone was one she'd chosen for her parents, although it hadn't rung since she'd assigned it to their contact a few weeks earlier.

Taking a breath, she pulled the phone to her ear. "Mom. How are you?"

"Hello, sweetheart. All is well here. Your dad and I have been busy, busy with work. And you?" her mom asked in return, effectively bringing up the subject of work in one single breath.

Kaitlyn wasn't surprised. Work begot achievement, which begot success. And her success determined how much her mother had to boast about with her country club friends.

"Have you come to your senses yet? Ready to get back to work here in New York?"

Kaitlyn closed her eyes. So much for the laundry room being her "safe place" here in the inn. "Just the opposite, actually. Did you get the invitation I sent? For you and Dad to spend Christmas here at the Sweetwater Bed and Breakfast? Just say the word, and I'll reserve a room," Kaitlyn offered with forced cheer.

Her mom clucked her tongue into the receiver. "No, no. We have plans to go to the Bahamas this year, remember?"

Kaitlyn did remember but she'd thought maybe there was a chance they'd change their minds after receiving the invitation. She'd included a picture of the inn that she'd taken for the brochures. In the photograph, the mountains towered in the distance. Sunny beaches were nice, but during the holidays, snow and mountains were fitting. So was the idea of spending it with your family.

"Come to the Bahamas with us?" her mom urged. "I'm sure you can still get a ticket, although it might cost you an arm and a leg this late in the season. Or cost you the inn that you're so determined to revive."

Kaitlyn was literally seeing stars. "Mom, has it occurred to you that I'm actually happy here, doing something that wasn't your idea? I love hosting at this B and B."

"You used to say you loved your job in New York too."

There was a condescending tone in her mother's voice that made Kaitlyn clutch her cell phone even tighter.

"I'm sure if you spoke to your boss, he'd take you back, sweetheart. You might have to start at the bottom rung again and work your way back into their good graces, but…"

"Haven't you heard a word I've said? I'm not going back to my old job," Kaitlyn ground out with just a touch of irritation. Okay, more than a touch, in the same way that Bradley's moves on her had been more than an innocent sweep of his hand.

"I don't get it. You had a job that other designers would kill to have."

"Okay, Mom. If you really want to know," Kaitlyn snapped, "I didn't quit. I was fired."

Her mom sucked in an audible breath. "What? Why? What did you do?"

"Oh, I don't know. I was sexually harassed by America's favorite action hero, maybe." Kaitlyn's eyes suddenly stung.

"Are you talking about Bradley Foster?" Her mom had known that Kaitlyn was working for him. "Are you sure? Maybe you misunderstood?" she asked in quick succession. "He's married, isn't he?"

Kaitlyn blinked. "Yeah, because no married man ever tried to cheat on his wife," she said sarcastically. Hurt feelings blistered up. They'd been festering with every conversation she'd had with her mom since she left Beautiful Designs and the city.

"This must be some sort of mistake," her mom continued. "What were you wearing when this happened?"

Kaitlyn's mouth dropped open, and she pulled her cell phone back for a second to stare dumbfoundedly at it. "Clothes, Mom," she said when she finally brought it back to her ear. "I don't typically work naked, you know...Listen, I need to go."

"Kaitlyn, we're not done talking about this."

Oh, but Kaitlyn was. And if her mother questioned her one more time, she was going to toss her iPhone at the wall. Not wise, considering that it cost her a small fortune. "I have a guest who needs me," she lied. "Bye, Mom." She quickly disconnected the call and shoved her phone into her jeans pocket.

Well, that had gone well. *Not.*

The nerve of her mom questioning her. Why was it always the woman's fault if a man crossed a line? And of all the people who should believe a woman, it was her own mother.

Kaitlyn clutched the front of the washer, feeling it vibrate through her hands and up her arms. She gulped in a breath, then another, and another.

"Are you and the washing machine having a stare-down?" Mitch asked.

She whirled to face him. "Just when I thought I'd gotten used to you sneaking up on me."

"Sorry. I tried to make noise as I approached but you were pretty absorbed in whatever you were thinking."

Kaitlyn looked down at her hands. "Yeah."

"Everything okay?"

He was always asking that. Always trying to fix her problems. She didn't want to weigh him down with any more of her baggage. "I'm fine," she lied. Then she looked back up and offered a smile, which wasn't hard when he was around. "Thought you'd be at the police station."

Now his expression turned crestfallen. "I was."

"Long day?" she asked, reading something in the lines of his face.

"Something like that." He shrugged. "Anyway, Alex forced me to leave. He won't let me work more than a normal shift."

"A bit of a workaholic, are you?" She'd already learned that about him. He always took care of whatever she needed. Never complained. She'd never seen him at rest, come to think of it. Well, except for after they were spent from making love.

"I like to stay busy," he said.

"Well, the B and B is running on autopilot at this point. I have nothing for you to do. Unless, of course, you want to mingle with the guests." She poked up a brow, knowing his answer.

"I don't." He leaned against the dryer beside her. "Not my thing."

"That's what you keep saying. But you looked like you were enjoying yourself the other night when I caught you playing cards with the new couple."

His mouth quirked to one side. "Putting me in charge of entertaining guests would be bad for business."

"You haven't scared people away yet." She winked. "Every room is booked, thanks to Josie's article."

"And you," he said. "People know a fraud when they see it. Guests are staying and enjoying themselves. That's because of you."

She leaned back on the washing machine. It was entering the spin cycle against her back, and with Mitch beside her, she might as well have been sitting on top of it. "And you. You helped. In the shadows."

It was his turn to lift a brow.

"Not *those* shadows," she said, thinking about their midnight trysts, which, yes, had been quite inspiring.

"So, what do you guys have on the agenda tonight?" he asked.

She turned to face him, her side vibrating off the machine. "A few of the guests are going to the Tipsy Tavern. The Nelsons are going out to dinner on their own. So, it's just us. Unless you're going to the tavern too."

His eyes darkened. "I was thinking about staying in. I prefer peace and quiet."

"Do you want me to leave you alone?" she asked, lifting her arm to trace a finger down his chest. She couldn't resist. The washing machine was going insane with its spin cycle, and her body was responding to it and the heat crackling between them. "There's a book I've been meaning to read anyway."

He pulled her to him and wrapped his arms around her waist. Her body complained against being torn away from the vibrating appliance but buzzed back to pure bliss in Mitch's embrace. "No. I like peace and quiet. And you. I like you most of all."

Her heart danced around like sugarplums in the beloved "Night Before Christmas" poem.

"The guests leave in twenty minutes. I was considering possibly climbing into the hot tub outside."

He leaned in and kissed her. His lips were warm. The friction of his beard scraped softly against the corners of her mouth. "That sounds perfect," he whispered. "I'm going to shower off while we wait. I worked up a sweat chasing a dog today."

Kaitlyn choked on a laugh as he pulled away, feeling loads better already. "Seriously?"

"Chasing dogs is evidently part of the job description. There's still a thief out there though, and I can't wait to bring him or her to justice."

"You're a good guy, Mitch Hargrove."

His gaze flicked down and out. He didn't believe her. She wished she could erase his past but she could no more do that than she could her own. Everyone had a past they wished were different. From what she'd seen, the town had already given him a clean slate. She wished he would give himself one too.

"Twenty minutes," he said as he walked out. "In the meantime, you can enjoy the rest of that spin cycle." With a wink, he left her on her own, which had been the only thing she'd wanted fifteen minutes ago when she'd walked in here. Now, being alone wasn't quite as appealing.

She glanced at her watch, wishing time away—even though lately she'd been wishing it to stop. So Mitch would never leave Sweetwater Springs.

* * *

Kaitlyn shivered as she stepped outside wearing a modest tankini bathing suit when a heavy winter coat probably would have been more appropriate.

Mitch stepped out behind her, two glasses of red wine in his hands. "I hope that Jacuzzi is warm," he said. "Wouldn't want you to catch a cold out here."

No chance of that, she thought, admiring his bare chest that narrowed to a pair of low-hanging swim trunks. She shivered again for an entirely different reason. Then she walked to the edge of the hot tub and dipped a toe in the water before stepping inside.

"Feel good?" he asked, handing her a wineglass once she was settled.

"Oh yeah," she moaned happily. "The temperature is just right."

He followed her in and took a seat next to her on the Jacuzzi's bench.

Sipping her wine, she looked up at the star-filled sky. "What an amazing view," she said in more than a little awe. "Romantic is an understatement for this place."

When Mitch didn't respond, she glanced over at him. He was staring at her with an unreadable look in his eyes. "I agree."

Butterflies chased around in her belly. After several weeks, they hadn't stopped. "Thought you weren't big on romance."

"Maybe you've sold me on the concept. Don't tell anyone though, okay? I have a reputation to maintain."

She giggled softly. "It'll be our little secret."

He set his glass down, and his hand disappeared under the water, finding her thigh.

She narrowed her gaze. "The guests could come back, you know? We'd be wise to keep our hands to ourselves just in case."

He grinned mischievously. "No one can see underneath these bubbles." His hand moved higher. "And I have an awfully hard time keeping my hands to myself when it comes to you. In case you haven't noticed."

"Oh, I've noticed." She put her glass down and leaned in to him.

He grinned. "I thought you were worried about the guests coming back."

"I'll take my chances." She crossed the rest of the distance and brushed her mouth to his. Both of their hands roamed under the thick layer of bubbles. She could feel Mitch's arousal as he pressed his body into her but they took their time, touching and teasing. No rush to do anything more. This was the ultimate foreplay until they retreated to the bedroom where they could be ensured privacy.

CHAPTER SIXTEEN

*I*t was after six o'clock when Mitch finally left the police station the next day. His body was sore and achy from being folded up in a car half the day and walking the sidewalk outside the row of downtown stores the other half, keeping a watchful eye for suspicious activity. They still hadn't caught the thief who'd stolen from five stores now. They would though. Mitch was intent on that.

"Hey," Kaitlyn said, rounding the corner of the B&B's kitchen.

Mitch stopped to stare at her. Despite her smile, there'd been something bothering her since last night when he'd found her in the laundry room white-knuckling the front of the machine with tears burning her eyes. Whatever the problem, she obviously didn't want to talk about it.

Holiday music streamed down the hall. "What's going on?" he asked.

"Mr. Timsdale from Ohio is teaching a two-step in the ballroom," she said.

Mitch had been the one to check in Mr. Timsdale and his wife yesterday. They were on their way to visit family and had decided to stay in Sweetwater Springs for a couple of days.

"The guests seem to love it," Kaitlyn said. "I might have to hire someone to teach ballroom dancing in there regularly. It could be another draw for the inn after the holidays."

He nodded as he considered the prospect, not that he'd have any say in what happened here after the holidays. "That's not a bad idea."

Kaitlyn tilted her head. "I've been meaning to ask: Do you happen to know anything about the ballroom? What did my grandma and grandpa do with it?"

Mitch shrugged. "They danced. That was probably Mable and Henry's favorite room in the house. They always considered opening it up to the guests but it never happened. It was their special place, Mable used to say. I sneaked in there a time or two and watched. They were pretty good."

Kaitlyn shook her head, a smile lifting her cheeks. "So much I don't know about them."

"I'm happy to fill in the holes where I can," he offered.

"Thanks. Well, I hope my grandparents don't mind me opening up their special place for guests. I actually have another idea for the ballroom. I'm going to show a movie in there later. I found an old projector and several films in the shed. There were even a few Christmas flicks in the mix."

"Yeah?"

She nodded, her face lighting up as usual when she had one of her moments of inspiration. "What do you think? A little *Home Alone* or *How the Grinch Stole Christmas*?"

"I'll have you know I am not planning to steal Christmas this year," Mitch joked. "Although I have been compared to the Grinch many a time." His teasing worked to make her laugh, which was exactly what he'd intended.

"I have another surprise too." She gestured for him to follow her down the hall toward the kitchen, which seemed to be the heart of the Sweetwater B&B.

He could already smell the scent of cinnamon strudels as soon as he crossed the threshold. "You've been talking to my mom again, haven't you?" he accused, his mouth watering as she pulled the oven door open and allowed him a peek at what was inside. "She told you that cinnamon strudels were my favorite dessert?" he asked.

Kaitlyn shut the oven door and turned to face him. Her cheeks were suddenly flushed, and he wasn't sure if it was from the heat of the oven or from him standing so close. "I wanted to do something nice, to thank you for everything you've done. You didn't have to help or do as much as you've done for the inn. And for me."

She'd already thanked him a dozen times. "I would've been some kind of schmuck not to."

"True. But you didn't have to care." She folded her arms. "Anyway, Mr. Garrison called this afternoon. Since the time stipulation of the will is nearly up, he's coming by to check on things tomorrow morning. I invited him to breakfast."

Mitch nodded. "I'll cook and let Alex know I'll be in to the station a little later. He won't mind."

"Perfect," she said with an easy smile. It still didn't reach her eyes, and he decided to make it his personal mission to change that tonight. Whatever was bothering her, he wanted to erase it from her mind.

"So, how much longer until the strudels are ready?" he asked.

"One minute."

"I can do a lot of things in one minute. Starting with this."

He pulled her to him and planted a soft kiss on her lips. He stroked a finger along the side of her jaw as his thumb rested on the jumping pulse at her neck. After a moment, he pulled his mouth away and looked at her, long and deep. Those eyes worked as a flame, and he was their moth.

How the hell was he going to walk away from this woman in a couple of weeks?

The oven's timer beeped in the background.

Kaitlyn cast a glance over her shoulder. "Don't want those to burn."

"Just a second." He pulled her in again, needing one more little taste. Because she was the sweetest thing he knew. His love for cinnamon strudels had been before Kaitlyn Russo. Now *she* was his favorite dessert.

* * *

The next morning, Kaitlyn bumped her body against Mitch's as he taught her the art of making eggs Benedict in the kitchen. The well-rested guests would start stirring soon.

She, on the other hand, was tired. She had snuck off with Mitch midway through *Home Alone*. They'd hurried down the hall like a couple of horny teenagers. Like the college-aged couple who'd stayed at the B&B during Thanksgiving week. After posting the DO NOT DISTURB sign—a cute little trinket she'd picked up the other day—and locking the door they'd buried themselves under the covers but hadn't gone to sleep until well after midnight.

"I could get used to this," she said dreamily as they cooked.

"You could get used to what? Delicious breakfasts every morning or me?"

"Both." At her confession, a moment of panic streaked

through her at the thought that Mitch might think she was somehow implying she wanted him to stay. She wasn't. But she relaxed when she saw the easiness of his smile. Everything with him really was starting to be so easy. Yes, she could get used to the tasty dining, but also to him.

They carried the food into the dining room where one couple had already come down. Another lingered at the staircase. She quickly set the table, leaving an extra spot for Mr. Garrison, who was supposed to be arriving anytime now.

"Take a breath," Mitch advised as she straightened one of the centerpieces. "He's just checking that I haven't gone AWOL. He doesn't care if the bed and breakfast is in pristine condition. Which it is, by the way."

"I know." Kaitlyn glanced around at the guests filling the seats. "It's just that Mr. Garrison knew my grandparents. He knew this place. I want him to be impressed with what we've done here."

"It was mostly you." Mitch lowered his voice in that intimate way that lovers did when they were paying the other a compliment. It sent gooey warmness all through her. "And he will be impressed. He'd be crazy not to be. In just a short time, this place has been completely transformed. It's more than a B and B. It's an experience."

Kaitlyn narrowed her eyes. "Wow. I love that. More than a bed and breakfast—an experience." She clapped a hand over her chest. "I've been working with Paris on some graphic design ideas for pamphlets to advertise the B&B. Emma from the Sweetwater Café said she'd put some out for me. She said her restaurant is one of the first places tourists hit when they come to town."

"You're getting cozy with all the locals, aren't you?"

She shrugged. "Well, if this is going to be my home, I should make friends."

"I think putting pamphlets out is a great idea."

"And I can send some to Josie in New York. She'd send people here. I can put them everywhere to keep this place hopping all year long." Renewed excitement surged through her.

"Careful what you wish for," he warned teasingly.

"I love it when it's busy." She just wished, for the millionth and one time, that she could keep him on staff.

She busied herself filling the guests' coffee mugs and making small talk as she waited for Mr. Garrison to arrive.

"He should be here by now," she said, coming up to Mitch halfway through breakfast. Before he could respond, her cell phone buzzed in her pocket. She pulled it out and read a text.

Running late. Be there in fifteen minutes.

Kaitlyn frowned.

"What's wrong?"

"Mr. Garrison is running behind. He's going to miss breakfast with the guests, and his food will be cold."

"Again," Mitch said, talking calmly, "he's not here to shut you down."

To shut *you* down. "Right," she said, nodding. "You're right."

Mitch reached for his own cell phone now. It was his turn to look disappointed. "Alex wants me to call him. I'll help you with cleanup in just a minute."

"Sure." Kaitlyn stood there by herself for a moment, listening in on the conversations at each table. Mitch was right. This was much more than a bed and breakfast. It was an experience. She'd done more than the interior design here. She'd designed a place where guests were taken back to a time when electronics didn't run every second. Good old-fashioned fun happened at this inn.

A moment later, Mitch returned to the dining room, looking apologetic. "There's been another break-in. I have to go."

"Now?"

"I'm sorry."

"But Mr. Garrison..."

"He'll understand," Mitch promised.

Kaitlyn was shaking her head. "He'll be here any minute. What am I supposed to tell him?"

Mitch leaned in and kissed her cheek, which made her thoughts totally slam to a halt. He'd never shown any display of affection in front of the guests before. "Just tell him the truth. We're doing great. We make a good team. And I'm out making the streets of Sweetwater Springs a little safer these days."

With that, he hurried out the door, leaving Kaitlyn all alone to prove to Mr. Garrison that she and Mitch were fulfilling the conditions of the will.

* * *

Mitch moved through Julia Kent's bookstore downtown, looking at the upheaval of knickknacks and books. He knew from the past robberies that the thief was only interested in money. The burglar was likely an amateur who'd watched way too many *CSI* episodes. Why else would someone tear through the place but not actually take anything except for what was in the cash register? Another amateur move was robbing a bookstore. Everyone knew bookstores didn't have a lot of cash on hand.

"Hey, Julia." Mitch walked over to the store owner who

was seated behind the cash register, looking flustered. Her face was red and blotchy as she looked off into space, apparently attempting to gather her thoughts.

"I'm not sure what happened," she told Alex. "The robber was wearing a black ski mask, only it looked more like a black knit hat pulled over his head with holes cut out for his eyes and mouth." She laughed softly. "I know that sounds ridiculous."

Mitch was holding a small notebook in his hand. "Did he say anything?" Mitch asked.

She nodded. "He told me to sit in this chair and not get up. He also told me to close my eyes and not open them until I heard the back door shut."

Mitch jotted those facts down. "So he went out the back door?"

"Yes. At least I think he did. I heard the back door close. That's when I got up, grabbed my cell phone, and dialed 911."

Alex squeezed her shoulder gently, a comforting gesture that Julia seemed to appreciate.

Petty thief or not, this burglar was scaring people. "If you don't mind, I'm going to take one more look around," Mitch said.

Alex nodded. "Take your time. I've got a few more questions for Julia while you do."

Mitch took his time walking around the store a second time. He watched his feet, looking at the floor around the bookshelves. He'd enjoyed reading cozy mysteries as a kid growing up here in Sweetwater Springs. Maybe that was one of the things that appealed to him so much about law enforcement. He liked to solve puzzles. Liked to figure out whodunit.

His gaze caught on a small, white rectangular ID lying

just beneath one of the bookshelves. Mitch's steps quickened, and he bent to pick it up. It was a driver's license. *How idiotic can this perp be?* The ID read Kyle Martin and had the photo of a young seventeen-year-old pimply-faced boy with fair skin and red-toned hair. The ID said that Kyle was approximately five foot eleven, one hundred and forty pounds. All of the victims had described their burglar as being around six feet tall and very thin.

Bingo!

Mitch couldn't bring himself to be happy about it though. This was just a kid. Why the hell was someone so young, with so much future ahead of him, throwing his life away on something like this?

Alex looked up as Mitch approached the counter again.

"Found something," Mitch said.

Alex raised an eyebrow. "Oh yeah? What is it?"

"I don't think you're going to like it." He slapped the ID on the counter in front of Alex.

Alex picked it up and frowned. "I know this kid. He's a bit of a troublemaker around town. I've had to talk to him a few times. The kid doesn't have a father, and his mom is always working." With this information, Alex offered an apologetic look, as if maybe Mitch would take it personally. "He's angry, and he hangs out with the wrong crowd."

"Burglary is a felony." Mitch shook his head. "At his age, he'll probably be tried as an adult."

"It's possible." Alex poked his pen back into his front pocket. "I know where they live. Looks like we're making a house call."

"Do we need to call this in?" Mitch asked. "Backup?"

Alex shook his head. "No. Kyle won't put up a fight. His mom, maybe."

Alex turned to Julia and promised to call her later.

"Thank you both," she said, offering a wobbly smile. "I'm just glad it's all over. I might not sleep for a week."

"Trust me. Sweetwater Springs is still one of the safest towns I know," Alex promised, patting a hand on Mitch's back. "Especially with Mitch here on the job."

They headed out of the store and climbed into Alex's SUV. Mitch closed his eyes for just a moment. He'd been a stupid teen once too. It hadn't gotten him thrown in jail but it could have. He shouldn't have been on the road the night he ran into Brian Everson. It was a stupid mistake that he'd never be able to correct.

Alex waited for traffic to pass, did a U-turn in the road, and then drove toward Kyle Martin's home.

CHAPTER SEVENTEEN

"Wow, Kaitlyn. You've really given it your own spin," Mr. Garrison said.

They had toured the dining room, living area, sitting room, and ballroom, and were now walking down the upstairs hallway and peeking inside the guest rooms that were currently unoccupied.

"Each room has its own theme," Kaitlyn said. "My friend Josie helped me come up with that idea. Mitch helped me pull it off."

"It's wonderful," Mr. Garrison said.

"Mitch has really been a lifesaver," Kaitlyn continued, rambling nervously. "I don't think I could've done this without him."

Mr. Garrison turned to her at the end of the hall. "And what about when he leaves? The conditions are satisfied on Christmas Eve. That's not far away."

"Well, then I have Gina Hargrove down the street. She's been a huge help as well."

"Ah, yes, Gina always enjoyed helping out your grandmother. It's convenient since she lives so close."

"Let me make you a cup of coffee."

"That sounds wonderful."

Kaitlyn led Mr. Garrison back downstairs where he sat on a metal stool at the kitchen island.

The brew was already in the pot. She grabbed two mugs and poured both three-quarters full. Then she grabbed cream and sugar and placed them at the center of the island before sitting down as well.

"Here you go." She pulled her own cup to her. It was her third cup this morning, which meant she was bubbling with energy and nerves, fidgeting almost uncontrollably, and talking at supersonic speed.

"You know, Mable was a matchmaker of sorts. I think that's part of what she was doing when she left the inn to you and Mitch."

Kaitlyn's eyes widened. "I thought she wanted us to run the B and B because of my creativity and Mitch's business mind."

"Sure, sure. That's what she said. But everyone who knew Mable knew she always had a hidden agenda. She set up a number of couples in this town, you know."

"No, I didn't know that."

"She's the person behind my first date with my wife."

"I had no idea my grandmother did that kind of thing."

Mr. Garrison chuckled. "Between Dawanda's cappuccino readings at the fudge shop and your grandmother, singles here have never had a chance. Have you met Dawanda?"

Kaitlyn giggled as she nodded. "Yes. She gave me a complimentary reading."

"And you didn't run from Sweetwater Springs screaming? Means you're one of us now."

Kaitlyn liked the sound of that. "It's part of the town's charm. So, you think my grandmother was trying to set me and Mitch up?"

"She never would've admitted to it, but..." Mr. Garrison shrugged. "I miss Mable's meddling ways."

"There's so much I didn't know about her. I wish we could've spent more time together."

"I'm guessing that's another reason she chose you. You can learn about her by living the life she lived. You're making it all your own, of course, but there's a certain lifestyle that comes with running a bed and breakfast. I'm assuming you want to continue on even when the conditions are met?"

Kaitlyn didn't hesitate. "Definitely."

"Because legally you and Mitch could sell this place. The way you have it running now, you'd probably make a pretty penny."

And she could go back to New York. Maybe reclaim her life and career there. "No. This is my home now."

Mr. Garrison seemed pleased by her declaration. "I sure do wish I could've talked to Mitch."

"I'm so sorry."

"Just good to know he's helping out. When Mable put him in the will, I had my doubts he'd even agree. It was a risky move, knowing Mitch's history here. Mable had faith he wouldn't leave you high and dry. That's just not the kind of man he is."

"He's also not the kind to stay once his promise is fulfilled." It was worded as a statement but Kaitlyn's tone of voice turned it into a question. She already knew the answer in her heart of hearts but some part of her needed confirmation from someone else. "I mean, he loves working at the police station. His mom is here. He seems happy. I know he has a past, but..."

Mr. Garrison frowned. "You and Mable are more alike than you know." With that, he stood. "I'll check in with Mitch later, before the condition of the will is officially up. We'll need to fill out some paperwork to turn this place completely over to you."

And that was his answer to her question.

Mr. Garrison shrugged. "Or not. Have a great day, Kaitlyn."

She followed him to the door. "Thank you. You too." Closing the door behind him, she blew out a breath. She wished Mitch had been here, but she thought she'd done well on her own. Hopefully, Mr. Garrison was convinced that she and Mitch were satisfying Grandma Mable's terms so far.

* * *

There were two cars in the Martins' driveway as Mitch and Alex pulled up to the curb. A clean, older model Honda Accord and a dirty, dented-up Toyota Corolla with missing rims. He guessed they belonged to Cassie and Kyle Martin, respectively.

"Let's have a chat with our burglar, shall we?" Alex said to Mitch, knocking on the front door.

A moment later the door opened, and a petite woman with bobbed black hair and a cautious expression peered back at them. Mitch glanced down at his uniform. He was willing to guess this wasn't the first time an officer had been to her door. He was also willing to guess she already knew this would be about her son.

"Hello, Cassie," Alex said with a friendly nod.

"Hi, Chief Baker." Her gaze moved to Mitch.

"This is Officer Mitch Hargrove," Alex told her. "He's new to the department."

"Good morning," Mitch offered, already feeling bad about what they had come to do. Although she was young, Mitch could see in Cassie's eyes that she'd endured a lot in her lifetime.

"I was wondering if we could speak to Kyle."

Her lips pressed together, and her eyes narrowed. "Is he in some kind of trouble?"

Alex offered a stiff smile. "For the moment, we just want to talk to him. Is he home?"

She nodded and gestured for them to follow her inside the house. "I'll go get him. You can wait on the couch."

Mitch and Alex sat on the edge of a faded couch with several tears patched up with duct tape. There were more than a few dings and holes in the walls too. They weren't a rich family, and this wasn't the best of neighborhoods. Being a single parent wasn't easy. He knew that from watching his own mom. Mitch had felt the pressure of making ends meet back then. Maybe Kyle was also feeling it.

A few minutes later, a tall, lanky kid—definitely not an adult yet, even though he was nearly eighteen—stepped out into the living room.

He cast a wary gaze between Mitch and Alex. "My mom said you wanted to talk to me," he said more to Alex than Mitch.

Alex nodded from the couch. "That's right. This is Officer Hargrove. We need to ask you a few questions."

"Yeah, whatever," the kid said with attitude.

"Why don't you sit down first?" Alex suggested.

Mitch remained quiet because the family was more familiar with Alex.

Kyle sighed and plopped into a worn recliner across from them. Mitch saw Ms. Martin lingering within earshot.

"I believe this is yours." Alex slapped Kyle's driver's license down on the coffee table between them.

Kyle's gaze swept over it. He shrugged, looking between them. "I lost it a couple weeks ago."

The kid was a bad liar. "I found it in the bookstore that was robbed downtown earlier today," Mitch told him.

Ms. Martin gasped in the background.

"Wasn't me. The thief who stole my license must like books too."

"He didn't steal books. Just cash." Alex kept his gaze trained on Kyle, who was doing his best to look uninterested.

"Thanks for finding it for me. No risk of getting a ticket for driving without one anymore." At this, the teen offered up a smile but his eyes were still dull and lifeless.

"Your fingerprints were at the bookstore too," Mitch lied. They hadn't had time to run fingerprints yet. Alex would probably have something to say about Mitch's white lie later.

Kyle shifted uncomfortably.

"There's more than a traffic ticket at stake," Alex continued, not correcting what Mitch had claimed.

"Kyle?" Cassie Martin stepped up to her son now. "Did you rob a bookstore? Is that where the money came from?" she asked.

Mitch looked at her. "How much money?"

He could tell she was hesitant to answer. Doing so would likely implicate Kyle. "My son is a good boy. If he did this, it's only because he was trying to help me. He's a good boy," she repeated.

Mitch's eyes flitted to meet Kyle's and then returned to her.

"I'm sick," Cassie confessed. "I have cancer, and the treatments will be expensive. I can't afford them, and even if I could, I wouldn't be able to work because the treatments would make me sicker. Not at first, at least. Kyle has been working long hours, doing side jobs, and raising money to help me get well." Her lips trembled. "He really is the best son a mom could ask for."

"Listen," Kyle spoke up, "I'll pay the money back, okay? All of it. I never meant to do anyone harm."

"Kyle!" Cassie's hands covered her mouth. "Why would you do such a thing?"

"Because I don't want you to die, all right?" Kyle shot back. "I need you. I would do anything to keep you well." He lowered his head into his hands. "I know it was stupid. Am I going to jail?" he asked in a small voice.

Mitch could hear his own teenaged self asking a couple of law enforcement officers that same question a decade earlier. He remembered the feeling of wondering if his next ten to twenty would be behind bars. Worse than that feeling was knowing that he was the reason that the rest of someone else's years would be in a wheelchair.

"You'll have to come down to the station, yes," Alex said.

"You're arresting him?" Cassie's dark eyes filled with thick tears. It reminded Mitch of when his own mom had arrived at the hospital after the accident. A couple of police officers came to talk to Mitch in his room. Once he was discharged, they wanted him to come down to the station for questioning. In Mitch's case, it had all been an unfortunate accident. But Kyle had purposely robbed several stores. Yeah, his reasons seemed almost noble if you looked at it from a teenager's viewpoint, but he'd still committed crimes.

"I'm afraid we have to," Alex said. "But considering the circumstances and Kyle's age, we might be able to work out a deal with Judge Ables. Can't make any promises about that though."

"It's okay, Mom. Don't worry about me." Kyle gave a

wobbly smile to Cassie, who had tears streaming down her cheeks now. If she couldn't afford medical treatment, she couldn't afford bail money either.

"He's right," Mitch told her. "We'll take care of Kyle. You need to save your strength for your own fight, and you won't be doing it alone. Sweetwater Springs takes care of its people."

"I don't like to ask for handouts," she said, lifting her chin. "It's not other people's responsibility to worry about me."

Mitch stood. "No, it's other people's privilege to help someone in a time of need. We'll figure it out. Together." The word *we* on his tongue surprised him. He hadn't been part of the Sweetwater community since he'd left town after high school. Ever since he'd returned here, he'd made a point of not including himself, especially when he referred to the bed and breakfast.

Alex nodded. "The police station and fire department have been known to join forces for fund-raisers. I'll arrange that side of things." He glanced over at Kyle. "Fund-raisers are legal, and I'm guessing we can rake in a lot more than can be taken from a bookstore register."

Kyle smiled weakly. "Thanks for helping her. She's all I have."

Mitch's stomach twisted. He knew that feeling of helplessness. Kyle didn't have to take on the burden of helping his mom alone though.

The three of them headed out to the police SUV and got in.

"Have I completely screwed up my life?" Kyle asked midway through the ride to the station.

"Everyone deserves a second chance. One mistake doesn't define you, son," Alex said, glancing at Mitch. "Unless you let it."

* * *

Kaitlyn's cell phone had rung four times since she'd started this new project. No doubt it was her mom—the last person she wanted to talk to right now. So she continued hanging fairy lights outside under the eaves of the covered porch. She'd seen something similar in a magazine recently, and it had looked so romantic. Perfect for the holidays too. The lights also reminded her of her first kiss with Mitch by Silver Lake under a blanket of stars. She'd never forget that moment, sweet and perfect.

The back door opened, and the man himself walked outside. Kaitlyn stared at him for a moment, trying to make sense of the picture in front of her. Mitch was dressed in his police uniform and holding a bouquet of flowers. The image did not make sense in her mind.

"What are you doing?" she asked.

He held out the assortment of brightly colored daisies. "For you. I stopped at Halona's flower shop on the way."

"They're beautiful." She stepped off her ladder and walked to him. "What did I do to deserve this?"

"Oh, I don't know. Put up with the likes of me."

She laughed, taking the flowers and sweeping them under her nose. "You're not so hard to put up with."

"I'm sorry I wasn't here this morning. I know it was important to you. How'd it go with Mr. Garrison?"

She looked up at Mitch, remembering how Mr. Garrison had told her about Mable's matchmaking ways. Was this her grandmother's grand finale of matchmaking? "It went fine. He was sorry you weren't here, of course, but he understood. So do I."

Mitch's wooden posture softened. "So I can skip the groveling part?"

She laughed again. "Yes, please skip over that part. You don't strike me as someone who'd get down on your knees anyway. I did figure out a way you can make it up to me though."

He raised one brow, and if she wasn't mistaken, he looked a little worried. "Yeah?"

Kaitlyn held her bouquet under her chin, the soft scent still lingering in the air. "It was your mom's idea actually."

Yep, that was definite concern lining his forehead. "You've been talking to my mom? Now I'm worried."

Kaitlyn laughed. "She came over earlier to watch the place while I went grocery shopping. And before you ask, yes, she looked fine. You can see for yourself when she gets here in a minute."

Mitch folded his arms in front of him. "Why is my mom coming here?"

Kaitlyn suppressed the small quiver of guilt in her belly. Since she and Mitch had inherited this B&B, he hadn't watched it for her on his own once. Yeah, he'd done a lot of repairs and handled any of the maintenance that the inn needed but Mitch hadn't played host. "The downtown stores are staying open late tonight for last-minute shoppers. Your mom and aunt Nettie invited me to go with them, and I would really like to."

Color drained from Mitch's cheeks. "So who will be watching the inn tonight?"

She lifted her brows, waiting for him to come to the natural conclusion. "It'll only be for a few hours. I've set aside a movie to play in the ballroom for entertainment. And hot chocolate."

"I don't entertain."

"So you've said." Kaitlyn smiled softly. Gina had warned her that Mitch would try to get out of this but she'd told

Kaitlyn to stand her ground. He was capable, and it was just as much his responsibility as hers, at least until Christmas Eve. "I'm sure you'll do fine."

The doorbell rang before he could continue to argue.

"That's them now. Do you mind getting the door while I put these flowers in a vase? Thank you, Mitch," she said, walking past him. Not that he'd agreed. She'd let his mom do the final persuasion. He didn't seem to be able to tell Gina no.

Once Kaitlyn returned from the kitchen, the other two women were waiting excitedly by the door for her. Mitch, on the other hand, looked like a pound puppy, frightened and caged. Gina tugged Kaitlyn's hand through the door, tossed a wave over her shoulder at her son, and then they made their way through the biting cold of the night.

"Don't feel bad for a moment," Gina said, patting her arm. They all climbed into Gina's sedan in the driveway. "It's good for him."

"And shopping is good for us," Nettie said, climbing into the front passenger side.

Kaitlyn took the back seat. "I do have Christmas shopping to finish up, including gifts for the angel I selected off the tree during Lights on the Lake."

"The downtown stores will have everything you need. I'm certain of it," Gina said.

Ten minutes later, they parked in the overflow lot for the row of stores and made their way through shop after shop. Kaitlyn picked out a hand-knitted scarf for Josie and a second one for her mom, even though she probably wouldn't see them over the holidays. She found a baby doll that cried and peed for the little girl she'd pulled off the Angel Tree, along with extra outfits and a toy stroller. Her dad was getting a new tie per usual.

At Dawanda's fudge shop, Kaitlyn got some dark chocolate fudge for Paris, who had been not only her first guest at the inn but also one of her first friends here in Sweetwater Springs.

There was only one person left on her list to buy for. Mitch. Gina had gotten him several shirts and a mug featuring a picture of a thermometer indicating an improved mood at the bottom of the cup after he'd drunk all his coffee. But Kaitlyn had no idea what to get him. Hopefully it would come to her before the big day.

Arms full of bags, the three women finally made their way back to the car and drove back to the inn.

"How do you think Mitchy fared on his own?" Nettie asked Kaitlyn, angling her body to talk to her in the back seat.

"Honestly, he's a better host than he thinks. I'm sure he did just fine."

"And how hard is it to turn on a movie and serve some drinks?" Gina said on a laugh. "Maybe he'll realize he has a knack for it after all and decide to stay."

Kaitlyn's heart sank as she watched the lighted homes blur by while they drove. Some little part of her had hoped the same thing when she'd left Mitch to watch the inn tonight. It was the season of hope after all—even if she thought that one particular Christmas wish was hopeless.

CHAPTER EIGHTEEN

$\mathcal{M}$itch checked his watch. Then his phone. Where were they?

He'd started the movie and served the cocoa. He'd even smiled and asked a few of the guests if they needed anything. There were only two couples downstairs tonight because the Nelsons had also gone shopping and the Amabiles had gone to dinner. Even with only four people to entertain, he was counting down the seconds until the real innkeeper returned.

He heard the front door open and took off down the hall toward the women's laughter.

"Oh, hi, Mitch." Kaitlyn removed her coat and hung it on the rack beside the door. "Everything okay?"

Her brow wrinkled with concern as she looked at him. He supposed if he looked in a mirror right now he'd have a strained look on his face. Put him in charge of a few hardened criminals and he'd be A-okay. Leave him with two bubbly, chatty couples who expected him to mirror their enthusiasm, and he felt like he was going to come out of his skin.

"Of course," he said, feeling relief wash over him at just the sight of her. "Looks like you guys had a good time."

Kaitlyn looked down at the assorted bags in her hand. "I might've gotten a little carried away," she admitted.

"Nonsense," his mom said, waving a hand. Then she stepped up to kiss Mitch's cheek before removing her coat as well.

"Staying?" he asked.

"Nettie and I thought we'd watch the last of the movie, if you don't mind."

"And Kaitlyn promised us that you'd make hot chocolate," his aunt Nettie said, also removing her coat. "Plus, I thought I'd catch you in action as a B and B host." She winked at him playfully. Then his three favorite women headed to the ballroom together, taking the couch that lined the back wall.

A little jealousy flared up inside him as he leaned in the doorway, where he'd stood most of the night. Kaitlyn was his, not theirs.

"Cheer up, lad," one of the guests said, stepping up beside him. Mr. Peters was in his midfifties and had come here for an anniversary retreat with his wife. "You're supposed to be happy that your girlfriend is getting along with your family. Trust me—it's rare," he said in passing and headed back to his seat beside his wife.

Mitch had wanted to tell Mr. Peters, *She's not my girlfriend*, but couldn't. Because by all definitions, that's exactly what Kaitlyn had become. They were long past a fling and very much exclusive. He even felt possessive of her with his own family members. And the fact that she was sitting beside his mom and aunt and having such a good time was kind of attractive in its own odd way.

Ever since this morning when he and Alex had talked to Kyle, something had been niggling around in the corner of his mind. This community supported each other. That's what he'd told Ms. Martin. People deserved second chances. That's what Alex had told Kyle. So why couldn't that be true for him too? Despite his best efforts not to, he loved this community. Everyone here had supported him after the accident. Well, except for the Everson family, but who could blame them? They loved Brian.

Mitch had been thinking about his own past since he'd left Kyle at the juvenile detention center. He'd never apologized to Brian in person. There'd been a civil lawsuit against Mitch at the time, and his lawyer had advised him to stay as far away from the Everson family as possible. Mitch had won the case because it was just an unfortunate accident. The facts supported him. But he'd never gone to face Brian like a man afterward. He should have. He'd never apologized for what had happened and the part he'd played in it. Maybe if Mitch's father had been alive, he'd have told him to man up and do just that.

Mitch swallowed thickly. It was finally time to pay Brian a visit. It wouldn't be easy but it was the right thing to do. He was tired of running from his past. Tired of being ashamed for something that happened a long time ago. He'd been just a kid, like Kyle, and he was ready to make things right.

The sound of Kaitlyn's laughter drew him in. Glancing over, he saw the three women looking at him. It was obvious whatever they thought was funny pertained to him. He straightened from where he leaned in the doorway and headed to the couch. "Okay, I give up. What's the joke?"

His mother had a hand to her chest, and he thought she

looked happier than he'd seen her in a long time. Family, friends, and laughter were a salve to the body and soul. "I was telling Kaitlyn about the girl across the street when you were growing up."

Mitch groaned. "Mom."

"You had such a huge crush on her, even though she was two years older than you."

Mitch rubbed his forehead. "All the guys on our street had a crush on Alison Winters."

"Aw, how sweet," Kaitlyn said. "You still remember her name."

"Oh, it was sweet. He would even leave little notes and special trinkets on her doorstep," his mother continued, much to his chagrin.

Mitch groaned again. "That's it. I'm supervising the rest of your conversations tonight."

"But I was just about to tell Kaitlyn about the time you ran away from home."

"She doesn't need to know that story, Mom. Let's just say I was seven years old and I didn't make it very far."

That time, he thought. When he'd run away from home at the age of eighteen and joined the marines, he'd gone across the world. And the things he was running from had come along with him every step of the way.

Tomorrow, he decided. He'd stop running from his ghosts tomorrow.

After the guests had gone back upstairs and his mom and aunt Nettie had gone home, Mitch joined Kaitlyn in the kitchen. He watched as she loaded the hot chocolate mugs into the dishwasher. "I think my mom really likes you."

She turned to face him. "Well, I really like your mom. She reminds me a lot of my friend Josie back home."

"So Josie is a fifty-year-old woman who is a workaholic and likes to cook and tell embarrassing stories about her son?"

Kaitlyn closed the dishwasher door and pressed the On button. The motor groaned in the background as she straightened and stepped over to him. "Not exactly. They're both feisty though. And they make me laugh. Your aunt Nettie is pretty awesome too."

"Well, I love to see you laugh," he said. "Even if it's at my expense."

Tilting her head to the side, her eyes hooded sexily. And he knew exactly what she was in the mood for. *He* was in the mood for the exact same thing.

Her cell phone rang on the counter, which made her smile fall away.

"What's wrong?"

She shook her head. "I'm sure that's yet another call from my mom."

"You can't avoid her forever."

"I know. I'll talk to her later. All that shopping wore me out."

As if on cue, she yawned, and the hooded look in her eyes was gone. She *really* did look tired now.

"You go on to bed," he said. "I'll finish cleaning up the kitchen."

"Really?" Her eyes widened a little bit.

"Yeah. I'm still partial owner here, at least until next week."

That was supposed to make her smile but instead her frown deepened. Did she wish he would stay as much as he was starting to wish the same?

That was crazy though. Impossible.

"Good night," he said, urging her to bed. "I'll see you in

the morning." If he could manage to keep his hands off of
her until then.

* * *

Kaitlyn had told Mitch she was tired, and that was true, but
she didn't feel like sleeping. Her mind was on overdrive suddenly. Her cell phone dinged with an incoming text. She
reached for it, read the screen, and considered throwing the
phone against the wall, not for the first time today.

> Kaitlyn, you're acting like a child. Call me back and
> let's discuss the situation.

"The situation?" Kaitlyn said on a scoff, fury funneling in her belly. She stared at her mother's words in
disbelief.

Another two points go to Bradley Foster. He'd groped
her, cost her a job, and now he might cost her the relationship with her own mother.

Kaitlyn plopped back on the bed and stared at the ceiling.
There was a time when her mom had been her best friend.
She would take Kaitlyn to the park every weekend, and her
mom would make a huge deal over finding the perfect picnic
spot to lay their huge, red-checked blanket. Then they'd eat,
talk, and laugh so hard that Kaitlyn sometimes wondered
if her food would come bubbling back up. Once they were
done eating, her mom always loved to lie back and stare up
at the clouds.

It was Kaitlyn's favorite game back then as well. "That's
a dinosaur," she'd chirp, pointing at a puff of cloud.

"I see an elephant over there."

Kaitlyn blinked up at the high wood-paneled ceiling of

her room now, considering the memory. In the markings of
the wood, she could almost make out designs in the same
way she had with the clouds as a little girl. She wasn't a
child anymore though. That was the point and the thing that
her mom didn't quite get. Kaitlyn could make her own decisions and live her own life.

And she knew when a man crossed the line with her.

The bedroom door opened, and Mitch stepped in, his eyes
trained on her. "Thought you were going to sleep."

Kaitlyn sat up in bed. She was still dressed and held
her cell phone in her hand. "I guess I'm not tired after
all."

He nodded, not moving for a moment.

"Thank you, by the way." Her anger was starting to
fade now that he was here. Her breathing smoothed out
just a little bit. "For the flowers and tonight, for washing
the dishes and cleaning up the kitchen. And for being
here."

"It was nothing, really," he said.

She'd seen his panicked look when she'd asked him to
host the guests for movie night. He could have refused.
There was no way she could make a strong man like him
stay downstairs and play nice. He'd done it of his own vo-
lition because she'd asked him to. At his core, he was one
of the good guys just as he'd claimed several weeks ago as
they'd fought in the front room.

He hooked a thumb behind him. "Want me to give you
some space? I can sleep on the couch or—"

"No. I only need space from the world right now, not you.
You can stay." In fact, Mitch had a way of making the entire
world fall away once that door was closed. "Why don't you
hang the DO NOT DISTURB sign?" she suggested.

His left brow lifted just slightly, and she found herself

smiling. He was wrong. He was good with people. Good with her. "Yeah?" he asked.

She lifted her hands and started to unbutton her top. It wasn't fury funneling in her belly anymore. No, it was desire, and it threatened—*promised*—to sweep them both up in its cyclone. "Better turn that lock," she said, as her fingers popped the third button down.

He did as she asked and then flipped off the lights. The night-light came on automatically, filling the room with just enough light so they could find each other. Even without the light's help, she'd have tracked down the woodsy, highly sensual scent of him. In just a few short weeks, her body knew this man. Craved him.

His arms locked around her, and then they made love like it was the most natural thing in the world. When he held her, it felt like a promise that everything was going to be all right, and she believed it. She believed what she saw when his eyes bore into hers, even though she wasn't quite sure what they said. Something wonderful though.

At some point in the night, she fell asleep in Mitch's embrace. Her eyes flickered open to read the clock on the nightstand. One a.m. The inn was quiet, and Mitch's breathing was steady on her shoulder as he hugged the back of her.

Smiling softly, she returned to sleep.

When her eyes fluttered open again at five a.m., the weight of his arm was gone. She turned to find his side of the bed empty except for a note on the pillow. She rolled forward and grabbed it.

You're beautiful when you sleep. See you tonight.

Mitch

It wasn't the warmest or the fuzziest, but even so, her insides buzzed happily. She could get used to this, she thought again, shuffling across the room toward the bathroom.

Except no, she couldn't.

* * *

There was a piano sitting on Mitch's chest.

At least that's what it had felt like since he'd walked into the Everson Printing Company and asked to speak to Brian more than thirty minutes ago. Brian wasn't there yet because Mitch had arrived as soon as the store had opened this morning. The young employee behind the counter said he expected Mr. Everson to arrive anytime.

Mitch's gaze flicked to the door that led to the back room. He'd hid like a coward when Brian had come into Dawanda's Fudge Shop on his night downtown with Kaitlyn. He was ashamed of that behavior. For one, he was a marine, a cop, and he wasn't supposed to duck or hide from anything. He was supposed to face his challenges head-on. That's exactly what he planned to do today. And whether Brian accepted his apology or not, this was a step in the right direction.

Brian had always been a nice guy in high school. Mitch had looked up to him and his three brothers. Everyone had, it seemed. Brian Everson was the star athlete of the Everson clan. By all predictions, he was going to bring a gold medal home for long-distance running in the Olympics the following year after he graduated. But no one had predicted the accident on that icy mountain road.

Mitch pulled out his phone and texted Alex.

I'm coming in late today. I have an errand.

Alex's response was quick.

> I told you to take the day off. People are going to think I'm taking advantage of my newest officer if you don't.

Mitch frowned. What was he supposed to do with a day off? And he was a new officer at SSPD but also temporary. Alex should work him while he could.

Before Mitch could argue, the door to the back room finally opened, and a female clerk came out. She spoke briefly to the younger male clerk whom Mitch had talked to earlier. Then their gazes flitted over, and Mitch knew they were talking about him. The male clerk nodded and headed in his direction.

"I'm sorry, sir," he said, looking apologetic and not meeting Mitch's eyes directly. "Mr. Everson is really busy this morning and is unable to meet with you."

That piano on Mitch's chest turned into a baby grand. "Did you tell him who I was? That Mitch Hargrove wants to speak to him?"

"Yes, sir," the clerk said.

"I see." With a sigh, Mitch stood. "I'd like to leave my phone number and where I'm staying, in case he wants to get in touch later." Mitch knew Brian wasn't too busy to talk to him right now. There weren't even any customers yet. Part of Mitch wanted to go behind that counter, open the door to the back room, and find Brian anyway. Brian needed to hear his apology. And Mitch had things he needed to get off his chest; like this baby grand piano, for one.

Mitch left his contact information with the clerk and walked out into the parking lot. Now what? Alex had insisted he take today off, and Mitch suspected if he ignored that order and showed up anyway, Alex might just shove him in one of those jail cells in the back.

Sliding behind the steering wheel, Mitch stared out at the open road. The mountains could be seen clearly today, almost purple in the bending sunlight. The first thing that came to mind for how to spend the day was being with Kaitlyn. But he needed to collect his thoughts when it came to her. He'd known there was a possibility that Brian wouldn't forgive him but he hadn't considered that Brian might not even talk to him.

He could go to the juvenile detention center to visit Kyle Martin. The court was trying to figure out what to do next in that situation but Cassie was pleading to have her son home for the holidays.

Kyle probably needed some time with his jumbled thoughts too. Not some older know-it-all who thought he had any good advice to give. Obviously, looking at the way Mitch had twisted up his own life, he didn't.

So instead, Mitch drove his truck to Evergreen Park. He was dressed in a T-shirt and loose-fit jeans along with a pair of sneakers. Just right to go for a short hike up the foothills to see the springs. Hopefully Brian would contact him later, once he'd had time to think. Something told Mitch that wasn't going to happen though.

It'd been wishful thinking that had brought him to the Everson's Printing Company this morning. Now it was back to reality.

CHAPTER NINETEEN

Breakfast was served. The kitchen was cleaned. The guests were all off doing various things and seemingly happy.

The bell above the B&B door sang out, and in walked Paris in his usual black jeans. Instead of a black shirt, today he wore a festive red-and-black checked, button-down flannel. The transformation from biker to mountain man had begun.

"Hey," he said.

Kaitlyn smiled. "Hey. How's it going at Ms. Hamilton's?"

Paris frowned as he placed his laptop on the coffee table in the living room. "Let's just say I miss you and this inn. And I mean that in a completely platonic kind of way. I don't want to get on Mitch's wrong side again."

Kaitlyn laughed as she scooted over for him to take a seat beside her. "You were never on his wrong side."

Paris grunted and sat down. "He didn't like me when I first got here. I get it. He saw me as a threat on his territory."

"I doubt that. If Mitch had it his way, this inn never would've been his territory."

"I wasn't talking about the B and B." Paris gave her a sidelong wink and then pulled the laptop to him. "So, I think I have a handle on what you want. I put this together late last night. If you don't like it, be honest."

"I will." She nodded, bubbling with anticipation. She'd hired Paris to help with some promotional materials for the bed and breakfast early last week. She would have reached out to him regardless, but after looking at his website, she'd fallen in love with his work. Who knew her first guest had been such a graphics whiz?

He tapped a few keys and pulled up a design he'd prepared for the B&B with the name written in a fancy yellow script. Purple-toned mountains rose behind the words. It was simple, tasteful, and she didn't want to blink.

"It's perfect." She stared at the image until it blurred. Even then, it was gorgeous. "I mean it," she said, finally looking over. "I love everything about it."

He smiled gratefully. "I can tweak it if there's something you want to play up or down."

"Paris, this is even better than I had envisioned. It'll look amazing on the front of a brochure. You are very talented. Thank you so much." She leaned in and gave him a huge hug.

"It was nothing. Really. And I'm serious," he teased, pulling away. "I don't want to be on the other side of Mitch's fist if he walks in on us."

Kaitlyn swatted Paris's shoulder. "Don't be silly. How much do I owe you?" Whatever it was, it was worth every penny.

Paris shook his head. "Merry Christmas, Kaitlyn. I may have been your first guest here, but you were my first friend."

Her mouth dropped open, and emotion gripped her, strong and fierce. "I can't accept something so nice."

"You can, and you will. Didn't anyone ever teach you it's rude to turn down a gift?"

Kaitlyn drew a hand to her chest, so touched by his gesture. "Well, I got you something as well. Nothing nearly as generous as your graphic design, but I did want to give you a gift." She hurried over to the Christmas tree in the corner, where Paris's present was wrapped in shiny silver paper with a large red bow. "Merry Christmas, Paris," she said, handing it over.

He took his time opening it, and it occurred to her that maybe Paris didn't receive too many presents. He'd grown up in the foster care system. He didn't have family, and he was new in town. This might be the only present he got this year.

"It's not much," she explained, once Dawanda's fudge was revealed.

"Are you kidding? Dawanda's fudge is the stuff that wish lists are made of." He grinned and stood. "Thanks."

"You're welcome. And Paris, if you don't have any plans, please feel free to come over here for Christmas breakfast. I haven't decided on the final menu yet but it'll be festive and you're always welcome here."

"Sounds good. I'll even wear my Santa hat," he promised as he started to pack up his computer. "I'll send you the final graphic tonight."

"Great."

Kaitlyn walked him to the door and then turned as the phone began to ring.

"Uh-oh," Paris said. "Looks like more guests are calling to book their stay."

"I hope so. We're full over Christmas already. But there's

always room for one more for breakfast. Don't forget," she told him.

"I won't."

Kaitlyn closed the front door behind him and then ran to catch the phone. "Sweetwater Bed and Breakfast. Can I help you?"

"Yes. Is this Kaitlyn Russo? Mable Russo's grand-daughter?" a woman asked on the other end.

"Yes, it is."

"Hi there. This is Summer Rivera. We met at your grand-mother's funeral a few months ago. Do you remember? I heard you took over the B and B. How is it going?" she asked in one long string of words.

"Fine, thank you." Kaitlyn struggled to recall meeting anyone by the name of Summer Rivera. There'd been so many people at Mable's funeral though. It'd been a whirl-wind day, and she'd shaken a hundred different hands. Then she'd immediately flown back to New York, never dreaming that she'd be dropping everything and moving here only a month later.

"Well, I was calling to officially welcome you to town and to see if you would be carrying on your grandmother's generous tradition of donating cakes to the Hope for the Hol-idays Auction."

Kaitlyn twirled her finger in the cord of the phone. "Oh. I'm afraid I don't know anything about that."

"The Hope for the Holidays Auction is something the town puts on every year. We choose a family in need and auction off all kinds of things, including your grandmother's homemade cakes. They were always very popular at the auc-tions."

"Oh." Kaitlyn leaned back against the wall. "Well, I can guarantee I'm nowhere near as good a baker as my grandmother, but I'll certainly agree to making a couple cakes for the cause."

"Terrific!" Summer cheered. "This year we're supporting a single mother with cancer. Mable usually made at least ten."

"Ten?" Kaitlyn repeated, wondering if she'd heard correctly.

"At least, but often more than that because they brought in so much money for charity. And her gingerbread cheesecake was the most popular. If you could make a few of those, that would be spectacular."

Gingerbread cheesecake? "Well, I'm...well..." Protests stuck in Kaitlyn's throat. How could she possibly refuse to donate to a charity her grandmother had supported? "Okay," she finally said. "I'm sure I can make that happen."

"Oh splendid. You are a dear, just like Mable always said. The auction is next Wednesday. I'll be in touch."

* * *

The movies Mitch liked the best were the ones with a ticking time clock. Time ticked down and the hero, Daniel Craig, Jason Statham, or any one of those action stars—to exclude Bradley Foster, whom he'd never liked—had to race to some sort of finish line to save the world.

Mitch had his own ticking time clock, and it was nowhere near as exciting. It'd been over twenty-four hours, and Brian hadn't called him. He didn't want Mitch here, and Mitch respected that. Mitch couldn't deny that he had feelings for Kaitlyn though. Deeper feelings than he'd ever had for any woman before. Was he just supposed to walk away?

He pulled into the parking lot of the Sweetwater PD and waved at Tammy as he walked inside.

"Hold on. Alex wants to speak to you," she said.

"What about?"

"Dunno. It's never good when the boss summons you though."

Mitch slapped a hand on her desk playfully. "Unless the boss also happens to be your best friend." He headed down the hall to Alex's office and offered a courtesy rap on the door before pushing it open. "You summoned?" he said dryly.

"Yeah. Hey, Mitch." Alex leaned back in his chair. As usual, he was dressed in a nice button-down shirt and a pair of faded jeans. Chiefs didn't have to wear the uniform if they didn't want to. Mitch was jealous of that. After all his years in the marine corps, he didn't much like uniforms. Even so, he supposed he'd be wearing one at his security job next month too.

"I'm still here for another week." Mitch plopped in the chair in front of Alex's desk. "If you tell me you don't need me anymore just because the Sweetwater Springs thief has been caught, you and I are going to have words."

Alex stared at him. "I'm not letting you go. In fact, I'm trying to keep you. Jackson Curtis resigned this morning."

"What? Why would he do a thing like that?"

Alex shrugged. "Well, between you and me, Jackson is going to ask his girlfriend to marry him. And she doesn't like the idea of marrying a man in this line of work."

Mitch laughed out loud. "Really? It would be different if we were in a big city but this is Sweetwater. Our most sought-after criminal is a seventeen-year-old boy trying to save his mom from cancer. I'd hardly call this a dangerous job." At least not compared to what he'd been up against as an MPO.

Alex leaned back in his chair. "I've been shot at," he said.

"I've had a knife pulled on me. I mean, yeah, it was a ninety-year-old woman wielding the knife but she could've done some serious damage." Alex cracked a grin. "This life isn't for everyone. I always knew I wanted to grow up and be in law enforcement just like my dad."

Mitch nodded, remembering well how Alex had wanted nothing more than to play a good game of cops and robbers growing up. Mitch had played right alongside him. Mable had always joked that they'd been cut from the same cloth.

"And I always knew for me that would mean not getting involved with someone."

"That doesn't even make sense, man," Mitch argued, sitting across from Alex.

"I watched how my dad's long hours here at the station affected my mom. I promised myself, when I decided this was the career I wanted, I would leave relationships to everyone else. That's just me. Most of the other employees here are happily married, and I'm happy for them."

Mitch shook his head. "I give up. Why are you telling me all this?"

"Because I want to offer you a job. Probably not as exciting as the security contract you have lined up in Virginia, but I know you and Kaitlyn have something good going. Thought you might consider staying awhile longer. We could use a guy like you. Especially now."

Mitch didn't say anything for a long moment.

The thought had already been niggling around in the back of his mind. He'd tried to ignore it because of the promise he'd made to the Eversons.

"Just say you'll consider it," Alex pressed.

Mitch gave a small nod. "I'll consider it."

"Great. That's halfway to a yes."

"Or halfway to a no, depending on how you look at it."

Alex pointed a finger. "I'm an optimist when it suits me. Now, get to work, Officer Hargrove. Sweetwater needs you. And if you see a ninety-year-old woman with a knife, heed my warning and take her seriously."

Mitch chuckled as he stood up. "Will do, Chief."

* * *

"Don't worry about the cakes," Gina told Kaitlyn a couple days later as they sat across the table from each other. "I'll come over on Wednesday morning and help you. I have Mable's gingerbread cheesecake recipe too."

Kaitlyn slid a cup of peppermint tea in front of Mitch's mother, who'd stopped by after cleaning one of the neighbor's homes. "Really? I won't turn down the help, if you're offering."

Gina chuckled. "I know your grandmother has big shoes to fill but Mable didn't do all of these things on her own, you know. She had help. Mine and Mitch's. Townspeople stopped in to give her a hand too after Henry died."

Kaitlyn grabbed a cookie off a plate that she'd set out for the guests. "Thank you. For everything. I'm not sure what I would've done without you and Mitch these last couple of months."

"Well, I'm sticking around so don't worry about that."

Mitch, on the other hand, wasn't sticking around, and they both seemed to know it. Even if Kaitlyn was still a tad bit in denial over that fact.

"What's that over there?" Gina asked, gesturing toward a wooden pallet that Kaitlyn had picked up outside the grocery store the other day. She'd covered it with chalkboard paint and hung it on the wall.

"I made that to display movie choices for the guests.

Movie nights in the ballroom are popular lately. Not everyone comes down but some do. Mable and Henry had quite the collection of films too. I thought I'd let the guests start voting between a couple of choices."

"Well, you are as smart as you are creative. I love the idea."

"Thanks." Kaitlyn smiled to herself, taking another bite of cookie. At Beautiful Designs, her ideas had always been shot down by her boss. Here, there was no one to tell her what she could or couldn't do. With her newfound freedom, her ideas seemed to be flowing faster than she could jot them down in her little notebook.

Gina pushed back from the table. "Thanks for the tea, dear, but I better head back to the house and see what Nettie is up to."

"How long is your sister-in-law in town for?"

"Oh, at least through Christmas," Gina said, grabbing one more cookie. "Honestly, it's been nice having her around. I've resorted to talking to myself over the years, which I guess could be considered a little crazy. Now I still talk to myself but there's someone else in the room. Makes me feel a little less off my rocker."

Kaitlyn laughed as she followed Gina to the door. "I've always heard talking to yourself is a sign of intelligence."

"Really?" Gina looked intrigued. "Well, I'll see you bright and early on Wednesday. We'll make a day of it. It'll be fun."

"Sounds perfect." Kaitlyn hugged Gina and then watched her head down the steps. There was a marked chill in the air from earlier. The forecast was calling for snow in the next week. Just in time for Christmas. And who knows? Maybe if it snowed hard enough, Mitch would have to stay a tad bit longer.

With a *brrrrr*, Kaitlyn closed the door, barring out the chill. She started toward the fireplace to stoke the flames but stopped short when she heard a crash upstairs. It'd come from the *Anne of Green Gables* room.

Another crash jolted Kaitlyn where she stood. Then she took off running. Even from the bottom step, she could hear the raised voices.

"It's okay," Kaitlyn assured one of the other guests, who was peeking outside her door at the commotion. She wasn't sure if that was the truth or not. Her steps quickened as she heard a choice word puncture the air. "Ladies! What's going on?" Kaitlyn asked as she entered the room.

Doris Manchester, an older woman who wore a visible hearing aid, pointed a shaky finger across the room at Sally Huddleston, the guest whom Kaitlyn had checked into the *Gone With the Wind* room yesterday morning. "I told that woman her guitar playing was bothering me."

"Well, I paid for a room just like you," Ms. Huddleston said. Ms. Huddleston was probably in her early fifties. If Kaitlyn remembered correctly, she was a music teacher at a private school in Ohio. "That means I get to play my instrument anytime I want."

"But I paid for a room and I came here for some peace and quiet."

"Then turn your hearing aid off!" Ms. Huddleston shot back.

Ms. Manchester's mouth fell open. Then both women turned to look at Kaitlyn as if waiting for her to make things right.

Kaitlyn looked between them, her mouth gaping open too. She had no idea how to fix the situation.

"If she plays her guitar one more time, I'm going to march into her room and break the damn thing," Ms. Manchester threatened.

Ms. Huddleston gasped as if the other woman had tossed a toad in her direction.

Kaitlyn held up her hands. "Hold on, ladies. I'm sure we can work this out."

"I want another room away from this woman," Ms. Manchester demanded.

"Fine by me," Ms. Huddleston said. "And if you touch my guitar, I'm going to call the police."

"You wouldn't."

"I certainly would," Ms. Huddleston promised.

At that very moment, a Sweetwater Springs police officer just happened to walk into the room.

* * *

"I heard the voices from the front door," Mitch said. He'd taken the steps two at a time when he'd walked in and heard the commotion. "Is everything okay?"

Kaitlyn blew out a long breath. "Oh, you know, just a little disagreement," she said, even though her voice sounded tight.

"No." Ms. Manchester turned to Mitch and jabbed a finger in the air at Ms. Huddleston. "That woman threatened me. Lock her up!"

"I did no such thing," Ms. Huddleston huffed. "She said she was going to break my guitar!"

Mitch tossed a sideward glance at Kaitlyn. "Do we have any rooms that we could move one of these nice ladies to?"

"We're full," Kaitlyn said, looking completely flustered.

"I see." He poked his tongue at the side of his cheek as he tried to think. There was no good solution, which was sometimes the case. These two women either had to stick it out in neighboring rooms or one of them had to leave. "Well, if either of you are unsatisfied with your stay here, you can feel free to leave and your stay so far will be at no cost." They'd both already stayed one night so this seemed like a deal to Mitch.

"I'm not leaving," Ms. Huddleston said.

"Neither am I," Ms. Manchester added. "I read about this B and B in a magazine. This is a romantic holiday experience, and I'm old. I could die at any moment. I need romance."

Kaitlyn stifled a laugh.

Mitch frowned at her. Laughing at an angry old lady was never wise. He remembered Alex's warning about avoiding old ladies with sharp knives. He quickly assessed whether Ms. Manchester had one.

"Do you think that you could play your guitar in another room?" Kaitlyn asked. Her question was hesitant as if she was concerned the women were going to turn on her at any moment.

Ms. Huddleston cocked her head to the side. "And where would that be?"

"Well, the ballroom is empty during the day. You can feel free to play guitar in there. There's even a nice couch set up along the wall."

"I suppose I would be agreeable to that."

"Great," Mitch said, grasping on to her agreement. He was, after all, a man, and men liked to find solutions to problems. "Would you like me to carry your instrument down for you?"

Ms. Huddleston's eyes widened. "No one touches my instrument except me."

Mitch took a step backward. "No problem." He was just happy the standoff had been mediated. As he walked back through the populated hall, he spoke to the guests. "Everything is fine. Please go back to relaxing and enjoying your stay here."

"Wow." Kaitlyn grinned at him. "That sounds like something an actual bed-and-breakfast host would say."

"I'm nowhere near a B and B host but I did get offered a job today."

Kaitlyn was matching his every step down the stairs. She paused at the landing. "Alex?"

"Yep."

"I'm not surprised."

Excitement swam through him. Then the memory of Brian Everson sending him away snubbed out that feeling. "I'm not sure I can accept the offer."

Kaitlyn's expression turned crestfallen. "But you love working there. And you and Alex are friends. It would be a dream come true if I could work with my best friend, Josie, every day."

"I don't know. Seeing Alex daily might drive me crazy." He was only teasing, of course, and deflecting from the real issue. Alex was a great guy, a true friend, and he'd be a good boss too. "I told him I'd think about it."

Kaitlyn's face brightened just a touch. "I hope you do."

He and Kaitlyn had never discussed him staying before, and she'd never let on that she wanted him to stay. But right now, seeing the hope shine through her eyes, he thought maybe she did.

"Did you cast your vote yet?" Kaitlyn asked then.

"Vote?"

"It's movie night. I hung a chalkboard in the dining room this morning with some options for movies to watch tonight. I asked the guests to cast their votes."

"You are full of ideas, aren't you?" He lifted a finger to slide a hair away from her cheek, locking it behind her ear.

Just that simple touch made his fingers itch for more. He wasn't sure he would ever get enough of the woman standing in front of him.

"Just feeling inspired these days," she said, almost shyly. "There's something about this town and the people. It's impossible not to fall in love with it all." Her gaze hung on his.

She was talking about the town and the people. Not him. But she was looking at him with those bedroom eyes that inspired the hell out of him. He'd taken this thing between Kaitlyn and him too far, half of him thought. The other half protested that he hadn't taken it far enough. Not yet.

The silence of his phone in his pocket was deafening. *Come on, Brian. Call!* he silently pleaded as he looked at Kaitlyn. *Please call.*

CHAPTER TWENTY

$\mathcal{K}$aitlyn was in a daze as she set out the breakfast she'd prepared for the guests in the dining room. When she'd awoken this morning, Mitch was gone. There'd been a note on the kitchen counter telling her he'd gone to the station early to work on a case. He hadn't mentioned any new case lately though. She couldn't help wondering if he was already distancing himself in preparation to leave next week. She hoped not. They had so little time left together, and she wanted to savor it, moment by moment.

Her phone rang in her pocket, jolting her from her stupor. She pulled it out and glanced at the caller ID, still not ready to speak to her mom. Instead of her mom's picture, it was Josie's that filled her screen.

Kaitlyn stepped out of the dining room for privacy and put the phone to her ear with a smile. "Hi!"

"I hope I didn't wake you," Josie said.

Kaitlyn laughed. "I was already up. I'm surprised you're awake at this hour though."

"Are you kidding? I haven't gone to sleep yet," Josie admitted.

That statement didn't surprise Kaitlyn one bit. Even with Josie's night owl ways, she always seemed to be so put together. She never had dark circles under her eyes or a single hair out of place. Josie was a machine, and Kaitlyn admired the heck out of her friend.

"I've been meaning to call and catch up," Josie said. "How are things going down there?"

"Busy."

"Glad to hear it. And what's going on between you and Mitch?"

"His job here is done on Christmas Eve, and he's still planning to leave."

"Oh." Josie sounded surprised. "It sounded like you really liked this one. After all you've been through these last few months, I was wishing you a little happiness in the love arena."

"Me too." Kaitlyn pulled in a breath. "But life keeps going. I don't need a man to make me happy."

Josie snorted. "Now you sound like me."

Kaitlyn couldn't remember the last time Josie had been in a serious relationship. Maybe never. Josie sometimes went out "for drinks" with a guy but it never amounted to more than a casual date. Josie had never been one to give her heart to anyone, which Kaitlyn had always found strange. Josie was one of the most caring, generous people she knew. She had a lot to offer in a relationship if she were interested in having one.

"Mitch is starting a new job in January," Kaitlyn added. "I don't really have any choice but to accept that he's leaving and to move on."

"I'm sorry. Maybe you should give online dating a try,"

Josie suggested, the keys of her laptop still clicking in the background. "We just ran an article in *Loving Life* on couples who've found love that way. Did you know that one-third of marriages start with online dating?"

"As I said, I don't need a man right now." Or she did, but only a certain man would do. "I do, however, need more contact with my best friend."

"Agreed. I'll put a reminder in my phone so we can chat at least weekly."

This made Kaitlyn roll her eyes, although she was still smiling. "Sounds good."

She and Josie talked a little while longer, and then Kaitlyn disconnected and went into the dining area to make sure everyone was okay. There was a lively discussion going on about the movie they'd watched last night.

Ms. Manchester was against happily ever afters even though she'd been married to her husband for forty-six years. "No one said we were happy," she said gruffly to the group.

Mr. Manchester just wrapped his arm around his wife's shoulders and squeezed gently. "We're more than happy," he declared, soliciting an *aw* from the other guests. "I'm over the moon that this woman has stayed with me for so long."

Ms. Manchester melted into his side, and when she turned to face him, her expression softened. "I still prefer the movies without happily ever afters. It's more realistic."

Kaitlyn could agree. Her feelings for Mitch were the closest she'd ever had to being in love, and the thought of him leaving physically hurt. It would be hard to watch him go and say nothing. But what could she say? She understood his reasons. She'd been a fool to let herself feel as much as she did, and it would take a while to recover. Love wasn't something she wanted to participate in again for a very long time.

So, no, she wouldn't be dipping her toe into online dating, as Josie had suggested.

Kaitlyn glanced around at her guests. Instead, she'd live vicariously through the couples who booked rooms here at the inn, and maybe that would be enough.

* * *

Mitch was having a bad case of déjà vu. Once again, he was sitting in the Everson Printing Store and waiting to see Brian. In the middle of the night, he'd awoken to a recurring nightmare about the accident. Only this time, Brian was dead and so was Mitch's mom. Life was ruined, and as usual it was all his fault.

Mitch hadn't been able to go back to sleep after that. Instead, he'd gone for an early morning jog, showered, and had driven back here. He wouldn't give up so easily this time. After all these years, Brian deserved his apology. And Mitch deserved closure.

The young clerk with pimpled skin kept casting awkward glances toward Mitch in the waiting area. Then the back-room door opened, and the female clerk came out just like last time. Instead of turning to the younger male, however, she walked directly to Mitch and smiled warmly.

"Good morning, sir. Mr. Everson is ready to see you in his office now," she said.

Relief poured through Mitch. He was going to at least have a chance to tell Brian how sorry he was about the events that had taken place that fateful night when one lie had cost so many so much. This was something he should've done a long, long time ago. "Thanks."

Mitch stood and followed her through the storeroom door and down a well-lit hallway to the last office on the left. A nameplate on the door read EVERSON in big block letters.

The clerk offered a courtesy knock before turning the knob and opening the door for Mitch to enter. As he stepped into the office, he expected to see Brian in his wheelchair. Instead, a graying man behind a large oak desk stood and shoved his hands on his narrow hips.

"Hello, Mitch," Frank Everson said. Just like when Frank had come to see him at his mom's house when he was seventeen years old, there was no smile or offer to shake hands.

"I came to see Brian." Mitch stepped farther inside the room but didn't sit. And he didn't plan on sitting. Frank was not the man he came to talk to.

"I thought you and I had an agreement, son," Frank said.

"I'm not your son," Mitch bit out.

"Right. My son is in a wheelchair, thanks to you."

Guilt and anger warred within Mitch. One emotion begged him to back down, walk away. The other prompted him to stand rooted in that office. "With all due respect, sir, it was an accident. I never meant to hurt Brian, and you know that. All I want is to talk to him, man to man."

Frank frowned, his eyes hard. "You were careless, irresponsible, and foolish back then. And you made a promise to my family, which it looks like you're not man enough to keep."

Mitch folded his arms in front of him. Frank was right. He had been foolish and irresponsible. But what Alex had said for Kyle Martin was true for him too. One mistake didn't define a person. Mitch was tired of letting his past hold all the power. The accident was the reason his mom had taken on so much work. The reason he'd left town and joined the military instead of staying and going to the police academy with Alex. The accident had dictated every choice Mitch had made since he was seventeen years old. It had to stop now. "I want to tell Brian that I'm sorry."

"Why? To ease your guilty conscience? No, you don't get to do that." Frank walked to the office door and held it open—Mitch's cue to get the hell out. "The Everson family still has a lot of power in this town, Mitch. Your mom lost her job but there's more to be lost unless you honor your promise and leave Sweetwater Springs."

Mitch clenched his teeth so hard that pain shot up his jaw. "Is that a threat, sir?"

"Take it any way you like. I'd take it as a promise."

Mitch didn't offer a goodbye as he stormed down the hall and out of the building.

* * *

Ten cakes to donate to the Hope for the Holidays Auction. Piece of cake.

By Wednesday at noon, the entire kitchen looked like it'd exploded. There was cake batter, flour, and every color of frosting smeared across Kaitlyn's apron. It was likely also on her face and in her hair.

"We are a sight," Gina said on a laugh as she slipped the last Bundt pan into the oven. "I'll help you clean up this mess while it bakes," she offered, pulling back and straightening as she shut the oven door.

"No. You've already helped more than enough. I can get all this." Kaitlyn spanned her arms out to encompass the full kitchen because not one spot had been neglected in their mess. "Really. Go home and relax."

Gina narrowed her eyes. "Now you're starting to sound like my son." She pointed a finger in Kaitlyn's direction.

"Speaking of which, you keep an eye on him and make sure he doesn't tear into one of these cakes."

Kaitlyn grinned. "Maybe I'll make one more cake just for him. He deserves it after all he's done here."

Gina chuckled, flour dusting the air as she did. "Mitch will always do what he thinks is right. Following Mable's wishes and helping you fix up this B and B was the right thing to do, no doubt about that. Mitch wouldn't have been able to live with himself if he'd left."

"He's gone above and beyond what Mable asked of him though."

"Yep. That's Mitch's way too." Gina lifted her apron from around her head.

"I suspect he gets all those wonderful traits from you," Kaitlyn said, smiling warmly at the woman. "Thanks again for coming by today."

"I was glad to do it, dear. Call me anytime. But right now, since you insist on sending me away, I'm heading home to shower."

Kaitlyn followed her down the hall and through the front room.

When Gina opened the door to leave, Mitch was standing on the other side.

He looked between Kaitlyn and his mom. "What's going on here?"

His mom went in for a hug. "Now that's no way to greet the woman who suffered fourteen hours in labor with you."

Kaitlyn's grin fell short at Mitch's grim expression.

"You've been cooking?" he asked his mom in an accusatory voice.

Gina pulled back. "Kaitlyn was nice enough to allow me to help with the Hope for the Holidays cakes. I offered, and she did me a huge favor by accepting. I hope you're not prepared to lecture me on cake baking, because I'm not yours to order around."

His eyes narrowed on Gina. "Not my orders. Doctor's orders. It's supposed to be your day off."

"Doctor, schmoctor. I told you that Dr. Jacobs cleared me to return to my normal activities. A low iron level isn't going to kill me, Mitch, and I've been taking my supplements dutifully. Now stop your fussing. I'm going home to make sure Nettie is behaving herself."

"You're the one who needs to behave," he said in a less-than-teasing tone.

Gina hugged Mitch one more time, leaving a thick film of flour on his shirt. Then she waved and headed down the steps.

Kaitlyn felt an *uh-oh* tremor through her because Mitch still didn't look happy for some reason, and she didn't think it was due to his mom cooking with her for the last few hours. "Your mom really loves being here. She offered to come over and help me bake," Kaitlyn explained. "I couldn't tell her no."

"Yes, you could have. She's supposed to be slowing down, not taking on more work."

Kaitlyn stepped past him and closed the front door in case Gina was still within earshot. "I made sure she didn't do too much. Cooking is not exactly strenuous activity, Mitch." Even though cooking ten cakes had turned the kitchen into a sauna, and Kaitlyn's arms were already sore from all the batter stirring. "We had a nice time. I love your mom's company. The guests seem to enjoy her too."

He shook his head. "Did you also have her scrub the floors and toilets while she was here?"

Kaitlyn pulled back. "What?"

"She's not going to be your hired help after I'm gone," he bit out. "Do you understand?"

Kaitlyn didn't understand. Not at all. The Mitch she'd gone to bed with last night had been sweet and gentle. The one she was looking at right now reminded her of the burly guy she'd sat down and argued with in this very room a couple of months ago. "I think your mom is old enough to take care of herself. She's survived just fine without you all these years."

Kaitlyn didn't mean that to come out so harshly but Mitch tensed like she'd tossed a bucket of ice water on his head. "I'm sorry. I know you had your reasons for leaving town before. All I meant was—"

He held up his hand. "I know what you meant. And I'll be gone this time next week. I just need to know that Mom will be okay. Not accepting every job offer that comes along. She doesn't need the money. I'm making sure of that."

"I didn't pay her," Kaitlyn said. Although she wasn't sure having Mitch's mom work for free was any better in his mind. "She did it for charity." Kaitlyn swallowed back her hurt feelings. "Maybe it's not about the money. Have you ever considered that? Maybe she likes to work. I know it's hard to understand for someone like you but maybe your mom enjoys being with people."

"Someone like me? You mean heartless? Cold?" he asked.

Who is this man? She didn't recognize him. Had something happened this morning? "That's who you pretend to be, at least. But I've seen a different side of you," she said, softening her voice. She didn't want to fight, even if it was obvious that was exactly what he was looking for. He was picking a fight with a sledgehammer right now. "Your mom doesn't want your money, Mitch. She wants you to stay." As much as Kaitlyn wanted the same. "You can, you know."

His dark eyes narrowed. "Can what?"

"Stay. I know we haven't discussed it," she began, suddenly spurting out what she'd been hoping to bring up tonight over dinner. Definitely not in a moment where Mitch was upset and worried. But her words came anyway, almost without her permission. "I can still buy you out of your half of this place. You can pay off your mom's house. But you can also stay. You don't have to leave Sweetwater Springs." She fidgeted nervously with her hands. "I mean, I know the security job is offering a lot more money, but…"

"Staying was never part of the plan, Kaitlyn."

This was not how she was supposed to be bringing up this conversation. They were supposed to be flirting over a delicious dinner and maybe on their second glass of wine. Then she would broach the subject that, in her fantasies, he'd only been waiting for her to bring up. Because staying was what he wanted too. He'd vow to make amends with the ghosts of his past, for his sake and hers. Then, knowing they wanted the same thing, he'd walk around the table, kiss her, and tug her down the hall to the bedroom. That was what was supposed to happen.

"But plans were meant to be broken," she said weakly. It sounded like a plea even to her own ears.

Mitch kept his gaze steady. The warmth she'd seen so many times was gone. He really did look cold and heartless right now. "Not these plans."

CHAPTER TWENTY-ONE

Reason one for why Mitch couldn't stay: He had a high-paying job that would set his mom up for life.

Reason two: The town may have forgiven him but Brian Everson hadn't.

Reason three: If Frank Everson's threat had any credibility, Mitch had to leave. He'd never forgive himself if he was the reason Kaitlyn lost the Sweetwater B&B. Wasn't that the reason he'd agreed to the will's stipulations to begin with? To save this place for a woman he didn't even know at the time? Now that he knew her, he was willing to do whatever it took to preserve her family's business.

Like a fool, he'd gotten too close. He'd allowed himself to have feelings for Kaitlyn. To hope that maybe what she was proposing could be true. But it couldn't. He knew that, and she needed to know it, and believe it too.

"This was never meant to be a real thing," he said, already seeing the shine of her eyes. If she started to cry, that would be his undoing. *Please don't cry*, he mentally pleaded. Ending things would be hard enough as it was. But necessary. "We had a good time but we always knew it would end. Time's up."

There is that damn ticking time clock.

She didn't respond at first. Her tears stayed at bay as she blinked back at him, a flurry of emotion storming in her irises. "I see," she finally whispered. "This was a business partnership, and you and I were having a good time on the side."

Mitch nodded, feeling like the world's biggest jerk. "That's right."

"I know that. I was just saying that if you wanted to stay for your mom's sake, you could. But like I said, she's a grown woman. She doesn't need you." Kaitlyn lifted her chin, and he suspected she was speaking for herself as well. And judging by the coolness of her eyes now, she also didn't want him anymore.

"I see. It might be best if I go ahead and pack up my things. I can stay at Alex's place until the conditions in the will are met."

"That's probably best," she agreed, refusing to meet his eyes now.

"Just let me know when Mr. Garrison plans to stop back by, and I'll be here."

She gave another curt nod. "Okay."

He started to turn and walk away but then hesitated and looked at her. "Kaitlyn, for what it's worth…"

She held up a hand. "Don't. It's fine. Obviously, it wasn't worth very much."

* * *

Mitch was walking away from the best thing that had ever happened to him, and he knew it. Kaitlyn was the first person to make him feel whole since the accident. She'd filled this huge crater in his soul. How the hell was he supposed to turn away from that and never look back?

He got into his truck and drove to Alex's house. Tuck's Jeep was parked beside Alex's police SUV in the driveway. Between the two of them, Mitch was sure he could find a place to stay tonight. His mom didn't have room and he didn't feel like fielding questions from her or Aunt Nettie about what had happened between him and Kaitlyn anyway.

Mitch walked right inside, not bothering to knock on the front door. "I would think a police chief would know to lock his front door," he called as he cut through the living room.

Alex turned to look at him with surprise from the kitchen. "I would think anyone stupid enough to break and enter would know not to do so at a police chief's house."

"Hey, Mitch," Tuck said before biting into a sandwich at the table.

"Hey, man," Mitch replied.

"Want a PB&J?"

"No, thanks." Mitch pulled out a chair and sat down, feeling fifteen years older suddenly. Like he'd been served his own jail sentence. "Do you think one of you could put me up for the next couple of nights?"

"Uh-oh. Did you and Kaitlyn get in another fight?" Alex asked.

"I wouldn't say fight. I just broke up with her."

Both Alex and Tuck looked at him as if he were crazy.

"I thought you were smarter than that, buddy," Alex said. "I never would've offered you the job at the police station had I thought you were that dense."

Mitch lifted his gaze. "And I'm not taking the position with the SSPD."

Alex cast a grim expression. "Why is that?"

"I have my reasons."

"I doubt any of them are good ones," Alex said.

Mitch was so tired of defending himself. He wasn't even sure if he believed his own reasons anymore. "All I know is I can't stay. So, back to my question. Which one of you is going to let me stay with them tonight?"

"We're going out," Tuck told him, wiping a smear of purple jelly from the corner of his mouth. "Why don't you come with us? And whoever doesn't get lucky is the one that gets to bring your sorry butt home."

Mitch looked between his friends. Alex didn't mind dating but like he'd told Mitch when he'd offered him the job at SSPD, he wasn't ever going to get serious with anyone. His career was too important to him. Tuck talked a good game, but whenever they went to the bar, he typically just drank his beer and watched everyone else. He didn't hit on the ladies, even though Mitch was sure Tuck could have anyone he wanted. Perhaps, once you've experienced a love like Tuck and Renee's, your heart stalled. Is that how it would be for Mitch? Now that he'd been with Kaitlyn, no one else would ever compare?

"Fine," Mitch said. "I'll go out." A night of drinking sounded like a good idea right about now anyway. And between his two friends, it was a good bet he would have his pick of where he wanted to stay tonight.

* * *

Kaitlyn listened for the front door to close. The guests were all gone. Some had gone to dinner, others to the Hope for the Holidays Auction, where Kaitlyn had planned to be herself. Claiming she was sick, she'd asked Gina and Nettie to go in her place. Gina had sounded undone with excitement.

Tears slipped out of the corners of Kaitlyn's eyes as she lay back on the couch. For the last two months, she'd wanted nothing more than a full inn but tonight she was glad she was all alone here. It would be unbecoming of a host to bawl her eyes out in front of the guests. Grandma Mable would surely agree with that.

Kaitlyn felt like she'd been discarded along with the table scraps. Her own fault. Mitch had always been up-front about his intentions. At least with his words. His actions had offered her a glimmer of hope that she'd recklessly grabbed on to though. She'd allowed herself to fantasize about something more between them, and in her wildest fantasies, she and Mitch had created the ultimate partnership.

She grabbed a box of Kleenex along with a large bag of chocolates because if you were going to have a pity party, you needed to do it right.

Twenty minutes later, once all her tears were dry and the box of Kleenex and bag of chocolates were empty, Kaitlyn showered and headed into the kitchen to pour herself a healthy glass of red wine—just what the doctor ordered for a broken heart. Climbing onto the couch in the living area, she turned on the TV. She was hoping to find a Hallmark movie and live vicariously through the actors and actresses on-screen. Their problems could be fixed in a two-hour time slot on television. Hers couldn't.

Halfway into a lighthearted tale of two fated lovers, the doorbell rang. Kaitlyn froze. The guests weren't expected back anytime soon and they were free to walk in.

A new guest?

She did have one vacancy in the *Pride and Prejudice* room.

Thank God, she'd showered after her crying episode. The mascara streaks were washed away and hopefully some of the puffiness of her eyes had gone down too. She didn't want to scare off any potential guests.

The doorbell rang again, and she realized she was taking too long to answer. Jumping up from the couch, she ran over to the door, opened it, and froze. "Mom? Dad? What are you doing here?"

Her parents stood on the porch with luggage in hand.

"We needed to see if you were okay," her mom said. She was dressed in a bright-red parka, black leggings, and boots all the way to her knees. Even so, her slight frame trembled in the cold.

"You could've just called," Kaitlyn said.

"I did. You didn't answer." Her mom gave a sheepish smile.

"You didn't have to come all the way down from New York. What about your Bahamas cruise?"

"It's Christmas, darling. This is where we should be this year." Her mom stepped over the threshold and wrapped Kaitlyn in a tight hug. Then her father let go of his luggage and wrapped them both in his wide, encompassing arms. It was surprising, and it felt really good. So good that Kaitlyn almost dissolved into tears for a second time tonight.

"Come in, you two," she finally said, sniffling. A second box of tissues was in order.

Her parents retrieved their luggage off the porch and brought it inside.

"Wow, sweetheart. This place is amazing." Her mom stared in awe at the front room, her gaze falling on the large Christmas tree, sparkling magically in the sitting area. "Did you do all this by yourself?" she asked, turning back to Kaitlyn.

"Um, no. I had help." Kaitlyn didn't want to get into the details of her last two months. Not tonight.

"Your decorating skills really shine in this place," her father agreed.

A compliment from him was akin to gold. From her mother, platinum. "Thanks."

Both of her parents looked at her with serious faces.

"I'm sorry I questioned you," her mom said quietly. "You would never invite such negative attention—I know that. Are you all right? Did that man hurt you?"

Kaitlyn swallowed. "Yes. No. I'm fine."

"We can threaten your former employer with a lawsuit," her father said, looking for a solution as usual. "You were sexually harassed by a client, and Beautiful Designs wrongfully terminated you. That's unjust."

Her mother nodded in agreement, her entire expression pulled down by the gravity of her sadness. "We'll pay for a lawyer, dear. We'll fight this. Bradley Foster can't do this to you or your career. You've worked too hard to be knocked down like this."

Kaitlyn had only worried about defending a lawsuit against herself. She'd never considered filing one against Bradley or her former employer. She didn't want to get wrapped up in legal battles though. And she certainly didn't want her old job back. "I don't want a career in New York. This is where I want to be now."

She waited for her parents to argue and rattle off what was best for her the way they always had. When she'd chosen electives in high school, they'd always vetoed the ones she wanted most and strongly advised the ones they said "would take her further in life." When she'd chosen a small college off the grid, they'd told her in no uncertain terms that she'd be attending the top college in New York state for interior design. One of the best in the country.

Instead of challenging her now though, her mom wrapped

her arms around her and hugged her tightly once more. "I think this is the perfect place for you." She pulled back and looked at Kaitlyn with shiny eyes that caught the twinkle of all the Christmas lights in the room. "And I can't wait to see the rest of the inn."

"Your grandma would've been so proud, honey," her father added. "Your mom and I are proud too."

Kaitlyn hadn't thought she had any tears left to cry but several streamed down her face suddenly. "Thank you."

He cleared his throat. "Now the big question is, Do you have a room available for us tonight?"

Kaitlyn laughed as she wiped her cheek. "You're in luck."

* * *

Going to the Tipsy Tavern with the guys last night had been a welcome distraction, so Mitch was back again tonight, drinking soda this time.

A waitress came up to his table and laid a beer down in front of him. Lucky for him, Nadine was off tonight. That was one thing Mitch could be thankful for. Another was two friends willing to put up with his scrooge-erific demeanor.

"What's this?" he asked. "I didn't order alcohol."

"Courtesy of the woman at the corner table," the waitress told him.

Mitch's gaze followed the direction that she was pointing and saw three women staring back at him. They all appeared to be in their midfifties and waved as he looked over.

"What do you want me to tell them?" the waitress asked.

Mitch didn't want to hurt the women's feelings by sending the drink back, and something told him they weren't flirting. "Nothing. I'll walk over and talk to them myself."

"Suit yourself," the waitress said with a half shrug and then turned and continued to the next table.

Tuck raised an eyebrow. "Seriously? You dump Kaitlyn, and now you're going to go seduce a bunch of fifty-year-olds? No offense—they're beautiful fifty-year-olds but they're pretty much your mom's age. That's a little weird."

"I'm not seducing anyone." Mitch pushed back from the table. "I'm just going to thank them for the drink." Working at the bed and breakfast and at the police station these last several weeks had softened his antisocial tendencies. He had to admit he kind of liked meeting new people now, even if he wasn't in the best mood tonight.

Without another word to Tuck or Alex, he grabbed the beer and walked over to the women's table. "Hi, ladies. Just wanted to say thanks for the gift."

The woman on the left nodded. She had overstyled white-blond hair that made a helmet around her round face. "You don't remember me, do you?"

Mitch zeroed in on her in the darkened tavern. Something about her eyes was familiar but he couldn't put his finger on where or how he knew her. "I'm sorry," he said, shaking his head.

"It's okay. I was your language arts teacher in high school."

"Mrs. Lambert. Right," Mitch said, remembering her immediately with the hint.

"You were more interested in the girls than my lessons back then." She shared a glance at the other two women.

Mitch gave them a closer look too. Both had also worked at Sweetwater High, although he didn't think he'd ever been in either of their classes. "I paid more attention than you know," he said. "I rather enjoyed reading *Moby Dick*." And it was weird saying the word *dick* in front of his old high school teacher.

All three women laughed.

"So, you're back in town?" Mrs. Lambert asked.

"No, actually, I'm leaving in a couple of days."

A frown settled on her lips. "Oh, what a shame. You know, I always worried about you after what happened. I worried about Brian for a while too, but I stopped being concerned for his well-being a long time ago."

That statement struck Mitch as odd. The tavern was crowded so maybe he misunderstood. If there was anyone to worry about, it was Brian. He was the one whose entire life had veered off course. He was the one who was supposed to be an Olympic gold medalist by now. The one in a wheelchair for life. "What do you mean?"

"Well, Brian took something terrible that happened to him and found his purpose in life. If he had become an Olympian like he had planned, he might not be where he is today."

Mitch's brows knit more closely together. Fifty years wasn't old but he was beginning to wonder about Mrs. Lambert's mental status. "You mean the printing store?"

Mrs. Lambert nodded. "Yes, among the other businesses he owns."

"You mean his family owns," Mitch corrected.

"No, *Brian*. He's quite the businessman," Mrs. Lambert told him. "Of course, owning your own business is nice but it's his work with the Special Olympics that I'm most impressed with. The way he coaches those children is so inspiring. The newspaper has done several write-ups on him over the years."

The other two women nodded in unison.

"Brian coaches for the Special Olympics?" Mitch asked.

"I didn't know that." How would he though? He'd closed himself off from knowing anything when it came to the Everson family.

"Yes," the third woman at the table said. She had a librarian look about her, with thick glasses and shoulder-length, pin-straight hair. Mitch thought maybe she actually was his school librarian once upon a time. "His wife too. She has a physical disability as well, you know."

"No." Mitch hadn't known that either.

"She doesn't use a wheelchair too often but sometimes when her multiple sclerosis flares up, she does."

"Oh, Brian seems to adore Jessica," Mrs. Lambert said, beaming under the dim lights of the bar. "I've never been a fan of Brian's father, Frank, but those two couldn't be more different. I mean, even though Brian doesn't get along with his father, he still lets him run the printing store."

Mitch pulled out a chair and sat down at the table with the women now. His body was suddenly too heavy to hold up. "Brian and his father don't get along?" he asked.

"Well, no," Mrs. Lambert said. "Not for some time now. His father was always so sports oriented. Even after the accident, he pushed Brian to enter the Olympics. It was never Brian's dream to be an Olympian though. He wrote a narrative paper in my class once telling me so. He asked me not to share it so I didn't." Mrs. Lambert shook her head. "I guess the cat's out of the bag now so it's okay."

Mitch was trying to wrap his head around this new information. Even though he hadn't planned on drinking tonight, the beer in his hand looked appealing right about now. He pulled it to his mouth and took a long pull. When he set it back down, he asked, "So Brian doesn't work at the printing store with his father?" Because that little tidbit stood out.

"Well, I'm sure he drops by there from time to time but he

has so many businesses. He practically owns all the downtown shops," Mrs. Lambert continued.

Mitch leaned forward. He'd been policing the stores on Main Street for weeks. He'd seen Brian at Dawanda's Fudge Shop once but that was as a customer. He'd seen Brian's sister Penny too.

"All those store owners would have lost their life's work if Brian hadn't swooped in and bought it all. Some bigwig commercial businessman wanted to snap up all that realty, and he would've too."

"That would've ruined some of Sweetwater's charm," the woman on the right said, shaking her head with a cluck of her tongue.

Mrs. Lambert nodded in agreement. "Brian was a real hero to save it all. And you," she said, pointing her finger. "We hear you're a hero these days as well. You caught the thief who was wreaking havoc down here."

Mitch shook his head. "He wasn't much of a thief, if you ask me." Just a scared kid who reminded Mitch a whole lot of his younger self.

Mitch wrapped his fingers around his beer as his mind raced. It was Frank Everson who'd turned him away both times Mitch had tried to see Brian. Did Brian even know Mitch wanted to talk to him?

Mitch stayed and chatted with the ladies just a few minutes more, and then he got up and returned to the table with Alex and Tuck.

"Thought you weren't drinking tonight," Tuck said, lowering his gaze to the beer in Mitch's hand.

Mitch set it down in front of him. "Brian Everson owns the downtown shops we've been patrolling," he said, looking at Alex.

Alex stared at him for a moment and then gave a slow

nod. "On paper, but the shop owners still have complete control. They all had substantial flooding after the last year's winter storm. The costs to repair were steep and a commercial realtor wanted to buy it at a steal. The store owners couldn't possibly have afforded to turn him down, if not for Brian."

"Why didn't you tell me?"

"A lot of people around here don't know. Besides, you've always insisted you didn't want to hear about the Everson family," Alex told him. "I respected that."

Mitch nodded. He'd shut down every conversation pertaining to Brian over the years. It was too painful. His philosophy had been that what he didn't know couldn't hurt him. "I want to know now. Where can I find him?"

Alex pulled out his cell phone and tapped the screen. "The man is everywhere. Sometimes I go long stretches without seeing him, and sometimes I run into him several times a day."

Tuck agreed. "The wheelchair doesn't slow Brian down one bit. He's even been climbing with me a time or two."

Mitch raised a brow. The image he'd carried in his mind along with all the guilt wasn't accurate. Mitch was more paralyzed than Brian, it seemed.

"I have his contact information in my phone," Alex said. "You want his number?"

Mitch hesitated and then nodded. He'd already been shot down twice in his efforts to talk to Brian. Maybe the third time would be the charm.

CHAPTER TWENTY-TWO

*K*aitlyn awoke the next morning with mixed emotions. Mitch was no longer in the space beside her like he'd been for the last few weeks. Along with the empty space in her bed was a void in her heart. She'd never been in love before so she guessed she'd also never felt the full extent of a broken heart.

It hurt. A lot.

After dragging herself out of bed, she went to the bathroom and then retrieved fresh clothes from her chest of drawers. A few minutes later, she walked into the kitchen to get started on breakfast: a sunrise frittata. She wanted to start off her parents' day with the full bed-and-breakfast experience. After that, she planned on giving them a tour of the inn. She hadn't gone into detail last night about what had happened with Bradley but she suspected they'd have questions. They told her they believed her story though, and would stand beside her no matter what she decided to do.

Honestly, she just wanted to let the past go. It was a mess

but everyone had messes. Some weren't as easily forgotten, like Mitch's. She understood that. What she couldn't come to grips with was the way he'd treated her when he'd ended things the other day. She wanted to believe he thought he was doing her a favor by being such a brute but maybe that was just the real him, the Mitch she'd first met two months ago, standing in the front room and adamantly stating that he wouldn't be agreeing to the stipulations of Mable's will.

But he'd changed his mind. And after a while, he'd changed. She'd watched the transformation. He'd become happy here. At home here.

Unwilling to waste a moment more dwelling on something she couldn't change, Kaitlyn carried the breakfast plates to the table and greeted everyone, playing the part of the happy hostess. Since she'd arrived, she hadn't had to pretend that was true. Today, however, it took effort.

"Good morning, dear." Her mom beamed from the table, sitting beside her father. As usual, her mom was perfectly put together. Her hair was already styled and her makeup applied tastefully.

"How did you sleep last night?" Kaitlyn asked, joining her parents after all the guests had been served a plate.

"Like a baby," her father said with an appreciative nod.

"Oh, the bed was so soft. And it's amazing how quiet it is here. You'd think being in a house full of people would be dreadfully loud but it wasn't."

"Well, you're used to being in a home smack-dab in a city full of millions, Mom. Sweetwater Springs is a small community."

"It is. And it's a nice change of pace." Her mom forked a piece of her frittata into her mouth and closed her eyes. "Oh, George. You must try this food our daughter has prepared. It's so good."

He dutifully took a bite, and Kaitlyn couldn't help the satisfaction mounting inside her at impressing her parents. "Delicious," he affirmed. "She definitely didn't get her cooking talents from you, Marjorie," he told Kaitlyn's mom, whose mouth popped open before laughing.

"No, I'll admit that's true," her mom said.

After breakfast, Kaitlyn took them through each room of the inn while her mother oohed and aahed at all the furnishings.

"You always did have so much imagination," her mom commented.

Kaitlyn ended the tour of the house in the ballroom and told them about the movie nights they'd had here and her plans to possibly hire someone to teach ballroom dance lessons in the future. "It really has been so magical seeing this place come alive. I know exactly why Grandma Mable loved this B and B so much."

"Your grandparents didn't buy this place until after I left for college," Kaitlyn's father said. "I never spent enough time here to really fall in love with it."

Kaitlyn's mom placed a hand on her shoulder. "I might not have supported you coming to stay here at first but I was wrong, honey. If this place makes you happy, then your father and I will just have to plan on coming down here every couple of months to see you. An added bonus is we can stay in a different themed room every time we visit."

Kaitlyn's father chuckled. "You've been saying we need to have more romantic getaways. I hear this is one of the most romantic towns in the country."

"For the holidays, at least." Kaitlyn grinned. "Sweetwater is planning their annual Sweetwater Festival this spring. I hear it's an amazing time. You two should come down for that."

"Maybe we will," her mom said, casting a glance at Kaitlyn's dad.

Kaitlyn hoped they would as she led them toward the back door. "Do you want me to show you outside?"

"Sure," both her parents said with what sounded like sincere excitement.

"We'll have to get our coats," Kaitlyn said. "It's freezing out there. But I've started making plans for the landscaping once it warms up." She'd be carrying out those plans on her own, however. From here on out, she and this inn were on their own.

* * *

Mitch nearly missed the turn into his mom's driveway. With his cloud of thoughts hanging heavily on his mind, he was on autopilot, driving toward the B&B and Kaitlyn. But he'd broken up with her. It was for the best, he kept telling himself, even if he couldn't seem to convince his heart. It felt like someone had used that vital organ inside his chest as a punching bag over the last four days.

After parking, he walked up the driveway carrying a treat for the two women inside.

His mom and aunt Nettie were sitting at the dining room table playing a game of Rook when he walked in.

His mother immediately lifted her head and sniffed the air. "Dawanda's fudge," she said, her eyes rounding like a five-year-old child's.

"And you're excited to see me too, right?" he asked, dipping to kiss her temple. As he did, he scrutinized the color of her complexion and the skin under her eyes. She really was doing better these days. The symptoms she'd had when he'd first come to town had been alleviated with rest and supplements. That would make leaving for his security job so much easier.

"Of course, I'm excited to see you," she said. Mitch turned to his aunt. "Hey, Aunt Nettie. Is Mom behaving?"

"What do *you* think?" Nettie asked.

"I think I'd be worried if you said yes."

Nettie emptied the bag of fudge onto a paper plate at the center of the table. "You were always my favorite nephew. And if you keep supplying us with this stuff, you always will be."

"You plan on staying awhile?" he asked, pulling out a chair and sitting down across from them.

Nettie looked up at him and then flicked her gaze to his mom.

This tripped his gut's radar. "What?" he asked, looking between them.

"I haven't told him yet," his mom said, looking a shade guilty.

"Told me what?" He sat up straighter, suddenly going through the worst-case scenarios of what she would say. Maybe he'd let his guard down too soon. Maybe she wasn't doing better after all.

His mom frowned. "Stop your worrying," she ordered. "It's written all over your face. What I have to say is no big deal. Nettie is just moving in with me, that's all."

He raised an eyebrow as his thoughts caught up to speed. "Why? I thought the doctor said you were just exhausted. You just need to slow down, which means *not* taking on more jobs," he said, reminded that his mom had been helping Kaitlyn at the Sweetwater B&B a lot these days.

His mom raised a hand. "The doctor says I'm fine, yes. But my small health scare got me thinking that I'm tired of being alone. What if you hadn't shown up when I collapsed?" She shook her head. "Not only that, with you here, I realized that I'm lonely in this house all by myself."

"And I've been lonely living in my RV," Aunt Nettie added.

"We're not getting any younger," his mom explained. "People need someone to grow old with, and, well, we've decided we want to be that for one another."

"Sure beats waiting on another loser to break my heart." Aunt Nettie laughed as she licked remnants of a piece of fudge off her fingertips. Mitch's aunt had never married. Growing up, he'd watched her get close a time or two but it had never worked out. "An added bonus is that I get to see my nephew from time to time." She winked. "If you come around," she added, and then took another bite out of her fudge square.

"He will. Mitch has a girl here," his mom shared.

His mom and aunt really were like two best friends when they got together. Mitch almost felt like a third wheel in this conversation.

"Actually, Kaitlyn and I have decided it's best if we end things. I've been staying with Alex for the last couple of days."

"What?" His mom was visibly upset.

"Don't worry. I'll be back to visit you and Aunt Nettie." And Alex, Tuck, and Dawanda. He had family here. Friends. This was his hometown. "I'm happy for you two," he told his mom and aunt. "I think this is a good thing."

"It is," his mom agreed as he reached for a piece of fudge himself. Both his mom and Nettie swatted at his hand.

"I thought you brought this for us," Nettie complained.

"Word of wisdom," his mom offered. "Never come between a woman and her chocolate."

Mitch chuckled. "Noted."

"Another word of wisdom. Whatever noble reasons you think you have for cutting things off with Kaitlyn, forget them. Those are in your head. You need to listen to your heart."

"Mom, I'm going to Northern Virginia. I have a job lined up. One that will pay enough to let you stop working for good."

His mom put her fudge down—the first clue that he was in trouble—and narrowed her eyes. "Mitchell Douglas Hargrove, I never said I wanted to stop working. I love working. Go to Virginia if you must but I'm going to continue exactly what I'm doing. I'll slow down, maybe. Nettie is going to help me clean houses. We're going to be a team, right, Net?"

Aunt Nettie licked the sticky fudge residue off her index finger with a loud smack. "That's right."

"And stop sending me money. I don't need it. I never have," she said, reaching a hand out to rest over his. "The only thing I need is for you to be happy."

That's all he'd ever wanted for her as well. "Ditto," he said, unable to say anything more for a moment.

"Seeing you happy is what makes me happy, son," his mom said, offering his hand a little squeeze before reaching for another piece of fudge.

Mitch swallowed past the melon-sized lump in his throat.

"Fine," Aunt Nettie said, lightening up the sudden heaviness in the room. "I'll share a piece of my fudge with you." She broke a piece off and handed it to him. "But just this one time."

"Thanks."

Nettie shrugged a shoulder. "I just want you to be happy too."

After leaving his mom's house, he climbed into his truck

and leaned back against the headrest. Without Kaitlyn, he wasn't sure if he'd ever feel true happiness again.

His cell phone dinged in the center console, and Kaitlyn's name lit up the screen and everything inside him for a moment. "Hello?"

"Hi," she said in a flat voice.

"Hi." He wanted to tell her that he missed her. That he was sorry. He was a fool. Nothing had changed between them though. Even though he had Brian's contact information in his phone, he hadn't called. And there was nothing to indicate that Brian would welcome talking to him any more than Frank Everson had.

"I need you," Kaitlyn said, igniting hope in a spring he'd thought had dried up. His heart responded with a hard kick. He didn't deserve to be needed by her but it felt good. Like air at peak elevation.

"Mr. Garrison called. He's stopping by for breakfast one last time tomorrow. He wants to make sure we've met our end of the deal. You weren't there last time," she pointed out.

"I'll be there tomorrow."

"Good." With that, she hung up on him.

* * *

Kaitlyn had set up Mr. Garrison's spot at the table beside her. She'd intended for Mitch to sit on Mr. Garrison's other side but somehow he'd moved to sitting across from them.

She kept her gaze down on the food in front of them.

"This is delicious. Who made it?" Mr. Garrison asked, looking between them. "Kaitlyn or you, Mitch?"

Mitch had only walked in the door five minutes before Mr. Garrison arrived. And in those five minutes, Kaitlyn had successfully avoided looking at or talking to him.

She hated him.

She *loved* him.

She hated that she was in love with him. So in love that she couldn't taste the food she was chewing because it hurt to be near Mitch. Hurt to be around him after he'd broken her heart into a million little pieces that she feared would never reassemble.

"Kaitlyn cooked this morning," Mitch said. Then he rattled off several stories about their time together here at the inn. How he'd helped her master Grandma Mable's made-from-scratch biscuits. The repairs he'd done. The tree they'd put up right after Thanksgiving.

Kaitlyn didn't say a word. She was barely listening because she didn't want to revisit the time they'd spent here together. Whoever said it was better to have loved and lost than to have never loved at all was wrong. Shakespeare? She guessed he would've liked this story because the ending wasn't a happy one.

"Sounds like Mable was right. You two have been a good team," Mr. Garrison said.

From her peripheral vision, Kaitlyn saw Mitch nod. She didn't move. They had been a good team. They really had.

"Tomorrow is Christmas Eve. I know you had a plan to sell your half of the B and B to Kaitlyn at the end of the timeline, Mitch." Mr. Garrison reached for his cup of coffee. "Is that still what you'd like to do?"

Kaitlyn swallowed painfully, waiting for Mitch to respond, but it seemed to be taking forever. Finally, she looked up. "Yes, that's what we both want," she blurted out.

Mr. Garrison looked up from his coffee. Then he turned to Mitch. Kaitlyn finally looked at Mitch too. It was hard to hate him when she met his eyes. There was so much to find there: pain, sincerity, warmth.

Not love for her though. They were business partners, and even that relationship was ending tomorrow.

"Yes. I'm not cut out for running a bed and breakfast. This is what Kaitlyn was born to do. She takes after Mable in that way. She can make anyone feel at home. She's smart, creative, and tireless in the work here." His gaze slid to hers and stuck. "She's pretty amazing."

Fresh pain poured through her. How could he be so nice after the way he'd walked out the other day? After the way he'd turned off the feelings they'd shared so easily?

Mr. Garrison took one more sip of his coffee and scooted back from the dining room table. "Okay, then. I'll need each of you to stop by my office anytime tomorrow or thereafter. You'll both have papers to sign."

"Do we have to come together?" Kaitlyn asked, standing from the table as well.

Mr. Garrison frowned. "No. I know you'll have your hands full here at the inn, and Mitch has obligations elsewhere with his new job. Just anytime you're free. I can even swing by here with the paperwork if that'd be easier for you, Kaitlyn."

"Thank you." She walked Mr. Garrison to the door.

"I know I've already said it but your grandparents would be proud. They're probably smiling down on this inn right now."

Kaitlyn hoped that wasn't true. They'd done well with the inn, yes. But Kaitlyn wouldn't wish for Mable to see what a mess her attempted matchmaking had made.

Mr. Garrison shook Kaitlyn's hand and then reached for Mitch's, who was standing right behind her now. So close she could smell his familiar pine smell, like a freshly cut Christmas tree. Kaitlyn squashed all the attraction that buzzed to life inside her.

After Mr. Garrison descended the porch steps, she closed the door and addressed Mitch, keeping her back to him. "Your job here is done. You can go."

He didn't move.

She turned and walked past him, back into the dining room to clean up the dishes.

"I meant what I said. You're in your element here. And you are amazing," Mitch said, following her.

Her jaw tightened. "So amazing that you can hardly wait to leave." Her eyes darted to his. "So, get on with it. Leave."

$\mathcal{C}$HAPTER TWENTY-THREE

$\mathcal{M}$itch glanced around the restaurant. It was relatively quiet for the moment. The lunch crowd wouldn't hit for another half hour. When he'd mentioned that he was meeting Brian Everson, the hostess had seated Mitch along the window, where there was more space and handicap accessibility.

Mitch interlocked his hands in front of him on the table and blew out a pent-up, nervous-as-hell breath. He was a little shocked that Brian had even agreed to meet with him when he'd called earlier. Mitch just needed to say his piece. He wanted to look Brian in the eyes and tell him how sorry he was about everything that happened on that cold, icy night that changed so many lives.

Friendly voices filled the air as the restaurant's entrance opened and Brian rolled in with his wheelchair. Mitch kept his head down and listened to the greetings.

After a moment, the hostess headed back down the aisle, leading Brian toward Mitch.

Mitch took a breath and looked up, meeting his former

classmate's youthful face. It was almost as if nothing had changed in the last decade. But appearances could be misleading. For instance, looking at Mitch, one might not be able to tell that he was terrified right now. But he was. Sitting across from Brian was scarier than any scene he'd ever walked in on as an MPO. Mitch had learned to hide his emotions well over the years, starting after the time his dad passed away.

Brian extended his hand first. "Hey, Mitch. Looks like you beat me here," he said in a friendly voice.

Mitch smiled stiffly. "Hey, Brian. I've only been here a few minutes." Lunch had been Brian's suggestion but maybe meeting for drinks would've been a better idea. Then Mitch wouldn't be facing at least an hour of what promised to be an awkward conversation. "Thanks for agreeing to meet with me."

"Of course." With ease, Brian positioned himself at the table across from him.

"What can I get you to drink?" the waitress asked.

Brian tapped a finger to his mouth thoughtfully. "I think I'll have a sweet tea, if you don't mind."

"Of course, Mr. Everson," the waitress said with a bright smile that told Mitch Brian came often and tipped well.

"I'll have the same." Mitch willed his heart to slow down as the waitress scribbled on her notepad.

"You got it. I'll be right back with those," she promised in a cheery voice before walking away.

When she was gone, Mitch looked Brian in the eye for the first time since the accident. Ten years seemed to evaporate before him. "I'm sorry," Mitch said.

Those two words broke out of him and threatened to shatter his very existence. His heart hammered despite his efforts to stay calm, cool, and relaxed.

Brian smiled back at him. It wasn't a fake gesture. Brian's smile radiated from more than his lips. It poured through his twinkling eyes and beamed from the glow of his skin. "Me too."

Mitch sat there a second, trying to process that response. He would have understood a *go to hell* more readily. "What?"

"I should've reached out to you. I know it wasn't easy dealing with the aftermath of the accident. I also know my family fired your mom. My dad threatened you and asked you to leave the only home you ever knew. I'm sorry for that, Mitch. No one should ever feel run off from their hometown."

"But I'm the one who ran into you. I'm the reason you're in that chair," Mitch said, working hard to control his emotion.

Brian laughed softly. "Well, if it's true, then maybe I ought to thank you as well."

"You are confusing the hell out of me right now, man," Mitch said. He could feel the corners of his mouth pulling up in a tiny smile though.

"Come on, Mitch. Life doesn't just happen."

"It doesn't?" Because that's exactly how life seemed to go. Things just happened, and sometimes they sucked.

"I don't think so, at least," Brian said, sounding a lot like Dawanda. "If that accident had never happened, who knows where I'd be."

Mitch stared across the table at the man he barely knew. If the accident had never happened, Brian would have walked into this restaurant. He might have two or three gold medals on display in his home.

"Sure, I was angry when I first found out I was paralyzed. It wasn't fair. I spent my entire life up to that point training for something that I couldn't do anymore. But because of my accident and my training before that, I'm able to help hundreds of kids now."

"So I hear," Mitch said.

The waitress sat the drinks down in front of them. They both thanked her and waited to continue talking until she had walked away.

"I've spent the last decade trying to pay penance for your injuries. Now you're telling me it's okay."

Brian took a sip of his sweet tea. There was a thoughtful look on his face. "Yeah, it's okay. Honestly, I snuck out of my parents' house that night. I shouldn't have been on that road either." He shook his head. "It was all just one big mistake. Or it was orchestrated by some higher power for a reason we'll never begin to understand."

Mitch had been feeling sorry for Brian all this time but now some part of him was jealous. Brian was happy. Mitch could see it on his face. It wasn't an act. It was real.

For the next hour, they talked like old friends over burgers and fries.

"I'm not sure if you're planning to stay in Sweetwater Springs for any amount of time," Brian said, "but I can guarantee my family won't stand in your way. This is just as much your home as it is ours. And my dad is all talk, little action."

"From what I hear, you hold all the power around here now," Mitch said.

Brian gave his head a shake. "I don't know about that. I own a lot of property, yeah. I might even run for mayor next year."

Mitch's brows rose. He wouldn't hesitate to vote for the guy in front of him if he was a citizen in this town.

"What my dad never understood is that power doesn't

come from threatening people. It comes from serving them."

When the bill came, Brian insisted on paying for Mitch's meal.

"I can't let you do that," Mitch argued.

"You can pay for mine next time. I enjoyed catching up with you. Let's do this again, man," Brian said. He laid enough cash down to more than cover the charge and they left the restaurant.

Mitch hit the unlock button on his truck. "Honestly, I'm supposed to be leaving in the next couple of days. I'm not sure when I'll be back."

"Supposed to be?" Brian asked. "You don't sound so sure about that."

Mitch shrugged. "Either way, next time I'm in town, I'll call you. We'll definitely grab a bite. Seeing that you bought my lunch today, I owe you."

Brian shook his head. "You don't owe me a thing." And that statement held more meaning than just who had paid for lunch.

Mitch watched Brian get into his vehicle and load his wheelchair effortlessly. He was doing okay. More than okay.

When Mitch got back into his truck, he expelled a heavy breath. A weight had been lifted off his chest and shoulders. Brian didn't blame him for what happened. Mitch didn't need to steer clear from him, and the Everson family was no threat to the Sweetwater Bed and Breakfast. Frank's threat had been as empty as the current gas tank of Mitch's truck.

He'd fuel up first. Then he'd work on figuring out his life. There was no reason he had to leave unless that was truly what he wanted. If he were creating his own wish list for Santa, what he truly wanted was Kaitlyn.

Could she ever forgive him though? He'd cut her off like

a loose end. The hurt in her eyes was something he'd been revisiting in his head for the last couple of days. He'd never meant to hurt her but it'd seemed like the right thing to do at the time. A sacrifice for the greater good. He couldn't just walk back into the inn now and say, "Just kidding. I want to stay."

Can I?

* * *

Bah humbug.

It was the day before Christmas, and that's what Kaitlyn was really thinking as she smiled across the breakfast table at her guests, including her parents. Festive music jingled in the air along with the delicious aroma of cinnamon and butter from the pastries she'd served this morning. There was lively conversation going on at the table about what the guests had done last night.

"We were thinking we'd go out tonight," Kaitlyn's mother said. "What do you suggest we do, Kaitlyn?"

Kaitlyn blinked them all back into focus. "You could go downtown to Dawanda's Fudge Shop. It's world-class."

Numbness radiated through her, from her cheeks, still puffed up from smiling, to her toes.

"And ask for a cappuccino," Gina said, walking into the room with a pot of coffee. She'd shown up this morning, bright and early, to help with breakfast. Kaitlyn was more than capable of doing this on her own but she'd been grateful anyway. Gina said Mitch wasn't staying with her but didn't elaborate. Maybe he'd called Alex or Tuck. Or maybe he'd gone home with that waitress from the Tipsy Tavern for another baggage-free one-night stand. What she and Mitch had was supposed to be baggage-free as well.

. It would all be over soon though. Mitch would go to Mr. Garrison's office to sign the necessary paperwork to sell his portion of the inn to her. She could wait until after Christmas to do her part. They wouldn't even have to see each other again. The idea of that made her breakfast sit unsettled in the pit of her stomach. She'd fallen in love with him, despite her head knowing that it was a bad idea. Her heart had overridden that truth.

"A cappuccino would hit the spot," her father said at the table, pulling her attention back to the here and now.

"It's too bad you missed the Hope for the Holidays Auction the other night," Gina continued, making easy chitchat. "We raised over ten thousand dollars for one of our families in need. One of Kaitlyn's gingerbread cheesecakes brought in over three hundred dollars itself!"

Kaitlyn's smile was sincere for the first time this morning. "Really?" she asked. She hadn't heard that detail yet.

"Oh yes. Our ten cakes alone brought in a thousand dollars combined."

"That's wonderful!" her mom said. "Was it Mable's recipe?"

Kaitlyn nodded. "The money from the auction is helping Cassie Martin, a single mother from town who's battling cancer."

"That's right." Gina sat at the dining room table with her own cup of coffee. "My son has been helping out at the police department these last few weeks. Cassie's son got in a little bit of trouble with the law, trying to acquire money for his mom's cancer treatments. Once Sweetwater Springs found out she was sick, well, the whole community rallied around to help. That's just how townsfolk here are. Your mother was one of the finest for that," Gina told Kaitlyn's dad.

"Her heart was always in the right place," he agreed.

"Sweetwater Springs sounds like a great community," her mom said, eyes suspiciously shining. "Is Ms. Martin's son still in trouble?"

Gina shook her head. "Since he's a minor, Judge Ables let him off with a stern warning and a whole lot of community service."

"Really?" Kaitlyn asked. "I didn't know that either."

Gina nodded. "It's amazing how things work out."

"Three hundred dollars is a lot to pay for a cake," Kaitlyn's dad said, "but I'd pay as much to taste Mom's recipe one more time. It really was the best."

"Who knows?" Kaitlyn said, swallowing past a tight throat. "Maybe Santa will bring you one this year."

"Speaking of Santa, we need to finish up our shopping," her mom said. "What do you want this year, Kaitlyn?"

Nothing that her parents could buy in downtown Sweetwater Springs. Kaitlyn either wanted Mitch or a shiny, brand-new heart. "Just having you two here with me this holiday is enough."

* * *

The doorbell rang later that afternoon while Kaitlyn sat reading a book. With her parents occupying the last room, the inn was full. The sign out front indicated as much. Hopefully, Kaitlyn wasn't going to have to disappoint a prospective customer and turn them away.

When she opened the door though, Kaitlyn was greeted by two familiar faces. "Halona and Theo, what a lovely surprise!"

Halona held out a large poinsettia plant. "Here you go.

This is from my flower shop. I always brought Mable one this time of year."

"That's so nice of you. Please, come in." Kaitlyn led them through the front room, noticing that young Theo stuck close to his mother's side. Kaitlyn hadn't asked but she didn't think there was a father in the picture. She'd run into Halona several times over the last month and she'd always been alone or with her brother, Tuck. "Would you like some tea and cookies?"

Theo's eyes widened but he didn't make a sound.

"I'll take that as a yes," Kaitlyn said with a grin. "If it's okay with your mom." She looked at Halona.

"Of course. Cookies are his favorite. He'll love you forever," she promised.

Kaitlyn took them to the dining room and placed the poinsettia at the center of one of the tables. "You two have a seat. I'll grab the refreshments." She walked to the serving table that she kept stocked for the guests during the day and made two cups of hot tea. She grabbed the plate of cookies and turned back to her visitors.

"It looks great in here," Halona commented.

"Thanks. It's been a lot of work, but totally worth it." Kaitlyn slid the plate of cookies beside the poinsettia and then placed Halona's cup of tea in front of her. "Do you bring gifts to a lot of townspeople?" Kaitlyn asked, sitting across from them with her own cup.

Halona nodded. "We like to thank the business owners who support the flower shop. Mable always sent her guests my way for special occasions. She didn't really have a choice, I guess. I'm the only florist in town."

Kaitlyn laughed. "Well, I'm sure she would've sent guests to you anyway."

Theo chomped happily on his treat as they chatted.

"I grew up with Mitch, you know," Halona said after a lull in the conversation. "I always hoped he'd find peace after the accident." She looked down at her hands and then to her son. "We lost Theo's father in an accident last year. He and I weren't married but Theo has taken the loss hard. I wonder if there are some things that people just don't ever recover from."

Kaitlyn's heart pinched hard for the child sitting in front of her. "I'm so sorry to hear that."

Halona broke off a piece of her cookie. "Thanks. Mitch seems different these days than he has during his past visits home. I was wondering if it had anything to do with you."

Kaitlyn shook her head. "I don't think so. We aren't really talking anymore."

"Oh." Halona's beautiful features twisted. She looked sincerely disappointed. "Well, seeing his difference gave me hope that people can let go of the things that haunt them."

Kaitlyn wanted to believe that too. Even if Mitch was leaving, even if he'd broken her heart beyond repair, she did hope he found peace one day. She wanted him to be happy wherever he was.

She looked at little Theo. She wished him peace too. It couldn't be easy for him losing a parent so young. Finishing off his last bite, he stared at the plate of cookies.

Kaitlyn lifted one and offered it to him. "Here you go, sweetheart. One more won't hurt. But after that, I have to save the rest for Santa. He's coming tonight, you know."

Theo's eyes rounded.

Halona ruffled the hair on top of her son's head. "Oh, we know. We have cookies at home for him too."

By the time Kaitlyn opened the door to say goodbye to her visitors, the temperature had notably dropped outside.

Santa was coming, and according to the local meteorologist, so was a snowstorm.

Mitch, on the other hand, was likely packing his bags to leave at this very moment.

* * *

In addition to being Christmas Eve, today was Mitch's last day on the job with SSPD. Since he was still in town, he'd told Alex he'd work so that the officers with family could be home.

The day had been uneventful so far. Everyone in Sweetwater Springs seemed to be celebrating quietly with the ones they loved. Mitch had spoken to his mom earlier. She'd gone to the inn to help Kaitlyn and was planning on spending the afternoon with Nettie. Two peas in a pod, they were. He really didn't have to worry about her anymore. She was taking care of herself, splitting her workload with Mitch's aunt, and was living a good life.

Mitch pulled the SSPD cruiser he'd been driving for the last month up to Cassie Martin's house. Kyle was on the front porch stringing festive multicolored lights.

Mitch put the car in park and headed up the driveway. Hearing him approach, Kyle glanced back, his gaze turning wary when he saw Mitch dressed in uniform.

"Whatever it is, I didn't do it this time," the teen called out, continuing with his task.

Mitch laughed softly under his breath. "I'm not here for the department, although I hear you're doing a good job keeping up with your community service sentence."

Kyle shrugged. "Beats serving time in juvie."

"Decorating the day before Christmas, huh?" Mitch asked, taking the end of the string of lights and holding them up to the banister for Kyle to attach.

"Better late than never, my mom always says. Plus, some women brought a bunch of decorations over for us. They offered to help put them up too, but my mom volunteered me to do the work. The women said the decorations would be good for my mom's spirits. If that's true, then I'll do it."

Mitch nodded. He understood exactly how the kid felt. Ever since his dad had died, Mitch had felt the same way about his own mother. Whatever it took to make her smile. To keep her safe. Secure. He'd failed at that task often enough but it had always been his not-so-secret mission in life.

"Your mom is lucky to have you," he told Kyle.

"Yeah, well, I'm lucky to have her too. She's all I got."

Mitch understood that as well. At least, that's how he used to feel. All this time, he'd had more than he realized though. He'd had Mable and Henry. Aunt Nettie. Dawanda. Alex and Tuck. Even Halona. There was a whole town full of people here that had readily welcomed him back these last two months, even though he'd abandoned them in some ways.

"Just don't forget to be a kid, okay?" Mitch said.

Kyle's gaze slid over to him. "I'm not a kid."

"Right. Don't forget to enjoy your youth a little, then. Do things for yourself while looking out for your mom. Live your life and be happy, because that's what she really wants for you." Maybe it was the holiday making him sappy but his throat tightened as he gave Kyle his best advice.

Kyle didn't look all that impressed. "What are you? One of the wise men?"

"Kyle Martin!" Cassie said, waving a finger as she stepped out the screen door and onto the porch. "That is no way to talk to Officer Hargrove." Mitch was glad to see the single mom in good spirits. Hopefully, this time next year, she'd be cancer-free.

"Mom, you're supposed to be resting."

Mitch closed his eyes as he listened. If the similarities between his family and this one got any stronger, he'd wonder if God was pulling his chain. Or Mable in heaven with her meddling ways.

"And it's cold out here. You're supposed to stay warm inside," the teenager nagged.

Cassie tsked, ignoring him. "Merry Christmas, Officer Hargrove," she said.

"Please, call me Mitch. Merry Christmas to you too. How are you doing?"

"Good, thanks to you and the community. I have high hopes for the new year too." She smiled brightly. "I have pie in the house if you'd like a slice."

"Afraid I can't stay," he said. "I'm on the job. Just thought I'd play the role of one of the wise men while passing through."

Kyle cracked a smile.

And since Mitch was still feeling wise and sappy, he pointed a finger at the teen. "Also, don't do drugs and stay in school."

With a wave, he started to walk away until a little yellow furball darted out of the bushes. Once it stopped moving, he saw that it was a golden retriever mix.

"That's the stray that's been coming around here all week," Cassie called from the porch. "He doesn't seem to belong to any of my neighbors so I wish I could take him inside, but my immune system is low right now. Do you want a puppy, Mitch?" she asked with a hopeful lift in her voice.

"I'm afraid I'm not in the market for a dog," he said, turning back to Cassie.

She hugged her arms around herself. "I'd hate for the poor thing to be out here when it snows tonight."

Mitch's gaze dropped to the pup, who repeatedly propped his paws on Mitch's leg and then returned to all fours. It woofed softly. "I can take it back to the station and see if someone there wants him."

"That would be great," Cassie said. "Thank you so much, for everything."

Mitch stooped and collected the soft little wiggler into his arms and double-checked that it was indeed a boy. Then he returned to his cruiser and set the puppy in his passenger seat. Apparently tired from his surge of energy outside, the puppy lay down and put his head on his front paws.

"Good boy," Mitch said. He started the car and continued through the streets, all welcoming and festive with lights and wreaths. *Loving Life*'s article hadn't fudged anything. Sweetwater Springs truly was a great place to spend the holidays. He'd forgotten that. Or he'd pushed it out of his mind because it hadn't seemed like an option for him. It was romantic too. His thoughts took a stroll through the memories of his time here with Kaitlyn. The cappuccino reading at the fudge shop. Their trip to Merry Mountain Farms to get a tree. Even though it'd been cut short, Lights on the Lake had been festive and romantic too. He regretted that every Christmas season couldn't be spent here, with Kaitlyn, doing the same.

A short drive later, he walked into the station with the puppy under his arm.

"Who's this?" Alex asked, looking up from the paperwork on his desk as Mitch entered his office.

"Your new pet," Mitch said.

Alex was already shaking his head. "Nice try, but no. I don't have time for a dog right now. Especially a puppy. He's cute though. You should keep him."

Mitch didn't have time either. He set the puppy on the floor to run around for a moment and then placed his gun and badge on Alex's desk.

Alex nodded. "Still scared shitless, huh?"

Mitch shoved his hands on his waist. Once upon a time, those would've been fighting words but they were true. "Yeah," he admitted. "I messed up with her, and there's nothing to say I won't do it again." He couldn't use his mom or even the Eversons as an excuse for leaving town this time. This was all on him. He was sick of feeling like the bad guy no matter how much good he did.

"If you could have seen the look on Kaitlyn's face." Mitch shook his head, hating himself for causing her more pain. She'd been through enough over the last few months with Mable's passing, getting fired, and giving up the life she was accustomed to in New York to come to the mountains of North Carolina. "It doesn't matter my reasons; I handled it all wrong. I should have told her that I…I…" He stumbled over his words. There was only one word that completed that sentence.

Love.

He swallowed thickly. "I should've told her that I loved her," he said quietly, more to himself than Alex.

Alex didn't look surprised when Mitch blinked and looked up at him.

Had Mitch really been that thick skulled? He knew he cared about Kaitlyn. Admired the heck out of her. Knew he was wildly attracted to the woman and could possibly never get enough of her, if given the opportunity. But the way he felt for Kaitlyn Russo went beyond all of that. Over the last two months, he'd fallen in love with her.

Alex leaned forward on his elbows. "Great. So why don't you go tell her that right now?"

Mitch didn't move. He felt like he'd just been hit over the head with a large block of ice.

"Listen, I don't need one of Dawanda's cappuccinos to

predict you'll screw up and hurt her plenty more times," Alex said. "You will. But if you leave town tomorrow, you'll hurt her even more. You deserve to have this, buddy. You are a good man and a good officer." Alex slid the badge back in Mitch's direction and looked up.

So much for Mitch's wise man act. He was the biggest fool of all. Picking up the badge, he nodded at Alex. "Looks like I'll be reporting for duty tomorrow."

"Tomorrow's Christmas, buddy. Spend it with the people you love. And maybe that puppy over there."

That was good advice and Mitch planned to do just that. He hadn't known what, if anything, to say to Kaitlyn to fix how he'd behaved. There'd been no fixing it in his mind. Now he knew the answer though. All he had to do was tell Kaitlyn the truth. He loved her. That he was an idiot. And then he planned on begging for a second chance. He wasn't going to run away from his mistakes this time. He was going to face them head-on.

Mitch stepped over to his little friend, who was spinning in circles while chasing his own tail. He could relate. Scooping him up, he headed down the hall away from Alex's office and past the reception desk.

"Merry Christmas, Mitch," Tammy called after him.

"You too, Tammy. I'll see you in a couple of days."

"Glad to hear it!"

The cold air surrounded him as he stepped onto the sidewalk. The sun had dipped below the mountain peaks now, making another ten-degree drop at least. He needed to hurry before daylight dwindled completely and he missed his chance to make things right today. He had one more important person he had to go see before Kaitlyn though.

CHAPTER TWENTY-FOUR

Kaitlyn sat in front of the Christmas tree, watching the lights wink at her. The inn had only three couples tonight. All of them had joined Kaitlyn and her parents earlier this evening for the Christmas Eve service at the community church. At this hour, the guests had retreated to their rooms, leaving her to enjoy a private nightcap. She was grateful for the solitude because tomorrow she needed to wake early and make a breakfast worthy of Christmas Day. Gina and Nettie were coming to help, of course. Paris would be there too. It was going to be a full, wonderful day. She wouldn't even have time to think about Mitch.

Hopefully.

A mournful sigh burrowed in her chest, close to her heart. This time next year she probably wouldn't even remember what he looked like. How he smelled. The way his voice took on a deep timbre in the bedroom when he curled in behind her, wrapping her in his arms and making her feel like there was no safer place in the world.

Kaitlyn lifted her glass of red wine and took a healthy gulp. Appropriate for her current mood, it tasted bittersweet on her tongue. She tried to steer her thoughts to something happy, and the name of the child she'd chosen off the Angel Tree at Silver Lake came to mind. Kaitlyn imagined the little girl joyfully opening her new doll and all the accessories she'd picked out. The Angel Tree was a tradition Kaitlyn wanted to participate in every year. Giving to someone else was the very heart of Christmas.

She finished off the last sip of her wine and decided one more glass might be nice. After that, she'd turn in.

As she headed toward the kitchen, Kaitlyn grabbed a fire poker and moved the logs around to keep the flames burning in the fireplace. It'd begun to snow a few hours ago. When she awoke tomorrow, the ground would be a soft blanket of white. It would be a magical white Christmas. Her first in Sweetwater Springs, but not her last.

Something scratched at the front door. Kaitlyn whirled, nearly dropping her wineglass. It was just the winter storm, she decided. Then the scratching sound came again. She stuck her wineglass on the mantel and tightened her hold on the fire poker. Her heart thrummed like a drummer boy nestled inside her chest. She was being silly. She wasn't alone at the B&B. No one would be foolish enough to break in.

The doorknob turned.

Kaitlyn swallowed. Potential guests would knock. The only person who wouldn't knock wouldn't be coming back.

The door opened, and Kaitlyn gasped as a pale-colored puppy with a large red bow around its neck barreled through the entryway toward her. She immediately put the fire poker down and dropped to her knees to pet its soft fur. "Aren't you the cutest thing?" she said, laughing as it climbed onto her lap and proceeded to lick her cheek. "Where did you come from?"

As if on cue, she heard the front door close and Mitch entered the room.

"What are you doing here?" she asked.

He was dressed in a heavy coat dusted with fresh snow. His beard was also dusted and sparkling with soft white flakes. "This little guy has nowhere to go," he said, gesturing to the squirming puppy in her arms. "He was hoping you'd have room for him at the inn."

Kaitlyn's mouth dropped open. She hadn't even considered getting a pet.

"His name is Mr. Darcy," Mitch added.

"Well, how can I say no to that? That's perfect." She looked up and connected eyes with Mitch. Big mistake.

"Merry Christmas, Kaitlyn," he said quietly.

Tears threatened at the base of her throat. She held Mr. Darcy tightly against her suddenly aching chest and stood to face him. "Thank you. If that's all, I was just about to head to bed. Tomorrow will be a busy day here." Busier with Mr. Darcy running around, but she didn't mind that. What she did mind was Mitch standing there and looking at her that way.

"I have something else for you." He held out a thick orange manila envelope.

She placed Mr. Darcy on the floor and took the envelope with shaky hands. She knew exactly what this was.

"I stopped by Mr. Garrison's after my shift," he said.

"Great." She swallowed thickly. "Thank you. I'll go to the bank after Christmas and start the process of taking out a loan to pay you."

"No need for that. I'm not selling my half of the bed and breakfast to you anymore."

Kaitlyn whipped her head up. "What?"

"I know." He held up a hand to fend off any arguments

she was about to fire back at him. "We had an agreement but I'm backing out of it."

"You want to keep the B and B?" Her mouth fell open.

"No. I'm not keeping my half either. I'm giving it to someone. It's a Christmas gift of sorts."

"A Christmas gift?" she repeated. This had all come down to Mitch giving his half of the inn away as a present?

Kaitlyn opened the envelope hurriedly. She didn't want another partner. If it wasn't going to be Mitch, she'd rather go into debt and buy him out. She yanked the documents out and read, her eyes tearing up when she saw the name printed on the bold line. "I can't believe this."

Somehow Mitch was standing even closer to her now. "I hope you're not disappointed."

She shook her head. "This is..." Kaitlyn was desperately trying not to cry.

Don't cry. Don't cry.

"I am doing my very best to hate you right now, and you're making it nearly impossible." She blinked back her tears and looked at the name of her new business partner again. Gina Hargrove. "She's going to be so happy, Mitch. You are a really good son."

A good man too, she thought. The kind of man she wished she could have as her own. He was strong, hardworking, thoughtful, and one of the most giving people she'd ever met. He'd give the clothes off his back to someone in the middle of that mounting winter storm outside if it was asked of him.

The only thing he wouldn't give fully, unconditionally, was his heart to her. Maybe that's why he'd brought her a puppy tonight. It was her consolation prize for falling in love with him.

He took a step toward her. "There is one stipulation in that contract."

Kaitlyn couldn't even see the fine print anymore. Her eyes were so blurred with tears. "There's always a stipulation," she said on a small, humorless laugh.

"Now that I don't own the inn anymore, I kind of don't have a place to stay either."

She hugged the manila envelope against her chest, pressing it against her rapidly beating heart. "Well, I'm sure you'll find something when you get to Virginia."

"That's the thing. I'm not going to Virginia anymore. I thought I'd stay and help Alex keep the streets of Sweetwater Springs safe from women wielding fire pokers."

"Really? That's great, Mitch." For him and Gina, and the town. But what about her? Could she really see him and not be with him? Would she be able to move on from what they'd had together if she were constantly running into him at the grocery store or coffee shop?

A million thoughts were swirling around in her head like wind-battered snowflakes on their downward spiral toward the ground.

"I also thought I'd stay on the small chance that you ever forgave me for being such a fool."

She cocked her head to the side. "Christmas *is* a time for miracles, I guess."

He grinned. "And love. It's also a time for love."

Everything inside her froze. Every muscle, every breath.

"I love you, Kaitlyn," he said in a low, gruff voice. "I'm in love with you."

Tears swam in her eyes now, too many to hold back. They streamed off her cheeks faster than she could wipe them away with her shaking hands. "I love you back."

"Well, *that* is a miracle." He reached inside his coat pocket and pulled out a piece of mistletoe.

"From the Merry Mountain Farms," she said, looking up into his eyes. She loved those eyes. Loved this man.

"I wanted to use this on you so badly that night it made my head spin."

She lifted his arm to hold the sprig over her head. "So kiss me now."

Dutifully, as always, he bent and brushed his lips to hers as Mr. Darcy circled them and woofed excitedly at their feet. Pulling away, she met Mitch's gaze, and her heart answered with love. *He* was her home. And there was no place she'd rather be than with him for the holidays.

EPILOGUE

Two months later

The grand reopening celebration for the Sweetwater Bed and Breakfast was going well so far. Over the last couple of weeks, Kaitlyn had sent out flyers to everyone in town for the all-day open house event. She had Mable's famous homemade cookies and tea available, and several townspeople were huddled in one corner of the room enjoying themselves while admiring the designer touches that Kaitlyn had made. Other guests were exploring the newly opened walking trails behind the inn.

"This is a wonderful turnout, don't you think?" Gina asked, coming up beside her.

"It really is." Kaitlyn adored having Gina as her partner in this business. She was hardworking, and she genuinely loved doing for others. She made the guests feel at home, and she was full of stories about Mable and Henry's days at the inn. Kaitlyn felt like she was getting to know her grandparents a little more by spending time with Gina.

"My two favorite women," Mitch said, stepping up beside them with Mr. Darcy, considerably bigger now, at his side. He leaned in and gave Kaitlyn a soft kiss on the cheek. "Hey, beautiful," he whispered in her ear and then lifted his head to look at Gina. "Hey, Mom. Where's Aunt Nettie?"

"Oh, she's showing one of the women from our book club the garden outside. It's such a pretty place this time of year."

The garden had been Nettie's idea. It was a masterpiece of vibrant colors that attracted birds and butterflies and guests.

"Mom, do you think you can manage the event on your own for a little bit?" he asked then. "I need to borrow Kaitlyn."

Gina put a hand on her waist. "What kind of silly question is that? Of course I can. You two go on ahead. Mr. Darcy and I will handle things in here."

Kaitlyn laughed softly as he tugged her down the hall and toward the bedroom. "Can't this wait, Mitch?"

He stopped in front of the closed door. She'd closed it to make sure today's visitors didn't wander. The entire inn was available for the open house with the exception of their private quarters.

"I've waited long enough," he told her. "I can't wait any longer."

* * *

Mitch was still pinching himself over how much his fortune had changed in the last couple of months. He'd gone from a jaded loner who was lost in the world to working at the Sweetwater Springs PD during the day and coming home at night to the most caring, gorgeous, intelligent woman he'd ever met.

Dawanda had been right. He'd fallen quick and hard, and he was staying in Sweetwater Springs forever. Well, minus the romantic escapades he planned to take Kaitlyn on, starting with their honeymoon.

If she said yes.

He reached for the doorknob of their room now. This morning, while Kaitlyn and his mom had been busy preparing the final touches in the B&B to welcome the entire town, he'd holed up in their bedroom. He wasn't an interior designer by any means but he was proud of what he'd pulled off in a small amount of time.

"Okay. Close your eyes," he told her.

"What? Why?" Kaitlyn looked at him with uncertainty.

"I thought you trusted me."

Her dark hair fell over her cheek as she cocked her head to one side. "I do."

"Then close your eyes," he said again, smiling back at her. She was gorgeous, inside and out. He loved her more than he knew he could love anyone. And the feeling only kept growing, expanding inside him, threatening to crack his entire chest wide open.

Kaitlyn closed her eyes, and Mitch waved a hand in front of her face to make sure she wasn't peeking.

"No cheating," he instructed and then opened the bedroom door and led her inside. For a moment, he was nervous, wondering if it was enough. Kaitlyn's rooms were expertly designed down to the smallest detail.

But no. This was perfect.

"Open your eyes," he said after angling her body to face the bed.

Her eyes fluttered open and bounced from the bed to the

wall and the ceiling above it. Her lips parted slightly as she looked around. "You did all this?" she finally asked.

"Our room needed a theme, don't you think?"

The bedspread was still one of Mable's quilts. Mable had been integral to their relationship. Sneaky even after death, she was the one who'd brought them together. Above the bed, Mitch had strung just a few strands of twinkling lights. They reminded Mitch of their first kiss under a blanket of stars by Silver Lake. He'd tried so hard to ignore his attraction to Kaitlyn that night, which seemed so long ago now, but he hadn't stood a chance.

He watched as she took in every detail.

"Is that the picnic basket we used at Evergreen Park the other day?" she asked.

He nodded. "Yeah." He'd used the basket to hold books under the nightstand.

Her gaze swept around the room where he'd hung various pictures of random moments together and the places they'd been in town. There was a picture of Dawanda's storefront. One of Silver Lake. Kaitlyn's gaze kept going back to the large eleven-by-eighteen picture above the bed. The one Mitch had taken on his phone and had blown up at the Everson printing shop with Brian's help.

"Kaitlyn and Mitch Forever," she read.

He'd carved it in a tree outside, right below the words he'd found while hiking the newly established walking trails out back: *Mable and Henry Forever.*

"In case you haven't realized yet, that's the theme of our room. I know we're not famous, but..."

"It's perfect," she whispered, turning to him, her eyes glistening with happy tears. He didn't mind making her cry if it was because she was happy. She deserved happiness, and so did he, he'd realized. Making Kaitlyn smile did that for him. Serving her, supporting her, loving her made him happy.

Taking both of Kaitlyn's hands in his, he continued forward on his mission. "I have traveled the world looking for a place where I could feel whole again. Never in a million years did I think that would be right back where I started." He slowly dropped to one knee in front of her.

Kaitlyn sucked in an audible breath, and he was fairly certain she could guess what was coming next, given how many of those romantic movies and books she enjoyed. He just hoped he lived up to her expectations. He wasn't perfect. He was human after all. Flawed. Those flaws didn't make him unworthy though. He understood that now.

"You are my world, Kaitlyn. I love you, and I want to spend the rest of my life showing you just how much. I want to grow old with you here, just like your grandparents did."

Reaching into the front pocket of his shirt, he pulled out a simple round diamond. Old-fashioned but timeless.

Kaitlyn gasped once more. "How did you get my grandmother's ring?"

"She left it with Mr. Garrison. He had instructions to give me the ring if things worked out between us. If they didn't, this ring was to go to you anyway."

"Sneaky woman," Kaitlyn said on a tearful laugh.

Mitch looked at the ring and then held it up to her. "Marry me, Kaitlyn, and I'll try to be the man you deserve."

She lifted a hand to touch his cheek. "You are the best man I know, Mitch Hargrove. *Our* love story is my favorite. All of those other couples I named the inn's rooms after have nothing on us."

He glanced at the ring and back to her, swallowing hard. "Still waiting here. Do I, uh, need to give this back to Mr. Garrison?"

"Don't you dare." She held out her left hand. "This is where it belongs."

"And you are where I belong," he said as he slid it onto her finger. Then he rose back to his feet. "I love you, Kaitlyn Russo soon-to-be-Hargrove," he whispered.

"I love you back, and I can't wait to be your wife."

He smiled back at her. "I was thinking a Christmas wedding might be nice."

She gasped with excitement. "With lights and poinsettias. We can get Halona to help with that. And we'll need a huge Christmas tree. The biggest on the Merry Mountain Farms' lot."

Mitch laughed out loud. "If you're there, I'm there. Tux and all."

She went up on tiptoes and pressed her lips to his in a soft kiss that evolved to something deeper. "I can't wait," she whispered, finally pulling away.

"Me neither." He gave a longing glance at the bed. There'd be plenty of time for private celebration later. Right now, they had a house full of people who cared for them and wanted to share in their good news.

Taking her hand, they went back down the hall to their home filled with family, friends, laughter, and love.

Grandma Mable's Gingerbread Cheesecake

The quickest way to Santa's heart is a slice of my ginger-bread cheesecake. Your home will always be the first on his list if you set aside a piece of this delicious dish!

Yields 12–14 slices and a whole lot of yumminess

Ingredients

Crust:

- 2 cups of ground gingerbread cookies (homemade is best, but store-bought gingersnaps are fine in a pinch)
- ¼ cup butter, melted

Cheesecake filling:

- 3 packages (8 ounces each) of cream cheese, room temperature
- 1 cup brown sugar
- 2 teaspoons vanilla
- 3 eggs
- ¼ cup unsulfured molasses
- ¼ teaspoon salt
- 2 teaspoons ground ginger
- 2 teaspoons ground cinnamon
- 1 teaspoon ground nutmeg
- ½ teaspoon ground cloves
- ½ teaspoon finely grated lemon zest (optional)
- A heaping helping of Christmas cheer!

Cranberry topping:

- 1 cup granulated sugar
- ½ cup orange juice
- 1 package (12 ounces) fresh or frozen cranberries
- Whipped cream, powdered sugar, or molasses (optional)

Instructions

1. Preheat the oven to 350 degrees. Line a 9-inch spring-form pan with parchment paper and grease the sides.

2. Double wrap the outside of your springform pan with aluminum foil for a water bath.

3. In a small bowl, add your crushed gingerbread cookies and stir in melted butter while naming Santa's reindeer (or for 15–20 seconds).

4. Press the mixture evenly onto the bottom of your springform pan and then 1/3 of the way up the sides. Make sure no one sees you licking the spoon afterward. That'll put you on the naughty list!

5. Bake until the cookie crust is set (the time it takes to write out two Christmas cards, or about 10 minutes).

6. Transfer the pan to a wire rack to cool completely.

7. Reduce oven temperature to 325 degrees.

8. In a stand mixer, add the cream cheese and beat until fluffy.

9. Add in the brown sugar and beat until fully combined, then add in the vanilla and the eggs one at a time. Make sure you scrape the sides of the bowl so that everything is evenly blended.

10. While humming "We Wish You a Merry Christmas," add the molasses, salt, ginger, cinnamon, nutmeg, cloves,

and zest (optional) and mix on medium speed until fully combined.

11. Pour the mixture into the springform pan. Then place the pan into a larger pan and fill the outer pan with an inch of hot water (to prevent your filling from cracking).

12. Bake at 325 degrees in the water bath for 60 minutes.

13. While the cheesecake bakes, it's the perfect time to prepare the topping. In a saucepan over medium heat, stir the sugar and orange juice until the sugar dissolves. Add the cranberries and cook until the skins pop. Let the cranberries cool to room temperature and then chill. (Or this is a great way to get rid of any leftover cranberry sauce that you may have from a holiday dinner. I won't tattle on you.)

14. After baking the cheesecake, place on a wire rack to cool for 1–2 hours at room temperature. Optional: while waiting for the cake to cool, settle onto the couch to watch your favorite holiday movie.

15. Transfer the cake to the fridge for at least 8 hours. If you've got an event that just won't wait (aka Hope for the Holidays), place the cake in the freezer for 1–2 hours.

16. Decorate your cake with the cranberry topping. For extra *mmm*s from your guests, serve with swirls of whipped cream blended with powdered sugar or molasses.

Warning: May cause spontaneous moaning, eye rolling, and possibly a marriage proposal if served to your significant other!

Enjoy,
Mable

About the Author

Annie Rains is a *USA Today* bestselling contemporary romance author who writes small-town love stories set in fictional places in her home state of North Carolina. When Annie isn't writing, she's living out her own happily ever after with her husband and three children.

Annie loves to hear from her readers. Please visit her at:

http://www.annierains.com/
@AnnieRains_
http://facebook.com/annierainsbooks

LOOK FOR MORE HEARTWARMING ROMANCE
IN THE SWEETWATER SPRINGS SERIES

Available Spring 2020

Fall in love with these charming contemporary romances!

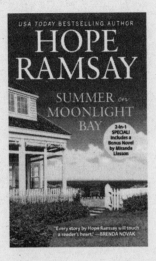

SUMMER ON MOONLIGHT BAY
by Hope Ramsay

Veterinarian Noah Cuthbert had no intention of ever moving back to the small town of Magnolia Harbor. But when his sister calls with the opportunity to run the local animal clinic as well as give her a break from caring for their ailing mom, he packs his bags and heads home. But once he meets the clinic's beautiful new manager, he questions whether his summer plans might become more permanent. Includes a bonus novel by Miranda Liasson!

WISH YOU WERE MINE
by Tara Sivec

When Everett Southerland left town five years ago, Cameron James thought it was the worst day of her life. She was wrong: It was the day he came back and told her the truth about his feelings that devastated her. Now she's having a hard time believing him, until he proves to her how much he cares. But with so many secrets between them, will they ever find the future that was always destined to be theirs?

ALL I WANT FOR CHRISTMAS IS YOU
by **Miranda Liasson**

Just when Kaitlyn Barnes vows to get over her longtime crush on Rafe Langdon, they share a sizzling evening that delivers an epic holiday surprise: Kaitlyn is pregnant. While their off-the-charts chemistry can still melt snow, Rafe must decide if he'll keep running from love forever—or if he'll make this Christmas the one where he becomes the man Kaitlyn wants…and the one she deserves. Includes a bonus novel by Annie Rains!

SNOWFALL ON CEDAR TRAIL
by **Annie Rains**

Determined to give her son a good holiday season, single mom Halona Locklear signs him up for Sweetwater Springs' Mentor Match program. Little does she know that her son's mentor would be the handsome chief of police, who might know secrets about her past that she is determined to keep buried. Includes a bonus novel by Miranda Liasson!

Follow @ReadForeverPub on Twitter and join the conversation using #ReadForver.

IT STARTED WITH CHRISTMAS
by Jenny Hale

Holly McAdams loves spending the holidays at her family's cozy cabin, but she soon discovers that the gorgeous and wealthy Joseph Barnes has been renting the cabin, and it looks like he'll be staying for the holidays. Throw in Holly's charming ex, and she's got the recipe for one complicated Christmas. With unexpected guests and secrets aplenty, will Holly be able to find herself and the love she's always dreamed of this Christmas?

CHRISTMAS IN HARMONY HARBOR
by Debbie Mason

Evangeline Christmas will do anything to save her year-round Christmas store, Holiday House, including facing off against high-powered real-estate developer Caine Elliot, who's using his money and influence to push through his competing property next door. When her last desperate attempt to stop him fails, she gambles everything on a proposition she prays the handsome, blue-eyed player can't refuse. Includes a bonus novella!

THE AMISH WEDDING PROMISE
by Laura V. Hilton

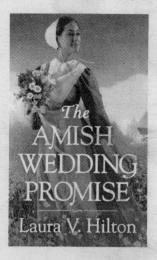

After a storm crashes through town, Grace Lantz is forced to postpone her wedding. All hands are needed for cleanup, but Grace doesn't know where to start—should she console her special needs sister or find her missing groom? Sparks fly when the handsome Zeke Bontrager comes to aid the community and offers to help the overwhelmed Grace in any way he can. But when her groom is found, Grace must decide if the wedding will go on...or if she'll take a chance on Zeke.

MERMAID INN
by Jenny Holiday

When Eve Abbott inherits her aunt's inn, she remembers the heartbreaking last summer she spent there, and she has no interest in returning. Unfortunately, Eve must run the inn for two years before she can sell. Town sheriff Sawyer Collins can't deny all the old feelings that come rushing back when he sees Eve. Getting her out of Matchmaker Bay when they were younger was something he did for her own good. But losing her again? He doesn't think he can survive that twice. Includes a bonus novella by Alison Bliss!